"Let go." Mattingley's voice from above, steady, commanding.

Her feet in their soft slippers felt the gritty sandstone of the cliff. The harness was firm under her arms. She took a deep breath, let go, swung dizzily for a moment, then felt her hands scrape against rough rock as she plunged steadily downwards.

It was an eternity; it was an instant. She had never been so frightened in her life. And she had not even asked who was waiting below.

She could hear voices now, the muffled splash of oars. They were drowned suddenly by a wild burst of music and shouting from the quay and then a scream so horrible that her hands and feet stopped obeying her and she plunged for a few moments, helpless, banging against an outcrop of the cliff. Then, mercifully, she was grasped by steadying hands, pulled sideways, and deposited safely in the bottom of a small boat....

THE LOST GARDEN

JANE AIKEN HODGE

FAWCETT CREST • NEW YORK

A Fawcett Crest Book
Published by Ballantine Books

Library of Congress Catalog Card Number: 82-73266

ISBN 0-449-20253-4

This edition published by arrangement with Coward, McCann & Geoghegan

Manufactured in the United States of America

First Ballantine Books Edition: November 1983

Author's Note

This book was inspired by the romantic careers of two eighteenth-century Spencers, the famous Duchess of Devonshire and her sister, the Countess of Bessborough. They both married highly eligible, dull husbands, bore their children and made the best they could of their own lives. The Duchess of Devonshire and her husband lived as a remarkable threesome with their friend Lady Elizabeth Foster, whose son and daughter by the Duke grew up with the Duchess's and Lady Bessborough's legitimate children. The Duchess had a brief and the Countess a long affair, each with a brilliant younger man, but the children of these liaisons did not appear in the Devonshire House nurseries, where the Countess of Bessborough's were constant visitors, and Lady Elizabeth's two were passed off as those of friends. The secret of their birth was an open enough one in adult aristocratic society, but was kept from the children until they were well into their teens.

My Caroline's situation owes something to the stories of both Spencer sisters, just as Cley and Chevenham House were inspired by Chatsworth, Holkham and Devonshire House, but there the likeness ends. I like to think that though their circumstances are historical fact, my characters are my own. Mrs. Winterton is not Lady Elizabeth Foster, Caroline is neither Caroline Lamb nor Caroline St. Jules, and the Duke of Cley is most certainly not the Duke of Devonshire.

❧ *Prologue 1788* ❧

Rain FELL LIKE streaks of lead. Thunder crashed across the valley. Lightning, following almost at once, lit the interior of the carriage with its sudden flash, showing two women, livid-faced, each grasping her luxurious armrest.

'*Madame, j'ai peur!*' The French maid let out a fresh exclamation of terror at each new volley of thunder.

'*You're* afraid!' Frances Winterton had been biting her lips against the sharp onset of pain. '*You* don't like the thunder! How do you think I feel?'

But the maid, chosen for her lack of English, merely looked at her with dumb incomprehension.

Outside, the storm had brought nightfall two hours early, and the coachman could only just see the torrent of water where a bridge should have been. Reining in his horses, he swore to himself. The Duke had insisted he leave the footman behind for the last stage of this secret journey, and choose the youngest possible post boy. So now, here he was; madam, by the looks of her, starting her pains, the bridge washed out between him and his destination, and no adviser but the idiot-looking boy whom he had chosen for just that stupidity back in Hereford.

The house he was seeking was only miles beyond the River Teme, but what use was that with the bridge washed out? 'Is there anywhere else we can cross?' he shouted between the next two peals of thunder, and got a frightened headshake, the boy's eyes gleaming with terror in the now almost continuous lightning. The coachman swore again and began slowly and carefully to turn the coach in the narrow road. A mismanaged business from the start, he thought angrily, and no fault of his. Madam should have gone abroad as the Duchess had that time.

And here was madam, leaning out of the window into the drenching rain, to ask, 'What happened? Why are we turning?'

'Bridge washed out, ma'am. I'm sorry.' He was. A man

1

could not help being sorry for her, such an engaging little bit
of a thing, and in so much trouble.

'James, what are we going to do? I'm . . . I'm afraid . . .'
She clenched her teeth as a new pain washed over her.

'Find help,' he told her. 'I saw a house, a good-sized one,
not far back. We'll have to go there. There were lights, plenty
of them.'

'Gentry?' she asked faintly. 'A party? James, I can't . . .'
And again the pain silenced her. Close together, they were.
He remembered his wife and thought they had better hurry.

'Don't fret yourself, ma'am,' he told her. 'You're Mrs.
Brown, remember, on her way to her sister, and not a bit of
livery or a sign on the coach to give you away. A chance in a
million if you're recognised down here.'

'Please God you're right. Oh,' she bit back a cry, 'James,
hurry.'

The house was set well back from the road and as he approached it from this angle lightning showed the squat tower
of a church behind it. Probably the vicarage. Well, bit of luck,
there should be help there.

As he turned the carriage into the short drive, the front door
of the house flew open and a tall man came hurrying out into
the rain, then stopped, as a flash of lightning showed him the
strange carriage. 'Not the doctor!' he exclaimed, ignoring the
rain that was soaking his white hair. 'It's full three hours now.
Which way did you come?'

'From Hereford, sir. Going on to Wales, we was. But we
had to turn back, a mile or two down the road; the bridge is
washed out.'

'The bridge! Gone? And you've seen no other carriage?'

'No, sir. Not a sign of life on the road. I was hoping you
could help us. It's the mistress, she's on her way to her sister
the other side of the river. She's very near her time, sir.'

'Oh, dear God.' The white-haired man actually appeared to
be addressing his divinity. 'Another one. My poor wife's been
in labour these twenty-four hours and more. And the midwife
gone to Hereford and Dr. Mancroft at a death bed on the other
side of the river. I don't like the look of her.' He spoke man
to man, difference of rank forgotten in his deep crisis.

'I'm truly sorry . . .' The coachman was interrupted by the
sudden opening of the carriage window.

'What is it?' asked his mistress. 'Why are we stopping? Oh,
thank God,' she saw the house and the white-haired man staring

up at her. 'Sir, I must beg your hospitality and your wife's. I'm . . . I'm not well.'

'Neither is she,' said the white-haired man bleakly. 'She's been in labour twenty-four hours, and no help to be had this side of the river. I'm more than sorry, madam,' he paused courteously, expecting a name.

'Mrs. Brown.' A spasm of pain flickered across her face. 'And . . . at least we can help you. My maid is an experienced midwife. If you will only give us shelter, she will tend to your wife.'

'Oh, thank God!' He looked up momentarily, then turned to shout a volley of orders to the servants who could be seen lurking as close as they dared to shelter.

Half an hour later, the woman who called herself Mrs. Brown was sitting by the fire of a comfortable bedroom drinking hot soup and listening to her maid's voluble French.

'It's bad, madame.' The girl summed up. 'It's gone on too long; she needs a doctor; more help than I can give. I fear for the life of the little one. But how are you?'

'Easier, thank you. The pains have slowed. I think I could sleep a little.' Her French was very nearly as good as the maid's.

'The very thing.' She helped her mistress into bed, saw that there was a bell ready to her hand and urged her to get all the sleep she could, but ring at once if the pains increased again. 'The kind Monsieur Trentham downstairs says he and his housekeeper will be watching all night. We will not lack for help if we need it. But, *mon dieu*, for a house with two children in it already they are strangely ignorant of what to do.'

'Two children?'

'Yes, in as many years. Monsieur speaks almost as good French as you do, madame.'

'A man of the world?' She pulled herself up on her pillows. 'Oh, dear God, he'll betray me.'

'Not he, madame. He's not of the world. He's a man of God. *Dévot*, I think. He is praying for his wife, down in his study. Shall I ask him to pray for you too?'

'I certainly need it. Oh, Denise, what will become of me?'

'Courage, madame. You'll have no trouble, you'll see. You're built for it. Tomorrow we will have a fine little boy, and then what a happy man the Duke will be.'

'And the Duchess?'

'That's between you and her. But she's such a saint, that one, I really believe she will rejoice for you if it's a boy. Now,

I must go back to my other patient. Rest well, madame, and trust in me.'

'I don't know how I'd manage without you, Denise.'

'No more do I,' said her maid.

Three days later, 'Mrs. Brown' received her host for the first time. Denise had propped her up among her pillows and wrapped her up in the swansdown négligé the Duke had bought her. 'How do I look, Denise?' She studied her reflection in the hand mirror.

'*Ravissante* as always, madame. But I doubt that monsieur will notice.' Was there a note of warning in her tone?

Mr. Trentham looked exhausted. 'I owe you my wife's life,' he said, when the first greetings were over. 'It was the hand of God sent you here, Mrs. Brown.'

'A rough hand!' She smiled up at him, her huge dark eyes brilliant in the ivory face, glossy curls falling in controlled disorder among the swansdown, a most extraordinary contrast to the drained, sallow face of the wife he had just left. 'But I must not jest about sacred things,' she went on, always quick to sense an adverse reaction. 'I am so very sorry about your poor little girl.'

'The Lord gave,' he said. 'The Lord has taken away. And at least I still have my wife, thanks to your maid. And to God.'

She bit back another of the dry remarks the Duke so much enjoyed and widened her eyes at him. 'And I have to thank your wife for feeding my poor little scrap,' she said. 'I am sure you see the hand of God there, as I do.' No need to tell him that she had never meant to feed this inconvenient child herself.

'Yes, indeed.' He agreed with her earnestly. 'But you must not be blaming yourself. You were worn out, ma'am. Your family should not have let you undertake such a journey at such a time. As to your little charmer, I think her needs have saved my wife's reason. She took our loss hard; I was afraid for her. And then, your Caroline, so beautiful, so hungry, so good. She loves her already.'

A little silence fell between them, as he wondered what to ask and she what to tell. He pulled a chair close to the bed and sat on it, looking at her at once keenly and kindly. 'Mrs. Brown.' He made it almost a question. 'Will you let me talk to you like a father, my dear?'

'A father!' she exclaimed. 'I never had one. And not much of a mother either.'

'Then you have all the more need for friends. Tell me your

trouble, my child. I am a man of God. It is my duty to help those in need, and He has sent you to me most directly. Tell me how I can help you?'

'I hardly need to tell you, do I?' She was crying, but quietly, slow tears that made the large eyes larger still. 'You understand it all, do you not?'

'Well, most of it, I am afraid. Your servants have been discretion itself, but that very discretion . . . And the timing of your journey. Were they mad, your friends, to send you off so late—and alone?'

She managed a tremulous smile, the tears still silently flowing. 'He . . . he could not make up his mind,' she said. It was so like the Duke to have made and discarded one plan after another until at last, characteristically, it was her dear friend the Duchess who had stepped in, made the arrangements, sent her down to the pensioned-off housekeeper who lived, so disastrously, on the wrong side of the River Teme. But how could one explain the Duke? 'He's not used to things being difficult,' she said.

'My dear, it is my duty to tell you that you must give him up, whoever he is. Stay here; stay with us.' As he said it, he felt a flash of fear. What would his wife say? 'We will help you,' he went on bravely. 'Think of a story for you. You're so young. Stay with us, my dear. God is a kind father. Stay with us.'

'Oh, but I can't! They could not go on without me. The poor Duchess . . .' She put a hand to her mouth and looked at him with big, scared eyes. Had she meant to let it out?

'The Duchess? Oh, don't look so scared, child. Your secret's safe with me. Call this the confessional, if you like. Let me be your father in God. Tell me all about it. It will go no farther, not even to my dear wife. And it will help you, I am sure, to clear your mind. Talking always helps.'

'Oh, yes! And yet—we've talked so much, the three of us. Well.' She was delighted to feel herself actually blushing. 'Not all together, of course. I love them both, you see. It is very wicked of me?'

'Love is never wicked, but it can be selfish. I think you should ask yourself whether yours is not that. Surely, if you really loved both the Duke and the Duchess you would see it as your duty to leave them. Especially now that you have a new duty, to your little girl.'

'But I can't,' she said. 'I've promised them I'll go back.'

'Both of them?'

'Yes. They need me, you see. When I'm not there they don't know how to go on together. They quarrel. And then there are her debts. He gets so angry. I can always talk him round. Dear sir, try to understand. They saved me. From my husband. He . . . he was not kind to me.' A nervous hand pushed dark ringlets away from the side of her face and revealed an old scar. 'I ran away from him. In Bath. Nowhere to go. My Aunt and Uncle Purchas hadn't like my marriage. My mother was abroad. Well, she always is. It was dark. I . . . I . . . there was a man in the street, following me; then the Duke came. Oh, sir, he was splendid! He took me home to the Duchess. I've lived with them ever since. I love them. Both.' It came with a note of defiance.

'How old are you, child?'

'Twenty-five.' She had decided to let her age stand still there.

'And all your life before you. You could go abroad, to your mother. You'd be a married lady, separated from her husband, with a child.'

'Mother would not have me. Nor would I go to her. You wouldn't wish me to if you knew the kind of life she leads.'

'Oh dear!' He sighed. 'Your aunt and uncle then? Purchas, did you say?'

'Ah. They're good. They'd have me. And forgive me, too. I couldn't bear it. A Sussex squire and his pious wife. Church twice on Sundays. Jams and jellies and soup for the villagers. You can see my Aunt Purchas trying to like me, but she can't do it.' She smiled, her face transformed, alive, amused. 'Well, you can't blame her. I'm the family skeleton. I'm a disgrace in myself, you see. My mother never did manage to marry, though she tried hard enough. Poor Uncle Dick, as if that wasn't bad enough, I remind him of the old days, of his first wife, my Aunt Ruth. Oh, I loved *her*. If she had only lived, I'd have been quite different. Everything would. But my new Aunt Purchas was always ashamed of me. She was a Quaker, one of the Gurnings. No wonder she was glad to marry me off to the first man who came along.' And then, aware suddenly of how much she was shocking him, 'So, you must understand, it doesn't much matter what happens to me. And I can make the Duke and Duchess happy. I really can. They need me. It's a place for me; a life for me. I'm going back there. Don't ask me not to. Please . . .'

'And the child?' His voice was stern now.

'She's to go to an old servant of the Duchess's. A very good sort of woman, with married daughters. It was all arranged. Only . . .'

'You left it too late.'

'Yes. The Duke wanted to come too, you see. Only . . . he's always so busy. Politics, and the club, and—you know the kind of thing.'

'Yes, I know.' He felt infinitely sorry for her, but that had nothing to do with his duty as a clergyman. 'Well, if none of your family will have you, you will just have to stay with us.' His heart misgave him as he said it, but he went bravely on. 'My wife loves your daughter already. I know she will want to go on feeding her. You will have to stay that long. It will give you time to see your position in its true light.'

'Oh, no,' she said quietly. 'Don't you see? It's a kind of miracle. My not being able to feed the child. Your wife taking her. I was afraid I would not be able to part with her. Now it's easy. Please, won't you keep her? She'll be better with you than she ever would with me, or with the woman in Wales. It's the hand of God, as you said. Please, sir, say you'll keep her?'

'Keep her? You mean for good?'

'I don't know.' She looked up at him pleadingly. 'The Duke couldn't make up his mind. He thought maybe, later, we could think of a story. The child of French friends, perhaps. Something like that. He's a devoted father,' she said.

'The Duchess has children?'

'Oh yes! Two girls. They long for a boy—for an heir. Her first child was a son. He died of smallpox when he was four, poor little thing. That was before I met them. Oh, I'm so glad mine is a girl. I could not have born for it to be a boy. For the poor Duchess. I've been so afraid . . ' For a moment, she believed she was telling the truth.

'It's the Duke of Cley, isn't it?' He pronounced it to rhyme with fly. And then, seeing her shrink back in the bed, the tears beginning to flow again, he raised a soothing hand: 'Don't look so scared, child. Your secret is safe with me. As to the child, poor little creature, it is hard to know what to do for the best. This servant you were planning to leave her with, do you know her?'

'No, sir. But the Duchess says she is a very good sort of a woman.'

'And fit to bring up a child who may one day move in the highest circles?'

'I don't know, sir.'

'No,' he said gently, reserving his anger for the Duke. 'How should you? Well, you had best give me her name and I'll have some enquiries made. If she won't do, perhaps I will be able to think of someone else.'

'If only you would take her yourselves! Denise says she's good as gold. And healthy. She'd be no trouble. And, of course,' she smiled and blushed, 'the Duke would pay well for her keep.'

'I'm sorry,' he said. 'You must see that it is quite impossible. If it were a question of having the poor little thing for life, I might be mad enough to consider it. My wife does love her most dearly already.' His smile was kind. 'I've quite lost my heart to her myself. The most perfect baby I ever saw. But you must see, Mrs. . . .' he paused. 'Not Brown?'

'No, Winterton. You have perhaps heard of my husband.'

'I am afraid so. Even down here in the valleys one is not free from the London gossip. You have my deepest sympathy, ma'am. I take it there is no chance of his accepting the child as his?'

'Impossible,' she said. 'I've not ever heard from him since he fled the country to avoid his creditors. And'—again that pleading look—'I know you think me a bad mother, but I'd not saddle the child with him for a father. Oh, if only you . . .'

'I'm sorry.' He rose as a servant scratched at the door to announce that the doctor had come.

'At last,' he said. 'I'll take him to Mrs. Trentham first, if you don't mind?'

'Of course not. But she is really better?'

'I think so. Thanks to your maid, and your little girl. If you had not arrived when you did . . . I do thank God for you, Mrs. Winterton.'

'You won't tell the doctor?'

'I promised you, child.'

A little later, he was closeted with the doctor in his study. 'A near thing.' Dr. Mancroft sipped his wine. 'A deuced near thing. You must not think of risking another, sir. If that French girl had not had her wits about her, I don't like to think what would have happened. Pity about your little girl, but I doubt if even I could have saved her.' He had seen too many deaths

to take this one hard. 'Lucky accident, that,' he went on, 'the
other lady being here. She's making a splendid recovery, by
the way. No problems there. Up and about in a few days, I
have no doubt. Told her I thought she'd be fit to travel in a
week or so. She seems deuced anxious to get back to town.
No reason that I can see why she shouldn't. So long as she
leaves the baby, that is. What are you going to call it? Fetching
little thing. No wonder Mrs. Trentham's so taken with it. Saved
her life, you know, that baby did. You mustn't think of letting
the mother take it away.' He put a knowledgeable finger to
the side of his nose. 'Not that I imagine she'll be wanting to.
Pretty clear case, eh, to a couple of men of the world like you
and me? Lucky for her you've got no option but to keep the
child.'

'No option?'

The doctor finished his wine and turned serious. 'Had a
hard time, your wife. Deuced hard time. Be a liar if I didn't
tell you so. Not quite so composed in her mind, still, as I'd
like to see. Doesn't seem to want to see the other children,
had you noticed?'

'Yes. They mind, too.'

'Just so. That baby's all in all to her, right now. Just between
ourselves, I'm not sure she doesn't half think it's her own.
Well,' expansively, as the rector poured him more wine, 'women
are strange creatures. And at these times . . .' he shrugged largely.
'Not their most rational. By no means,' he concluded with
some emphasis.

'Let me understand you.' Mr. Trentham put down his glass
and leaned forward. 'You are saying that it would be inadvisable to part my wife from the baby at this time.'

'Inadvisable! My dear man, it would either drive her mad
or kill her.'

1

'CAROLINE! CAROLINE!' called Giles Trentham. 'Carrie, Carrie!' cried his sister. 'Time to come out now. We give up. And mother's rung the bell twice. Time for supper.'

Caroline did not stir. She had found a hiding place, down at the bottom of the garden, where cultivated flowers gave way to meadowsweet and comfrey and tall wild flags. Since Giles had fallen in and been dangerously rescued at the age of eight, they had not been allowed as near to the River Llanfryn as this, but today she had found the gleam of its fast water irresistible. Tucked invisibly away under the yew hedge which was clipped one side and wild the other, she could smell the rich scent of the vicarage garden, the blend of gillyflower and hyacinth and small heart's ease, while she watched the swift flow of the water.

It was one of the times when the world around her seemed so piercingly beautiful that she could hardly bear it, must stay quiet, feeling her happiness, listening to it, as she did to the voices of the older children, still calling her, but farther off now, from the orchard that sloped away to the west of the rectory. 'Carrie, Carrie,' came Sophie's voice, faintly now, and then Giles: 'You know she doesn't like being called that. Caroline, please come out now. Mother will be cross.'

Somehow, today, Giles's voice was part of the extraordinary sweetness of things. It drew her out of the trance of happiness, the spellbound watching of the river. Slowly, still half mesmerised by the rush of the water, she pulled herself up, hand over hand, through the lower branches of the yew, and so emerged on to the gravelled path that defined the bottom of the garden. The scent of blossom was stronger here, and she paused to take one deep, ecstatic breath, before she called, 'Coming!' and began to run up the rustic steps.

She caught up with the others on the terrace, and fourteen-year-old Sophie gave her one horrified look. 'Oh, Carrie, what

10

will mamma say? Your dress is torn again, and your hair! Where in the world have you been?'

'Down by the river,' said truthful Caroline. 'I had to climb through the yew hedge.'

'For goodness sake don't tell mamma that,' said Giles. 'You know you're not allowed there, Caro!'

'It's so pretty,' she said unanswerably.

In the house, the bell rang again. 'Come along,' said Giles. 'Let me speak for you, Caro, and you won't have to tell a fib.'

But when they went in from the hot sunshine to the cool of the stone-walled house, they found things in a turmoil. The bell had announced not supper but guests. Nurse Bramber was awaiting them in the back hall, arms akimbo, face red with anxiety. 'There you are at last! There's company come. Your mother's been calling for you this half hour and more. Oh, lud, Miss Caroline, what have you been doing now! Come upstairs this minute. I've your sprigged muslin laid out ready. Miss Sophie, I am trusting you to make yourself fit to be seen. And you, Master Giles, your best suit in ten minutes, or I'll know the reason why!'

'Lord, Martha, how you do fuss,' said Giles. 'Anyone would think it was King George the Third himself, calling, instead of some prosy friend of father's.'

'Farmer George, is it?' She was leading the way up the back stairs now, puffing as she went. 'No, nor yet that good for nought son of his. And as to a friend of your father's! It's not one I've seen before, nohow. The finest gentleman you ever did see, and the two ladies with him might have come straight from court. So, hurry, children, do, they asked most particular to see you.'

Fifteen agitated minutes later, the three children descended the stairs, neat as ninepence, as Giles put it, in their Sunday best. Sophie, whose curls were natural, had merely had them combed through, but Caroline's fine dark hair had been ruthlessly re-braided by Nurse Bramber, and tears of protest still showed in her large eyes. She was pale from a rigorous scolding and the brisk cleansing of the various scratches on wrists and ankles about which, fortunately, Nurse Bramber had not had time or breath to question her. The glow of happiness she had felt down by the river was gone, leaving her sad and strangely lonely.

'Come on, then.' Giles knocked firmly on the drawing-room door and pushed it open.

For once, Nurse Bramber had not exaggerated. The two

ladies who were talking to mamma were beautiful as fairies,
as the angels in the big picture in papa's study. Their clothes
were made of stuffs so fine that Caroline, who liked to have
a word for everything, had no idea what they were called. And
the man talking to papa was indeed the finest gentleman she
had ever seen, though she thought she liked papa's face better,
even though it was so much older and more lined.

'On our way to Llangollen,' the elegant young stranger was
saying, 'to see my cousin there, and thought we would take a
look in on you and your little family. Ah,' he turned his fair
head and saw the children, 'and here they are. And a handsome
parcel of youngsters, too. Now, let me see if I can guess which
is Miss Caroline.' He raised the quizzing glass to his pale eye,
considered the two girls for a moment and turned back to Mr.
Trentham. 'Not difficult after all. She's a little shrimp of a
thing, is she not, compared with your splendid youngsters.'

'Charles!' exclaimed the lady with the golden ringlets who
was sitting beside Mrs. Trentham on the sofa. 'What a thing
to say! You have put the poor child quite to the blush, I declare.
Come here, my dear,' she held out a hand to Caroline, 'and
tell me how old you are. I have a son at home who must be
very much of your age, and he is not very tall either. But I
love him dearly just the same.' She turned to the other lady
who was sitting very upright, very still, on a straight-backed
chair. 'Do you not think she has something of a look of our
Blakeney?'

There was an odd silence in the room, and Caroline felt herself
suddenly and most unusually the centre of attention. She looked
around, disconcerted, and met the steady glance of the second
lady, the one with the huge eyes and glowing dark hair. Her look
was kind. Wonderfully kind. It took Caroline strangely back to
that moment of pure happiness down by the river, smelling the
sweet flowers of the garden. Slowly, almost reluctantly, she
smiled at the beautiful, dark-eyed stranger, who was now holding
out a hand. 'Come to me, my dear,' she said. 'I would dearly
like to have a little girl like you.'

She smelled delicious, like the flowers. Clasped in a fragrant
arm, Caroline stood beside her chair and looked out at the
world she knew. Something very strange was happening. She
looked at her beloved family as if from a distance. Papa had
read them a poem by Mr. Milton that had made a great impression on her. Someone in it had stood high, high up, looking
down at the world. That was how it felt to be standing beside

this kind lady, who held her close, and went on talking lightly, pleasantly, to mamma and the fair lady.

It did not last. Suddenly, the gentleman was on his feet, slender in his blue coat. 'Time to be going,' he said. 'My cousin keeps early hours. Good of you to have made us welcome at so little notice, Trentham.' He did not sound as if this had surprised him. 'We'll give you a look in, if we may, on our way back to Norfolk? You'd like that, my love?'

He addressed the lady on the sofa, but it was the one who was holding Caroline who answered. 'Oh, yes, Duke, do let us,' she said.

'The Duke of Cley, no less,' said Giles, back once more in the safety of the nursery. 'And didn't he just know it! Treated my father as if he was . . . was nobody. And called you a shrimp, too, Caroline. I'd like to have told him you were the wisest shrimp in Christendom.'

'It's just as well you didn't.' Caroline flashed him a mischievous smile. 'I don't think he would have liked it above half.'

'No. He did fancy himself Sir Oracle, did he not?'

Caroline laughed. '"And when I ope my lips,"' she quoted. '"Let no dog bark."'

'Oh, you two!' said Sophie. 'Stop talking nonsense and tell what you thought of the ladies. The Duchess was the pretty fair one who sat by mamma, but I liked the other better, did not you, Carrie?'

'She wasn't pretty,' said Caroline, 'She was beautiful.'

She dreamed of the beautiful, kind lady that night, dreamed, amazingly, that she was showing her the garden and the river, telling her how it felt to sit there. She would understand, would share the happiness. Mamma and papa were always so busy. Besides, they were not really mamma and papa. Her own mamma had died when she was born, leaving her nothing but her blessing and a string of pearls, which she was allowed to look at on Sundays. She day-dreamed sometimes that that was all a mistake, that her mother came back, like a fairy in a story book. The strange lady had said she would like a little girl. How soon would they come? The man who was a Duke had not said, but she did not think he would stay long with the cousin who kept early hours. She stayed close to the house, not wishing to miss a moment of their next visit.

'What's the matter with you, child?' asked Nurse Bramber, a

week later. 'I said, "Go out and play while the sun shines," didn't I? And here you are, still moping in the nursery. Summer will be over soon enough, and the flowers gone. Out with you, and take the air while you can!'

'I don't know what's got into the child,' she said later to Mrs. Trentham. 'Never been a bit of trouble before, and now she no more minds me than if I was that chair. Creeping back, she comes, into the house, whenever my back is turned, and always on the listen.'

'On the listen,' said Mrs. Trentham. 'I wonder . . .'

She spoke to her husband about it that evening. 'Nurse says Caroline is always on the listen these days,' she said. 'As if she were expecting someone. Do you think they will come back, my dear?'

'I doubt it. I am afraid the Duke did not think much of our little Caroline. If he had given her a chance to speak, he might have understood something of her quality. But, frankly, my dear, I am glad he did not. I know I was reluctant to have her, but now I'd not part with little Caro for anything. I was afraid, when they were announced, that they might have come for her.'

'I felt sorry for her poor mother,' said Mrs. Trentham. 'What a lovely creature she is, and what a sad story. Still to be living that nohow kind of life with the Duke and Duchess after all these years. How can she bear it, my love?'

'I suspect she does not have your high moral principles,' said her husband fondly. 'To tell truth, I thought she looked happy enough.'

'And so did the Duchess,' said his wife. 'Extraordinary. And the Duke nothing out of the way, were he not a duke.'

'Ah, but he is,' said her husband. And then, 'My dear, I really do believe we are gossiping!'

'Is there much talk about them?' asked his wife.

'Bound to be. But not the kind I listen to, and no more should you. Caroline is our dear daughter, and that's an end to it.'

'Yes, but there is one thing . . .' She looked at him a little anxiously. 'She's not our daughter, you know, dearly though I love her. Sometimes I wonder about Giles . . . Bringing them up together like this. He stands her champion—have you noticed?—always. You saw as well as I did how angrily he coloured up when the Duke called the poor little thing a shrimp. If he'd been older, I verily believe he'd have called him out!

As it was, I was on tenterhooks lest he say something we'd all have regretted.'

'Giles and Caroline?' said her husband thoughtfully. 'No, no, my dear, brought up as they have been as brother and sister, they'll never think of each other as anything else. And anyway, would it be such a bad thing if they were to? She's got the finest mind, for a girl child of her age, that I ever hope to see. Now I'm teaching her, I tell you I am sometimes hard put to it to satisfy her. She has,' he paused, searching for words, 'a kind of zeal for truth.'

'I know,' said his wife, 'so poor Giles has to lie for her. And, dear, I do sometimes wonder whether you should spend so much of your precious time teaching that child.'

'I'm not sure it isn't the most useful thing I do,' said her husband. 'She's a very unusual creature. If she were a man, I would seriously expect her to come out as a philosopher or even a great preacher. Why, what's the matter?'

His wife had dissolved into laughter. 'Oh, my dear, you are so comic,' she cried. 'Our little Caroline! For pity's sake, never let Sophie or Giles know what you think; the poor child would never live it down. But at least the secret of her birth seems safe enough, thank goodness.'

'That widowed cousin of yours, Mrs. Thorpe, who bore the child and went away to die? Shame on me for telling such lies!'

'What a storm that was,' said his wife, remembering. 'By the time the bridge had been replaced and we were back in touch with the world again, we could have said anything we pleased. So at least Caroline will not have the slur of illegitimacy to contend with.'

'And yet I wonder if I have done right,' said her husband. 'I, in my position, to start such a tale of a cock and a bull. Dr. Mancroft would never leave teasing me about it, but what else could I do?'

'Ah, poor Dr. Mancroft,' she said. 'We miss him sadly. Though, mind you, I like young Dr. Thornton who has taken his place.'

'And so does our Sophie.'

'Sophie? At her age? Giles, you're joking me.'

'She's old for her age, my love.' He changed the subject. 'And so is little Caroline in some ways. I wish I saw her future clear. To tell you the vulgar truth I half hoped the Duke was come to make some arrangement about a settlement for her.'

'Lord knows the allowance he gives you for her is small enough, with the cost of living rising so, but I doubt if that young man ever thinks beyond the pleasures of the day, and his two ladies. I liked the look of the Duchess,' she went on thoughtfully. 'She had a good face, didn't you think? Not so beautiful as Mrs. Winterton, but much kinder.'

'Mrs. Winterton could charm the birds off the trees,' he said.

'Don't tell me she's put her spell on you too!' She was not quite joking.

'I'm an old fogey, my dear.' But they both knew it was not quite an answer.

Another week passed, and Mr. Trentham had to rebuke Caroline for inattention in her Latin lesson.. 'You have never failed to do your preparation before,' he said reproachfully. 'What's the matter, Caroline?' And was appalled when she burst into tears. 'Why, Caro?' A woman's tears always confounded him and he longed for his wife. 'What is it?'

'They're never coming back,' she sobbed. 'She was like one of the angels in your picture, and she smelled like the summer garden, and she's never coming back. She said she'd always wanted a little girl like me.'

Mr. Trentham was profoundly disturbed. 'I really believe the poor child has fallen in love with that mother of hers,' he told his wife later. 'Bother the woman. What business had she making up to her if she had no intention of doing anything more about it.'

'That woman would make up to anyone,' said Mrs. Trentham. 'I doubt she can help herself. And very likely she meant to come back, but the Duke would not be bothered. I'm afraid little Caroline was a sad disappointment to him. I suppose he expected a charmer like her mother and didn't even notice how much she favours him, poor child. As for Caroline, she will just have to make the best of things.' She rose and surveyed her middle-aged reflection in the glass over the chimneypiece. 'Have we done so badly by the child?' she asked. 'That she falls in love with the first pretty stranger she meets?'

'Not a stranger. Her own mother. I suppose there is an instinct in these things. And, my dear, you must not be making comparisons, nor yet blaming yourself. You know as well as I do that the boot was on the other foot at first.'

'Yes, I neglected you all shamefully for her, did I not? I

find it hard to believe, looking back. Well, I am paid for it now.'

Caroline waited in vain for any word from her beautiful new friend, and gradually the visit receded, to become part of the dream world where she spent more and more of her time as Sophie and her friends progressed from hide and seek and ponies to the enthralling subject of young men.

Two years later, just before Christmas, a smiling carrier delivered a huge parcel at the rectory door. 'One of your young ladies has a friend, and no mistake,' he told the maid who opened to him. 'All the way from Lunnon, it's come, and cost a mint, just in the carrying.'

'It's for Caroline.' Mr. Trentham read the direction.

'An unknown admirer?' Just home from Cambridge, Giles was very much the young man of the world. 'Let's see what he's sent you, Caro.'

'Nonsense,' said his father. 'We don't want that kind of talk in his house, Giles.'

'I'm sorry, sir. Only funning.' He was helping Caroline to unwrap the sacking from round the parcel. 'Don't you just hope it is books, Caro, but I am afraid it is not heavy enough. Ah, here's a note. Perfumed!' He handed it over and went on with his unravelling.

Caroline's hand trembled as she broke the seal. 'A present from London for my little friend in Llanfryn,' she read out.

'Is it from the Duchess?' asked Sophie, awestruck.

'I can't read the name.' Caroline gave the note to Mr. Trentham.

'No,' he told her. 'It's from the other lady who came. Mrs. Winterton. What has she sent you, I wonder?'

'There we are.' Giles removed the last piece of sacking and handed the oddly shaped parcel to Caroline.

'A doll!' exclaimed Sophie, as the last of the wrappings fell away. 'She thinks you a baby, Carrie, and I don't wonder.' For Caroline had burst into a passion of angry tears.

Later, Mrs. Trentham made Caroline write a letter of thanks to the beautiful lady she had thought like an angel. It was slow, painful work. The first three attempts were condemned out of hand. 'Caroline, use your imagination!' said Mrs. Trentham impatiently at last. 'Mrs. Winterton meant it kindly when she sent you the doll. You must not let her see that you do not like it.'

'But it's not true to say I do,' wailed Caroline.

In the end, Giles dictated her answer to her. 'It is the most
beautiful doll I ever saw,' the letter began. 'And that's true
enough,' said Giles, 'since you never saw one like it before.
And now, all you have to do is say something friendly. Like,
"Happy Christmas," or "I hope you are well," or something
about your studies.'

'She'd not care,' said Caroline mournfully. 'Not if she sent
me a present like that.' She took up the pen, and wrote in her
careful hand:

Dear Madam
    I thank you many times for remembering me, and
hope you will be very happy this Christmas, and always.

She wrote her first poem that night, a very gloomy one, and
it made her feel a little better, though she was to blush over it
in years to come.

Giles went back to Cambridge soon afterwards, and time
drifted on quietly at Llanfryn. Sophie put up her hair, longed
for balls, and refused to study with her father any more, con-
centrating instead on ladylike accomplishments. The music
master had washed his hands of Caroline after her third lesson.
'It is of no use at all, ma'am.' He was a lively Welshman very
much in demand for miles around. 'For the other young ladies
I teach, I can be doing something. I cannot give them voices,
but I can teach them to play so that it will not be being an
actual pain to hear them. But this one, no. I am sorry. I will
not be wasting my time on her.'

'Oh, very well,' said Mrs. Trentham. 'You will just have
to work harder at your drawing, Caroline, that is all.'

'But I cannot draw either,' said Caroline. 'Please, ma'am,
may I not spend the lesson hours at the studies for which Mr.
Trentham thinks I have some talent. I know he cannot spare
any more of his own time for me, but if I could just have the
use of the books, in my own room where it is quiet, I might
be able to prepare myself...' She stammered to a halt.

'Prepare yourself? For what, child?' Mrs. Trentham had
been surprised and shocked by the use of 'ma'am' instead of
'mamma', and her tone was more abrupt than she intended.

The pale face flushed crimson. 'To earn my living. I know
how dear everything is since this war has gone on so long, and
I can't seem to help it that I am always hungry. You have been
so good to me, always, and I am ashamed to be such a charge

on you. Just as soon as I can, I mean to go as a pupil teacher, perhaps at a school in Hereford, if Mr. Trentham could recommend me to one? So you see, the more I study, the sooner they will take me.'

'But, my dear child.' Mrs. Trentham was appalled. 'We have always looked upon you as one of our own.'

'Yes, but I'm not,' said Caroline with her usual daunting forthrightness. 'And since papa and mamma left me no money, I must think how I am to make my way in the world, and, truly ma'am, I shall like to be a teacher, since it is but a different way of studying, which is what I love best of all. So, please, will you speak to Mr. Trentham for me, and find out how soon he thinks I will be fit to begin?'

'Very well, my dear.' Mrs. Trentham's conscience was pricking her horribly. 'And in the meantime, you may certainly study in your room while Sophie is having her lessons, though I am afraid you will find it cold without a fire.'

'Oh, I don't mind that,' said Caroline.

'We should have thought of this sooner,' said Mr. Trentham when his wife consulted him in the privacy of their room that night. 'Poor little Caroline, what a deal of thinking she must have been doing. I am sure Sophie never bothers about the cost of living. Still less Giles.' He sighed. 'Did you tell her about the allowance the Duke pays me for her?'

'My dear, how could I?'

'And yet she must be told. I noticed, on Sunday, that she refused a second helping of roast beef, and I know how she loves it. Do you really think she is trying to be as little charge on us as possible?'

'My dear, I am afraid so.'

'Something has gone sadly wrong,' he said.

'My fault. I am afraid I have let there be a difference between her and our children. Do you know,'—she had not meant to tell him this—'she called me "ma'am" toady, instead of "mamma" as she used to. I'm so ashamed . . .'

'And you used to dote on her so.' He did not mean it as a reproach.

'Yes, I did. And then that woman came, and not one of you all had eyes for anyone else. And Caroline pining for her after she'd gone, like a lovesick baby, and you saying it was no wonder; she could charm the birds off the trees.'

'I?' He knew they had come to the heart of the matter.

'Yes, you!' She was crying now, tears long pent up. 'You,

who hardly think me worth a glance, since that woman came. The old woman who orders your meals and darns your socks. Do you think I did not mind it to see you ogling that strumpet? Giles, too! He couldn't keep his eyes off her. And now just look at the way he dotes on Caroline. Sometimes I think we made a great mistake when we took that child in!'

'But what else could we have done, my dear?' He was appalled at her increasing note of hysteria. He had jibbed at telling her of Dr. Mancroft's warning that she must not bear another child. No wonder if she had felt herself neglected. But what could he do?

Her voice rose. 'Must do what the great Duke wishes. He and his leman. Must bring up his bastard, even at the expense of our own children. Must . . . must . . . must . . .' She broke into hysterical laughter, and he rang urgently for Nurse Bramber.

Calling later that afternoon, Dr. Thornton recommended rest and quiet. 'She's at a difficult time of her life,' he told Mr. Trentham. 'Some megrims, some little fancies, are to be expected. Women must be indulged at these times. It will pass, I am sure, but in the meantime an easy life, as little anxiety as possible. I am sure there is no cause for real alarm.'

Spring came early that year. In their secluded valley celandines yielded to primroses and daffodils, and the river ran so full of snow water that Caroline could hear its murmuring voice from her bedroom. Lambs frisked in the tiny, odd-shaped fields the farmer had won back from scrub on the hills, and Caroline spent as much time as she could out of doors, watching her beloved garden come to life. Picking white violets down by the yew hedge, she had a new happiness. Mr. Trentham had brought her back a book from Hereford the last time he went there on parish business. It was called *Lyrical Ballads* and she found some of the poems in it strange, dull stuff, but there was one called *The Rime of the Ancient Mariner* that was pure magic. She was learning it by heart, stanza by stanza, and as she picked the tiny, hidden flowers, she murmured to herself:

> And now there came both mist and snow
> And it grew wondrous cold:
> And ice, mast-high came floating by,
> As green as emerald.

She had enough violets now for the vase by Mrs. Trentham's bed, and turned to hurry back to the house, as the shadow of

an April cloud moved across the hills. The shower caught her
on the terrace, and she was laughing with happiness and shaking
raindrops out of her hair when she bounced in at the back door
of the house.

'Hush, child.' Nurse Bramber met her in the hall. 'The
doctor's here.'

'Dr. Thornton? To see Sophie?'

'No.' The red face was set in odd downward lines, and
Caroline thought she looked like a witch in a story. 'He's with
Mrs. Trentham. She's had a bad turn.'

'I'm sorry.' A shadow like an April cloud passed over Caroline's mind, but they were getting used to Mrs. Trentham's
bad turns, and she went quietly away to her bedroom and went
on learning her magic lines:

> And through the drifts the snowy clifts
> Did send a dismal sheen:
> Nor shapes of men nor beasts we ken—
> The ice was all between.

The doctor came again next day, found Mrs. Trentham still
in bed and shook his head gravely, urging her to exert herself.
'I am counting on you young nurses to look after her and give
her mind a more cheerful turn.' His smile was for Sophie. 'I'll
come back tomorrow and see how she goes on.'

'Or how Miss Sophie does,' said Nurse Bramber, turning
to her when he was out of earshot. 'I saw you down the orchard
with young Mr. Staines the squire's boy this morning, miss!'

'Pish!' said Sophie. 'If you tell papa, I'll kill you!'

The apple trees blossomed, tossing pink and white through
the valley, and the familiar, beloved pot-pourri of scents was
building up in the garden. Caroline forgot the need to study
and fit herself to be a pupil teacher in the dreamy happiness
of lying in the hammock in the orchard reciting to herself:

> Oh happy living things! No tongue
> Their beauty might declare:
> A spring of love gushed from my heart,
> And I blessed them unaware.

Mrs. Trentham had made one of her surprise recoveries
on being invited to take Sophie to dine with Dr. Thornton and
his rich mother. It was a most unusual event and had been

tacitly recognised as such with a great deal of running from glass to glass and changing of caps and ribbons. Caroline, too young to go with them, was enjoying the rare luxury of being entirely alone. She had eaten her dinner in solitary state, with Miss Burney's *Evelina* propped beside her on the table, as a barrier against Nurse Bramber's conversation. Now *Evelina* had dropped on to the dry grass and she was lying somewhere on the edge of dream, trying to see how far she could get in reciting *The Rime of the Ancient Mariner* and wishing Mr. Trentham had not stopped buying books. He had always been used to bring something back from his visits to Hereford, finery for his wife and Sophie, and a book, as he would laughingly say, for him and Caroline. But that had been before Giles had gone to Cambridge, before the farmers had started looking so glum and the question of the tithes they paid the vicarage had become such a vexed one. They did not talk much about the long war with France at the vicarage, because talk of it tended to bring on Mrs. Trentham's bad turns.

She had almost had one over *The Rime of the Ancient Mariner*, and her husband had hastened to explain that it had been a present from the rural dean who had thought it sad stuff himself. Caroline sighed and picked up the battered old Latin grammar she had also brought out with her. It had *Giles Trentham, His Book* written in a bold hand on the first page, and she enjoyed following Giles's marginal notes as she struggled with the third declension. But Latin was much harder to learn than Mr. Coleridge's poem. Her mind was beginning to wander already:

> Instead of a cross, the albatross
> About my neck was hung.

She had written a ballad herself, the last time she had been left alone in the house. It was about a lone lady, who travelled the world on a white horse being kind to the poor.

> And still she wore, about her hair
> A shimmering veil of silk.

But she had not been able to find a rhyme for silk, and had torn it up the next day, and then regretted bitterly the waste of a good sheet of paper. Silk . . . milk . . . bilk would not do, nor would ilk because she did not precisely know what it meant, and meaning was very important to her.

A bee buzzed above her head; pigeons cooed; the book fell from her hand. She slept lightly, soothed by the small sounds of summer. The creak of the back gate waked her. Who would come into the orchard by the steep short cut from the road? She sat up quickly, swung down her feet and smoothed her braided hair with an automatic gesture bred by many scoldings. Then, jumping to her feet, 'Giles! What in the world? How did you get here?'

'Walked from Ludlow.' He looked exhausted, bedraggled. 'Where is everyone? Where's my father?'

'They've all gone to the Thorntons. Giles, what's the matter?'

'Everything,' he said. 'Oh, Caro, everything.' He sat down limply on the grass beside her. 'I've been sent down.' He stared at his feet as he spoke, as if he could not meet her eyes.

'Sent down? From Cambridge? Giles, why?' She did not entirely understand what it meant, but his tone told her that it was bad.

'Debt,' he said. 'And other things. Oh, Caro, I've been such a fool!' And then, 'The Thorntons? Is Sophie engaged then? Oh, that might help. Father may not be quite so angry.'

'I don't know,' she told him. 'Nobody said anything. I think, maybe, old Mrs. Thornton wanted to see Sophie.'

'To decide if she's good enough!' He flared up, then sank his head in his hands. 'To come home in disgrace just now! Caro, I won't do it to them.' He jumped to his feet. 'Pretend you never say me! I'll find some way. Promise me, Caroline, word of honour.'

'Promise what?'

'Not to say I came.'

'Giles, I can't. I don't tell lies.'

'You won't need to. Why should they ask if I've been here, when there's no reason in the world why I should have been. Just don't say anything.' He spaced out the words, slowly, for emphasis. 'That's easy enough. You've never been much of a talker. And then when I come back, with my fortune made, we'll laugh about it, won't we Caro?'

'But where will you go?'

'To the devil, the way I feel right now. No, no.' He saw her look of horror. 'Only funning, Caro. I'll look about me; join the army perhaps; lord knows they need men badly enough.'

'Your father would not like that. He means you to succeed him in the living here.'

'In a thousand years time! Please God!' He added belatedly. 'No, Caro, that's all over, all done with. He'll know soon enough. They are bound to write to him. No need to hurry with the bad news. But the Church is not for me, nor I for the Church. I have it! I'll go to Uncle George in Hereford. Why did I not think of that sooner? There, you have done me good already, little Caroline, got my mind working again. Of course: Uncle George. He's always been good to me. Sent me ten guineas when I first went up, and told me to be careful what company I kept. Oh, my God, careful!'

'Giles dear,' she said. 'I think your father would rather you came to him than to your Uncle George. I don't think he and your mother are very fond of Mr. Besmond, even though he is her brother.'

'Fond! I should think not indeed. Uncle George and his father opposed their marriage tooth and claw. Mammon, they think he is, or Belial or Beelzebub or something. But he's a rich man, Caroline, and my uncle, and he'll help me. I shall go to him at once. Say nothing to anyone, and I'll be back in a few days with better news. A week at the most.' His face fell ludicrously. 'Caro, love, can you lend me some money?'

'Me? Lend you money? You're joking me.' But she knew he was doing nothing of the kind. 'Much better stay and talk to papa,' she told him. 'I know he'd want you to.'

'And how he'd scold,' said Giles. 'I have it! Caroline, lend me your pearls.'

'My pearls?' She could not believe her ears.

'The ones your mother left you. You know where they are. In my mother's jewel case. They're yours, to do what you like with. Please, Caro? They'd pay my way to my uncle and he'll arrange to get them back for you. I promise he will.'

She did not quite understand what he meant, but she had never been able to refuse him anything, and after a little more persuasion went into the quiet house and upstairs to Mrs. Trentham's room. Nothing in the house was ever locked up. The jewel case, with its scanty contents, always stood on the dressing table in the big bedroom, and her neat fingers easily opened the little, so-called 'secret' compartment where the string of pearls was kept.

She loved the feel of them and was angry with herself for minding so much that she must give them to Giles.

'Thank you, little Caro.' He surprised her with a swift kiss on the cheek, then turned and hurried back the way he had come, down the footpath through the orchard.

Left alone, she picked up the Latin grammar, then dropped it again. Her peaceful afternoon was irredeemably spoiled. If only it had all been a dream, a bad dream. Perhaps, if she pretended hard enough, it would turn out to have been.

She was very quiet when the family came back from Mrs. Thornton's house, but they were so full of happy talk that nobody noticed. Mrs. Thornton had given her approval. Dr. Thornton had proposed for Sophie, and been accepted, and the wedding was to be quite soon, at Mrs. Thornton's express request. Mr. Trentham looked a little grave when he said that. The old lady had summoned him into her boudoir and explained the situation gruffly, abruptly. 'It's not the match I'd have picked for my son,' she had said. 'Forgive me, but I've always been used to plain dealing. I'd have liked an older girl, and a richer one, but the boy's mad for your Sophie, and I want to see him settled. I'm a dying woman, Mr. Trentham, and I'd like to see the new mistress into the house before I go. She's a sweet child; she'll do. My son don't want her told about me, and he's right, but I thought it only fair to explain to you.'

So Sophie was to be married at Michaelmas and the family talk was all of brideclothes. They must drive into Ludlow, Mrs. Trentham said, and visit the linen drapers there. 'What a happy, busy summer we are going to have. Of course I shall go.' She overruled her husband's protest. 'Sophie would make a sad mull of things without me. And, besides, the outing will do me good. I'm sure you can spare me the horses from the farm this once, Mr. Trentham.'

2

Left behind from this outing, Caroline found it hard to concentrate on her book. She had had a moment of horrible fright when Mrs. Trentham was getting ready and had reached for her jewel case. 'And now, something to dress up my old gown.' She had looked thoughtfully at the box's frugal contents. 'Might I, just this once, borrow your pearls, Caroline?' And then, changing her mind as she frequently did these days. 'No, I'll wear my cornelians.'

A week had passed without a word from Giles, and Caroline had pushed his visit so successfully to the back of her mind that this moment of fright had come as a rude awakening. And then, later in the morning, after the party had left, the post had come and Nurse Bramber had exclaimed: 'Here's a letter from Jesus College, but it's not in Master Giles's hand. I do hope he has got one of those fellowships Mr. Trentham used to speak of. That's a piece of news the master could do with and no mistake.' And then, 'Why, Miss Carrie, what's the matter? You look as if you'd seen a ghost in the glass.'

'It's nothing.' But she was sure that the letter brought news of the disgrace Giles had spoken of. Oh, the poor Trenthams . . . She was glad to put away her books and join Nurse Bramber in the fine sewing she was doing for Sophie's trousseau.

'That's never the carriage already?' Nurse Bramber dropped her work in her lap.

'Surely not. They'd hardly have had time for their luncheon at the Feathers.' But Caroline got up and moved over to the window that commanded a view of the short drive. 'It is they,' she said. 'I hope nothing is the matter.'

'They can't have done much shopping. Miss Sophie *will* be cross.' Nurse Bramber moved anxiously into the hall and opened the front door as the carriage drew up on the sweep. Something must be very wrong indeed. Mr. Trentham had the door open

26

and the steps down before the carriage stopped, and was soon carrying his wife into the house.

'Thank God, nurse!' He saw her waiting on the steps. 'Prepare Mrs. Trentham's bed. Quickly. And you,' he turned to the coachman, 'be so good as to go to Dr. Thornton's and ask him to come at once.' Pausing for a moment in the hall, to shift his half conscious wife to a more comfortable position in his arms, he looked down and saw the letter on the side table. 'Ah!' It almost seemed as if he had expected it. 'Caroline.' He paused. 'No, that must wait. I'd like to see you in the study as soon as we have got mamma to bed.' He turned away and carried her upstairs, followed by Sophie, who had emerged, looking at once cross and frightened, from the carriage.

Half an hour later, Mr. Trentham joined Caroline in the study, where she had crept, burdened by an indefinable, overwhelming sense of guilt, while the rest of the family scurried to and from ministering to Mrs. Trentham. 'She's resting now.' His face was bleak. 'I wish the doctor would come. Now, Caroline, I have to ask you a question.' He reached into his pocket, pulled out a small packet and handed it to her. 'When did you last see these?'

She knew it was her pearls before she had undone the paper. 'Last week.' She raised frightened eyes to his. 'When you were at the Thorntons. I promised not to tell.'

'Thank God for that. You gave them to Giles? He had your permission?'

'Yes, sir.' She was glad that it seemed to make him feel better. 'Not gave.' She went on to explain. 'Lent. He said he would return them when he had seen his uncle.' She could see that Mr. Trentham had the letter from Cambridge crushed in his hand. 'Is he in bad trouble, poor Giles?' she asked.

'Yes. But not a thief, thank God. He's gone to George Besmond? Well, I suppose that is something to be thankful for. Ah, there's the doctor. Caroline, I should scold you, but there is no time.' And he left her to her wretched thoughts.

Creeping out into the hall a little while later, she found Sophie furiously prowling about the house. 'Well, miss!' She pounced on Caroline. 'And what, pray, have you to say for yourself? Little thief!'

'What do you mean?' She looked down at the pearls, which she had twisted absentmindedly round her wrist. 'They are mine,' she protested.

'When you are grown up! Now look at the trouble you have

made. Gave them to Giles, I suppose! And he has no more
sense than to pawn them with Mr. Brown, the Ludlow jeweller.
Well, of course *he* knew with whom he was dealing. We are
not quite unknown in the district! Told papa he had been waiting
the chance to come out and tell him about it. Mrs. Thornton
had commissioned papa to have her rubies reset for me,' she
explained angrily. 'And now look what you and Giles have
done! Papa came out, white as a sheet, having spent all the
money meant for my brideclothes in redeeming your wretched
pearls. And blurted the whole out to mamma, asking when she
had last seen them. So of course she had hysterics and it was
all questions and sal volatile and we had to come home with
no shopping done and no money! I've never seen papa so angry.
What has Giles done? What did he say to you? And what
possessed you not to speak of it? If mamma dies it will be all
your fault. *And* how am I to get married without brideclothes?'
A new thought struck her. 'If mamma dies, I shan't be able to
get married! Caroline, I could kill you!'

'Giles made me promise . . .'

'Giles! Always *Giles*! We pinch and scrape so that he can
go to the university, and now look what he does to us! All
wasted! With a proper dowry I could have had Tom Staines!'
And then, horrified at what she had let out. 'Caroline, if you
ever breathe a word of that, I really will kill you. Promise?'

'Yes.' Caroline was beyond resisting yet another dangerous
promise. And, besides, Dr. Thornton had emerged from the
main bedroom and was coming downstairs talking encouragement to Mr. Trentham.

'Keep her quiet,' he was saying. 'Absolute rest. No worry.
I hope you have news of the young rascal soon, but do not let
her be fretting about him. And as to the brideclothes,'—he
saw Sophie awaiting him in the downstairs hall—'so long as
I get my beautiful bride, who cares about them!'

'You told him!' Sophie turned angrily on her father as soon
as the door had shut on her betrothed. 'How could you, papa!
If Giles is in bad disgrace Mrs. Thornton will forbid the banns,
as like as not. Is he?' she asked anxiously.

'I am afraid so. But no need to be anxious on your own
account.' His tone was a reproof. 'Young Thornton has said the
most handsome things and promised it shall make no difference.
He wanted to pay for your brideclothes himself, but of course
I could not allow that. You will always find, my dear, that it
is best to tell the truth and shame the devil.' He looked at

Caroline as he said this and she retired to her room in a new flood of tears.

A letter came from George Besmond two days later, having been delayed in the slow, cross mail from Hereford. It enclosed his own draft to cover the money Giles had received for the pearls, and an incoherent note of apology from Giles himself. Mr. Trentham looked very grave and showed neither letter to anyone.

'Mr. Besmond is sending Giles to India,' he announced at dinner.

'To India!' exclaimed Sophie. 'Oh, Giles has all the luck!'

'Will he come home first?' asked Caroline.

'No,' said her father.

'Mamma will mind,' said Sophie.

'I am afraid so, but Dr. Thornton says there is to be absolutely no excitement. And, besides, I do not wish to see Giles.'

'But mamma is better?' asked Caroline, still overwhelmed with guilt.

'Much better. You must not be looking so wretched, child. I know you only did it for the best, and indeed, as it has worked out, who is to say you were not right? I hope that India will be the making of Giles, and his uncle seems truly pleased that he went to him in his trouble.' He smiled a little wryly. George Besmond had enjoyed the little triumph of saving his nephew from certain disgrace, and had not spared his brother-in-law in his letter.

Luckily, Mrs. Trentham was still too weak to ask to see it. Warm June gave way to hot July, with the garden a blaze of hollyhocks and sweet-scented roses, but still she kept to her bed, and Dr. Thornton, who now visited most days, began to look anxious and urge that she be encouraged to get up and come downstairs. 'To sit in the air would do her the world of good,' he told Mr. Trentham after one of these visits. 'Your garden smells so delicious, it would cheer her up, I am sure.'

'I wish we could persuade her,' said Mr. Trentham, 'but perhaps until the shock of Giles's going has worn off a little . . .'

'Young wretch,' said Thornton. 'Has he any idea, I wonder, of the harm he has done?'

'I hope not.' Trentham silenced him with a warning glance.

But Caroline had heard. She had been surprised to be denied access to Mrs. Trentham's sickroom but had accepted Nurse Bramber's explanation that the fewer people the invalid saw

for the present the better it would be for her. Now, she began
to wonder anxiously whether there was not more to it.

'Papa.' She approached Mr. Trentham when he returned
from seeing the doctor out. 'Is mamma very angry with Giles
and me? Is that why I may not run errands for her?'

'Dear child,' he was looking haggard with worry, 'she is
not quite herself again yet. She does not feel fit for company.'

'Company! But papa . . .' She stopped, taking it in. 'I did
not understand,' she said. 'It's all my fault, isn't it?' She looked
up at him with tear-filled eyes. 'It is because of me that she
won't come downstairs? She doesn't want to see me? She thinks
it's my fault that Giles has been sent away?'

He could not deny it. Adoring Giles as she did, Mrs. Trentham had focused all her resentment on Caroline. 'She is not
quite reasonable at the moment,' he explained to the white-
faced child. 'Women get these fancies at her age, and must be
humoured. I am more sorry than I can say, my dear, but you
must try not to mind it.'

'Mind it?' said Caroline. 'But, papa, if that is why she will
not come downstairs, I must go away. You always said that it
was better to face things as they are. Only,' she swallowed a
sob, 'where shall I go?'

Dr. Thornton, who was no fool, had reached the same conclusion as Caroline, and put it to Mr. Trentham when he called
the next day. 'It is time Mrs. Trentham came downstairs.' They
had adjourned to the study. 'It is doing her no good to stay
cooped-up in her bedroom. There is some little fancy about
Caroline, is there not?'

'I am afraid so,' said Trentham ruefully. 'It's hard on the
child.'

'And bad for Mrs. Trentham. Has Caroline no relatives of
her own that she could visit for a while? I know you treat her
quite as your own, but surely . . .'

'It's not easy.' Trentham had been thinking anxiously on
very much the same lines and was glad of a confidant. 'I look
on you quite as a member of the family already. I'd be grateful
for your advice, Thornton.' He plunged into the story of Frances
Winterton's arrival, Caroline's birth and the one visit from the
Duke of Cley and his ladies. 'So far as I know,' he concluded,
'they are all the kin Caroline has aside from some cousins Mrs.
Winterton spoke of in Sussex, who've done nothing about her.
Her mother sent her a doll once, and the Duke makes her an
allowance but, to tell you the truth, that has become a problem

too, and one I am afraid that Mrs. Trentham has begun to resent. He has never increased it, you see.'

'And with the way the cost of living has risen during this endless war... awkward for you. And I can understand, too, that the Chevenham household is hardly one to which you would wish to send a ten-year-old child. A very curious ménage indeed, as I am sure you must know as well as I do. Amazing to think that that notorious charmer, Frances Winterton, is your little Caroline's mother. You would hardly call the child a beauty.'

'No. I am afraid she was a disappointment to the Duke when he came. Poor child, she was quite beglamoured by that worthless mother of hers. It was then that the trouble started, I'm sorry to say. She had been quite a favourite of Mrs. Trentham's before, but naturally she minded seeing the child pine and mope over a creature like Frances Winterton.' He did not mention his wife's jealousy of himself. That was his own affair, not to be mentioned even to a future son-in-law.

'A dangerous woman.' Thornton summed it up. 'One cannot help feeling sorry for the Duchess, though it does appear that she is really devoted to Mrs. Winterton. Well, hers was a dynastic marriage of course; no question of love between her and the Duke; and the gossips do say that she has found her own comfort. There was talk last spring about a young man— can't remember his name. Began with an 'm', I think. Doesn't matter anyway, but the Duke banished his wife to his Irish estates. Mrs. Winterton went too, mind you.'

'A very odd business,' said Trentham. 'But you can see why I hesitate to approach them on Caroline's behalf. Even if they should send for her, how would she go on, poor child, in a household like that?'

'Badly, I am afraid. Just the same, if Mrs. Trentham is not noticeably calmer in her mind by the end of the month, I really think you will have to do something.'

But before the month was up, a strange carriage came swinging up the vicarage drive.

'Jiminy!' Sophie was looking out the upstairs window. 'Did you ever see such horses! And the liveries! And the crest on the panel! Whose is it? Can you see?'

'There's no one inside,' said Caroline, as the carriage swept smartly to a halt.

'Yes, there is. Look!' One of the huge footmen had jumped

down to throw open the carriage door. 'What a little dab of a woman for such a grand carriage! Who in the world can it be?'

'Someone in trouble, I expect,' said Caroline. 'They always come to papa.' And wondered, as she often did these days, whether she should go on calling him that.

A rousing peal on the bell sent Nurse Bramber scurrying to open the door, and the two girls, leaning over the banisters, got a good look at the neat, black-clad visitor as she was led across the hall to Mr. Trentham's study.

'I like her face,' said Caroline, when the study door was safely shut behind the stranger. 'She looks kind.'

'Do you think so? I think she looks like someone's governess, and a strict one at that. As if she could see right through you.'

In the study, Mr. Trentham had seated his guest in the straight-backed chair she preferred and was looking at the letter she had handed him. 'From the Duke?' he asked.

'No, sir. From the Duchess.' The woman, who had announced herself as Miss Skinner, folded her hands composedly in her lap. 'If you would be so good as to read it?' It was not exactly a command, and yet he did almost feel as if he were relegated once more to the schoolroom.

The letter was a warm and pressing invitation from the Duchess for Caroline to come and pay them a long visit. 'We are quite ashamed, dear Mr. Trentham,' she wrote in her flowing hand, 'to have neglected the child so shamefully, but our excuse must be that we knew what good hands she was in. Now we all long to see her, and are even wondering whether you might not permit her to share the education of our great parcel of children. We have quite a household now, with our own two dear girls and Blakeney, and the little son of a French friend of ours who committed him to our care before the outbreak of this endless war. We have prevailed upon Miss Skinner, a very highly educated lady indeed, to undertake the care of the girls, and thought it might be to Caroline's advantage to share her good offices. So, dear Mr. Trentham, I am sending her to you, in the hope that she can smooth out any little anxieties you might have on the child's account, and then escort her back to Cley, where we mean to pass the rest of the summer.' And then, below the elaborate signature, a postscript. 'The Duke sends his regards and bids me say that, naturally, if you allow us the pleasure of educating the child, he will wish to be responsible for her future.'

'A very kind letter.' Mr. Trentham finished it and looked up to meet the steady eyes of his guest.

She smiled at him. 'The Duchess showed it to me,' she said. 'Perhaps you would allow me to expand on it a little?'

'I should be most grateful. It's a hard decision. We have looked on the child as our own.' How much, he wondered, did she know about the circumstances of Caroline's birth?

'I am a very old...' she paused and smiled at him again. 'I almost said friend of the family. I lived for many years with the Duchess's mother, to whom I was indebted for my education. She has been...'—another pause—'a little anxious about her daughter and grandchildren. They have lived, as you doubtless know, a wandering kind of life, first in one resort of fashion, then in another. It has not been entirely in the best interests of the children. Now all that is to be changed. The children are to have their own establishment at Cley, and I have agreed to take charge of it. There are rumours of a peace with France, as you doubtless know. If it should come, as please God it does, the Duke and Duchess, and, of course, their friend Mrs. Winterton, will most certainly go abroad at once, and I shall have entire control in the schoolroom. I think I can promise little Caroline a good education, Mr. Trentham, and'—another of her significant pauses—'if I may say so, a moral one.'

'Thank you.' He knew a great deal about the Duchess's mother, who was famous for her learning and good works. 'You are perhaps related,' he said now, 'to Mr. Gerald Skinner, the author?'

'My brother. I kept house for him for a while before he married. Mr. Trentham,' she went on earnestly, 'these are hard times. I have the Duke's assurance for you that you will never regret letting little Caroline join his family.'

'The other children?' He was thinking about the wandering, fashionable life they had lived.

'A trifle spoiled.' She smiled her friendly smile. 'But nothing a little discipline will not remedy. They are lovable children, Mr. Trentham. I am sure I can promise you that Caroline will be happy as a member of the family.' Her tone, more than her words, told him that she knew precisely how close a member Caroline was. She leaned forward. 'Mr. Trentham, it is not a situation of which people like you and me can possibly approve, but I beg you will believe me when I tell you that I think that nothing but good can come to Caroline from the change.'

'The Duke intends her to stay?'

'Oh, yes. The talk of a visit is merely by the way. It's part of the agreement.'

'Agreement?'

He had felt her considering him as they talked. Now she came to a decision. 'I feel I can speak frankly to you, Mr. Trentham. No need to say that it is in entire confidence. There has been some difficulty between the Duke and Duchess. Not just her debts... She and Mrs. Winterton spent almost the whole of last year on the Irish estate. Now, they are re-forming the family. Your Caroline's presence is part of the new plan.'

'I see.' He was afraid he did. Every instinct revolted at the idea of sending an innocent child to such a household. He looked up and saw Miss Skinner's friendly eye on him, reading his mind.

'She really will come to no harm,' she said. 'You have my word for it.'

He had heard the sound of an arrival, and rose to his feet. 'Will you excuse me? It is the doctor, come to see my wife. You will stay the night, of course, Miss Skinner, and if I may, I will give you my answer in the morning.' He turned to give the necessary orders to Nurse Bramber, who had opened the door to announce Dr. Thornton. 'And, nurse,' he concluded, 'where is Caroline?'

'In her room, I think. Reading one of those books of hers.'

'May I go to her?' asked Miss Skinner. 'And may I tell her?'

'Yes.' He looked distracted. 'Yes, I suppose so. Yes, of course. She has a right to know of the invitation.'

'Thank you. I must not keep you from the doctor. I am sorry to hear of your wife's indisposition.'

'Nurse Bramber will explain,' he said, and left them together.

Nurse Bramber had intended to be very much on her dignity, but the stranger's smile was so friendly and her questions so sympathetic that she soon found herself pouring out the whole story of Mrs. Trentham's illness and its cause. She glossed over Giles's disgrace as best she could. 'It's all done with now. His uncle's sent him to India, but it has left the mistress with this dislike to poor little Caroline. Really, ma'am, the invitation you bring comes as a blessing, though I shall be sad to see the child go. She's a funny little thing, but lovable.'

'Then if I might see her? Perhaps in her own room, if she sleeps alone.'

'Oh, yes, rooms is what we have got in this old rectory. It's hands to clean them we are short of. Though the girls are good as gold. Specially Miss Caroline. She minds being a charge on Mr. Trentham, you know, now times are so bad. But you would know nothing of that.' Her respectful eye had taken in every detail of Miss Skinner's elegant black travelling dress.

'On the contrary.' Miss Skinner had risen to her feet. 'I kept house for my brother, who is a clergyman, for several years. I know very well what it is like, and the expense of launching children in society . . .'

This, inevitably, led to a digression by Nurse Bramber on Sophie's projected marriage, and by the time Miss Skinner tapped lightly on the door of Caroline's bedroom, she had a very good idea of how things stood in the Trentham family. At Caroline's surprised 'come in,' she pushed open the door and found the child sitting at her open window writing away busily at a little battered desk.

'How do you do, Caroline.' She held out a friendly hand. 'I am Miss Skinner, come to you with a message from the Duchess of Cley.'

'The Duchess?' Caroline jumped to her feet and made a neat little curtsy, feeling herself in one of the strange, continuing stories of her dreams.

'Yes, the Duchess of Cley. She was a dear friend, you know, my dear, of your mamma.' And aside from the tense of the verb, that was true enough, thought Miss Skinner wryly. 'She has sent me to invite you to come and pay a long visit to her own children at Cley.'

'Oh!' It was a long breath of pure amazement. 'Me?' She looked down at the cotton dress that had been altered, first for Sophie and then for her. 'Me, visit a duchess? At Cley?'

Miss Skinner watched with interest as the child thought about it. Not a beauty by any means, she thought, but a taking child.

'Cley?' Caroline said again. 'That's in Norfolk, is it not? I found it on the map in papa's study once. There was a lady, sent me a doll. A beautiful one,' she added on a note of apology that spoke volumes to her perceptive listener. 'I wrote to thank her at Cley. It's quite close to Holkham, isn't it, where Mr. Coke lives?' She was remembering now, back to that long-ago visit and the sweet-smelling lady who had held her so close in her arm. 'Will she be there?' she asked. 'The lady? Mrs. Winterton?'

'Yes, indeed.' Miss Skinner thought this was going to be easier than she had feared. 'She is a dear friend of the Duchess.'

'Oh?' said Caroline again, taking it in. 'And there are children?'

'The Duchess has two little girls older than you, Lady Charlotte and Lady Amelia, and a boy, Blakeney, who must be about your age. And they have another boy living with them, the child of friends in France. He and Blakeney are just back from Harrow, and I teach the girls. I think I would enjoy teaching you, my dear. Tell me what you know about Mr. Coke?'

'Coke of Norfolk? The great commoner?' Caroline's face lit up. 'Oh, I know all kinds of things about him! He went to see the King in country clothes, just think of that, because it was his right as a country member, and of course the King didn't like it above half. That was before the poor King went mad because of losing the Americas. Do you think that served him right, ma'am?' she asked eagerly. 'He's better again now, I know, but Giles always said it was more than he deserved, only I don't think I believe in retri—' She paused, colouring scarlet, the word eluding her.

'Retribution,' supplied Miss Skinner. 'No, I agree with you, my dear. Things are not quite so simple as that.' She thought that the child would come as something of a surprise to the Chevenham girls. And to their father. 'At all events,' she went on, 'I can see that you are as good a little Whig as the Duke could hope for in a guest. And as to Mr. Coke, he is a friend of the family, and if you come to Cley you will most certainly meet him.'

'Oh.' Another deep, thoughtful breath. The child stood there for a moment, taking it all in. Then her eyes flashed to the open window with its frame of yellow roses. 'My garden,' she said, 'I shall lose my garden!'

'There are gardens at Cley, my dear.' The amusement in Miss Skinner's tone held a hint of irritation.

'I beg your pardon, ma'am.' The child surprised her by recognising it. 'I am sure there are splendid ones. Only, you see, this is the one I grew up with. I know where to look for the first primrose. And the last rose. It's . . . it's *my* garden.'

There was more to it than that, Miss Skinner thought. Later, when she met the rest of the family over dinner, she wondered if Caroline had perhaps used the garden as an escape from the rather commonplace Trentham girl, whose behaviour to herself she found sad and interesting. Caroline had recognised her at once as a friend and an equal. Sophie, on the other hand, taking her mother's place at the table, treated her with the elaborate courtesy of superior to mere governess.

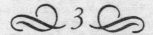

CAROLINE HAD NEVER been farther than Ludlow in her life, and the long, luxurious journey across England to Cley was one she would never forget, though at the time she was in such a mixèd daze of shyness and homesickness that only isolated incidents stood out clearly. They travelled by easy stages, and she was amazed at the calm competence with which Miss Skinner dealt with innkeepers, post boys and the like. But then, life was clearly quite different when one travelled in a crested coach with two footmen.

They spent two days staying with Miss Skinner's brother outside Cambridge. He had recently been given a good living, Miss Skinner told her, and the Duchess had suggested the visit. 'She thought we might do some shopping in Cambridge. A few things for the house that can be got better there than in Lynn and one or two little things she thought you might need. You won't mind?' She had recognised and respected the streak of pride in Caroline. 'Mr. Trentham wished to help in outfitting you, but I had to tell him I had the strictest orders from the Duchess.'

'She seems to think of everything,' said Caroline. 'She must have been very fond of my mamma.'

'And means to be just as fond of her daughter. And so does Mrs. Winterton too.' This was one of the moments when she disliked her commission, fearing questions she could not answer.

'Mrs. Winterton,' said Caroline, 'I remember her best. She

smelt like a garden.' And bit back the tears that would come
when she thought of the garden at home. Would she ever find
a safe place again, like the one between the yew hedge and
the river?

It was strange to be in Cambridge at last and know that
Giles was already at sea on the long voyage to India. Miss
Skinner took her to see his college, as an interval among a
perfect orgy of shopping, as it seemed to Caroline. Miss Skinner apparently thought otherwise. 'That should do for the time
being,' she said, when the new dresses were delivered on the
second evening of their stay. 'You'll wear the rose-coloured
dimity tomorrow, and the new bonnet and pelisse.'

'Will we get there tomorrow?'

'No, the next day. We don't want to arrive worn out, do
we? Not to the kind of welcome we are likely to receive. The
children will be eager to see their new companion.'

'Oh.' Caroline seemed to shrink into herself, and Miss Skinner felt a twinge of anxiety.

'She's such a feeling little creature,' she told her brother
and sister-in-law that night after Caroline had been sent off to
bed. 'The new impressions of the journey have been almost
too much for her. I've sent one of the men ahead with a note
to the Duchess warning her that it's a very tired child I'll be
bringing. It would be a pity to have too high expectations, and
have them disappointed.'

'The Duchess?' asked her astute brother. 'Or the Duke?'

'Oh, the Duke. He's the kind of man nobody ever calls
anything but "Duke" or "Your Grace".' It was one of the
comforts of the strange life she led that she need have no secrets
from this reliable brother of hers. 'And the Duchess's children
are such handsome creatures. Mrs. Winterton told me that he
called Caroline a little shrimp the only time he met her.'

'She's a very engaging little shrimp,' said Mr. Skinner.
'Did you see how she listened to the talk at dinner? She didn't
miss a thing. I thought for a moment she was going to join in
when we were talking about Mr. Coleridge and his poetry. Did
you see? She was scarlet in the face with wanting to.'

'I'm afraid there won't be much talk of poetry at Cley.'

'I suppose not. She's got a deal of character, that child.
While you are fretting about what they will make of her, maybe
you should also be thinking just a little of what she will make
of them.'

'Oh, I do. I've been anxious about that. And anxious too

that the mere sight of Cley may be too much for her. I've tried to prepare her for it by showing her Warwick Castle and one or two other places on the way, and we'll be passing Holkham, of course, but she's not got the slightest real idea, you know.'

'How should she have? But she's got backbone, that child. Whatever she feels, she will behave with that curious touch of dignity she has.'

'A perfect lady,' said his sister. 'Is it not strange?'

They spent the last night of their journey at the best inn at Lynn, and Caroline started out next morning nervous and self conscious in her new clothes. 'Oh!' she forgot it all in her first sight of the sea. 'Miss Skinner! I had no *idea*!'

'I knew how you would feel.' Miss Skinner smiled and pulled the checkstring. 'I grew up in London, and rivers just do not prepare you for this . . . this vastness. We'll stop for a moment and take a closer look. A pity it is such a misty morning,' she went on, as the footman let down the carriage steps, 'or you would be able to see the other side. This is not quite the sea, you know, but the Wash. At low tide it would be all mud. I am glad it is high for you.'

'The Wash? Where King John lost his baggage? It's like living in history! And Cley is near the real sea?'

'Yes. We will be driving along the coast this afternoon. The first Duke of Cley built his house here because King William the Third asked him to oversee the drainage of the marshes. The first house was quite a small one, in the Dutch style. He had lived in exile in Holland, after the Duke of Monmouth's rebellion, in which he was involved. They were very good friends.' She paused.

'Giles told me about poor Monmouth,' said Caroline, surprising her. 'Was he really Charles the Second's son?'

'So it was said. And, if so, he and the first Duke of Cley were half brothers.' She was grateful to Giles, who figured largely in Caroline's conversation, for giving her the chance to convey this piece of information.

'Like the Duke of St. Albans.' Caroline surprised her again. 'Giles told me about him too.'

'Giles seems to have told you a great deal.'

'We were friends.' A hint of tears in Caoline's voice. 'He told me all kinds of things. He said I listened like a boy. I wish he hadn't had to go to India.' She sniffed resolutely. 'Please tell me more about the Dukes of Cley. Was the first Duke part of the Glorious Revolution?'

'Yes. He came over with William and Mary. He had married a Dutch lady, the sister of a friend of King William's, and knew a good deal about how they drained their land.'

'Was he made a duke for that?'

'No, that came later. He was a soldier, too, and fought beside the Duke of Marlborough at Blenheim. They were good friends for a while, but their wives never did get on. People say the first Duchess of Cley planned their new house to rival Blenheim Palace. She was a very rich lady in her own right.' She did not add that the Dukes of Cley had made a practice of marrying rich women.

'Like Blenheim?' said Caroline. 'But that's a palace, isn't it? Is Cley so very big?'

'Huge. I used to get lost in it all the time.' She laughed and patted Caroline's hand. 'Don't look so scared, child! The family have a wing of their own, and you won't get lost in that.'

Caroline drew a deep breath. 'A whole wing!' And then, eased by Miss Skinner's friendliness. 'Will they like me, the children? Will they mind my coming?'

'Not a bit of it. They are used to visitors, and you are to be a very special one. They were looking forward to it when I came away. I am afraid they find life a little dull now they are all the time at Cley, and any diversion is welcome.'

'And I'm to be a diversion?' Caroline was quiet for a long time.

The morning mist had cleared into a brilliantly fine day and they stopped for their picnic luncheon at a place where the road commanded a wide view of brownish green salt marsh and deep blue sea. 'The air smells different here.' Caroline took deep breaths of it as the footman laid out rugs by the side of the quiet country road. 'I like it! I like the country, too. Sophie said it would be flat as a pancake, but it's not, is it? And there's so much sky. And as for the sea...' She took another ecstatic breath. 'I can't think of words for it.'

Miss Skinner showed her Holkham Hall that afternoon, grand and gleaming behind its newly planted screen of trees, and again she found herself without words. 'It looks like a temple,' she said at last. 'Giles had pictures of them in his Homer. Is Cley like that?'

'Not really. Mr. Vanbrugh had a different idea of building. But it's just as big.'

'Oh dear!' said Caroline.

The going had been heavier than the coachman had expected

and it was late afternoon when they drove through the thriving little town of Blakeney, from which the heir to Cley took his title.

'The people are bowing to the carriage!' exclaimed Caroline. 'I feel like a queen.'

'The Duke's a good landlord,' said Miss Skinner.

'Like Mr. Coke. Does he dress up and pretend to be a labourer, and find out that way what is really going on on his estate?'

'Well, no,' said Miss Skinner, awed by the idea of the autocratic Duke in peasant's smock.

Soon after they left Blakeney the road joined a high stone wall, running along the gentle slope that rose from the salt marshes. 'There,' said Miss Skinner. 'The estate wall at last. Not long now.'

'The trees here are higher than at Holkham,' said Caroline, disappointed. 'Can we not see the house?'

'Not until we are through the lodge gates. Cley's older than Holkham, remember. The trees here are about eighty years old. Gracious me,' she exclaimed, as the carriage drew to a jolting halt. 'What's the matter?'

'It's highwaymen, miss!' The footman looked in at the window, a broad grin belying his words.

'Your money or your life,' said a boy's voice. And then, impatiently, 'Out of the way, James, or I'll shoot you!'

The footman vanished, with a look of comic dismay, and his large figure was replaced by that of a slim boy in slouch hat, cloak and mask who edged his horse up close to the carriage, rested a deadly looking duelling pistol on the lowered sash of the window, and repeated his demand of, 'Your money or your life!'

'Blakeney.' Miss Skinner's tone was arctic. 'How dare you! Give me that firearm at once. How do you know it's not loaded?'

'Of course I know,' said the boy. 'Don't spoil sport, Miss S! You brought her, I see.' He removed hat and mask in one sweeping left-handed gesture, and made a low bow to Caroline. 'Welcome to Cley, Miss Thorpe. We've come to escort you, but you're late. The girls got tired of waiting and went home. You've lost your bet, Gaston,' he turned to speak to someone behind him. 'She's tiny, much smaller than I am.'

'Let me see.' The solid-looking, dark-haired boy had taken off his mask but also held a pistol. 'So she is,' he said disgustedly. 'What a take in. I was sure she would be tall. That's ten good shillings you've cost me, Miss Thorpe.'

'Give me those weapons at once,' said Miss Skinner. 'And make sure they are not cocked before you do so. Oh, dear God!' The pistol Blakeney held had gone off as it rested on the rim of the carriage window and she looked aghast at a neat hole in the window opposite. 'Are you hurt, Caroline?'

'No, ma'am, but something's happened to my bonnet.' She had been leaning forward to look at the two boys when the pistol went off, and the shot had gone clean through the high brim of her bonnet, which was now drooping round her face. Oddly enough, instead of being frightened, she was enormously amused by the horrified expressions of the two boys. 'Your faces,' she said with a little gasp of shocked laughter. 'If you could just see your faces!'

'You said you'd unloaded them!' Blakeney turned on his companion. 'You told me!'

'Tell-tale, tell-tale, Blakeney's a tell-tale!' mocked his companion. 'How could I imagine you'd be such a fool as to cock the thing? I just thought it would be a lark to fire a shot if the coachman didn't stop.'

'I didn't cock it,' said Blakeney. 'It must have hit the window frame. Miss Skinner, Miss Thorpe,' he turned suddenly from angry boy to serious, very young man, 'I beg you will accept my profoundest apologies for this accident.' And then, a boy again. 'I must say, Miss Thorpe, you're a brick. Charlotte or Amelia would have squeaked and fainted. You're like Queen Elizabeth, I think, great heart in tiny body.'

'Oh, thank you,' exclaimed Caroline. 'That's the best compliment I ever had.'

'That's all very well,' said Miss Skinner. 'And I admire Miss Thorpe's courage quite as much as you do, Blakeney. But the fact remains that you near as possible killed her. What are we going to say to your father?'

There was a little, shocked silence before the bigger boy spoke. 'Why, nothing, Miss Skinner. The men will be quiet about it because they know their orders are to drive on if they see a highwayman. It's as much as their job's worth if the Duke learns they stopped for us.'

'Yes, but I knew you, sir,' said a reproachful voice from the box.

'It won't do, Gaston,' said Miss Skinner. 'I'm sorry, but it won't do. There's Miss Thorpe's bonnet to be explained, for one thing.'

'Hasn't she got another one?' asked Gaston. 'All she has to do is change it.'

'It's my only one,' said Caroline ruefully. 'It was a beautiful bonnet.' And knew, watching Gaston's face, that she had made an enemy.

'I'll buy you a new one the very next time I go to Lynn,' said Blakeney. 'And indeed I am sorrier than I can say, Miss Thorpe. It is all my fault.' He spoke now to Miss Skinner, 'And so I shall tell my father. It was my idea to hold you up, and it should have been my responsibility to check the pistols.'

'Handsome of you, Blakeney,' said Miss Skinner drily. 'It's late. Drive on, Stokes,' she told the coachman who had been unashamedly listening. 'And if I were you boys, I'd ride ahead and tell your story to the Duke before we arrive. It won't improve with keeping.'

'Oh, I *say*!' protested Gaston.

'Thank you, Miss Skinner,' said Blakeney. 'You're right. We'll tell them to expect you shortly.' He motioned to the coachman to wait a moment and leaned in at the carriage window. 'I still think you're a brick, Miss Thorpe,' he said. 'May I call you Caroline?'

As the two boys rode away, Miss Skinner reached out a friendly hand to Caroline. 'That was brave of you, my dear. I'm proud of my new pupil.'

'Oh, thank you.' Reaction was setting in. A cold little draft blew on to her face from the hole in the carriage window, and she felt herself begin to shake as she realised what had nearly happened. 'Might I really be dead?'

'Best not think about it,' said Miss Skinner bracingly. 'Here we are at the lodge gates.' They were being held open by two grinning children. 'And in a moment you will get your first sight of Cley, but we're very late. I am afriad we must not stop to look.'

The carriage emerged from the screen of trees that lined the park wall and as it turned with the curve of the driveway Caroline gave a gasp of astonishment at sight of the house squatting hugely on the crest of the slight slope up from the marsh; a vast, dark silhouette, fringed with tower and turret and Gothic ornament. 'But. . . but it's worse than a palace,' she exclaimed, frightened as she had not been by the pistol shot. She clasped Miss Skinner's hand. 'You won't leave me?'

'We're much later than I meant to be, but maybe it will all be for the best. The family should be at their dinner and we can get you straight up to the children's apartments.'

'They have their own?'

'Yes. In the family wing. Family and guests have the two south wings. You're family, of course,' she reassured, as the carriage swept past the turning that led to what was obviously the main front of the house. 'That's the state entrance,' she pointed. 'We're going around to the family courtyard. That's right.' She took the ruined bonnet from Caroline and helped smooth her braided hair. 'They're almost bound to be at dinner.' She was encouraging herself as much as Caroline. 'The Duke insists on town hours,' she explained. 'Except on open days, of course.'

'Open days?'

'When he entertains his neighbours. But that's on Wednesdays. Ah, here we are at last.' The carriage had rounded the vast bulk of the family wing which seemed to Caroline larger itself than the ruins of Ludlow Castle. As they turned into the courtyard and under a low arcade, the sun came out from behind the clouds, slanting down into the yard, striking sparks from big windows and giving a rosy glow to the brick of which the house was built.

'It's all built of brick,' Miss Skinner explained. 'Mr. Vanbrugh who designed it found the clay on the estate. Thank you, James,' the footman had opened the door, and, behind him, Caroline saw other footmen swinging open heavy doors at the head of a sloping flight of steps. 'Chin up, my dear.' Miss Skinner turned swiftly to pinch spots of colour into Caroline's pale cheeks. 'You'll be quite a heroine, you'll see.'

The doors opened into a cold marble hall lined with huge statues, and Caroline, gazing round her, wondered what the main entrance could be like if this was the family one.

'The Duke is a great collector,' said Miss Skinner, eyeing the statues without enthusiasm. 'But here come the children. I thought they'd not be long.' She advanced smiling to greet the two girls who had appeared at the top of yet another sloping flight of steps. 'Lady Charlotte, Lady Amelia.' She kissed them in turn. 'Here is your new schoolmate, Miss Thorpe.'

'But we are to call her Caroline,' said Lady Charlotte, the taller of the two girls, who were both pink-cheeked, golden-curled and dressed in identical tucked muslin dresses, one with a blue sash, one with a pink. 'You are to call us Charlotte and

Amelia,' she told Caroline. 'And Blakeney says you are a regular Trojan. Did he really shoot clear through the brim of your bonnet?'

'He did indeed.' Miss Skinner held up the bonnet for the girls' inspection. 'Where is he now?'

'With father,' said Charlotte. 'He had to wait until dessert was served, poor Blakeney, and it has just gone in, and we are to join them as soon as Caroline is ready. It is just the family,' she told Caroline. 'Papa and mamma and the Winter Ton.'

'Charlotte!' said Miss Skinner in a voice Caroline had never heard her use before, even to Blakeney.

'I beg your pardon, Miss Skinner.' Charlotte dropped a quick curtsy but did not look in the least repentant, Caroline thought. 'You see what bad habits we get into when you are away, you dear old Skinner. We can't go on without you at all, but mamma says Caroline is going to be an example of propriety to us, having grown up in a country rectory. Did you really, Caroline? And have to pinch and scrape and think twice about every new dress? I declare it might be more amusing than having to dress up every Wednesday in a different one to entertain the county. And then to be in debt for every last one of them, as poor mamma is. There's been more trouble, Skinny dear, while you have been away.'

'Lady Charlotte,' said Miss Skinner repressively, 'that is quite enough of your nonsense. If we are really expected for dessert I must take Caroline straight up to her room, and perhaps you will be so good as to tell your mamma we will be down directly.'

'May we not come and help Caroline to change?' asked the younger girl, taking her hand. 'How old are you? I thought you were almost as old as me, but you're not nearly so tall.'

'Age and size don't always go together, Lady Amelia,' said Miss Skinner as the whole party moved up into a square, panelled hall. 'Any more than age and intelligence do. No, Lady Amelia, you and Charlotte must go and join your parents. Caroline will be better by herself for tonight.'

'Tench is waiting for her with open arms,' said Charlotte. 'Doesn't your hair curl at all, you poor thing?' She looked with pitying sympathy at Caroline's neat braids. 'Oh, very well, Skinny, I'll tell mamma you are home and as starchy as ever.' And she whisked herself and Amelia through a door held open for them by an immobile footman while Miss Skinner hurried Caroline away down a long corridor and up a flight of stairs.

'I persuaded the Duchess that to begin with at least you had best be up here near my room. I hope you will not mind it.' She opened a door and revealed a corner room full of the last sunlight. 'Lady Charlotte's room is directly below. And Lady Amelia's beside it. And I am next door. Oh, bless you, Tench, you've contrived to unpack, I see. This is Miss Thorpe, who will be in your charge. Caroline, Tench will help you to change—yes, the muslin, Tench, and I believe there is a string of pearls.'

'Yes, miss.' Tench was a cheerful-looking woman with braided hair very like Caroline's own. 'But what am I to do with her hair?' she asked, almost on a note of despair.

'Nothing for tonight. We're late as it is. Those wretched boys! I leave her in your good hands, Tench. I must make myself fit to be seen.'

Twenty exhausting minutes later, Caroline was ready in just such another muslin dress as the other girls had worn. 'A pity really,' said Tench, tying her sash. 'White don't suit you the way it does the others. If I'd had the ordering for you I'd have got you pink, like that dimity you come in. Never mind, can't be helped. You look neat as ninepence, and that's something. Speak up if his Grace should speak to you. He's a mite deaf and don't like to admit it. You're white as a sheet, child.' She turned as Miss Skinner entered the room. 'Do you think maybe a touch of rouge, miss? Just the smallest in the world?'

'No,' said Caroline. 'Please not. Papa says rouge makes him think of the scarlet woman.' And flushed crimson at her own boldness.

'I quite agree with Mr. Trentham,' said Miss Skinner. 'Thank you, Tench, she will do nicely. Come, child.' She led the way back to the panelled hall where they had parted from the two girls. 'This room divides the children's part of the wing from the rest of the family's,' she explained, as two footmen threw open the door through which the girls had previously vanished.

It opened on to a hall with more of the statues that made Caroline feel so uncomfortable. She caught Miss Skinner's hand. 'I do not think papa would quite like these,' she said.

'You'll get used to them. My brother says art justifies any-thing.' She did not add that her brother thought nothing of the Duke's idea of art. 'Do you know my dear,' she went on now, 'I believe I would not be talking all the time of what your papa thinks of things.' And on this warning note they passed between two more footmen and entered a dining room blazing with light. The candles in the huge chandelier that hung over the dining table were echoed by more in sconces round the walls, and all of them reflected over and over again by immense gold-framed looking glasses on three sides of the room. On the fourth wall, red velvet curtains closed out the last of the day-light.

The cloth had been removed, and heavy silver dishes gleamed against the mahogany, holding such a cornucopia of fruit and sweetmeats as Caroline had never even imagined. Glasses sparkled, bottles gleamed in ornate silver containers . . . And almost masked by the silver and candles, a group of people shining in silks and satins, silent now, suspended, all eyes fixed on her.

'Here she is at last.' The Duke sat at the head of the table, facing Caroline as she entered the room. A small man, but magnificent in deep blue satin and a full wig, he looked unlike anything she had ever seen, an illustration from a story rather than a real person. '"Great heart in tiny body," you say, Blakeney? Well, she's tiny enough. So you're the Trojan, are you, Miss Thorpe? Can stand fire with the best of us?'

'I'm afraid I was frightened, after.' Caroline had dropped a deep, general curtsy.

'What . . . what does the child say?' He turned to the woman on his left, whom Caroline remembered as her sweet smelling friend, now magnificent as her host in low-cut crimson satin and a blaze of rubies. 'I can't bear a child who mumbles,' the Duke went on.

'I expect you frighten her more than the shot did,' said the lady. Mrs. Winterton, of course. Caroline suddenly understood the two girls' cruel joke about the Winter Ton, though in fact Mrs. Winterton was elegantly slender, a glowing dark-haired beauty. 'I don't suppose the child has ever seen a gentleman in full dress before,' she went on. 'Come here, my love.' She held out a hand to Caroline, and Blakeney, who had been sitting beside her, got up to make room, giving Caroline a swift little smile of encouragement as he did so. The other boy, Gaston, was sitting, black-browed with rage, beside the plump, blonde lady on the other side of the Duke, who must be the Duchess. She, too, was resplendent in blue silk and diamonds but she looked tired, Caroline thought, and sad.

She turned to the glowering boy beside her. 'Now's your time, Gaston. And yours, Blakeney, to apologise to Miss Thorpe for frightening her so, and to ask her to name your punishment.'

'That's it,' said the splendid Duke. 'Two young rascals, not fit to be out with guns! Must apologise, must make amends. What shall it be, Miss Thorpe? Hit them where it hurts, eh? No more riding, no more shooting, that kind of thing?'

'Oh, no, please.' Caroline made herself speak clearly. 'I don't want them punished on my account. It was all just a joke, you know.'

'Must be punished, though,' said the Duke. 'Took my duelling pistols without a by your leave or with your leave. And loaded one of them too. Must have. I never leave them loaded. Blakeney, what do you say to that?'

'I most certainly did nothing of the kind, sir.' Blakeney was standing behind Caroline's chair.

'No more did I,' said Gaston.

'Calling me a liar, now, hey? The two of you!' He turned angrily from one to the other and Mrs. Winterton put a restraining hand on his arm.

'Please, sir, they both looked dreadfully surprised,' said Caroline. And then, belatedly, remembered Gaston's damning remark about meaning to fire a shot if the carriage had not stopped. Blakeney must remember it too. His hand touched her shoulder, very gently. Miss Skinner would remember, too. She looked round for her and found that she had vanished.

'Looked surprised, did they?' said the Duke. 'Well, by God, so they should. Nearly killing a young lady. Well,' he raised his quizzing glass to look her over, 'not quite a young lady yet.'

'She'll grow.' Mrs. Winterton patted Caroline's hand. 'And she has quite forgiven our bad boys her fright, have you not, Caroline?' Her smile was at once a plea and an enchantment.

'Yes, indeed, I wish we could say no more about it.'

'Spoken like a lady,' said the Duke. 'Very well. Boys, you're forgiven.' He turned to the Duchess. 'You'll be wishing to get back to your embroidery. Let me alone to give the boys a scold over their port.'

'THERE YOU ARE, Caroline.' Gaston looked in at the school-room door and found her sitting alone, struggling miserably with the lesson in perspective the art master had set her. Charlotte and Amelia were out on their ponies, having very reasonably refused to take her with them until she looked like something more than a sack of potatoes on horseback. 'The Duke wants to see you,' Gaston went on. 'In his office. Lord, I wouldn't be you for toffee. He looks cross as ten sticks.'

'The Duke? Me?' In the confused and homesick wretchedness of her first weeks at Cley, Caroline had not learned enough of the habits of the great house to realise how very improbable such a message was. Since she was equally frightened of Gaston and of the lordly footmen, it did not strike her that the Duke would never make a member of the family his messenger. 'He's angry? Oh, Gaston, why?'

'How should I know? In his office, mind. Right away, he said. I suppose you know where it is?'

'In the turret?' She had a feeling Amelia had said something in passing about the isolated suite of rooms where the Duke spent a good deal of his time, but so many people had told her so many things . . . She stood up, the habit of obedience strong in her. 'At once? Oh, Gaston, do I look tidy? Is he very cross?'

'He will be if you don't hurry,' said Gaston. 'And do for goodness sake remember, Caroline, that family don't knock.' He laughed. 'He wouldn't hear you anyway. Try and speak up, baby, or he'll be crosser still. You know how he hates it when you mumble. He'll probably be in the inner room, by the by. No use waiting in the lobby.'

'Oh, dear. Will you come with me, Gaston?'

'Not likely,' said Gaston. 'I'd cut across the garden, if I were you. It's quicker.' Having thus ensured that Caroline met as few people as possible on her way to the apartments that were rigorously private to the Duke, Gaston left her to her fate and went whistling off to the stables.

He had picked his time well. It was late morning, when all the staff who could get there congregated in the servants' hall for a well-earned dinner after the morning's labours that had got most of them up long before dawn. Caroline saw no one except a belated garden boy who merely gave her a puzzled look in exchange for her polite good morning. Reaching the garden door of the octagonal turret, she took a deep breath, remembered Gaston's warning, and boldly opened it. It gave on to a lobby paved with big black and white tiles, and Caroline paused, looking timidly up at huge, naked statues, trying to gather her courage.

At once, Gaston had said. The catch of the next door was stiff and she opened it with difficulty, only to reveal another empty room, obviously the Duke's office. A huge desk faced her, and the room smelled strongly of tobacco and dog. One of the duke's spaniels came and thrust a friendly nose into her hand as she stood, trembling and looking at yet another door. Go straight in, Gaston had said, don't knock. But, surely, he had meant the room she was in. Only where was the Duke?

She thought she heard voices from the next room. He must be there. Best get it over with. But, this time, instinct was too strong for her, and she knocked on the forbidding mahogany. Someone heard her. There was an exclamation from inside—a woman's voice? And then a long pause before the big door swung open to reveal the Duke, magnificent in frogged crimson dressing gown.

'What the devil?' He was even angrier than she had expected as he looked down at her.

'P...p...please sir.' Trying to speak loud, she stammered. 'Gaston said...'

'Gaston! An emergency, you thought!' He turned furiously to address crimson curtains round the huge four poster bed that dominated the luxurious room. 'A mare's nest! Get out!' He looked at Caroline with loathing. 'Get out, brat, learn some conduct, and stay out!'

Caroline crept to her room, too frightened to mention the disastrous adventure to anyone, and never learned what happened after that, but Gaston and Blakeney left early for school a few days later and she sometimes felt the Duke looking at her with what seemed like hatred. Mrs. Winterton, too, who had been wonderfully kind at first, seemed to have lost interest in her, and only the Duchess continued invariably kind. She was having trouble with her eyes and often sent for Caroline to read aloud to her, saying that she found her gentle voice soothing. 'But you must try to speak up for the Duke,' she reminded her. 'I am afriad it makes him impatient when he cannot quite hear.'

'All kinds of things make him impatient, don't they?' And then, blushing crimson, 'I beg your pardon. I should not have said that.'

The Duchess smiled at her very kindly. 'Well, better not. Or, only to me, Caroline. Be sure and come to me, child, with any little troubles you may have. With Gaston, maybe? I'm afraid it must be strange for you, in this great house.'

After that, Caroline's happiest hours were the ones she spent safe in the Duchess's rooms, reading her favourite Shakespeare to her. Arriving unannounced one day, she was appalled to find her friend in tears.

'It's nothing.' The Duchess held out her hand. 'Don't mind it. I have a piece of sad news, Caroline. A baby I loved very much has died, a long way away, in Ireland, and I cannot even go to the funeral. Look.' She held out a soft curl of fine, dark hair. 'It is all there is left.'

'Oh, ma'am, I am so sorry.' Instinctively, she went into the Duchess's arms, and they cried together.

But the Duchess could not protect her from Gaston's teasing through the long summer holiday.

'Miss Skinner,' she had found her alone. 'May I ask you something?'

'Why, yes, of course my dear.' What could be coming?

'Please, when am I to go home?' And then, stammering again, 'I do not wish to seem ungrateful, but it is Sophie's wedding soon. I am sure mamma will need me, and . . . and . . .' She was developing just a hint of a stammer, Miss Skinner noticed with concern.

'Yes, my dear?'

'I am forgetting all my Latin! Oh, please, don't laugh at me. Not you too! You see, when I grow up, and that will be very soon now, I will have to be a teacher like you, only I thought I would like to teach in a school, and it would make all the difference to have Latin.'

Miss Skinner sighed inwardly. What could she say? She knew that the Duchess and Mrs. Winterton had been trying in vain to get the Duke to make up his mind what to do with Caroline. He had never explained Gaston, though all the adults knew perfectly well that the boy was his own son by a French *gouvernante* encountered in the family of friends. Gaston had been in the family so long that the children accepted him without question, though she herself was often anxious about the way the Duke favoured him. It was bad for the boy, she thought, and hard on Blakeney, and then comforted herself wryly with the fact that the Duke did not much look like favouring Caroline. That was probably why he was being so slow to decide about her, and there was nothing in the world anyone could do about it. If Mrs. Winterton could not bring him about, the thing was hopeless.

Naturally the child was homesick. Charlotte and Amelia found her dull and made no secret of it. She was not interested in dress. She could not talk about ponies, or London. She could not make fringe, or draw, or play the harp or even the pianoforte, and, worst of all, she had a habit of looking through them with large, thoughtful eyes that they did not like at all. Miss Skinner thought sadly that it had made the two of them better friends than they had ever been before. But it left Caroline very much of a poor little fish out of water.

When he was at home, Blakeney was wonderfully kind to her, almost as if he felt the kinship between them, but Gaston had taken one of his black dislikes to the poor child, and, she suspected, lost no chance of setting the Duke against her, so that she really sometimes wondered if it might not be for the best if the Duke should, in fact, decide to make some sort of provision for her and send her back to those good Trenthams at Llanfryn. But, for the moment, there was Caroline gazing hopefully at her, the big brown eyes enlarged by the threat of tears.

'I think mamma really will be needing me now,' she said. 'I know I'm not much good at the things Charlotte and Amelia like to do, but Nurse Bramber says I'm worth my weight of gold in the stillroom. And then there will be the invitations to Sophie's wedding. Papa says I write almost as good a hand as he does.'

'I am sure you do, my dear. But as to Sophie's wedding, I think perhaps you should not set your hopes too high. I am sure the Duke intends your visit to be a long one.'

'The Duke is like God, isn't he? It's frightening, rather.

Oh, Miss Skinner, I do wish this house was not quite so big. Or so full of people. Are there always so many visitors?'

'Why, yes, when the family are here. That's the way they live. You'll grow used to it.'

'Will I? Sometimes I think, when we go down for dessert, that they look at me as if I were . . . oh, I don't know, a travelling bear, or one of those monkeys at fairs.'

'It's just friendly interest. They know you are the Duke's little protégé.' But it was more than that, of course. The children might not know about Caroline's birth, but the adults in the Chevenham house circle most certainly did.

'It may be interest.' Caroline suddenly sounded very grown up indeed. 'But I don't think it's friendly. And I'm not the Duke's . . .' she boggled at the strange word. 'It's the Duchess who is always so kind. I do love the Duchess!'

'We all love her,' said Miss Skinner.

Later, she sought out Mrs. Winterton when that lady was dressing, and laid the case before her.

'Poor little thing.' Frances Winterton leaned back to let her maid attend to her glossy ringlets. 'Of course she's homesick. Lord,' she smiled thoughtfully at the ravishing reflection in the glass. 'I remember when my Uncle Purchas fetched me to Denton Hall how wretched I was. And how badly I behaved!' She laughed. 'I ruined his wedding breakfast! Put pepper in the syllabub and spilled the cream. No! That was Cousin Hart's wedding. Uncle Dick married Aunt Ruth later that day. She was kind to me, Aunt Ruth. I loved her. If she had lived . . . No use thinking about that. As to Caroline, she's a disappointment to the Duke, I am afraid. Pity she didn't take after me. And no good telling him she and Blakeney both favour him.' Smiling at herself, she caught Miss Skinner's eyes in the glass. 'Do you really think it would be best for the child to go back?'

'Ma'am, I'll not lie to you. I do. She's . . .' Miss Skinner paused, feeling ill-timed colour flush her cheek. 'She has been brought up very strictly. If she stays here, sooner or later, it is bound to come out . . .'

'That she's my bastard.' She felt her maid Povey's fingers twist in her hair. 'Oh, come, Povey, don't pretend you don't know; that everyone doesn't know except the children. Which makes you right, of course, you wise Skinner. My fault, as usual. I could have got the Duke to make provision for her, instead of asking her here. But I did so want to see her. A pity she's not a more attractive child. You can't blame the Duke for being disappointed. I really believe he expected her to be the image of me!'

'She has your charm,' said Miss Skinner.

'Do you think so? The Duke doesn't. Well, he can't hear a word she says.'

'Poor child,' said Miss Skinner. 'I'm afraid she is still terribly shy. I found her in tears the other night. She was missing her garden, she said. But I think there was more to it. I'm afraid Gaston had been teasing her again. It's a great pity he's taken such a dislike to her.'

'Tiresome boy! Well, maybe I had better suggest to the Duke that he give her a dowry and send her back to sink or swim in Herefordshire. Povey, you're pulling my hair.'

It was Wednesday, open day at Cley, the day Caroline dreaded most in the week. Anyone who was anyone in the county could come to Cley that day, walk about the grounds as if they owned them, and dine, if they were brave enough, with the Duke himself. In the family, he made no secret of his dislike of the open days, but they were a political necessity, and if he suffered them, so must everyone else. The children must wear their best clothes and circulate among the crowd 'doing the pretty,' as Mrs. Winterton put it. The boys might sometimes escape this duty, but then they had to appear at the crowded early dinner the Duke so disliked, while the girls were excused at least from this.

Today, Charlotte and Amelia had let Caroline join them in the phaeton Charlotte liked to drive through the admiring crowd of her father's tenants. She had been given the little carriage with its matched grey ponies for her twelfth birthday, and fancied herself as a whip.

'And it means we don't have to talk to anyone beyond "good day" and "goodbye,"' she said with satisfaction, steering her way neatly between the ornamental water and the Chinese pavilion. 'Just listen to them saying what a picture we present. And so good to our little friend, too.' An excellent mimic, she lapsed into the broader speech of a Norfolk farmer's wife.

'You're very quiet, Caroline,' said Amelia. 'What's the matter?'

'She's always quiet, our Miss Mouse,' said Charlotte. 'I expect she's still pining over the unkindness of the Winter Ton. We could have told her, couldn't we, that dear Frances sets out to charm everyone who comes her way, and loses interest once they're her slaves.' She giggled. 'Do you remember how she threw out her lures at Farmer Coke?'

'And got a set-down for her pains,' said Amelia. 'I enjoyed that.'

'Father didn't. Move over, Caroline, you're squeezing the breath out of me.' She smiled and bowed as they approached a group of tenant farmers and their wives, visibly ill at ease in their Sunday best. 'Good morning, Mrs. Charlesworth . . . Mrs. Stokes . . . Mrs. Smithson . . . Yes, a very fine day, but hot.' She flicked the ponies' ears with her whip and got them clear of the little group. 'Did you smile and bow, Caroline?'

'It's not my place,' said Caroline miserably, fighting back the tears that had threatened ever since her disappointing interview with Miss Skinner.

'I suppose not,' said Charlotte. 'Considering what a good friend your mamma was of our parents, we don't hear much about her, do we? I expect there was some rip-roaring scandal, really, and the less said the better. Just another of mamma's lame ducks, like the Winter Ton. Do you know, Amelia, I learned something about Darling Frances the other day. I heard Miss Berry telling someone about her mother. Apparently she was a great goer at the time of the Gordon Riots. Set her cap at some rich American cousin of hers with a comic name. What was it now? Purchas, that's it. As if they were parcels or something. And at the eleventh hour his wife turned up to forbid the banns, and they discovered she'd had an affair with someone else long before and our Frances was the result. No wonder if she's not much better than she should be.'

'You oughtn't to talk about her like that,' said Caroline, surprising herself. 'She's your mother's friend.'

'And our father's,' said Charlotte. 'But you wouldn't understand, Miss Mouse.'

'Don't Charlotte,' said Amelia. 'You're making her cry.'

'You can't cry here. Really, of all the babies!' Charlotte whipped up the ponies and took them across the grass at a sharp trot to deposit Caroline at the edge of the family's garden. 'Run indoors and wash your face, cry baby.'

Reaching the sanctuary of her own room, Caroline found Tench waiting for her, looking anxious. 'There you are, child. Mrs. Winterton wishes to see you at once, in her boudoir.' She gave Caroline a quick look. 'What's the matter? Sun too strong for you, love?'

'No. Yes.' She accepted the handkerchief Tench offered

and quickly dried her betraying eyes. 'Mrs. Winterton's not gone down for dinner?' It was Duke's law that all grown up members of the household appear on open days, and the warning bell had sounded as she came upstairs.

'No.' Tench was twisting her hair into reluctant curls and retying her sash. 'The post came just as she was going down, and she made her excuses and sent for you.'

'The Duke will be angry.'

'Yes. Make haste, my dear, and don't keep Mrs. Winterton waiting.'

'No.' Caroline nervously smoothed out a crease in her muslin dress and hurried down to the next floor wondering why she was suddenly sent for. Charlotte had come uncomfortably near the mark in what she had said in the garden. In her first weeks at Cley, Caroline had fallen totally under Frances Winterton's spell, as she had once before. And Frances Winterton had been wonderfully kind at first, sending for her, talking to her, listening to her, and doing her best to make things easy between her and the formidable Duke, whom she often met in Mrs. Winterton's room. She was ashamed, now, to think that she had only grown homesick when these visits stopped.

Timidly entering Mrs. Winterton's silk-hung boudoir, she saw at once that today's visit was going to be different. Mrs. Winterton was not sitting on her chaise-longue as usual, but standing by the window that looked out over the family garden, the only bit of the property that was closed to visitors. 'My dear,' she turned as Caroline entered, 'come and sit beside me.' She took her hand and pulled her down beside her on the pink velvet of the chaise-longue. 'You must be a brave girl. I am afraid I have bad news for you.'

'Bad news? From home?'

'It's poor Mrs. Trentham.'

'She's ill again? I must go to her. Please. At once.'

'Not ill. It's worse than that, I'm afraid. She's dead, Caroline.'

'Dead? Mamma?' She sat quite still, her hand rigid in Mrs. Winterton's. 'She's . . . gone? But what will they do? Oh, poor papa. And Sophie. Her wedding? Oh, the poor things.' She let go of Mrs. Winterton's hand and stood up. 'Mrs. Winterton, please . . . will you, can you explain to the Duke that I must go home at once? That they will need me now.' And was ashamed, as she spoke, of a little, selfish surge of joy at the thought of going home at last. She had missed her garden's summer glory, but she would be home to see it fall asleep for the winter.

But Mrs. Winterton was shaking her head. 'I am sorry, my dear, but that is not the plan at all. Mr. Trentham writes to ask if the Duke will be so good as to keep you here.' And I shall have trouble enough persuading him to do so, she thought.

'Keep me? Always? Here?'

'Yes.' Her voice was bracing. 'You see, everything will be different now at Llanfryn. Mr. Trentham writes that Sophie is to marry the doctor she is betrothed to at once, and their old nurse will housekeep for him at the vicarage. Poor man, it will be a great change for him.' Or a happy release? A kind woman, when kindness did not inconvenience her, she hoped Caroline need never know that Mrs. Trentham had died by her own hand.

'And there is no place for me?' The cry of pure despair reminded Frances Winterton of her own lonely, desperate childhood, unwanted child of an uncaring mother. She took Caroline's hand and pulled her back down beside her. Should she tell her she was her mother? Suddenly, she was enormously tempted. But how totally it would commit her. Anyway, the Duke had forbidden it. It would be madness to do so, and she felt instantly relieved at having the matter settled for her. The Duke would be angry already because her place at the dinner table was empty. It flashed across her mind that the Duke's anger was just the same whether it was a question of disobedience to an important or a trivial order. But the Duke was the Duke. If she told Caroline, against his orders, he might do anything. For the child's sake, she must hold her peace, and persuade him to make the best of things.

'There is a place for you here,' she said. 'We all love you, dear child, and have always hoped you would make your home with us. Now, it must be settled.' She looked at her diamond-studded watch, the Duke's first present. 'I must go down, or he will be really angry.'

Later, Blakeney, returning at last from his ordeal at the hands of his father's tenants, looked round the children's luxurious sitting room. 'Where's Caro?' he asked. 'Mrs. Winterton says we must all be especially kind to her today.'

'Yes,' said Charlotte. 'That dreary "mamma" of hers down in the west has died. So we must be kind to the poor baby, and keep her with us always, what a bore.'

'But where is she?' persisted her brother.

'Lord knows.' Charlotte had just mastered the art of the elegant shrug. 'Glooming in her room, perhaps?'

But when he knocked on Caroline's door there was no answer. He sought out Tench, but she had not seen Caroline since she tidied her for her interview with Mrs. Winterton. 'Maybe she's out of doors, my lord,' she suggested. 'She do like to run out into the garden in all weathers. If I've spoken to her once, I've done it a thousand times, and you might as well talk to a pillar of salt.'

'You mean that no one has seen her since Mrs. Winterton gave her the bad news?' Angry, Blakeney sounded like his father, and Tench gave him a quick, scared look. 'That has not been well thought of, Tench.' And knew, as he spoke, that it was none of her fault. 'I'll look for her in the garden.' He smiled at her. 'Don't look so scared, Tench dear. I know it's not your fault.'

'Oh, thank you, my lord. Take her an apple, why don't you? She's had no dinner, and she loves apples. She'll be in the family garden, of course. She's scared of the public, poor little mite. She do hate open days.'

'Does she? I didn't know.' He took the apple she held out, polished it absentmindedly on his breeches and made his way out by a side door into the family's enclosed garden. High yew hedges masked its open side, and an elaborate orangery linked it to the family wing. Standing on the shallow steps that led down to the Fountain of Neptune, he looked across the trim box hedges of the old-fashioned knot garden. 'Caro?' he called, tentatively.

No answer. He would not shout and make a disturbance of it. She was nowhere in the knot garden. The grotto, perhaps? He had never liked it himself, finding it dank and musty, and had thought she shared his distaste. Apparently she did; there was no sign of her there. He emerged again into the knot garden and once more, hesitantly, called, 'Caro, where are you?'

Dead silence. Dead? Now he was really anxious. She should not have been left alone to her sorrow all the long afternoon. He crossed the knot garden, jumping its hedges, and walked along the high yew hedge, wondering if perhaps she had run out into the main grounds, now empty again, the last guest gone. To the ornamental pool with its deep salt waters fed by a tidal inlet? He shuddered and began to run, only to pause, listening. Had there been the tiniest rustle from inside the yew hedge? He remembered the secret place he and Gaston had hollowed out, years before, when they were little boys. The thick yew had grown back since they had cut their secret entrance at the end where the hedge met the house, and it was a struggle to force his way in, but he thought that someone had indeed been through quite recently. 'Caro,' he called again, softly. 'It's only me, Blakeney.'

She had made herself a kind of burrow in the heart of the hedge and was curled up in it like a small, desperate animal. 'Are they very angry with me?' She raised a tear-dirtied face to his. 'I'm glad it's you, Blakeney. I was beginning to think I'd never dare come out.'

'Of course no one's angry with you, Caro!' And saying it, he thought angrily that in fact no one had even missed her. 'We're all so very sorry about your sad news. You must think of us as your family now. That's what my father intends. Your mother was a dear friend of his and my mother's, you know. You must let us look after you.'

'Live here always?' Caroline looked at him pitifully, tears still lingering in her drowned eyes. 'I don't think Charlotte and Amelia will like that much.'

'They'll have to,' said Blakeney, 'if the Duke says so.'

'He can't make them like it,' said Caroline. 'Or like me. Please, Blakeney dear, could you not persuade your father that I would rather be set in the way of earning my living?'

'You? Little mouse. You earn your living? How, may I ask?'

'The way Miss Skinner does, as a governess, or maybe even teaching in a school. I think I'd like that, Blakeney, I really do. I know you think I'm a mouse, but that's because I'm always having to be grateful, don't you see? I haven't anything of my own, to be sure of. If I was a teacher in a school, I would be as fierce as anything with the pupils, because I would know who I was, where I stood.' She looked at him with the honesty of despair. 'Even at home, with papa and mamma.' She choked on a sob. 'Even there, I always knew I was different. Papa understood. He helped me to study, so that I would be ready to make my own way when I was old enough, but now it's all pianoforte and deportment and fine embroidery, and, Blakeney, I'm no good at any of it. It's such a waste! And, of course, Charlotte and Amelia scorn me. I don't blame them a bit. I'm not good at any of their things.'

Blakeney had been lonely enough when he first went to

Harrow to understand something of what she meant. 'What are your things then?' he asked.

'Reading, and learning, and thinking about people. I want to be some use in the world, not just a pretty thing with ringlets, playing the harp.' Besides,' again that look of sharp honesty, 'I never will be a pretty thing, however hard Tench papers my hair. I'm all wrong for this kind of life, don't you see? Look at today. Open day. I hate it so. Charlotte and Amelia drive about, and let people admire them, and say pretty things to them, and smile, and make them happy. I can't do that. And anyway,' she concluded irrefutably, 'I've no right to do it. It's not my place. They're the Duke's daughters. Lady Charlotte, Lady Amelia. I'm nobody. With no one of my own. And the sooner I go back to being that, the better it will be. Please, Blakeney,' she said again, 'Do you think you could make your father understand that?'

'Oh, Caro,' he looked at her with sympathy. 'You must have been here long enough to know no one can make the Duke do anything. He's the Duke.'

'I know. I'm sorry. It was stupid of me to ask it. But what am I going to do, Blakeney?'

'You want to read and study.' He had been thinking hard about her position. 'Well, that's not impossible, you know. Not in this house.'

'But it is! I've got no books. No books at all. I even left my *Lyrical Ballads* behind. I thought it was just a visit!'

He recognised it as a cry from the heart. 'Books mean so much to you? Well, there's something we can do about that. Come along, and I'll show you something.' He reached out a friendly hand to pull her to her feet. 'Lord, you're filthy. You *are* going to get a scold.'

She smiled at him rather tremulously. 'So are you! And your new satin breeches too, for the open day.'

'Never mind about that! No one's going to see us for a while. But clean your face a bit.' He handed her a spotless pocket handkerchief. 'Right now you could walk straight on stage as Hecuba, Queen of Troy. Not that you would know about her.'

'But of course I do.' She had accepted the handkerchief and was scrubbing away at her grimy, tear-streaked face. 'Papa always called her the mobled queen, because of the line in *Hamlet*, you know, but we never did decide just what it meant.'

'Lord, you really are a bluestocking. Thank you.' He tucked

the now filthy handkerchief into a pocket. 'Let's go then. Can you manage?' He held back a stiff branch of yew for her.

'Of course I can. You go on and I'll follow. Giles always said it was one's own stupid fault if one was hit by a branch the person in front let go.'

'And quite right too. Who's Giles?' He asked as they emerged from the tunnel in the hedge and he turned to lead the way along the side of the house.

'My brother at home, but he went to India.' And then, 'Not my brother!' With a catch in her throat.

'If you are going to cry again,' said Blakeney severely, 'I shall wash my hands of you, here and now.'

'I'm not crying. But where are we going?' He had opened an inconspicuous, low door in the rusticated wall of the family wing.

'You'll see.' He led the way down four steps into a long corridor quite unlike any part of the great house that she had seen before. Bare brick walls, big stone flags underfoot and a feeling of damp cold even now with hot summer just giving way to mellow autumn. 'This is the way the servants get into the family garden,' he explained. 'Had you never wondered?'

'The whole house frightens me. I don't much like thinking about the bits I don't know. But, the poor servants, do they spend all their time down here in the cold?'

'It's not all so bad as this. The servants' hall's down that way.' He pointed as they reached a junction in the long corridor. 'They keep up a good fire in there, I can tell you. But the rest of it's like this. I thought I might have matting put down when I am Duke.'

'Oh, Blakeney, just think of you being Duke!'

'I'd as soon not. I'd much rather be a great commoner like Mr. Coke than have to sit in that dreary old House of Lords. But father will live for ever, of course.' He turned to lead the way up a steeply winding spiral staircase, remotely lit by a window far above. 'There's the door to our floor.' He paused to let her catch up with him, then went on up. 'And there's the one to yours. I'll show you where it comes out on the way back. But now you must pay close attention to where we are going, or you will never find the way by yourself.'

'But where are we going?'

'You'll see,' he said mysteriously, as they reached the top of the winding stair and turned down a long, low-ceilinged passage. Lighted by flat windows in the roof it smelt mustily of disuse. 'Grandfather had this built. He got tired of having to go through the state apartments with footmen leaping about opening doors for him. Mother told me that. I wish I had known grandfather; I think I would have liked him very much. Mother loved him, she says. Now, look!' He turned a couple of corners and opened a shabby door.

Caroline gave a gasp. 'Blakeney!'

He smiled at her with delighted triumph. 'You said you wanted books. Well, there they are.' They were looking into a large room entirely lined with bookshelves except on the side where long windows looked towards the sea, and even there, full length gilt-framed looking glasses between the windows reflected the loaded shelves. 'Grandfather's collection,' he explained. 'He loved to read, and he loved to be quiet, so he built this library up here above the state apartments and nobody was allowed into it except by invitation. Everyone used to come and stay at Cley then. Pope and Gibbon and even Dr. Johnson. You'll find all their works here. Is that the kind of book you meant?'

'Oh, Blakeney!' She was moving along the shelves, looking at the leatherbound sets of volumes, pausing to touch a book here, to look closer there. 'Pope?' she asked. 'Would *The Rape of the Lock* be here?'

'All his poems,' said Blakeney. 'He gave grandfather a set. Mother showed me. Poetry's over here, where the light is best. Grandfather loved poetry, mother says.'

'Oh, Blakeney!' she said again as she followed him across the room.

'Shakespeare.' He ran a finger along a handsome set of gilt-edged maroon volumes. 'Dryden. Take your pick, if it's poetry you fancy.'

'Oh, yes,' she breathed. 'But, Blakeney, may I take them off the shelves?'

'Well, of course.' Impatiently. 'That's what they are for, isn't it?'

'But they're so beautiful! May I really read them?'

'Of course you may. No one else does. Old Pomfret the tutor used to come creeping up here in the bad old days before Gaston and I went to school, but no one comes here now. It's all yours.'

'I don't believe it!' She gazed around her, wide-eyed. And then: 'But how? When? They won't let me.'

'I'll talk to mother about it. She'll contrive something. She's a trump; she always does if I ask her.'

'Blakeney, will you really?'

'Of course I will, goose. And you will wash your face and put on a clean dress and come down to supper and look cheerful.'

Her face clouded over. 'Oh, poor mamma.' She said, conscience-stricken. 'I had quite forgotten.'

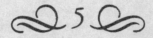

FROM THEN ON, everyone knew that if Caroline was needed she could be found in the old Duke's library. 'Oh, let her have her fling if it will keep her happy,' the Duke had said impatiently, when the Duchess approached him with her odd request. 'Better a bookworm, I suppose, than the cipher she is now. No wonder if our girls find her a dead bore.' He thought for a moment. 'Blakeney spoke of it, did he? Send him away for a bit, do you think? To his cousins, maybe?'

'He goes to school next week,' said the Duchess.

'So he does. Quite slipped my memory. Well, that's all right then.'

Caroline was sad to see Blakeney go, feeling him her one real friend in the house, but his absence was compensated for by that of Gaston, who had managed to plague her in so many small, apparently innocent ways. Anyway, she was too intoxicated by her secret life in the great library to mind even Blakeney's absence much. He had seen to it, before he left, that she was supplied with paper and pens, and had the certainty of a fire when winter came, and she was simultaneously engrossed in reading the complete works of Shakespeare and writing an elegy for Mrs. Trentham. As she had chosen to compose this in the complicated stanza form used by the poet Spenser in an absolutely enthralling poem called *The Faerie Queen*—that was better than any fairy story—this was an absorbing occupation and the family grew used to having to send a page to summon her to meals.

Nobody asked what she did in the library. The Duke and Duchess and, of course, Mrs. Winterton, spent most of that winter at Chevenham House in London, where the two girls and Blakeney joined them for Christmas. Caroline should have gone too but was thought to have outgrown her strength, and spent a peaceful holiday at Cley with Miss Skinner. She had finished the elegy for Mrs. Trentham now, and had embarked on an ode to Blakeney, which would have surprised him very much if he had ever had a chance to read it.

She had had no news from the Trenthams, and had minded, but when she asked Miss Skinner if she might write to them at Christmas, she had said, 'Better not, my dear. The Duke prefers that you let the past be the past.'

Miss Skinner had been unhappy about this decision of the Duke's, and yet, if Caroline were to be let correspond with the Trenthams, she was almost bound to learn that her adopted mother had thrown herself into the River Llanfryn. She was such a feeling child, Miss Skinner thought, that she should be spared this knowledge if it was at all possible. And, besides, Mr. Trentham, associating his wife's mental illness with Caroline and Giles, had made it clear that he would prefer to have nothing more to do with her. Unhappiness had made him cruel, Miss Skinner thought, and did her best to make amends to Caroline with an extra happy Christmas.

But Caroline, minding it all more than even Miss Skinner realised, sometimes thought she hated the Duke even more than she did Gaston. She had been reading Milton's *Paradise Lost* and had a recurring dream about her lost garden at Llanfryn. The Duke and Gaston were the angels who stood, swords in hand, at the gate and kept her out. Or were they devils? She wrote a poem about the Duke after reading Pope's *Dunciad*, was ashamed when she read it through, and burned it; but it did her good. She was learning to use poetry as a safety valve, and found it easier to endure Charlotte and Amelia's small superiorities when she knew that they were figuring, in bold caricature, in the verse comedy she was engaged on. The Duke appeared in it as Lord Omnipotent, and when he next came to Cley she surprised him by failing to blush and look away when he spoke to her.

'That child is getting some countenance at last,' he told the Duchess. 'We may do better for her than a country parson after all.'

'I do hope we can,' said the Duchess. 'I think Frances has her heart quite set on a good match for her.'

'Time enough to be thinking of that when we have got Charlotte and Amelia off our hands,' said the Duke. 'I promised Frances that her little shrimp should come out along with Amelia.'

Lady Charlotte's coming out was postponed twice, in 1802 because the Duke insisted on taking advantage of the peace with France to go abroad, and in 1803, when the war broke out again, because of an ill-timed outbreak of the measles. It was not until 1804, when Caroline was sixteen, that they all went to London at last for Charlotte's presentation and coming-out ball, which was to be held at Chevenham House in Piccadilly. This time there was no question of Caroline's being left at Cley.

'It's no use, my love,' said Miss Skinner when Caroline begged her to intercede for her with the Duchess. 'The Duke has decided that you and Amelia are to come out together next year and he intends you to begin learning the ways of London society. He has quite made up his mind.'

'I see,' said Caroline. Lord Omnipotent again, she thought.

'And he is right, too,' said Miss Skinner bracingly. 'It is time you got a little town bronze, and, anyway, I am quite sure that when you get to London you will enjoy it. There will be the theatre, and I know you will like that, and just think of the new books. Chevenham House is in Piccadilly, you know, no distance at all from Hookham's Library. You will be able to change your book whenever you want to. And I am sure the Duke will not mind if you spend some part of your allowance in buying books.'

'He won't notice,' said Caroline, with truth. 'But will I get an allowance, Miss Skinner?' The Duke did not believe in independence for young women, and even eighteen-year-old Charlotte was still forced to apply to her mother for money for any small purchase she wished to make. Not a single volume had been added to the old Duke's library since his death. Caroline, too shy and too proud to ask, had longed in vain for funds to replace her lost volume of *Lyrical Ballads*, or buy her own copy of Mr. Southey's *Thalaba* which she had read avidly when the circulating library sent it to Mrs. Winterton.

'I hope so,' said Miss Skinner. 'I know the Duchess has talked to the Duke about it. She agrees with me that it is a part of a young woman's education to learn how to manage her own money.'

'It's good of her to ask the Duke,' said Caroline. Everyone in the house knew that the Duchess's gaming debts were an ever-increasing source of trouble between her and her husband. They were silent for a moment, each aware of the other's thoughts. 'It's not fair,' said Caroline at last. 'Did you hear the Duke the other day, betting Mr. Carteret that he could not run twenty-five miles in four hours? £500 he bet on that, and he complains when the Duchess loses her own money at cards.'

'Not hers, child,' said Miss Skinner. 'His, since she married him. I do beg you never to speak like that. The Duke must be master in his own house, as you well know.'

'He is,' said Caroline. 'And of course I would never dream of speaking like that to anyone but you, but you know as well as I do, Skinny dear, that it is only because he makes such a fuss over her losses that the Duchess has been reduced to trying to conceal them from him, and so got into the hands of the moneylenders. And, anyway, whose fault is it that she has nothing to do to amuse herself but play at cards with that clutch-fisted set of hers? If he spent more time with her and less with Mrs. Winterton...'

'Caroline!' said Miss Skinner in tones of horror.

'It's no use, Skinny, now I've started I've got to say it, just this once. What right has he to set himself in judgment over her when he neglects her so? Oh, I know he's *polite* to her; it would not befit his dignity as a Duke to be anything else; but it's Mrs. Winterton he smiles at. I think the Duchess is a heroine to endure it.'

'She loves Mrs. Winterton,' said Miss Skinner, now thoroughly alarmed at the course the conversation was taking.

'I know. It's the most amazing thing. You'd think she'd want to scratch her eyes out, but she really does love her. I've watched, and thought about it, and it's true. I cannot understand it.'

'Nor should you be thinking about it,' said Miss Skinner. 'You and I, my love, as unmarried ladies, should not be passing judgment on those who are called to a different walk in life. Though, of course, I hope that you will be too in good time.'

'Frankly, Skinny, if marriage means the kind of life the Duchess leads, I think I'd rather be an old maid like you.' And then, impulsively, colouring up to her hair. 'Forgive me! I didn't mean!'

'Always think before you speak, child,' said Miss Skinner. 'But no harm in telling truth between friends. And so I will tell you that a single life is not at all necessarily a blessed one, even with such good friends as I have in the Duchess and Mrs. Winterton.'

'Oh, I know that well enough,' said Caroline. 'Because I don't talk a great deal, never think I don't notice things. It makes me mad as fire to see the way you are treated. You, who have more sense and more education than all three of them put together, and more morals, too, for the matter of that! And they treat you half the time as if you weren't there. As if you didn't exist.'

'Well, there you are,' said Miss Skinner. 'Unmarried ladies to all intents and purposes don't exist, so far as society is concerned, and as for governesses...So I do hope you will behave yourself in London, dear child, and try a little to get out of your bookish ways, and let the Duchess and Mrs. Winterton find you a good husband.'

'Is there really such an animal, Skinny?'

'Of course there is. Why, my brother is the very best of husbands.' She smiled, forgetting her anxiety over Caroline in pleasure at the thought of him. 'I am to go there for a little holiday, when you all go to London. Dear Edith is expecting her first child, after all this time, and I am to stay with them until she is quite strong again.'

'You're not coming to London with us? Oh, how will I manage without you?'

'Admirably, I am sure. Model yourself on Lady Charlotte, and you cannot go far wrong.' Her heart misgave her as she said it.

'On everything I'm not? Oh, Skinny!'

Just the same, it was impossible not to thrill to the first sights and sounds of London as the second-best Cley carriage rattled at last over the stones. Even Charlotte and Amelia, who had made the journey often before, admitted to excitement, leaning forward eagerly to peer through the gathering dusk and look for landmarks.

'It will be quite dark before we get to the house,' said Charlotte crossly. 'I do wish papa would ever leave when he says he is going to.'

'You should be grateful he started at all,' said Amelia. 'When he told mamma he had a twinge of the gout I thought it was all up with us.'

'So did I,' agreed Charlotte. 'But you can mostly count on Darling Frances to bring him round her finger if she really wants to. When she made those big eyes at him and lisped her little plea, I knew the thing was done.'

'How mamma stands it!' said Amelia.

'If you ask me, I think she finds papa a dead bore and is glad to have him taken off her hands. You know he can talk of nothing but dogs and hunting and those dreary old politics of his. And Darling Frances hangs on his every word and lisps her yes, and no, and, how amazing, and papa knows he is a great man, and mamma sits and thinks her own thoughts. I wonder if Charles Mattingley is in town.'

'Sure to be if mamma is. I don't know what he does with himself since papa forbad him Cley. He'll cheer things up a bit! I believe I will make him squire me to my first ball. Mamma can't object when she goes everywhere with him herself.'

'She won't like it,' said Amelia.

'I can't help that. He's much nearer my age than hers, and who knows but he may be on the look-out for a rich wife. Wouldn't that be a thing! Imagine marrying Mattingley, the unmarrying man!' She caught Caroline's eye and laughed. 'We are shocking Miss Mouse. I bet you a pair of French gloves that she falls neck over crop in love with handsome Mat when she sees him.'

'Who is Mr. Mattingley?' Caroline, sitting with her back to the horses, was beginning to feel queasy as the carriage rattled over the stones, and the powerful smells and sounds of London assailed her senses.

'Shall we tell her?' Charlotte and Amelia exchanged knowing glances.

'Better, I think,' decided Charlotte. 'She's such a little innocent she might say something that would put us all to the blush. Mr. Mattingley, dear child, is the good friend who consoles mamma for papa's affair with Darling Frances, otherwise the Winter Ton. Our ton of misery. Very thick, handsome Mat and mamma are. Oh, very thick indeed.'

'You don't mean?'

'Don't I just! There was a real turnout for the books when it first started, but that was a long time ago, before you came to live with us. Papa cut up very rough indeed and mamma and the Winter Ton had to go off and rusticate on the Irish estate.' She giggled. 'So clever Mat got a post in Dublin and dangled after mamma harder than ever. She was still quite

young and pretty then of course. She's gone off sadly these
last few years, everyone says, with all the worry over her
debts.'

'Yes,' chimed in Amelia. 'It's too hard that Darling Frances
can eat and drink just as much as mamma does and never get
fat at all, and there's poor mamma puts on weight if she so
much as looks at a lobster patty. I heard her scolding her dresser
this morning because her riding dress was too tight. I think she
forgets to bother when she's sunk down there at Cley with
father and Darling Frances billing and cooing under her nose.'

'I don't know what handsome Mat will say when he sees
her,' said Charlotte.

'Everything that's polite. He always does. It's what he will
do that counts. But do you really mean to have him, Charlotte?'

'Oh, I don't know,' said Charlotte. 'Maybe. Maybe not.
He's got a way of laughing at you, as if he cared, that I quite
like.'

'Anyway,' said Amelia, 'papa would never let you.'

'No, I'd have to make a runaway match of it, wouldn't I?
Just think what a lark that would be. Oh, look, there's Devonshire House! We're almost home. This is Piccadilly, Caroline, and the Park's down there.' She waved a hand to the left.
'If one could only see it.' It was dark by now, and flares outside
the houses on the north side of the broad street gave a fitful
illumination to the carriages that thronged it. 'Everyone's going
out for the evening,' Charlotte went on crossly, 'and we'll be
too late even for the play.'

'I expect papa planned it that way on purpose,' said Amelia.
'You know the theatre bores him to distraction, and, besides,
Mat's always there.'

'I bet you half a guinea he's at Chevenham House tonight,'
said her sister, as the carriage turned under an archway into a
wide paved square and drew up under the illuminated portico
of Chevenham House.

Next morning, the girls learned that the Duke had come to
one of his surprise decisions. Though they would not be presented, or officially out, Amelia and Caroline were to be allowed to go into society along with Charlotte. 'Might as well
get it all over with at once' was how he had put it to his wife.
'And they are all much of an age, after all.'

'Hard on Charlotte, perhaps?' suggested the Duchess dif-
fidently.

'Nonsense. She can take care of herself. And Frances thinks

it's time that chit of hers was dragged away from her books.
She's right, of course. I must have had windmills in my head
to let her spend her time bookworming in the old Duke's library.
God knows what notions she's picked up. She gave me a very
cool, queer look when she arrived last night.'

'She was travelsick,' said the Duchess. 'Charlotte and
Amelia made her ride backwards the whole way.'

'Quite right too,' said their father. 'Time the chit learned
to know her place. Pity we ever took her up, if you ask me.'

'We could hardly help it,' said the Duchess, controlling
herself.

'And that reminds me,' he went on. 'Frances thinks the girls
should dine with us now they are here. It will be a dead bore,
of course, but I think she is right. They've got to learn conduct
somehow, and I count on you and Frances to give them the
nod when you think it's time they left us.'

'You might say a word to your friends about their language.'

'Tchah,' said the Duke.

'There, miss, you'll have to do.' Tench twitched Caroline's
reluctant curls with a despondent finger. 'Run along now, do,
or the young ladies will have gone down already and I know
you don't want to have to enter the drawing room alone.'

'I should rather think not,' said Caroline. 'You're an angel,
Tench, you think of everything. But will I really do?' She
surveyed the pale, muslin-clad reflection in the glass dubiously.

'You look every inch the gentlewoman,' said Tench, and
with that cool comfort Caroline ran downstairs to the family
floor, only to find that Charlotte and Amelia had indeed gone
on without her.

'They was all ready, miss,' said Charlotte's dresser apol-
ogetically. 'Sent their love and said they'd look out for you.'

'But they won't,' said Caroline despairingly. 'Oh, Smithson, must I?'

'You know you must, miss. His Grace's orders. And there's
company come already. Best get it over with before there's
more.'

It was good advice. Caroline trod nervously down the stairs
and approached the door of the drawing room reluctantly, pausing for a moment to look at the huge portrait of the Duke's
mother as a huntress that hung over it. In the entrance hall
below, a little stir suggested that more guests were arriving.
Get it over with. The two huge footmen who stood on each

side of the door were looking at her expectantly. She put her chin up and approached it. Then an amazing thing happened. The one on the left winked at her solemnly with one eye. 'Good luck, miss,' she thought she heard him breathe, and was through the wide-opened double doors and into the brilliantly lighted room.

Bright lights always made it hard for her to see, and she stood for a moment, dazzled, listening to the hum of conversation, looking blindly for a corner to hide herself. A tall man moved leisurely away from an animated group of young bucks to intercept her. Very elegant in the close-fitting trousers worn by the younger set, he wore his own dark hair cut short. 'Let me guess.' He smiled down at her, dark eyes smiling too. 'It must be the missing maiden, the haunter of libraries.' He held out his hand. 'Charles Mattingley, very much at your service, Minerva.'

Despite what Charlotte and Amelia had said, he was quite old, she thought, which made him less formidable. 'Not so very wise, I am afraid.' She smiled back at him. 'But has the word really got about that I am a bluestocking? Am I sunk beyond recall?'

'Oh, I don't think so.' He tucked her arm under his and led her forward into the crowded room that was gradually coming into focus for her. 'Nothing that we cannot cope with if we put our minds to it.'

'We?' She looked up at him with the question.

'I have the Duchess's orders to see to it that you enjoy yourself tonight. What she did not tell me was that I should find myself enjoying the task.' It had only half surprised him that it should be the Duchess, rather than her mother, Mrs. Winterton, who had taken thought for Caroline's first London appearance, but he had been looking forward to his task as the most appalling of bores until he had been roused by an overheard scrap of talk between Charlotte and Amelia: 'Won't she just look the mouse she is, when she comes in with that blind look of hers,' had said Charlotte.

And, 'Not so much mouse as dormouse,' agreed Amelia, then turned, saw him, and was all radiant smiles.

It was true, he thought, steering Caroline expertly towards a quiet corner where she could get her bearings a little, there had been something a little blind about her gaze round the room. Had Frances Winterton ever thought to have the child's eyes examined? But then, did Frances Winterton ever think of anything but Frances Winterton? Impervious to her charms himself, it always amazed him to see how completely his dear friend the Duchess continued under her spell.

'There.' He placed Caroline with her back to a curtained window, and noticed how admirably the crimson velvet threw up her delicate colouring. 'I wish I was a painter.'

'A painter?' Surprised, she sounded less stiff.

'Yes. I would paint you against that red velvet, Miss Thorpe, and call the picture *Youth at the Helm*.'

'Is that a compliment, perhaps? Because if it is, it's almost my first.' And then, eagerly, 'Do you read Mr. Gray?' She coloured. 'I thought it was *Youth on the Prow*. Oh, why are you laughing?'

'At you, of course, admired Minerva. Yes, I do read Mr. Gray, and I did misquote him, and I am to tell you that no young lady ever corrects a gentleman, most particularly not when he has just paid her her first compliment.'

'Oh, I am sorry! But, please, why not? Wouldn't you rather get it right next time?'

'You think it so important to get it right?'

'Of course! I suppose "at" for "on" does not really make much difference, but "helm" for "prow"! The change in a word can make the whole difference to the feel of a poem.'

'You speak from experience, Minerva? Am I privileged, perhaps, to be talking to a poet?'

'Are you laughing at me again?' she asked suspiciously.

'Not the least in the world.' He noticed Charlotte's darkling eye fixed on them. 'But I am monopolising you, and that will not do. Let me see.' He looked about him. 'To whom shall I grant the privilege of meeting you? Ah,' a smile lightened the dark, expressive face. 'Would you like to meet a poet, Minerva?'

'A poet? Oh, yes!' She looked about her. 'Is it someone I will have heard of?'

'Not yet. But he is a coming man in poetry. I know it. He told me so himself.'

'Oh?' She looked up at him doubtfully. 'Have you seen any of his poems?'

'No, for the good reason that I did not ask to. But I am sure you will.' He reached out a long arm and touched the shoulder of a golden-haired young man who was standing with his back to them. 'Tremadoc, let me tear you away from Lady Charlotte and present you to Miss Thorpe, who can quote to you from Mr. Gray's *Bard*, if you will let her.'

'Miss Thorpe?' The young man turned round and showed Caroline the most beautiful face she had ever seen. This, she thought, was what a poet should look like. 'The bluestocking?' he asked, surprised. 'But you said she was plain, Charlie.'

'Don't call me that! We're not children now.' Charlotte turned a cross shoulder to him and concentrated all her attention on Mattingley. 'Tell me all the *on dits*, Mat dear, and let us leave the children to entertain each other.'

'Well of all the rude starts!' said Tremadoc to Caroline. 'I'm three years older than her if I'm a day. Just because I used to help her on to her pony when we rode in the Park. And that was only because mamma made me,' he went on. 'A Duke's daughter, after all, but I always thought them both dead bores. Now you're quite a different stable, Miss Thorpe, I can see that. Did you really spend all your time, down at Cley, reading in the old Duke's library?'

'All I could. But, please, tell about your poetry. I never met a poet before. Have you published anything yet?'

'Well, not to say exactly published, but I did have a little volume printed, just to give pleasure to my friends. Maybe, with your permission, Miss Thorpe, I might send you one?'

'Oh, would you really?' Her awed delight made him her slave at once. But now she was looking past him to where a young man in uniform was standing in the doorway, looking about him with bright, amused, enquiring eyes. 'It can't be Blakeney.'

'I don't see why not.' He did not like to lose her attention so soon. 'He's raised his own tame regiment of volunteers, I believe, and rather likes himself in uniform.' He turned to look over his shoulder. 'Very much the lord of creation, is he not? I tell you, Miss Thorpe, I get tired to death of these military boors and their lack of culture.'

'Blakeney went to Harrow,' said Caroline, and, aware that she was not paying him enough attention: 'Where did you go to school?'

'School? Oh, too barbarous. I was delicate, still am. My mamma would not think of letting me go to one of those rough and tumble public schools. I was educated at home. My uncle fussed, but my mamma could not bear to part with me. She's a very perceptive woman, my mamma. She understands my poetry better than anyone.'

She smiled up at him. 'Oh, are you not lucky! To have a mother who understands you!' And then turned aside to put out a hand. 'Blakeney! You're never passing without a word to me!'

He stopped and looked down at her, puzzled for a moment. He had gone abroad with his parents and Mrs. Winterton after the peace of Amiens and his father had seen to it that he had not been to Cley since. 'It's . . . It's little Caro!' he exclaimed. 'I'd never have known you if you had not spoken!' He took both her hands and pressed them warmly. 'My little library mouse turned into a young lady. And a pretty one, too.'

'Oh, Blakeney, don't sound so surprised! Just because Tench makes my life a misery with her curl papers!' She smiled impartially from him to Tremadoc. 'Now I have shocked you both. Am I supposed to pretend it is all done by nature?'

'Your exquisite colour most certainly is, Miss Thorpe,' said Tremadoc.

'Blakeney,' said the Duke, looming behind him. 'You are neglecting our guests. It is time to go in to dinner.'

Blakeney turned a smiling face to his father. 'I beg pardon, sir. I was congratulating Caro here on having become a young lady. *Au revoir*, Caro dear, I must take a dowager in to dinner. But I will call tomorrow and mean to hear all your news.'

'Call?'

'I have my own lodgings now,' he explained. 'In St. James's.'

'Of course. Stupid of me.' She was relieved to see that the Duke had moved away, obviously taking Blakeney's obedience for granted. 'Blakeney, you must find your dowager. Your father does not like to be kept waiting.'

'No, but it's good for him, just once in a way,' said Blakeney, and she wondered with awe if he was not perhaps the only person in the world who was not afraid of the Duke. 'Who is taking you in, Caro?' he asked now.

'I don't know. Nobody, I expect.' It had been troubling her a little.

'If I might?' Tremadoc took an eager step forward, but as he did so, Mattingley reappeared behind him.

'Miss Thorpe,' he said. 'The Duchess has given me the pleasure of taking you to dinner.'

'Oh, thank you!' She smiled from Blakeney to Tremadoc and moved off on the older man's arm, quite unaware of the impression she had made.

6

TREMADOC CALLED NEXT day, bringing his elegantly slim cream-and-gilt volume with him, and Caroline was overwhelmed by the attention.

'It's beautiful.' She stroked the volume lovingly before putting it down on the table where her work lay abandoned. 'I shall read it the very minute I am alone. One cannot read poetry in company. Do you not find it so?'

He had rather hoped that she would open it then and there and read his stirring verses aloud to him, but hastened to agree with her. 'No, it is too sacred, is it not? The divine flame? Do you, perhaps, write a little yourself, Miss Thorpe? I almost think you must, to be so understanding about the problems of a poet. And I believe young ladies do sometimes write quite passable verses. Of course, mine are in a strong vein.' He reached down carelessly and picked up the volume. 'I sing of war: its glory and its terror. I think you must be moved by the description of my hero, Mandragon, charging the enemy on his milk-white steed.'

'All by himself?' asked a mocking voice behind him. 'I hope his milk-white steed got him safe away again.'

'Mr. Mattingley,' said Caroline warmly. 'How do you do? Just look, Mr. Tremadoc has brought me his first volume of poems. Am I not a lucky girl?'

'Tell me that when you have read them,' said Charles Mattingley.

Charlotte and Amelia, returning from a ride in the Park to which they had not invited Caroline, were surprised and displeased to find her entertaining Mattingley and Tremadoc. They were soon joined by Blakeney, also glowing with fresh air from exercising with the Queen's Royal Volunteers.

'I have brought you a present, Caro.' He sat down beside her, while the four others stood in an animated group at the other end of the room. 'I bought it for you a while ago,' he went on. 'Thinking it perhaps the kind of thing you would like, but it is such an age since I have been to Cley, and I never was much of a hand at parcels.' He handed her a leatherbound volume. 'I do hope you will like it.'

'Blake's *Songs of Innocence*! And engraved by himself! Oh, Blakeney, how did you know! Miss Skinner told me about them. Her brother has them and I always longed to ask if I might borrow them for a while, but never quite dared. Oh, I do thank you!' She smiled up at him. 'I shall always value them particularly for your sake. Do look what Blakeney has given me,' she said to Tremadoc. 'Mr. Blake's *Songs of Innocence*!' And then, recognising his look of affront, 'What a happy day! Two volumes of poetry. Just think, Blakeney, Mr. Tremadoc has been so good as to give me his own poems. I shall not know where to begin.'

Charlotte and her parents were dining out that day, so Caroline found herself alone with a very cross Amelia. 'It's not fair!' She helped herself angrily to fricassee of chicken. 'Just one year's difference, and Charlie is to go everywhere, while I am to appear in company at home here, or, for a special treat, when we go to the play. It's lucky I've got you for company, Caroline, or I'd die of boredom. And there's Blakeney with his own establishment, and he's not even quite as old as you are.'

'He seems much older.'

'And the world his oyster. Oh, why wasn't I born a boy! Just think, I'd be the heir then, with everything handsome about me, and Blakeney just a younger brother. Wouldn't I just keep him and Charlotte in their place. Or even to be Gaston. The way father treats him he might as well be the son of the house. He's much kinder to him than he is to you, isn't he? I think he must have liked his parents better than yours. Lord, Gaston's handsome these days. Have you seen him yet? Oh, no, or course not. It was in the Park we met him yesterday. Uniform becomes him to a marvel. He makes Blakeney look a little shrimp like you.'

'I don't believe it,' began Caroline warmly, and was interrupted by the appearance of Blakeney and Gaston themselves.

'Just as I thought,' said Gaston. 'A couple of damsels in distress, boring themselves to distraction, and each other too, by the look of it. Ring the bell, Blakeney, there's a good fellow, and get us a bottle worth drinking while we tell the young ladies how little they have missed at Lady Benchley's rout.'

'A terrible squeeze,' agreed Blakeney. 'I cannot imagine that anyone will notice we have left. Ah, Sims,' he smiled his engaging smile at the rigid-looking butler. 'Mr. Gaston and I will take a glass of wine with the young ladies.' He turned, laughing, to Caroline as the man retreated, disapproval in every inch of his back, 'You are looking very fetching tonight, Caro. You should always wear colours. Now, do tell me.' He had drawn up a chair close to hers, while Gaston settled beside Amelia on the other side of the table, 'What did you think of Tremadoc's poems?'

'Oh, Blakeney, I am so glad to see you! To tell truth, I don't know what in the world to say to him! They're ... Blakeney, they are quite dreadful. They are all about war, and even I can see that he doesn't know the first thing about it. And he never talks about a horse, or a man, or anything plain. It's always a gallant steed or a noble warrior and it goes on and on and on. In blank verse, too, if you can call it blank verse.'

'Poor Caro! And he is bound to call tomorrow and ask how you like them. So we had best think what you are going to say.' He poured them both a glass of the wine Sims had brought. 'You will have to admit to having read them, I suppose. And I know how you hate to lie. Can you not say something about not being qualified to judge, being a woman and ignorant of military affairs?'

'Yes, thank you. That might do,' she said doubtfully. 'But whether it will satisfy him ...'

'Oh, nothing will satisfy him. That mother of his has so filled him up with praise that he really fancies himself the next laureate.'

'Well,' she said fairly, 'he could hardly be more of a butt than poor Mr. Pye. But, Blakeney, I have been longing to thank you for Mr. Blake's poems. Now, that really is poetry! I am going to get some of it by heart, just as soon as I have time, but it is difficult. He doesn't seem to care about the rules of scansion at all.'

'And you do?' He found himself thinking how very different this conversation was from the ones he usually had with young ladies.

'Well.' She looked at him doubtfully. 'Do you know, the strange thing is, after reading Mr. Blake, I'm not so sure as I was. Do you read poetry at all, Blakeney?'

'Not much.' To most young ladies he would have told a cheerful lie and hoped to get away with it. 'To tell truth, it was a college friend who told me about Mr. Blake. But I'll read some if you will lend me the book, Caro.'

'Of course I will! Just as soon as I have got one or two by heart—or copied them. There seems to be so little time here in London,' she said regretfully.

'But you are enjoying yourself?' He looked at her keenly. 'You're pale, Caro. It suits you, but...' He thought about it for a moment. 'Why were you not with the girls in the Park yesterday?'

'They did not ask me.' A quick glance had shown her Amelia deep in laughing talk with Gaston, who was indeed handsomer than ever. 'And, besides, there does not seem to be a pony for me in the stables here.'

'No pony! But that's absurd. I'll speak to my father.'

'No, please!' She held out a pleading hand. 'Blakeney, I am so beholden to him already, to you all...' If she had been pale before; she was white now, her lips trembling. 'Blakeney, please...'

'Don't look so frightened, Miss Mouse.' The childhood nickname came out by long habit and surprised them both. 'I'll think of some plan that will not embarrass you, I promise. And now we must be going. We are to meet the others at Drury Lane for the after-piece. We would be missed there. Come, Gaston, we must be off.'

'I am very well where I am,' said Gaston, with a languishing glance for Amelia.

'So am I.' He smiled down at Caroline. 'But you know we are expected. We agreed we would only give the girls a quick look-in, and see how long we have stayed.'

'The attraction was irresistible.' Gaston kissed Amelia's hand. 'But you are right, as usual, Blakeney. Should we grease old Sims' palm, and tell him we have not been here?'

'No need for that,' said Blakeney stiffly. 'Sims and I are old friends.' He saw nervous colour flushing Caroline's cheek, and touched it gently. 'Don't look so conscious, Miss Mouse, it's the way of the world, that's all. What the parent doesn't know, his heart does not grieve over.'

Caroline sat up late that night reading and rereading Tremadoc's poems and trying to think what she could say about them. But when he called next day, as Blakeney had predicted, she found it easy enough. It had never for a moment occurred to him that she would be anything but overwhelmed by them and he occupied himself happily in reading her his favourite passages until they were interrupted by Blakeney with a small bunch of primroses.

'I picked them for you in the Green Park.' He handed them to Caroline. 'It's an amazing year. Only February, and the spring flowers are all out. I've come to ask a favour of you,' he went on, as she sniffed ecstatically at the fragrant, creamy flowers. 'I've a mare in my stables that's no longer up to my weight; she'd be just the thing for you and needs exercise badly. I've taken the liberty of bringing her with me in the hope that I can persuade you to come out for an airing.'

'Oh, I'd like it above anything! Will you mind waiting while I change my dress?' And then, hesitating. 'But, Blakeney, should I?'

'Of course you should. Think how often we have ridden together across the marsh at Cley.'

'I wish we were there,' she said. She was not sure which she missed the more, the brown-green landscape she had come to love, or the constant sound of the sea.

Hurrying upstairs to change into her riding habit, she wondered if she ought to ask permission of the Duchess, but as usual that lady and Mrs. Winterton were both out. She found herself wishing as she so often did that Miss Skinner would come back from Cambridge, but her sister-in-law was far from well, and she kept writing to say she must stay longer.

'Riding with his lordship?' asked Tench, surprised, and then: 'Well, and why not, since the young ladies don't think to take you. Enjoy yourself, my honey, and get some colour into those cheeks of yours.'

'Why, thank you, Tench!' She was surprised and touched by the unexpected endearment.

'Never you forget, miss,' said Tench, her voice slightly muffled as she pulled on the heavy serge habit, 'that you've more friends in this house than you know of. We was drinking your health in the hall only last night. "A young lady as *is* a young lady," was what Mr. Sims called you.'

'Oh, Tench, thank you!'

'That's just it,' said Tench. 'Please, and thank you, as if we was people too. There,' she handed whip and gloves, 'off you go and enjoy yourself. You'll come to no harm with his lordship, that's for sure.'

Caroline found Blakeney and Tremadoc awaiting her in the

hall, and Tremadoc announced that he had decided to join them.
'My mother keeps lecturing me about fresh air and exercise,'
he confided. 'In the normal way I cannot be bothered with it.
The movement of a horse is not conducive to composition, I
find. But in such company, I am sure my muse must find me.'

'Your what?' asked Blakeney.

It was the hour for fashionable exercise and Hyde Park was
crowded with riders and carriages. Caroline, who had been
nervous in Piccadilly on Blakeney's frisky mare, Zoe, soon
found herself impatient at the dawdling, social pace of the
crowd. 'Can one never gallop?' she asked Blakeney.

'Not in the Park! But if this weather holds, we could make
up a party and go to Richmond, where admission is limited,
and one can gallop to one's heart's content.'

'And pick primroses?'

'Anything you wish.' He looked past her. 'There are the
girls. Perhaps we should join them.'

Charlotte and Amelia were accompanied by Mattingley,
Gaston and a tall, heavy-faced young man Caroline had not met
before. No introductions were made as the two parties coa-
lesced, but Caroline presently found herself riding beside the
stranger, a little behind the rest of the party. 'You're the adopted
sister, of course.' The young man edged his horse a little closer
to speak confidentially. 'Miss Court? Something like that. I'm
ffether.' He spoke with the absolute confidence of one who
expects to be known. 'I wish you will tell me what Lady
Charlotte thinks she is playing at.'

'Lady Charlotte? Playing? I do not understand you, sir.'

'"My lord,"' he corrected. 'Don't play the miss with me,
miss. Everybody who is anybody knows that it has been a
settled thing between the Duke and my pa ever since they met
at Woburn last autumn. Why else would the Duke have dragged
that whey-faced Amelia to town, if he had not known Lady
Charlotte was already spoken for? And now she chooses to
give me the go-by and cast out her lures at Mattingley, of all
people.'

'Mr. Mattingley is a great friend of the family,' said Caroline.

He threw back his head and roared with laughter, drawing
glances of disapproval from several nearby carriages. 'That's
rich,' he crowed. 'That's damned rich! Friend of the family.
I like that, Miss Court. Setting up as a wit, are you, being so

plain? Not stupid, I can see that, so I shall trust you with a message for my Charlotte. Tell her, I shall expect prettier behaviour from her at the opera tonight, or it's all off between us, whatever my pa may say. As for hers, he can go hang. Never did much like the stable, come to that. One of the Villiers girls was looking very fetching at me last night at the play. And you can tell Charlotte I said so,' he concluded, setting spurs to his horse and suddenly leaving her alone.

They had fallen a little behind the rest of the party as he talked and Caroline spoke an encouraging word to Zoe and dug in her heels to urge her forward.

'All alone, Miss Thorpe?' said a friendly voice, and she turned to see a stranger edging a neat bay up beside her. 'My friend the Duchess would not like that, I am sure, so you must just let me keep you company until we can rejoin your party.'

'You're very kind.' She smiled at him, liking what she saw. A phrase of Blakeney's, 'complete to a shade,' floated through her mind. 'But...' she coloured. 'I don't...'

'Know me,' he finished for her. 'Never mind, everyone else does, and I promise you, it will do you no harm to be seen in my company.'

'Oh, I'm sure of that,' she said warmly. 'You're so,' she looked in vain for a word, and concluded, blushing harder than ever, with 'exquisite.'

'You care about words, Miss Thorpe?' His smile was more friendly still. 'Well, I care about clothes. And appearances in general,' he went on, 'and if I were you, I would bring my own groom when riding here in the Park.'

'But I haven't got one,' she told him, surprised into frankness.

'Oh dear me,' he said. 'I must speak to the Duchess. Or, perhaps to the Duke? It's a bold man speaks to the Duke, but in a good cause, I am a bold man.'

'I'm sure you are.' She saw that the others had paused at last to wait for them.

Charlotte was looking miffed, but greeted Caroline's companion warmly. 'Mr. Brummell! When did you get into town?'

'Just yesterday,' he told her. 'Brighton smelled so strongly of the sea I could stand it no longer. Besides, all the talk was of a French invasion. A dead bore. And I am glad I came, now that I find my friends are back at Chevenham House. Will I see you at the opera tonight?'

'Yes, indeed. We are all going, I believe.'

'The inimitable Grassini?' he asked. 'It will be your first visit to the opera, Miss Thorpe?'

'To any theatre,' she told him. 'I am so excited I do not know how I shall get through the afternoon. Though to tell truth, I do not understand much about music.'

'I doubt if you will find that matters much.' He smiled, bowed and left them.

'Where did you meet Mr. Brummell?' Charlotte asked Caroline after they had parted with the young men and turned for home.

'I never had. Was it not kind of him to come to my rescue when I got left behind?'

'And you let him speak to you? A complete stranger! Caroline, I wish you will try for a little conduct. First to monopolise Lord ffether, and then to talk to any stranger who comes up to you! I am afraid I must tell mamma of this.'

'Do,' said Caroline, goaded beyond endurance, 'but first I must give you a message from Lord ffether. He stayed behind with me in order to send it. He says,' she crimsoned, realising as she spoke just how rude the message was, 'he says he hopes you will be kinder to him at the opera than you were last night at the play.'

'Only I imagine that was not just how he put it,' said Charlotte sharply. 'I know Lord ffether's charming ways. Well, I will show him what I think of him and his message.'

'The Duke will be angry,' said Caroline, suddenly sorry for Charlotte.

'The Duke won't be there. He detests the opera; even Darling Frances can't get him there.'

'But someone will tell him.'

'So much the better. It will give me a chance to tell him what I think of his arrangements for me. Just because our estates march, he thinks ffether the perfect match, without so much as consulting me. Well,' she admitted, 'it did not seem so bad when he spoke of it at Cley, but now I'm in town, with the world at my feet, why should I be bound by two old cronies' arrangements over a bottle of port?'

The Duchess had taken two adjoining boxes at the King's Theatre, Haymarket, for the opera season, and Caroline, tucked inconspicuously at the back of the one farther from the stage, soon understood what Mr. Brummell had meant when he said it would not matter much that she knew nothing about music. The prima donna was not the famous new Italian, Madame

Grassini, but the English singer Mrs. Billington as Iñez de Castro in an opera written for her by Bianchi. From the loud comments of the young men who stood behind the ladies' chairs, Caroline learned that the Grassini was thought to be the better singer of the rival primas, but Mrs. Billington the more beautiful. 'That's what Prinney thinks, anyway,' she heard Gaston say, with emphasis.

Unfortunately, she was sitting behind Charlotte, who had her hair dressed high, so she had not much chance of deciding about Mrs. Billington's attractions. When she could hear it, she could not understand the Italian of the opera, and when she asked Tremadoc, in the interval, what it was about, he shrugged his shoulders and said it was just a deal of Italian nonsense, not worth bothering with. 'I am thinking of writing an ode to Mrs. Billington,' he told her. 'How do you think it should begin?' And then, before she had time to open her mouth. 'I had thought of:

> Sound, Muse, sound out thy hectic strain
> Billington's on our stage again—

Or perhaps something a shade more heroic?

> Oh, Muses nine, fair company
> Deign now to hand your lyre to me.

'Miss Thorpe,' he said, 'what are you doing?'

'I was afraid I was going to sneeze,' she said meekly, taking from her mouth the handkerchief with which she had been stifling irrepressible laughter.

'Overwhelmed by the majesty of his verse?' suggested Mattingley's amused voice behind her. 'Your mother is signalling to you across the house, Tremadoc. I think perhaps she wishes you to join her in her box. A very obedient son,' he went on, when Tremadoc had sighed gustily and left them, 'I hope his mamma is not too surprised to see him.'

'You mean you made it up?'

'I thought if I did not rescue you, you might disgrace yourself, Miss Thorpe.'

'I was close to it,' she admitted, looking anxiously to the front of the box, where Charlotte had her shoulder ostentatiously turned to Lord ffether and was listening with exaggerated interest to something Gaston was saying to her.

'A striking young man, that,' he had followed the direction of her glance. 'And dangerous, I think. I am glad to see that he does not play off his charms on you.'

'Oh, I'm quite beneath his touch,' she said, and received one of his enigmatic smiles.

She rather hoped that he might decide to squire her to the carriage, having heard the long crowded wait in the crush room vividly described by Charlotte, who had been taken to the opera the year before. But he returned to the Duchess's box after the interval and, to her surprise, Tremadoc squeezed in beside her just as the curtain rose for the last act. He had received a resounding scold from his mother for paying attention to that 'little nobody of a Miss Thorpe,' and it had suddenly roused him to a declaration of independence. 'I shall see you out,' he told Caroline in masterful tones when the curtain fell at last, and regaled her, during the long wait until their carriage was called, with various new first lines for his ode to Mrs. Billington.

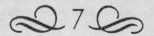

CHARLES MATTINGLEY PAID an early call on the Duchess next day, and found her still in the hands of her hairdresser. 'Exquisite,' he approved. 'Only you could carry off such a style. But I was hoping for a word with you before you are quite thronged with morning callers.'

'You certainly came early enough.' She nodded dismissal to her maid and the hairdresser. 'Dear Charles,' she held out her hand to him. 'It's always good to see you. Don't tell me, though, that you have come to read me a lecture about my losses at play. Surely that is the Duke's prerogative?'

'You're dipped again?' he asked with quick sympathy. 'I'm sorry to hear it. I wish I could persuade you to play for lower stakes.'

'And let the whole world say the Duchess of Cley cries craven? I thank you, no. The Duke told me, when we married, that he would go his way, and I mine. His way is expensive. Why should not mine be? After all . . .' She stopped short of reminding him that a great deal of their money had originally been hers.

'It's a hard life for a woman.' He raised her hand to his lips. 'In a way, that is what I have come to talk to you about.'

'About women's lives?'

'Yes. You asked me to have an eye to your little protégé, Miss Thorpe.'

'And most assiduously you have done so. Frances was twitting me about it only last night.'

'I wish Mrs. Winterton would mind her own business.'

'Well,' said the Duchess. 'You could say that Caroline Thorpe is Frances's business.'

'Mrs. Winterton hardly behaves as if she were. Anyone seeing you three together would think you were the child's mother, not she.'

'I almost feel as if I were. She's a most unusual creature, Charles. I love her very much. And Frances takes her part with the Duke, which is the great thing. But for her, I really think he would have left Caroline to moulder at Cley this winter, and then lord knows what would have become of her.'

'Well, what is to become of her?' he asked. 'Maria,' he did not often use her christian name, 'I do urge that you persuade the Duke to tell those children who they are.'

'Children? You mean Gaston and Caroline? He won't, my dear. He absolutely refuses. He says when they are engaged to be married will be quite time enough.'

'But suppose they should engage themselves to the wrong people?'

'The wrong people?' She thought about it. 'You cannot be imagining that Blakeney would be such a fool! Besides, they have grown up together: brother and sister. And the same is true, even more so, of Gaston and my girls. Besides, he is much too well aware of what he owes us to step at all out of line there.'

'I do hope you are right,' he said as her next caller was announced.

He took his leave soon after, saying with one of his half smiles that he proposed to give the younger party a look in.

'And make sure they are behaving themselves?' teased the Duchess.

But he had made her a little anxious, and she seized a

moment when she and Frances Winterton were changing for dinner to dismiss both their maids and raise the subject with her.

Frances responded with a peal of sardonic laughter. 'Blakeney and my poor little mouse? I never heard such nonsense in my life. Oh, he's kind to her. Your Blakeney is kind to everyone, Maria. But you know as well as I do how high the Duke looks for him. Between ourselves, I think he has set his heart on the Princess Charlotte. And, you know, our Blakeney would make an admirable consort.'

'That little hoyden?' asked the Duchess. 'I trust the Duke will think again. But you are right, as always, dearest Frances. Raised with such ideas, Blakeney would never think for a moment of your poor little Caroline.'

'Not so poor as all that,' said Frances, tartly for her. 'Have you not noticed, Maria my darling, that my little Caroline is having quite a success?'

'Young Tremadoc? Well, it would not be a bad match for her, if his mother would give her consent.'

'Which she never would,' said Frances. 'You know what airs that woman has given herself since you borrowed all that money from her husband.'

'I wish he was alive now,' said the Duchess.

'To lend you more?' Frances laughed. 'Maria, there is Gaston to think about as well as Caroline. That's a dangerous young man, I think.'

'Ah, poor Gaston,' sighed the Duchess. 'He really is a problem. I can understand the Duke's reluctance to tell him he is the son of a mere French *gouvernante*. But I am afraid he has filled himself with ideas about some very elegant bar sinister indeed.'

'Did you see him studying the Comte d' Artois, when he came to Cley? I could swear he was looking for a royal likeness. It's no wonder the Duke does not much look forward to telling him the truth. Oh well,' she concluded comfortably, 'if the news from Europe gets much worse, I have no doubt he will be sent abroad on some expedition or other with his regiment, and I won't say I shan't breathe a sigh of relief. He's trouble, that Gaston. If I were you, I believe I would keep an eye on Charlotte and Amelia. Have you noticed that he is dividing his attentions between the two of them?'

'And so much the safer. Besides, they know what is to be expected of them.' The Duchess dismissed the subject.

Downstairs, Charlotte and Amelia were quarrelling. 'It's not fair,' said Amelia. 'You've got Lord ffether. Leave Gaston to me.'

'You're welcome to ffether if you want him,' said Charlotte. 'I find him a dead bore.'

'All very fine to say I can have him. You know perfectly well it's not you he wants, it's papa's eldest daughter. Oh dear, I wish I was Caroline, able to marry whomever I liked.'

'Yes, but who'll ask her? With no family, no fortune and precious little countenance.'

'Tremadoc seems devoted enough.'

'She listens when he spouts that poetry of his. But his mother would never allow it, on the make as she is. I have no doubt the old harridan hopes Tremadoc is dangling after me.' She eyed herself lovingly in the glass. 'But, naturally, he knows that even you are quite above his touch.'

'Thank you for that "even"!' Amelia flounced out of the room.

Frances Winterton really intended, after that slightly disquieting conversation with the Duchess, to send for Caroline and drop a word of warning in her ear. But how difficult it would be to do, granted the Duke's absolute refusal to let Caroline or Gaston be told the truth about their birth. She put it off from day to day, and was soon distracted by the growing rumours that the King, who had been suffering grievously from gout, was going mad again, as he had in 1788. The leaders of the Whig party had been in high hopes, then, that their good friend the Prince of Wales would become Regent and bring them back to power at last. Now they discussed each new rumour with apparent concern and well concealed excitement. The King had taken to appearing in the oddest of uniforms: he had been to the play dressed as an admiral and received Sir Charles Poole in an out-dated uniform of Lord Howe's time. The daily bulletins from the Queen's House spoke of his condition as unchanged, but Sir Lucas Pepys and Doctor Reynolds, who had been added to the physicians already attending him, could only say that, 'His Majesty has had several hours sleep, and seems refreshed by it.'

Inevitably, Devonshire House, the great Whig stronghold a little further along Piccadilly, was the centre of frenzied activity, as Mr. Fox and his friends constructed one cabinet in the air after another. The Duke of Cley spent most of his time there, and Frances went too, to compare rumour and counter-rumour with her good friends the Duchess of Devonshire and Lady Elizabeth Foster. The Duchess of Cley had never cared much about politics and kept away. Bored and restless, she had what was almost a quarrel with Charles Mattingley about his too literal obedience to her orders about Caroline.

'I didn't mean you to sit in the chit's pocket.' She had met him, by her own appointment, at the room in Shepherd's Market he had taken expressly for their assignations.

'A very charming pocket.' His smile was a little sad, a little mocking. Surprised himself at how attractive he found Caroline, he recognised and regretted the Duchess's inevitable jealousy. Quite soon now, the time would come for them to part. In the meanwhile, no use quarrelling. He picked up her slender hand, one of her acknowledged beauties which had lasted better than face or figure, and kissed each fingertip in turn. 'A child,' he said. 'An attractive child who badly needs direction. I am afraid for her, a little. But enough of that.' It was too much already. 'Tell of yourself instead. Have you really been so unlucky at the card tables?'

'Unlucky!' The cry was worthy of the great Mrs. Siddons herself. 'It's a disaster, Mat. My only hope is in the Prince!'

'The Prince of Wales?' She had really surprised him now.

'He's always been my good friend. Now, with this chance of his becoming Regent, the Whigs are his to command. A word from him, and I truly think the Duke would pay my debts.'

'And you will ask for that word?' He looked at her thoughtfully. Everyone knew that the Prince of Wales was addicted to older women. Might the Duchess of Cley, who had aged so sadly, be about to replace Lady Hertford in his affections? If so, he had a delicate path to tread. He pulled her to him. 'Divine Maria, why are we wasting our time in talk?'

Later, looking down as she lay, relaxed and satisfied, in his arms, he thought that really it might be an admirable thing if he found himself able to make the gesture of yielding her up to the Prince of Wales. He had been used to call her his Rubens beauty, his Titian lady, now, regretfully, he thought her merely overweight. Even her famous complexion had succumbed at last to the toll of late nights and lavish food and drink. He always spared her lacquered face as much as possible in his love-making, but today the results had been disastrous. She would mind, horribly, when she saw herself in the glass. He must leave before she did, before the sad scene that would follow. 'My love,' he looked down at her with a deep affection he did not need to feign, 'I must leave you, alas. I have been summoned urgently to the country.'

'Your mother's ill again? I'm sorry, Charles. I know how you love her. I sometimes think it is more for her sake than mine that you have not joined the army.' She lifted her chin a little as if aware that it doubled itself as she lay. 'I'll miss you, Charles. The Duke and Frances spend all their time at Devonshire House, politicking. Do you think it is there that they . . . No,' she surprised him by a real laugh, 'the Duke's too lazy. I have no doubt they contrive somehow at Chevenham House as they did at Cley. Dear Frances, I expect if I asked her, she would tell me. Really, it would make things easier.'

'No,' he said. 'Never do that. But I'm glad you still feel that you could.'

'Oh, I love her,' she said. 'Much more than I ever even thought I did the Duke!'

More than you do me? But he had more sense than to ask the question aloud. Anyway, he knew the answer.

Mild February yielded to blustery March. The King was better, and Mr. Addington declared in the House that, 'There is not at this time a necessary suspension of the exercise of the royal authority.' The Whigs concealed their disappointment as best they might and paid calls of congratulation at the Queen's House. And Blakeney named a day at last for the long promised expedition to Richmond Park. His father had surprised him by taking him aside after the ladies had left the dining room one day and suggesting that he arrange some outing to throw Charlotte and ffether together. 'It's high time that business was settled. I've told her mother to say a word to Charlotte. You give them the opportunity, the thing's done, and we can get down to Brighton for a breath of air. Now the King's better, there's no point in dangling on here in London.'

'The girls will be disappointed, sir.' But Caroline would not, he remembered, with the little leap of the heart that now accompanied all thought of her. Caroline had told him only the other day how much she longed for the country and the sea. It would be a delight to see her glowing look when she saw the Sussex downs for the first time, the white cliffs shining down to the sea. 'I beg your pardon.' He realised that his father had said something and was waiting impatiently for an answer.

'I said, "The girls will do as they are told,"' repeated the

Duke. 'I don't like this wool-gathering, Blakeney. Anyone would think it was you who were about to put the question, not young ffether.'

'I'm sorry, sir. I was thinking I could make up a party to Richmond Park,' improvised Blakeney, longing, as he said it, to plunge in, tell his father how he felt about Caroline, persuade him that she was the only girl for him. Instinct held him back. The Duke liked to do one thing at a time. When Charlotte's fate was settled would be the moment to approach him about Caroline. Or was he putting it off because he feared the outcome?

He planned the Richmond party as a small one with the three girls squired by ffether, Tremadoc and himself, but Amelia objected at once. 'And have you and Tremadoc both dangling after Caroline? I thank you, no. Besides,' she went on, 'I'd think again on my own account if I were you, Blakeney. And on Caroline's. There's no future in it, Blakeney dear. I'm sorry for you both, but there it is, and the sooner you make up your mind to it, the better.'

'I don't understand you,' he began, but she interrupted him. 'Oh, yes you do. And why I'm the only one who has noticed it is more than I can understand. If ever I saw a case of April and May! She blushes if you so much as look at her, and as you can't keep your eyes off her, it's a miracle not even Darling Frances has seen it. There's none so blind . . . Skinny would have seen long since. What a bore that sister-in-law of hers is, dying in childbirth. I'd never have thought we'd miss Skinny so much. Things go on quite differently now she's not here. But someone's bound to notice you and Caroline soon. If you want your idyll to last a little longer, you'd better not do anything to draw attention to it. Besides, it would be downright discourteous not to ask Gaston to come too.'

'So long as he does not kick up one of his rumpuses.'

She laughed. 'At least he will make the day a more entertaining one, and you know it. But trust me to keep him in line, Blakeney.'

He hoped he could, and invited Mattingley to join the party, too, just, he told himself, to be on the safe side.

Mattingley accepted the invitation with one of his quizzical looks. 'Now I wonder just why you are inviting me. Is it to act as (God help me) chaperon and mentor, or is there more to it? Ah well, curiosity compels me to come along and find out. Can I take one of the young ladies up in my curricle? You will meet your horses at the Roehampton Gate, I suppose?'

'Why, no. I had thought the Richmond Gate, and then we can give the girls a collation at the Star and Garter Inn after their ride.'

'Why, a perfect orgy, Blakeney. I wish you would let me bring Miss Caroline, but I suppose it will have to be Lady Amelia.'

Blakeney could not help laughing. 'If you will be so good, sir.' He himself was to drive Caroline in the high perch phaeton he had just bought, and he meant ffether to drive Charlotte and, he hoped, get the real business of the outing over with before it had ever begun. But when he and Caroline arrived at the Richmond Gate, very much in charity with each other, and with the fine day that had rewarded his bold planning, it was to find ffether awaiting them with a thunderous expression and no Charlotte.

'Your sister,' he told Blakeney between angrily clenched teeth, 'chose to think I arrived late to fetch her, and did not wait for me.'

'Well, you were late,' said Blakeney reasonably. 'She was dressed and ready when we set off, and we came the long way round because I wanted to show Caro more of the river.' He looked about him. 'But where is Charlotte in that case?'

'That's what I would like to know,' said ffether. 'Your servants did not appear to be aware which gentleman it was who had taken her when she "got tired of waiting".' He put the last few words into angry quotation marks.

'Here she comes now,' said Caroline, who had listened anxiously to this exchange. 'And Mattingley and Gaston with her.'

'Such a squeeze,' exclaimed Charlotte, laughing, as Gaston helped her alight. 'Why, there you are at last, my lord. You must have driven like the wind. I vow I waited for you an hour or more, until these two gentlemen took pity on me. Amelia is following with Tremadoc.' She smiled placatingly at her brother. 'You know she is never ready when she is wanted, and his mother sent to say he would be late, so we three thought we had better come along and tell you what has become of your party. Must we wait for the others?' she concluded, looking to where the grooms were holding the horses. 'Amelia had not even decided which habit to wear when I came downstairs.'

But as she spoke, Tremadoc's curricle came swinging into

sight, driven at a spanking pace, with Tremadoc and Amelia quite obviously not speaking to each other.

It was not an auspicious start to the excursion, and Blakeney, hearing a hissed remark from Amelia to Charlotte, 'You hid my habit, you toad!' could only expect disaster, but to his deep gratitude Mattingley suddenly took command, spreading his charm, like soothing oil on the troubled social waters. He sympathised with Amelia; he complimented ffether on his showy bay, and at the same time directed a glance at once humorous and warning at Charlotte, which combined with something Gaston had just whispered to her to bring about a complete change in her manner. She turned to ffether, made him the prettiest apology in the world, and begged him to help her mount her impatient little mare. 'Since I did not have the pleasure of driving here with you, you must be my cavalier for the rest of the day,' she told him, And Blakeney, seeing him reply with renewed warmth, thought that his party might not be such a disaster after all. Perhaps Charlotte had been clever. A touch of jealousy might be just what was needed to bring ffether to the point.

At ease about this, he turned to help Caroline on to Zoe, only to find that Tremadoc had been before him and that she was looking a little wistfully back over her shoulder, as the two of them set forward for the rendezvous at the Pen Ponds. His eyes met hers for a swift moment of shared disappointment, which left him in such a glow of happinesss that he was able to turn all his energies to helping Mattingley soothe down the still disgruntled Amelia. Gaston, curiously enough, had mounted his horse and vanished. Well, it was just like Gaston to do something odd and tiresome, and he could not be bothered with his vagaries today.

Riding beside Tremadoc, Caroline had not thought it possible to be so happy. Surely that quick exchange of glances with Blakeney confirmed her throbbing instinct that he cared for her? She thought, now, that she had loved him from the first moment they met, when he had played highwayman on the road to Cley, but it was only in the last few weeks that a special something in his glance had taught her to hope that her feeling might be returned. The Duke would be angry, but her confidence in Blakeney was complete. If he meant to have her, he would.

In her glowing happiness, she gleamed and sparkled at Tremadoc, and finished the conquest begun by her patient ear for his poetry. For once, his mother's prohibition had had the opposite effect from what she intended. She had told him not to pay court to Caroline before he had seriously considered it, and her opposition had merely served to turn Caroline into a glamorous figure in his eyes, the heroine of a romance. Inspired by this, he had written a series of short poems about just such a heroine and lost no time in reading them to her. Unaware that they were, in fact, addressed to herself, she had been moved by an unexpectedly genuine note in his *Poems to the Mysterious Amoretta*. They were infinitely better than anything in his privately printed volume, and she told him so, without letting him see just how bad she thought the others. The result was inevitable. He had thought himself in love before, now he was as far in as was possible for anyone so self absorbed.

Perceptive for once, he had noticed that significantly exchanged glance with Blakeney, and it had served to enhance Caroline's value in his eyes. If Blakeney cared for her, and was looking visibly put out at not having her for his companion, she was a prize indeed. He had chosen a long way round to the rendezvous, and they were now out of sight of the others. He edged his horse closer to hers.

'Oh mysterious Amoretta,' he began.

'I beg your pardon?' It won him a quick, upward look of surprise that he found infinitely touching. Modest little thing. It had not struck her that she might be the heroine of his poetry.

He quoted himself:

> Oh, fair one, fairer than the night,
> Oh made to be my heart's delight
> Oh face that puts despair to flight
> Grant me the wish I wish tonight.

He was not entirely happy about that last line, but this was not, even he realised, the moment to be discussing that. 'Exquisite creature,' he reverted to prose, 'can it be that you still do not understand me?'

'I most certainly do not.' She was surprised at his tone, and made a determined effort to change the course of the conversation. 'I have been wanting to say to you that I am not sure that that last line quite keeps up the high romantic tone of the rest of your poem, Mr. Tremadoc.'

'Be damned to the last line! Divine Amoretta, will you not call me Geraint? Call me lover? Call me husband! Be mine,

Amoretta, be my life, be my happiness, be my love!' He reached out to grasp for her hand, but it eluded him.

'Mr. Tremadoc, you forget yourself!' She cast a quick anxious look behind, hoping to see Blakeney and Amelia, but there was nothing in sight but a herd of deer, peacefully grazing along the side of one of the little woods that dotted the park.

'On the contrary, lovely one, I remember myself. I understand myself at last. All my life I have been looking for my muse; for the peerless one who will inspire me to heights of poetry unimagined before. Amoretta, beloved, at last I understand that you are she!'

'I am neither Amoretta nor your beloved.' She tried to make her tone light, convinced that this was merely a passing whim, best treated as such. 'I am plain Caroline Thorpe, and I think we should be catching up with the others.'

'Or letting them catch us?' he asked, suddenly acute. 'No use looking over your shoulder for Blakeney, divine Amoretta,' he told her. 'I have come the long way around. You will not see him until we reach the Pen Ponds. And just as well, too,' he went on, reassuringly more practical. 'He is not for you, Amoretta, and in your heart you must know it. The Duke would no more let him make such a misalliance than . . . than . . .'

'Than your mother would you,' she concluded for him tartly.

'Ah!' He breathed a gusty sigh of understanding. 'So that's the trouble. Now I understand you, beauteous Amoretta. And you are right, of course. My mother did tell me to think no more of you, but it only made my flame burn more strongly. What do I care how base your parentage may be? You are my muse, my flame, my life, my heart!'

'I am nothing of the kind.' She was angry now. 'I have been bearing your nonsense, sir, but I will not bear your rudeness. Base parentage indeed! How dare you?' Her voice was angrier than she intended because he had struck a secret chord of fear. As she grew up, she had wondered more and more often, why no one ever said anything about her mother and father, who had been such good friends of the Duke and Duchess. She had longed to learn about them, especially since she had been in London society and become aware of just how important birth was. But who could she ask? Miss Skinner was still in Cambridge, fixed there by the death of her sister-in-law. The Duchess and Mrs. Winterton were kind enough, but she could not go to them. I will ask Blakeney, she thought.

Blakeney will tell me. Her cheeks glowed with sudden happiness. .

He misinterpreted the look. 'How dare I? I dare anything for your sake, Amoretta! I am your champion. Against my mother. Against the world! Only say you will be mine!' He reached out again and this time managed to catch her hand.

'Don't!' Now she was frightened. His pull was upsetting her balance in the side saddle. 'Let go!' She exclaimed. 'I'll never . . .' But the change of balance, and the feeling of tension in the air had unsettled the spirited mare, which bolted. For a while, all else forgotten, Caroline managed to hold on, grimly, breathlessly, then a brush with the branch of a tree finished the business.. For a moment she lay on the ground, shocked but conscious, aware with relief that she was only shaken, not hurt, then got slowly to her feet and looked about her. The wild flight had brought her to the little wood, scattering the herd of deer. Close to her stood a stag, huge of antler, pawing the ground, staring at her, and she realised with a shock of terror that her madly bolting horse had got her between it and the rest of the herd. She stood very still and stared back at the stag as boldly as she could.

Giles had outstared a bull once. How strange to find herself remembering Giles in this moment of terror. The stag lowered its head, cutting off that eye-to-eye challenge, and took a step forward. Instinctively she backed, felt something behind her, realised it was the tree that had caused her fall. She clutched its trunk with a backward hand and saw the stag hesitate. Where was Tremadoc? Surely he must have followed when Zoe ran away with her?

Silence. A nervous rustling behind her that must be the rest of the herd. The stag shook its head angrily and took a step forward, then hesitated, disliking the sweep of the tree's branches. So near, it seemed enormous. She held her breath, and as it lowered its head to charge, moved swiftly round the trunk of the tree. The stag backed off, circled the tree, came on again, angrier now. Once again, she managed to sidestep its charge. Would help never come? What was Tremadoc doing? The stag was coming on again; she dodged round the tree, slipped slightly, recovered herself, leaned against the rough trunk, breathing hard. How long could she keep this up? It was . like a mad dance, she thought, a children's game turned nightmare. The stag was getting used to the tree; it came closer, faster each time. An antler grazed her arm, bruising through the stuff of her habit. She could not keep this up much longer.

The thunder of a horse's hooves. 'Caro!' Blakeney's voice. 'Caro, I'm coming!'

Distracted, she was almost too slow in dodging, and once again felt the bruising impact of bone on bone. One last time? Blakeney was shouting now. She dared not turn her head to look, but knew he must be advancing at full gallop, meaning to scare the animal into flight. Behind her, she could hear the herd scattering; saw the stag realise this. It shook its head once, then turned and ambled gracefully away.

'Caro? Caro, are you hurt?' Blakeney dismounted, slipped the reins over his horse's neck, came towards her with arms outstretched. She went into them as if it was the most natural thing in the world. 'Caro.' He raised his head at last from the long wondering kiss. 'My love.' He said it slowly, testing the words.

'Blakeney.' She smiled up at him tremulously. 'You did feel it too?'

'From the very first,' he told her. 'That we belonged together.' It was not, perhaps, entirely true, but he thought it was. 'I've been working so hard,' he told her, 'to make a man of myself. To show my father,' he hesitated, 'to show the world I am worthy of you.'

'Oh, Blakeney,' she said sadly. 'It's the other way round, and we both know it. Will the Duke be very angry?'

'He won't be pleased. But it will make no difference. I love you, Caroline. Do you know,' he went on. 'I never loved anyone before. I had no idea . . . what it was like. What it is like.'

'Neither did I. No one.' And, as she raised her lips for his second kiss, thought with her incorrigible honesty that that was not quite true. Had she not, perhaps, far away and long ago, loved Giles just a little? The doubt was lost, drowned beyond recognition, beyond memory, in the ecstasy of his second kiss, surer now, stronger, turning her bones to water. 'Oh, Blakeney,' she sighed, 'what are we going to do?'

'Go back to the others.' He picked up her plumed hat from the grass. 'Try not to let it show. Not till I've told my father. He has the right to know first. But, Caro, my darling, are you sure you're not hurt?'

'A little,' she said honestly. 'But nothing to signify.'

'You were so brave,' he said. 'So cool. I have never been so frightened in my life.'

'Not half so frightened as I was.' She was beginning to shake now, and he saw it.

'We must find the others. We'll go home, of course. Would you like to stay here, while I find them?'

'No!' She clung to him and he could feel her tremble.

'Of course not. Stupid of me. But what happened to Tremadoc? What kept you so long? I had come back to look for you, thank God!'

'Thank *you*, Blakeney.' She blushed scarlet searching for words that came hard. 'Mr. Tremadoc . . . asked me to marry him . . . He tried to hold my hand. Zoe didn't like it. It wasn't her fault she bolted. I don't know what's happened to him.'

'He must have been thrown,' said Blakeney. 'He never was much of a rider. We had better go and look for him. And in future, Caroline, if anyone takes liberties with you, you will refer him to me.'

'Oh, Blakeney,' she raised her lips for one last kiss.

'We must go,' he said again, shaken as she was by the current that ran strong between them. 'Caroline!' And then, 'Ah, there will be time for that. Here, Zoe!' he called the mare, peacefully grazing not far off, and she ambled over willingly to his hand. 'You're not afraid,' he asked, as he prepared to toss her up into the saddle.

'Afraid of my dear Zoe? Of course not.'

'You're a heroine.' He mounted his own horse. 'You are sure you can ride?' He could see that she was holding the reins in an awkward grasp.

'Oh, yes. It hurts a little, but nothing to signify. But, oh, Blakeney, if you hadn't come!'

'I'll always come.' Mounted, he could see farther, but there was no sign of Tremadoc. 'We'd best look for Tremadoc first. He must be hurt, not to have come to your help.'

'I am afraid so.' She did not much want to see Tremadoc, and was relieved when they rode up a little hill and found him already being ministered to by Amelia and Mattingley. He had indeed been thrown, and was lying on the grass, curd-white with shock.

Sniffing at Amelia's salts, he raised reproachful eyes to Caroline. 'There you are at last,' he said. 'I thought you would have come to my help sooner.'

'She come to yours!' began Blakeney angrily, but a pleading

look from Caroline made him change his tone. 'She was thrown too,' he said briefly. 'You're badly hurt?' He addressed the question as much to Mattingley as Tremadoc.

'No bones broken, I think,' said Mattingley briskly. 'But a bad shaking. And Miss Thorpe?' A quick, anxious glance for Caroline.

'Miss Thorpe's a heroine,' said Blakeney warmly. 'She was thrown *and* chased by a stag. She was between it and the herd,' he explained. 'I found her gallantly dodging it round a tree.'

'A heroine indeed,' said Mattingley, his thoughtful glance travelling from her flushed face to his.

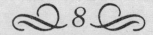

AFTER A QUICK discussion among the men, it was agreed that Mattingley should ride on to the Pen Ponds and explain the situation to Charlotte and ffether, who must be awaiting them there, while the rest of the party made their way slowly back to the Richmond Gate. 'The carriages will be down at the Star and Garter by now,' said Blakeney. 'But I'll send a boy to fetch them back for us. I expect you will get there before they do,' he told Mattingley.

But at that very moment, ffether himself came in sight, riding towards them at a furious pace. 'So she didn't join you!' He shouted it at Blakeney as he approached. 'Vixen! To be jauntering about in the Park by herself! Done it too brown this time.' He was breathless with anger and the sentences came out explosively. 'I fancy I am a little too much of a man of the world to be playing children's games.'

'You're speaking of Charlotte?' asked Blakeney, angry too. 'But she was with you.'

'Gave me the slip in the woods! Insisted on riding through them. To look for primroses, she said. Told me to ride on while she made some adjustment to her dress. Vanished! Hoyden.' He summed it up in one angry word. 'You can go looking for her, Blakeney. She's your sister. She can play games with you if she likes, but it's the last chance she has with me. I'll be on my way. No need to ask her to apologise to me. I wouldn't accept it. I wish you all a very good day.'

'No,' said Blakeney, before Mattingley could intervene. 'I'm sorry if my sister has played you a schoolgirl's trick, ffether, and I do indeed apologise on her behalf, but we cannot leave it like that. Where did you leave her? Which wood? She must not be riding about in the Park by herself.'

'She can ride to the devil for all I care,' said ffether.

'I think you do not quite understand.' Mattingley thought it time to intervene between the two increasingly angry young men. 'Miss Thorpe and Mr. Tremadoc have both been thrown. If we have to look for Lady Charlotte, we shall need your help, ffether. I fail to see what you find so comic,' he concluded stiffly, as ffether went into a peal of rather coarse laughter.

'Both thrown!' he exclaimed. 'In the Park! Well, I thought I'd seen everything. If I could not ride better than that, I'd keep to the riding house where I belonged.'

'Which wood, ffether?' asked Blakeney again, through clenched teeth.

'The big one over there,' he pointed carelessly with his riding crop. 'But I imagine she is at the Star and Garter by now. She had said something earlier about going there which I did not rightly understand. I take it it is her idea of a jest to go riding about the Park by herself like the veriest . . .'

'Schoolgirl,' interposed Mattingley, as ffether searched angrily for the right word. 'Well, a childish prank enough, but we must be grateful that it's no worse. Do you not think, Blakeney, that we had really best all ride to the Star and Garter? Miss Thorpe will be glad of rest and refreshment before we drive home, and so, I expect will Mr. Tremadoc. Do you think you could manage the ride, Miss Thorpe?'

'Of course I can,' she said eagerly. 'By all means, let us start at once. I do not like to think of Charlotte's being there by herself.'

'By herself?' asked Amelia. 'I'll bet you a guinea to a garter that Gaston is with her.' And then coloured crimson, obviously wishing the words unsaid.

'Gaston!' exclaimed Blakeney. 'Of course! Stupid of me. You'll give us your company to the inn, Lord ffether?' He made it a little formal, almost an apology.

'I thank you, no. I'll ride home. My carriage is at your disposal if you need it. If not, be so good as to tell my man to bring it back to Grosvenor Square.' He kicked his horse into a startled gallop and left them before either Blakeney or Mattingley could protest.

'Well, so much for that,' said Mattingley. 'And perhaps best as it is. If you are fit to ride, Tremadoc, I think Miss Thorpe is right and we should be making the quickest possible way to the Star and Garter.'

'Yes, indeed,' said Blakeney, as Tremadoc got groaning to his feet, 'Of all the extraordinary starts. I'd not have thought it of Charlotte.'

It was a subdued little party that started back across the Park towards the Richmond Gate. Caroline was beginning to feel the throb of pain where the stag's antlers had grazed her, and concentrated silently on the business of sitting her horse. Tremadoc, on the other hand, kept up a stream of sotto voce grumbling, which made her own pain even harder to bear, and she was deeply relieved when they reached the Richmond Gate and he announced that he could ride no further.

'You do not seem to understand,' he told Blakeney and Mattingley, 'that I am seriously injured. I shall stay here, and you will be so good as to send my carriage to me.'

'Well, thank God for that,' said Mattingley with an attempt at cheerfulness, as the four of them set forward again down Richmond Hill. 'I do feel, do not you, Blakeney, that the fewer of us, the better.'

'Yes.' Blakeney recognised with a sinking heart that Mattingley shared his own fears about what news would await them at the inn. 'Should I have asked him and ffether to keep their mouths shut, do you think?' he asked now.

'Useless, I'm afraid.' Mattingley was touched and amused by the appeal to his greater age and wisdom. 'Hopeless in Tremadoc's case. He's bound to tell his mother. And unnecessary, I should think, in ffether's. He will hardly wish to tell the world that your sister has made a public fool of him.'

'I suppose not. But it's the deuce of a business, sir. My father is going to be angry.' He could not help a swift, shamed thought that it made the time anything but hopeful for him and Caroline.

'I just hope that's the worst of it,' said Mattingley.

When they reached the Star and Garter his fears were confirmed. Enquiring for his sister, Blakeney was handed a sealed note. 'Dear God!' He passed it to Mattingley. 'Charlotte and Gaston.'

'What I feared.' Mattingley crumpled it in his hand. 'Blakeney, have I your permission to handle this? As a friend of your mother's, and, forgive me, an older man.'

'Sir.' Blakeney looked at him very straight. 'I would be more grateful than I can say.'

'Good. I'll make some enquiries.' He returned almost at once. 'They've not got much start. Left not much more than fifteen minutes ago. A closed carriage, only two horses. Going north, of course.'

'Not Gretna?' asked Blakeney, appalled.

'Where else?' He handed Blakeney a note he had scrawled to the Duke. 'Blakeney, do you take the young ladies home, give this to your father, tell him I hope to catch the young fools before they even get out of London, but, just in case, that I count on him to meet me at the inn on the Great North Road that Gaston mentions. It's an odd note, when you think about it. Why tell us they'll be at the Crown Inn? Don't look so anxious, man,' he put a friendly hand on Blakeney's shoulder. 'I know the carriage Gaston has taken, and he's no kind of a whip. Mine was built for speed and I've ordered four horses put to. Besides, I think he means to be caught. And I shall most certainly do so. We'll have to think then, the Duke and I, what is best to be done about this bit of folly.'

'Yes. Yes, I don't quite understand, but I do thank you, sir. I only wish I could come with you.'

'But you know you must not. The girls must be taken home. Caroline is behaving like a little heroine, but she must be exhausted. And I hope you know you can count on me.'

'I do indeed.' Blakeney shook his hand warmly. 'We'll not keep you a moment longer. Caro,' he turned to her with a quick, loving look that moved Mattingley to a passion of pity. 'Can you manage without a rest?'

'Of course I can. We must go straight home, and we must not delay Mr. Mattingley another minute.'

Driving swiftly across Richmond Bridge and through a well known pattern of side roads that should bring him to the Crown Inn before Gaston's lumbering carriage could possibly get there, Mattingley thought with angry sympathy of the disaster that faced the Duke and his family. All the Duke's fault, of course, for refusing to tell Gaston and Caroline the truth about their births, but what difference did that make now? If he was not very much mistaken, Blakeney and Caroline had come to some kind of an understanding in the Park. Poor children, he thought, and congratulated himself that Blakeney had been biddable enough to accept his quick arrangements. He very much hoped that by the time Blakeney got the girls home to Chevenham House, found the Duke and broke the news to him, he himself would have told the grim truth to Gaston, got rid of him, and so avoided the painful and maybe dangerous scene that might otherwise take place between him and his new-found father. Gaston had too much of the Duke's impatience of temper for such an encounter to be anything but disastrous.

He slowed his horses and pulled Gaston's note from his pocket to confirm the strong impression he had received, on first reading it, that Gaston had no intention of going to Gretna. He meant to be caught and to make his own terms with the Duke. Not a nice young man, thought Mattingley, and he must be very sure of Charlotte. He meant to have the Duke pay him handsomely to marry his discredited daughter.

But Gaston's scheme had already gone awry on one vital point. He must have expected the entire party to arrive at the Star and Garter and learn of the elopement. In that case, with ffether and Tremadoc present, there would have been no hope of hushing the matter up. But ffether and Tremadoc had not been there. And Gaston could not marry his half-sister. He had ruined himself, but not, with luck and good management, Lady Charlotte. At all costs, Mattingley thought, he must get to the inn before they did. Gaston meant to be caught, but not before he had fatally compromised Lady Charlotte. Seduced her? Raped her?

Mattingley whipped up his horses, his thoughts turning to Blakeney and Caroline, who were going to suffer so much when, as it now must, the truth about her birth came out. Poor Caroline.

Driving steadily on, he looked back at a series of pictures of her face today. She had been in a great deal of pain and concealed it admirably. And she had been glowingly, ecstatically happy. What would it feel like to see her look at him as she had at Blakeney? It would be pleasant. It would be most remarkably pleasant. His mind surprised him with a quick picture of the Duchess, passive in his arms. Suddenly, to his own amazement, he had made up his mind. 'I'll do it,' he thought. 'I'll marry her.'

The carriage was veering across the road. An admonitory touch of the whip to his leaders' ears had it back on course again, and he drove on, curiously contented, his mind made up. 'Here you may see Benedick, the married man.'

Everything went as he had planned. Quick enquiries at the inn reassured him that Gaston and Charlotte had not yet arrived. 'I am expecting two young friends,' he told the landlord. 'Your best parlour please, and a neat dinner for when they get here.'

They drove into the inn yard half an hour later, and Mattingley, watching them from a parlour window, thought they had been quarrelling already. Nothing surprising about that. They both had their father's temper. But it should make his tasks easier. 'There you are at last.' He walked leisurely into the hall of the inn to greet them. 'I was really beginning to fear that you had met with some accident. But, come in,' he went on hospitably. 'You must be famished, both of you, and dinner will be ready this instant.'

They were both staring at him, open-mouthed with surprise, now Gaston spoke angrily. 'Of all the damned, interfering...'

'Do come into the parlour,' said Mattingley. He had been wondering how to break the true facts of the case to Gaston, now he saw. 'Your sister must be exhausted from her long day.'

'So that's your game is it?' But Gaston was not quite master enough of the situation to delay them in the hall with its interested audience. 'Brother and sister, indeed!' He took Charlotte's hand. 'Lady Charlotte will tell you that that is not what we intend to be at all.'

'It's not a question of what you intend.' Mattingley handed Charlotte a glass of madeira. 'It's a matter of fact.'

'Fact? I do not understand you.' But the hand Gaston reached out for his glass was shaking. Had he suddenly seen it all?

'Yes. I'm sorry to be the one who must break it to you, Lady Charlotte.' He turned to where she had sunk into a chair and was looking from one to the other with frightened eyes. 'But you have just eloped with your half-brother.'

'My what?' She had gone very white.

'Your father's son. A pity the Duke did not choose to tell you sooner, but there it is. What's done is done. We must be thinking how best to extricate you from this coil. And,' he turned to Gaston, 'I understand your feeling that I am a damned interfering... You did not, I believe, supply the noun. Perhaps you would like to do so now? But I thought it would be better if I broke the news to you before your father got here.'

'I don't believe it!' But he did. And then, 'My mother?'

'The French governess in a family your father used to stay with when he was very young. She hoped for marriage. Played for it, I think, and lost. You would be wise to be warned by her unlucky example, Gaston.'

'A governess? No!'

Mattingley shrugged. 'By all means wait and ask your father, if you wish to. I sent a message to the Duke, of course. He should be here quite soon. I am sure he will tell you all you want to know about Mademoiselle Françoise. Her father was a blacksmith, I believe. She had come up in the world.'

'A blacksmith?' Charlotte emptied her glass, and spoke across Gaston to Mattingley. 'He told me he was of royal blood. When this was over we were going to France to make ourselves known to his family.' She looked at Gaston now with frank dislike. 'I should have known better, just looking at you. Of course, a blacksmith. How very comic. And I nearly ruined myself for you.' She turned appealingly to Mattingley. 'Who else knows?'

'Lord ffether went home from the Park gates,' he told her. 'And so did Tremadoc. Only Blakeney, Caroline, Amelia and I went on to the Star and Garter and found Gaston's note. And the girls don't know what's in it. Do you, for the matter of that?'

'Why, not precisely. He said it would come better from him.'

'So you did not know that he intended your father to catch up with you here? That he planned to make sure of the dowry before he married the bride?'

'No!' She looked at Gaston now with loathing. 'That was why you insisted on stopping here. I told him it was too soon,' she told Mattingley. Then back to Gaston. 'And all your talk of love false too? Dear God! You said we would pass as man and wife. Safer, you said. What would have happened to me, I wonder, before papa came, if Mr. Mattingley had not been here? You'd have had me on my knees, I suppose, begging for marriage? Mr. Mattingley, get him out of my sight.'

'I really think you would be well advised to go.' Mattingley told Gaston. 'No good can come of an encounter between you and the Duke now.'

'I might kill him,' said Gaston.

'Which would not exactly improve your position. Patricide has never been a popular crime. Give me any message you wish for the Duke, and I promise to do my best to make him listen to it.'

'Tell him I've gone to the devil. No, dammit, tell him I mean to live! I'll exchange to a regiment on active service, if he will continue my allowance. Otherwise I'll talk.' And as he said this, something struck him. 'And Caroline?' he said. 'Don't tell me she's another of his bastards! Dear God, that almost pays for all. Oh, poor little Blakeney! I wonder if he has put the question yet. Yes, Mattingley, you may tell my father that if he wishes my silence, he must pay for it. And in the meantime, can you lend me £50?' He turned with a sneer to Charlotte. 'One very good reason, my poppet, why we had to stay here was that I hadn't a penny to bless myself with after paying that first toll.'

'You eloped with me with no money?'

'Since that was all I had. Damned heavy doings at Watier's last night. I'd hoped at least to earn enough to buy you a pair of bridegloves, but it worked the other way. So, Mattingley, if you would be so good?'

Mattingley smiled his wry smile. 'I'll give you what I have,' he said. 'And I'll give the Duke your message. I am sure your idea of active service is an admirable one. He has always been fond of you. Distinguish yourself; stay away; I think you can at least hope to have your allowance continued. So long as you do not talk.'

'Thanks,' said Gaston. He turned to Charlotte. 'What a disappointing first night.' He made her a deep mocking bow, and left them.

Charlotte looked up, trembling, at Mattingley. 'He meant to ... to ravish me?' she said.

'I am afraid so, my dear. You have had a lucky escape.' No need to tell her that Gaston had undoubtedly expected her to welcome his advances.

When Blakeney's glum little party reached Chevenham House it was to find a scene of disorder. Mrs. Winterton had been taken ill; the Duchess was with her and Dr. Farquahar had been summoned. Blakeney handed Caroline over to Tench's loving care with a brief explanation of her accident, and sought out the Duke in the small downstairs saloon where he entertained his political friends.

'I'm sorry to hear about Mrs. Winterton, sir,' he began, the note still in his hand. 'I hope it's nothing serious.'

'A deuced ill-managed business,' said the Duke surprisingly. 'Parcel of women! What's this? Note from Mattingley?' He took and read it swiftly, swore an oath Blakeney had never heard him use before, and stood for a moment, back to the chimneypiece, angrily thinking. 'Damned fool of a girl,' he said at last. 'Made her own bed; serve her right if I let her lie on it. Can't, of course. But I'm damned if I'm leaving here before Farquahar comes. You'll have to go, Blakeney. Made a mull of things, one way and another, haven't you? Up to you to make amends. Mattingley seems sure enough he can keep the young fools till I come. Well, you'll go. Bring Charlotte home; we'll have to think of a story. God!' He put a distraught hand to his brow. 'Frances is the one who can think of stories. To have her ill now!' He felt it as a personal affront. 'Mattingley will think of something.' He looked at the note again. 'Has already. Brother and sister escapade. Gaston learned the truth about his birth; shock to him of course; all those royal notions; Charlotte comforting him as a sister should. Deuced improbable, but the world won't know that. Anyway, by the time you get there, the worst should be over. Mattingley will have told Gaston the truth; sent him away with a flea in his ear, I have no doubt. But if not, I'll not have you fighting him, Blakeney, understand that. He's my son, your brother, I won't have the two of you fighting.'

'Your son? My brother? Gaston?' Nothing in the eventful day had hit Blakeney like this. 'Sir, you can't mean it!'

'All a long time ago!' The Duke did not like to find himself taking this apologetic tone to the son who was gazing at him so straight with wide, horrified eyes. 'A boy's wild oat. Deuced pretty girl she was; governess—well,' he qualified it, 'nursery maid.' He laughed, man to man. 'I really believe she thought I'd marry her.' And then, discomfited by his son's shocked silence. 'Long before I met your mother, of course. Gaston's a little older than we said.'

'We?'

'Your mother knows all about it. Always has. Damn it, man, she's a modern wife.'

'She needs to be,' said Blakeney. 'And Mrs. Winterton?'

'Never did like Gaston,' said the Duke, relieved at this practical question. 'But Frances has got a lot of sense. God, I wish Farquahar would come! If I'd listened to Frances none of this would have happened. She's been at me this age to tell those two about their birth.'

'Those two?' Something turned to stone in Blakeney's breast.

'Why, yes. Thought you'd have seen it right away. Not a milksop, are you, Blakeney? Know what the world's about? Never noticed the likeness between you and Caroline? Fetching little chit when she's in spirits, but not a patch on her mother.'

'Her mother?'

'Frances, of course. Ah,' there were sounds of a carriage outside. 'That will be Farquahar at last. I count on you, Blakeney, to bring Charlotte home with as little fuss as possible. If Gaston should be still there, which I doubt, you will tell him I will continue his allowance so long as he leaves the country. And stays away.' He was at the room door, listening to the sounds of arrival. 'It is Farquahar, thank God. Oh, by the way, how did ffether take it?'

'Badly,' said Blakeney between clenched teeth, praying that he would not be sick where he stood.

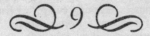

TENCH PUT CAROLINE straight to bed, and Caroline was glad to go. Her head was reeling from the events of the day, but the one, outstanding, important thing was what had happened between Blakeney and her. 'Oh, Tench,' she put up loving arms and hugged the surprised maid, 'I'm so happy.'

She fell asleep almost instantly, and Tench, who had stood for a moment anxiously watching her, tiptoed away to seek counsel with the Duchess's maid, Briggs.

'I could wring his Grace's stiff neck,' she told that sympathetic lady. 'That poor child. If his Lordship ain't spoke to her, he must have come pretty near it. Stars in her eyes, and hugs and kisses me. "I'm so happy," she says. I could cry!'

'And not for lack of warning,' said Briggs. 'Povey's heard her lady on about it often enough, but you know how his Grace is.'

'Stubborn,' said Tench.

'As a mule, and not much more brains. Men!' said Briggs,

with loathing. 'Povey says he's been quacking her lady this age. Wouldn't let her have the doctor. Said he knew the very thing for what ailed her.'

'Which he should,' Tench sniffed. 'Seeing she caught it off him. Lucky for the Duchess he neglects her so.'

'Mrs. Winterton's real bad now,' said Briggs. 'It was the Duchess sent for Farquahar.'

'She's a lady, yours. Does she know about Lady Charlotte?'

'I don't know. She's not left Mrs. Winterton's side all day. She'd have something to say if she knew his Grace sent his Lordship instead of going after Lady Charlotte himself.'

'But it would do no good,' said Tench. 'I just hope it ain't pistols for two!'

'Mr. Gaston would never!'

'Don't you be too sure. Think, Mrs. Briggs, if Mr. Gaston were to kill his Lordship, which heaven preserve us, he'd be the only son.'

'Wrong side of the blanket.'

'But the only son.'

Caroline slept through the night and woke with a throbbing head and aching arm. Tench was hovering near the bed, her expression anxious, a steaming cup in her hand. 'Miss Caroline,' she came forward as Caroline stirred. 'You've slept the clock round, pretty near. How do you feel?'

'Happy.' She smiled at the maid. 'Stiff. Hungry.' She took the cup, remembering it all. 'Charlotte? Is she all right? Did Blakeney bring her home? And how is Mrs. Winterton?'

'Better. I don't know what Dr. Farquahar gave her, but it did the trick. He's with her again now, deciding if she's strong enough for the journey.'

'Journey?'

'To Bath. She's to take the waters. Rest and quiet.'

'And Lady Charlotte?'

'Goes too. His Lordship brought her safe home last night, praise be.'

'You know, Tench?'

'Bless your heart, miss, we all know everything in the hall. That Gaston! He won't be playing you any more of his sly tricks now, and that's one comfort. Nor he didn't fight his Lordship neither, which was what Mrs. Briggs and I most feared.'

'Fight his Lordship! But, Tench, why?' And then, 'Oh, you

mean over Lady Charlotte? Do you think Gaston truly loved her, Tench?' The thought of her own love was warm about her heart.

'He don't love no one but himself, that Gaston,' said Tench. 'And I don't reckon Lady Charlotte is broken-hearted, neither. Just cross, if you ask me. Smithson says she was neither to hold nor to bind last night, and not much better this morning. If I were you, Miss Caroline, I'd keep to my bed until the worst is over. Oh, Mr. Tremadoc called first thing. Flowers and a kind message. And Mr. Mattingley.'

'And his Lordship?' Caroline had to ask it. 'Has he enquired after me? He saved my life, Tench. I long to thank him.'

'He's not been here today, miss.' Tench felt herself on dangerous ground and was relieved by a knock on the door. She opened it a crack, held brief talk with Briggs and returned to the bed. 'The Duchess is wishful to visit you, miss. Are you strong enough, do you think?'

'Like this? But, yes, indeed I am!' Could Blakeney have spoken already to his mother? 'Quick, Tench, my comb and a shawl. Is the room tidy? Yes, of course it is. I can count on you for that.' She let Tench plump up the pillows behind her, cast a quick, anxious glance at the pale, bright-eyed reflection in her glass, and said, 'Do, please, tell the Duchess I shall be most happy to see her.'

'Yes, miss.' What was the matter with Tench this morning?

The Duchess, too, looked heavy-eyed, doubtless with watching by Mrs. Winterton's bed. 'Dear child,' she said, 'how do you feel today?'

'Better, thank you. Oh, ma'am, Blakeney saved my life. I do long to thank him.'

The Duchess looked sadly at the eager, blushing girl in the bed. So Mattingley had been right in the swift warnings he had given her, while officially enquiring after Frances Winterton. Poor child, she thought, how shall I tell her? 'Dear Blakeney,' she said. 'I do not know how we could go on without him. His father is quite delighted with the way he behaved yesterday. Contriving everything so well for my poor, foolish Charlotte. It's been an ill-managed business, I am afraid.' She pulled up a chair close to the bed and sat silent for a moment.

Caroline looked at her in surprise. She had never seen the Duchess at a loss for words before. She took a little breath of courage. She had known that things would not be easy for Blakeney and her. Did the Duchess know something? Was the trouble starting? But they had promised each other. Were sure. It was but to wait. I love him, she thought. I trust him. And this is his mother. She smiled tremulously at the Duchess. 'Dear ma'am,' she asked. 'Are you very angry with me?'

'Angry? Dear child, why in the world should I be angry with you? With Charlotte, yes, and with Gaston, who have behaved so foolishly. And yet, whose fault is that? Frances and I have begged the Duke, over and over again, to let us tell you and Gaston the truth, now you are both grown up . . .' She stopped, twisting her lace-trimmed handkerchief in nervous hands.

'Tell us the truth? What do you mean? Forgive me, ma'am,' she had spoken sharply, and knew it. 'I have the headache a little this morning. It makes me stupid. I do not rightly understand what there is to tell Gaston and me.'

'That you are the Duke's children.' The Duchess brought it out in a rush. Then, watching with compassion as Caroline took it like the blow it was, she moved to the bell. 'Sal volatile, Tench. Miss Caroline is not well.' And, ashamed of herself, left Caroline alone. But what was there to say? What comfort to give? Much better to pretend nothing had happened between Caroline and Blakeney, though she was sure now that Mattingley was right, and that something had.

Caroline did not cry. Watching her white silence, Tench wished she would. If she would be angry, scream, have hysterics, blame someone, it would be better for her, Tench thought.

'I shall get up, Tench,' she said at last. 'I shall be better dressed.' And then, 'Tench, you have always been my friend. You knew?'

'Yes, miss. We always know, in the servants' hall.'

'I wish you had told me.'

'So do I. But it wasn't my place, miss.'

'No. I'm not blaming *you*, Tench. You're all I've got left to love.'

'Oh, miss!' Tench was crying a little herself. 'You mustn't feel like that. Think of your poor mother.'

'My mother? The Duchess never said . . .' In her passion of grief, she had hardly thought of this aspect of her case. Now, her mind flashed from remembered scene to scene. The beautiful visitor who never came back . . . That absurd doll . . . 'Mrs. Winterton,' she said. 'I do not think she is breaking her heart for me, Tench.'

'Well, poor lady, she's ill,' said Tench, and hoped Caroline would never know what was the matter with her mother.

Dressed, Caroline found she could not bring herself to go downstairs. If Charlotte knew, everybody would know. The servants too. Tench had said so. Sympathetic, knowing eyes . . . The Duke's bastard daughter. A little shrimp, he had called her. The Duke's disappointing bastard daughter. So plain as she was, of course it had never struck him Blakeney might like her. Like? Love. My half-brother, she thought. Ah, poor Blakeney. No wonder he had not come to the house today. He must have learned yesterday. Did he feel sick with horror, as she did? She was sure of it. So in her own misery, one thing stood out, one plain duty. How could she make things easier for Blakeney? Well, not easier, just less unbearable.

The answer stared her in the face. She must go away. But where? Not to Llanfryn. She had heard, only the other day, that Mr. Trentham was dead. And Sophie, sending the brief announcement, had left no opening for further correspondence. Her letter had been a door closing in Caroline's face. I have nowhere, she thought now. No one. Nowhere to go.

Back to Norfolk? Would the Duchess, who was always kind, let her go and live a hermit's life at Cley? She would like that, she thought, with a great wave of longing for the sea's voice and the wide green quiet of the marsh. But if she went there, she closed Cley's doors to Blakeney. She knew, had already faced it, that she and Blakeney must not meet again. When we are old, she thought, we can be brother and sister, but now, there is nothing. Would he write and tell her so? She thought he very likely would. We are so alike, she thought. It's no wonder if we love each other.

She must not think about Blakeney. There was something else, almost as painful, to be faced. Mrs. Winterton. Her mother. If she had not been ill just now, would she have turned to her for help? Of course not. Suddenly she was a child again, moping in the garden at Llanfryn, longing for the beautiful lady who never came back. Had her mopes turned Mrs. Trentham against her, she wondered now? Had it all helped to make her ill? Did Frances Winterton cause trouble wherever she went? Or do I? I will not be like her. And then, wryly realistic, thought there was not much danger of that. She was neither beautiful nor charming like her mother. Naturally, she had disappointed the Duke. Her father. And, disappointing him, had disappointed her mother too. Did Frances Winterton care for her only as a pawn in the strange game she played with the Duke and Duchess?

Thinking this, she felt sick. I must get away. Miss Skinner? Darling Skinny. But she was fully occupied with her brother and his motherless baby in the small house in Cambridge. I will not be selfish like my mother. So what shall I do?

Blakeney's note came that afternoon. It said almost exactly what Caroline had expected. She might have written it herself. Would she allow herself to answer it? He would like to have one line of her writing. She knew this. But it must be positive. She must have some plan, something to tell him, something to make his burden less.

Tench scratched at the door later in the afternoon. 'Miss Caroline, Mr. Tremadoc has called again. He begs you to see him for a moment.'

Tremadoc? A million years ago, yesterday, he had asked her to marry him. Well? 'I'll see him, Tench. Ask him to be so good as to wait a few minutes, then come and help me make myself fit to be seen.'

Geraint Tremadoc had never been crossed in his life, except by his mother. Caroline's refusal, the day before, had begun by making him furious. He had driven home from Richmond Park vowing to think of her no more, and rather intending to take to his bed for a few days and make an interesting recovery. He might even tell his mother about his rash proposal and bask in her relief at the escape he had had. But when he got back to the big house in Grosvenor Square he found only a note from his mother. Her one brother, a rich mill owner in Manchester, had been taken ill and sent for her. She did not know how long she would be away. She had, of course, given every order for his comfort.

But the house seemed very large and lonely without her bustling presence. He changed his mind about going to bed, went out to his club instead, heard the rumours about Lady Charlotte and enjoyed contributing his own bit of information to them. Yes (he was delighted fo find himself the centre of an interested circle of listeners) Lord ffether had been very angry indeed. No, neither of them had gone to the Star and Garter.

'So you don't know the end of the story,' said a young man whose name Tremadoc did not know. 'She wasn't there, of course. Gone to Gretna.'

'To Gretna?' Tremadoc could not believe his ears.

'Started for Gretna,' corrected a very young man in a yellow-striped waistcoat.

'With her half-brother!'

'Gaston Fouquet,' said striped waistcoat. 'Never did like him. Dashed unpleasant way of looking at one.'

'At least he didn't call Blakeney out,' chimed in yet another voice.

'Call Blakeney out?' Tremadoc managed at last to learn the main lines of the story. The truth about Gaston and Caroline's birth had been a well kept secret of the Duke's generation and one of which his mother had not been cognisant, since her connection with trade had barred her from the inner circles of society.

He went home at last, his head buzzing with information. Caroline was the Duke's daughter. More important, in some ways, was the fact that she was Blakeney's half-sister. So much for the calf's eyes she and Blakeney had been casting at each other. They would be a sad pair now.

So his chance? His Amoretta was a romantic figure again, a Duke's daughter, and in despair. It must be deuced awkward for them at Chevenham House. Should he go to the Duke? He imagined himself welcomed with open arms, the solution to one of their problems. His mother would be angry. His mother should not have abandoned him at no notice to go to his Uncle Tom. He felt very free, very independent. Caroline would look up at him adoringly, as she had yesterday at Blakeney. She had always been his best audience. He would write her an epic.

He put on his best waistcoat, the one with huge brass buttons, took particular care in choosing a gold-headed cane, and strolled down Audley Street to Chevenham House. The Duke was out. The Duchess then? The Duchess was with Mrs. Winterton, who was ill, and was seeing no one. He had the bit well between his teeth now, and asked for Miss Thorpe. Much more romantic, much more the act of a poet to propose at once, and let the old people go hang.

Caroline kept him waiting, which was unlike her, but he made allowances for her. She had had a bad shaking the day before; he must remember to enquire about her injuries. He remembered his own and sat down on a straight-backed, gilded chair. Chevenham House seemed oddly quiet this morning. He wondered, casually, if Mrs. Winterton was really ill. But that was no affair of his.

When Caroline appeared at last, he was shocked at her appearance. This was not his Amoretta but a pale, quiet girl with dark smudges under her eyes. Really, she was almost plain. Perhaps he would merely enquire after her health and beat a quick retreat.

'It's good of you to come.' She raised dark-circled eyes to his, and smiled a little, tremulously.

'Of course I came.' He had forgotten how small she was. The muslin sleeve of her morning dress revealed a purple bruise on her white arm. 'I frightened you yesterday,' he said. 'I came to say how very sorry I am. I am afraid you are hurt!'

'It's nothing.' She put a defensive hand on the bruise. 'I was so sorry about your fall. I do hope you are none the worse.'

'Not the least in the world,' he said. 'We men are used to getting in and out of scrapes, you know. I was out at the club last night,' he told her, very much the man of the world. 'I heard something I did not much like about Lady Charlotte. Lucky it was no worse, I suppose.' Suddenly he saw his way clear. She had blushed scarlet when he spoke of Lady Charlotte; her eyes sparkled with unshed tears; she was his Amoretta again. 'This is no place for you now,' he told her. 'I am come to offer you my heart, my home, my hand!'

'Oh, Mr. Tremadoc.' A tear detached itself from the corner of her left eye and rolled slowly down her cheek.

'Call me Geraint,' he said. 'Call me husband! Amoretta, be my muse, be my inspiration, be my dear. Come to me, sweet one, and I will look after you always.'

'You're . . . you're very good!' She was twisting a damp handkerchief between her fingers. 'I . . . I would dearly like to get away from here. But, Mr. Tremadoc,' she looked up and met his eyes through her tears: 'I must tell you. I do not love you. I love another.'

'I know all about that.' He surprised her. 'Quite impossible, you know, even if you hadn't been . . .' He stopped, colouring. 'Related. The Duke would never have allowed it.'

'And your mother?' she asked.

'Has no say in the matter. I'm my own master. Have been since I was eighteen. Besides, she's away. Went off in a cloud of dust yesterday to look after that mill-owning uncle of mine.' He laughed what he meant for a wordly laugh. 'Shall we give them a look in on our way to Gretna, Amoretta?'

'Gretna?'

'Where else?' The idea must have been at the back of his

mind ever since he had heard of Lady Charlotte's attempted
elopement. It would be the most romantic thing. Poet elopes
with Duke's daughter. They would be in all the gossip columns,
thinly disguised under initials. Gallant Mr. T and the daughter
of the Duke of C. A rhyme flirted at the corner of his mind.
No time for that now. 'Things are all to pieces here,' he told
her. 'The Duke seems to have gone away. Mrs. Winterton
is ill, and the Duchess is seeing no one. It is no time to be
talking to them of marrying and giving in marriage. You will
see; they will be only too grateful to have you arrange your
own destiny. Let me arrange it! Oh, my little love, I will
cherish you, care for you like a queen as we drive to Scotland.
I will put you on a pedestal, my goddess, and write you a
sonnet a day.'

'It sounds very uncomfortable.' For a moment, her sense
of the ridiculous got the better of her, but she caught his look
of chagrin and hurried on. 'You are goodness itself! Would
you let me bring Tench, my maid? I think she would come if
I asked her.'

'Of course you must bring her,' he said with some relief.
It had been beginning to strike him that the servants at Grosvenor Square were very much more his mother's than his. 'That
will make everything right. Your maid and my man Jenkins.
It will be quite a little holiday for you. Honeymoon!' he amended
swiftly. 'Only, of course, until we reach Gretna, you will be
a sister to me. What's the matter?'

'Nothing.' The thought of Blakeney, her brother, had been
almost too much for her. But in a way that settled it. She could
not stay here. Where else could she go? 'You really think
Gretna would be best?' she asked, and realised, as she said it,
that she had already, somehow, tacitly agreed to marry him.

'I am sure of it! I shall call for you tomorrow, heart of my
heart. There are arrangements I must make today. I shall come
in the morning, seemingly to take you for a drive in the Park.
You will send your maid to my house with your bandboxes.
You will have to think of some reason. A dress back to the
dressmaker, perhaps? Then we will pick her up there and set
out post haste for the border. Oh my love, I cannot wait to call
you mine.'

He was going to kiss her. Her cheeks burned, remembering
Blakeney yesterday, that passionate communion. But this was
so different that she almost found she did not mind it.

After he left, her heart failed her. Mad to have tacitly agreed to go. She would write and tell him so. She thought, in her heart, that he would be relieved. Even if he really loved her, he must on thinking it over feel as appalled as she did now at the idea of a trip to Gretna. His mother would be furious. It was no way to begin a marriage. She sat down to write to him, but was interrupted by Charlotte.

'Well, sister dear,' she said. 'How does it feel to wake up and find yourself a Duke's daughter? Are you expecting a throng of suitors now the glorious truth is out? I doubt you'll be disappointed. Oh, father will provide for you, I suppose. He must always have meant to do so, but I think you may find the gallants less than pressing.' She laughed. 'Imagine having Darling Frances for a mother-in-law. Mind you, it's an idea. Marry at once, there's a kind sister, and take your dear mamma to live with you. Then we can all breathe again here.' She took a quick angry turn across the room. 'It makes me mad as fire to see my mother hanging over that woman's sickbed.'

'She is my mother,' said Caroline. 'Dear Charlotte, please . . .'

'Don't "Dear Charlotte" me! You can't come round *me* with your quiet little pleading ways, so like your mother's, and so I tell you! We don't want you here! A daily reminder of all that's wrong with our lives! About father . . . Oh, I wish I was dead!' She sank on to a chair and burst into tears.

'Charlotte, I am so very sorry.' Caroline crossed the room to put a timid hand on her shoulder. 'Have you heard anything from Gaston?'

'From my dear brother? No. Nor do I expect to. But he'll be all right,' said Charlotte with one of her fits of clear sight. 'Father will forgive him in no time. Father dotes on him. It's your darling Blakeney who is going to be in trouble. I don't know what he said to papa last night, but I don't think the Duke is going to forget it in a hurry. He doesn't like either of you above half this morning, and I do think, Caroline, that the sooner you get away from here, for Blakeney's sake as well as everyone else's, the better. Surely you must have some friends of your own? What happened to those people down in the west? The ones with the garden you were always mooning over?'

'Mr. Trentham is dead,' said Caroline sadly. 'Sophie wrote to me the other day. She's married; she doesn't want me. You know the Duke didn't want me to keep in touch with them.' My father, she thought.

'Oh, the Duke! I could kill him, though he is my father—

and yours! We're all off to Bath in the morning, did you know? For Darling Frances's sake, and to hide my disgrace. My disgrace! Father's disgrace! And yours too, come to that,' she ended, rounding on Caroline. 'Don't think Amelia and I are going to be sisters to you, because we have talked it over, and we won't. So think that over, Miss Bastard Thorpe.'

Caroline fled for the refuge of her room. She found Tench there, angrily mending a torn flounce and, visibly, waiting for her.

'Mrs. Winterton is worse again.' If Tench saw Caroline's distress she thought it best to pretend not to. 'But his Grace is positive for Bath tomorrow. I think they'll go if it kills her. He's sent his Lordship on ahead. Like a courier. They had words last night, I understand. The Duke don't seem to know what to do with you, Miss Caroline.'

'He'd brick me up in a convent cell if he could,' said Caroline.

'I really believe he would, miss. You're not to go to Bath, that's for sure. The Duchess thinks you should go to her mamma in Derbyshire. I do hope they don't send you there, miss. Of all the dead and alive holes! And the old lady deaf as a post and pious as St. Peter.'

'But she won't want me,' wailed Caroline, a whole host of now-understood memories flocking into her mind. The Duchess's formidable mother had been a rare visitor at Cley and had never made any secret of her dislike for Mrs. Winterton, Gaston and Caroline. And, more significant still, on the rare occasions when the Duke and Duchess visited her in Derbyshire, Mrs. Winterton always had another engagement. 'She will refuse to have me,' said Caroline. 'Tench!' Suddenly, her mind was made up. 'Can you keep a secret?'

'For you, miss? Anything.'

'Mr. Tremadoc has asked me to marry him. We're going to Gretna Green. Tomorrow. And you're coming too, dear Tench, if you will.' And as she said it, knew a moment of prophetic despair.

10

GERAINT TREMADOC SUFFERED from travelsickness. His mother, he explained to Caroline, had always seen to the details of their journeys. Now Caroline would have to. He accepted her smelling salts gratefully, having forgotten his own, and left her and his man Jenkins to decide where they would change horses.

Jenkins showed signs of sauciness at first, but Caroline had not lived at Cley for nothing, and the man soon changed his tune. 'She's going to be the missus, all right,' he told the coachman, when they stopped for the first night. 'And how she and the old missus will get on, only God knows.'

'I reckon you and I have a pretty fair idea,' said the coachman. 'But what I say is, this un's a lady, and young. My money's on her.'

'And mine,' agreed Jenkins. 'And I don't mind that maid of hers either. She's a high flyer and no mistake.'

From then on Caroline found at least the mechanical details of the journey easy enough. But the prospect before her was increasingly appalling. She had been mad . . . mad . . . mad. Sitting, silent, hour after hour as the carriage jolted over the Great North Road and Tremadoc shivered and grumbled in his corner, she longed more and more desperately for rescue.

Rescue? Yes, Blakeney. Blakeney acting the part of a brother. Stopping the carriage; telling her not to be a fool; promising to take care of her. She had told him, in the note she had written the morning she left, exactly what their plans were. As she herself became day by day more aware of the madness of what she had done, she was convinced that, as always, he would see things as she did, would come to her rescue. After all, thanks to Tremadoc's travelsickness, they were travelling slowly enough.

It gave her all too much time to get to know the man she had agreed to marry, and the more she saw of him, the more

118

she longed for Blakeney, and rescue. In the carriage, he lay with his head against the squabs and groaned if she spoke to him. And when she tried to engage him in conversation over meals in the inns where they spent the night, she found they had nothing to talk about. Brought up at home under the doting eye of his mother, he seemed to have read nothing but poetry, and that without the slightest discrimination. Politics bored him, and when he found her anxiously scanning the papers in the coffee room of an inn he spoke to her sharply.

'But I wanted to see if it is true that Mr. Pitt is to form a government,' she explained. 'The Duchess thought he was bound to be asked, now that Mr. Addington's majority is down to twenty-one.'

'Whig, Tory!' He said impatiently. 'What difference does it make? My mother would be shocked to see you in the coffee room of a public inn.'

'I'm sorry.' It was not the moment to tell him that Pitt and Addington were both Tories. And she was getting unhappily used to his habit of referring to his mother as if she were a kind of arbiter of fate. She would have been desperate by now, if she had not been so sure of Blakeney.

But Blakeney had not received her note. After much anguished thought, she had written also to the Duchess, a note to be delivered after she and Tremadoc were safe on their way. The Duchess, distracted with worry about Frances Winterton, had read this note quickly and handed it to the Duke.

'Gone off with Tremadoc, has she?' He scanned it quickly. 'Well, that's a relief, I suppose. Takes care of her. No blood in that family, but money. And, I'll tell you something.' Just occasionally the Duke actually had an idea. 'Bit of management, we should be able to set it about that there was only one elopement, young Caroline's. Get Charlotte clear off, d'you see? More than she deserves, but useful.'

'Yes,' said the Duchess doubtfully. 'Poor little Caroline . . . But the way things are . . . I don't know that Frances will be best pleased, though.'

'Glad to get the chit off her hands,' said the Duke with robust realism.

'Caroline left a note for Blakeney,' said the Duchess.

'Did she so?' He thought about that for a moment. 'Well, now, m'dear. He must have it, of course. But . . . not for a week or so, do you think? No need for it to follow him to Bath. I mean him to see us settled there, then come back to town and his duties with the Volunteers.' There was no need for him to explain to the Duchess that the less he saw of Blakeney after last night's exchange of words, the happier he would be.

So, ten days later, no rescue had come, and Caroline heard herself saying the fatal words that made her Geraint Tremadoc's wife. She had not believed it could be so horribly easy. At every stage she had expected, hoped for some insurmountable obstacle, but there had been none. It would have been small comfort to her to realise that her own cool, ladylike behaviour had contributed a good deal towards this result. She had been trained always to behave like a lady, never to make a scene, and her training had held. Finding herself Mrs. Tremadoc, she now allowed her husband's chilly kiss, civilly thanked the grinning blacksmith who had pronounced the fatal words, and fainted.

'Not very flattering,' were the first words she heard as she recovered consciousness.

'I expect it was the relief, sir.' Tench's voice, and Caroline blessed her for her tact. She was lying on a shabby sofa in the uncomfortable little inn where they had spent the night. It was all over. She opened her eyes and looked up at Tremadoc. 'Forgive me, my dear,' she managed the endearment with an effort. 'I am afraid it has all been too much for me.' She looked about the sordid little room. 'I am quite better now. Please, may we not start for home at once?' And wondered, as she said it, just what home would be like.

'Just what I thought.' He agreed with obvious relief. 'Tench, tell Jenkins we'll start at once. I rely on him, tell him, to see to everything, since Mrs. Tremadoc is not well.'

'Mrs. Tremadoc,' she said as Tench left them. 'How strange.' She held out a hand to her husband. 'I will try my very best to be a good wife to you.'

'I am sure you will.' He was. 'But first we must get some colour back into your cheeks, Amoretta. Do you know, I think perhaps it would be best not to stop at my uncle's in Manchester. After all, my mother has probably left there by now, and I am sure you will be better off at home in Grosvenor Square.'

'Have you written to your mother?' She had been longing to ask this, but had not felt entitled to do so until now, when she was actually his wife.

'Not yet. I thought it best to wait until I could tell her the knot was tied. I'll write her from Carlisle tonight. To my uncle's, and a note to Grosvenor Square in case she is back there already.'

'Will she be very angry?' Caroline had met Mrs. Tremadoc only once and remembered her as a rather formidable figure in purple bombazine.

'Angry? A little, perhaps.' He, too, was beginning to realise just what they had done. 'But a Duke's daughter, after all.'

When they reached the Crown at Carlisle Caroline was surprised and relieved to find that Jenkins had again asked for separate rooms for them.

'I can see that you are not quite yourself yet.' Tremadoc must have noticed her swift look of surprise. 'Besides, I must write to my mother tonight.'

Over breakfast, he admitted that he had failed to do so. 'A deuced awkward letter to write. But here is a trifle of a sonnet for you, Amoretta.'

'Oh, thank you.' She read it with an admirably composed countenance. 'I do hope your mother will not hear the news from someone else first,' she said, when she had paid him the expected compliments. 'I left a letter for the Duchess, you know.'

'Yes,' he said. 'Quite so. I will write tonight.'

Once again, he arranged separate rooms for them, and once again failed to write to his mother. 'I was feeling entirely too sick and shaken from the day's journey,' he told her next morning. 'How you can take travelling so lightly, Amoretta, is more than I can understand. But I wish you will try, today, not to disturb me by so many exclamations about the beauty of the prospect!'

'I am sorry, she said humbly. 'I was so excited to think that we were travelling through the country Mr. Wordsworth writes about. I promise I will be quiet as a mouse today.'

'Do,' he said. 'I am planning an epic poem, when the shaking of the carriage allows it, which will be quite different from anything your Mr. Wordsworth has ever written.'

'I am sure it will,' she said.

He had still not written to his mother when they reached London at last, and they were still sleeping in separate bedrooms. Was he waiting for his mother's approval, she wondered, or did he, perhaps, find the next step in matrimony as daunting as she did? The inevitable close contact of the journey had merely emphasised the fact that they were total strangers to each other. Madness to have married, and she began to wonder if he did not feel this too. Was he even hoping that the powerful mother who had organised his life so far would free him from the bonds in which he had tied himself? There were such things as annulments, she believed, though she did not know just how they were obtained.

'Here we are at last,' he said with false joviality as the carriage turned into Grosvenor Square. 'Now we will be comfortable again.'

'I wonder if Mrs. Tremadoc is there.'

He turned to give her a strange look. 'You are Mrs. Tremadoc! It's your house now.'

There was a carriage waiting outside the house. 'James, my man of business,' he told her. 'Now I wonder why in the world?'

'We will know in a moment.' She smoothed her hair with a hand that would shake. She had passionately hoped that they would find no one in Grosvenor Square, that there would be time to have her things sent over from Chevenham House. Absurd to mind that she had had to go away with so few clothes and now looked unmistakably travelstained, but she did. It was somehow a last straw, in this awkward situation, to know that she looked so far from her best.

He was handing her down from the carriage. He looked pinched with fatigue and, she thought, fear; and in the midst of her own discomfort she found time to be sorry for him and ashamed of the way she was using him. She pressed the hand that held hers. 'It won't be so bad, not if we stick together,' she said.

The doors of the big house had swung open; a huge butler was awaiting them.

'Well, Barnes,' said Tremadoc, as they trod sedately up the steps together, 'Is your mistress home?' And then, recollecting himself, 'Here is your new mistress.'

'Yes sir,' said Barnes. 'Yes, madam is in the small saloon with Mr. James. She *will* be glad to see you.'

Something's wrong, thought Caroline, something is very wrong in this house. Not just our mad marriage. There is something the servants know and we don't.

Did Tremadoc feel it too? 'Would you like to go upstairs, my dear?' he asked. 'Or will you come and meet my mother and Mr. James?'

She thought he wanted her to go upstairs. 'I would like to meet your mother.' She kept her hand firmly in his as they crossed the hall to where a gawking footman had thrown open another door.

Mrs. Tremadoc was all in black. For a wild moment, Caroline thought she must be in mourning for her son's marriage, but her first words explained it. 'Geraint.' She held out a shaking hand to her son. 'Your uncle is dead.'

'Uncle Tom?' He could not believe his ears. 'Impossible! A man in the prime of his life...'

'By his own hand,' she interrupted him dramatically. 'I will spare you the horrible details. This is no time for that.' She turned, still holding Tremadoc's hand and held out her other one to Caroline. 'My dear...' To Caroline's amazement, her voice was now warm and loving. 'Such an awkward greeting for my new daughter, but I thought best to have it all out at once. And now, let me see my new child! Such a naughty puss to steal away like that; they are quite at sixes and sevens at Chevenham House; but you are to be forgiven of course. And my bad Geraint too, who swept you off your feet. What a coil we have been in here, thinking what was best for you bad children, and you, I have no doubt, thinking of nothing but your own happiness.' She had actually been untying Caroline's bonnet strings as she talked, and now planted a firm kiss on her cold face. 'But you look exhausted, child, and so does my poor boy. Travelling never did suit him, which shows, does it not, how desperately in love he was. Quite the romantic story of the day, my dears, and thanks to a few words from the dear Duke where they most mattered, I think we will brush through it well enough. That Mr. Mattingley has been a good friend, and so has his friend Mr. Brummell, who seems to have taken quite one of his fancies for you, my love. But what a brute I am to keep you talking here, when you must be longing for the comforts of home. Come to your room, Daughter Caroline. We'll leave the men to talk their business, shall we?'

Still volubly talking, she led Caroline upstairs to the big bedroom with its huge damask-hung four poster which, she confided, she had abandoned on learning of their marriage. 'Nonsense, my dear,' she said, when Caroline protested, 'You are the mistress of this house, and I the old devoted dowager. I found myself a corner up one more pair of stairs where I shall be snug as can be, so long as my dear new daughter lets me stay. What a tiny thing you are,' she exclaimed, as Tench, who had already begun unpacking a big trunk that stood in the middle of the room, rose to help Caroline out of her pelisse.

'I sent for your things from Chevenham House just as soon as I learned from the dear Duchess how things stood,' she rattled on. 'Just think of my bad boy not leaving me a line of explanation! We must scold him about that, you and I, but not tonight. Tonight everything is to be happiness. And now I will leave you. We dine at six, my love, quite *en famille*, and I am sure you and my bad boy will wish to make an early night of it.' And on this note she left them.

Caroline and Tench looked at each other. 'Well,' said the maid at last, 'You could knock me down with a feather.'

'Me too,' said Caroline, sinking into a chair. 'I don't understand it, Tench.'

'The Duke must have turned up trumps, I reckon,' said Tench. 'You're nicely enough settled here, that's for sure.' She opened a door. 'Mr. Tremadoc's dressing room. I'm hanging your things in here, Jenkins can have the cupboards there. I'm surprised he's not here yet, fussing about and getting in a body's way.'

'Yes,' said Caroline absentmindedly. She had been looking with what she recognised as hope at the small bed in the corner of the dressing room. There was no lock on the communicating door. Absurd. Why should there be? 'I must dress, Tench dear,' she said.

'Yes, ma'am,' said Tench. 'I've had your dress hanging up but there's not a crease in it. Whoever packed it for you knew her business. Well, they all love you at Chevenham House, and no wonder.' She returned from the closet with a great froth of white over her arm.

'My ball dress? Oh, Tench, should I?'

'Yes, ma'am, that you should. Dining the first night in your new home. We must show the flag, ma'am, don't you see? Mr. Tremadoc ain't said anything about jewels, I suppose?'

'Jewels? Why, no.' It occurred to her with new force that Tremadoc had said very little about anything practical.

'Then you'll just have to wear your pearls, and very pretty and suitable too.'

Her mother's present. She had loved them as a child, the only tangible evidence of the mother she had lost. She had found her now. Frances Winterton. The Duke's mistress. As Tench clasped the pearls round her neck she thought they had brought nothing but trouble. If she had not lent them to Giles he would have stayed and faced his father. Poor Giles. Where was he now?

Tremadoc joined them just as Tench had pronounced herself satisfied with her appearance. 'We must send for the hairdresser in the morning, but for tonight, with the flowers, it will do.'

'It will do admirably.' Tremadoc smiled at his wife's face in the glass. 'I believe I have never seen you in such looks! I am delighted to find you ready, my dear. My mother is awaiting you in the drawing room. She has a million things to say to you. And I will join you just as soon as Jenkins makes me fit to be seen.' There was something in the way he looked at her bare shoulders and low neckline that she did not quite like. Ridiculous. He was her husband.

Emerging from her room into the upstairs hall, she caught the murmur of voices, suddenly stilled, in the hall below. In the surprise of Mrs. Tremadoc's overwhelmingly warm greeting, she had forgotten her first feeling that there was something odd going on in this house, but as she trod down the balustraded stairway and saw the footmen, stiff in the hall, she was more sure of it than ever. A minute ago, they had had their heads together, talking about something so exciting that it could not wait until they were off duty. What could it be? Well, she thought, Tench will find out. Tench will tell me when she gets me ready for bed. Thank God for Tench.

Mrs. Tremadoc was resplendent in black velvet and jet. 'My dear,' she came forward to give Caroline another of her firm kisses. It smelt of something faintly sweet, unidentifiable, associated in Caroline's mind with illness. 'You look like a princess.' Mrs. Tremadoc held her off by the shoulders and Caroline felt like a bale of merchandise being inspected for quality. 'I am glad that you, too, felt this was a night for all our finery. I am only sorry,' she produced a black bordered handkerchief, 'that I must depress your spirits with my blacks.'

'I am so sorry,' began Caroline, 'your poor brother . . .'

'No, no.' A firm hand on her arm stopped her. 'Not tonight, my dear; tonight is for happiness; for my Geraint and you. Sit down, child, and tell me all about my new daughter and how she stole away my son's affections.' And then, as if aware that this was not the happiest of notes to strike, she plunged into a string of breathless questions about the events of the journey, which Caroline answered as best she might, wondering a little about the million things Tremadoc had said his mother had to say to her.

It was a relief when he joined them and they adjourned to a sombre dining room furnished with more ostentation than taste. There was something extraordinarily oppressive about this house, she thought, as Tremadoc pulled out a chair for her. 'No, no,' she protested, 'I am sure that is Mrs. Tremadoc's place.'

'Dear child,' said that lady. '*You* are Mrs. Tremadoc now.'

The meal seemed endless. The food was both over-elaborate and ill-cooked, and Tremadoc merely toyed with his. 'These collops are scorched!' he exclaimed. 'And the sauce has curdled. I tell you, ma'am, we ate better on the roads than here. You know how delicate my digestion is!' He turned and said something to the footman behind his chair, who left the room and presently returned with a ruby coloured decanter. 'This will set me to rights.' His hand shook as he raised the glass to his lips.

'My dear,' protested his mother. 'Remember...'

'I remember everything,' he told her with what struck Caroline as almost a look of hatred. 'Have some yourself, mamma.'

'Do you know, I really believe I will,' she said. 'My poor nerves are quite discomposed with joy! It is a tonic medicine my poor son and I are compelled to take from time to time,' she turned to explain to Caroline. 'I am afraid you would think it very nasty.'

'This lemonade is quite delicious,' said Caroline, untruthful for once. Something must be very wrong indeed in the kitchen, she thought, if the lemonade came up to table unsweetened.

By the time she and Mrs. Tremadoc rose to leave the dining room the decanter was almost empty and Tremadoc's cheeks were flushed and faintly shining. His talk was rapid and enthusiastic as he described the epic he had planned on their journey. 'It's to be *The Downfall of Bonaparte*.' He rose unsteadily to his feet. 'But I have not quite decided who shall be my hero.'

'Do not stay too long considering,' said his mother with a quick glance from the level of the liquid in the decanter to the footman behind her son's chair. 'We shall expect you when you have finished your glass, Geraint. You know port never agrees with you, and I am sure my dear daughter is ready for her bed.'

'And so am I!' Still standing, Tremadoc refilled and drained his glass, then moved over to take Caroline's arm with a hand that felt damp with sweat. 'You will excuse us, ma'am?'

'Of course I will, dear children. It's all honeymoon with you, I can see. Sleep well, my dears!'

Something in her tone made Caroline flush up to her hair, and as the three of them climbed the stairs to the drawing room floor, Tremadoc's arm still in hers, she was aware of servants, watching, listening, full of salacious curiosity. It's horrible, she thought, disgusting. But soon I will be with Tench. Tench will help me.

Help her how? She did not know. And when she and her husband reached their bedroom he sent Tench away. 'I shall wait on my wife tonight,' he told her. 'Off to bed with you, woman.'

'But, sir!' Tench actually began to protest. 'My lady . . .'

'My wife!' He was suddenly white and shaking with rage. 'You will leave us, if you wish to keep your place.'

'Yes, sir. Yes, ma'am.' Tench made a flurried curtsy, gave Caroline a long, strange, loving look and left them.

'There!' said Tremadoc. 'Master in my own house. Told her I would be. Husband and wife. One flesh. Whom God hath joined . . .' Suddenly, disconcertingly, he giggled. 'Not much like God, that blacksmith, was he? No wonder if you fainted. But not flattering! Not flattering at all, my mamma says. Journey's over now. Very patient man. Now we're here. Now it's time. Man and wife.' He pushed her, not gently, down on to the big bed and she felt his hot hands looking for the fastenings of her dress. 'Dammit!' The buttons down the back were too small for his shaking fingers. 'Dammit,' he said again. 'Man and wife.' He set his hand to the low front of the dress.

'Don't!' But it was too late. One surprisingly savage pull and the dress ripped clear down to the waist.

After that, it was all unspeakable muddle. Somehow, swearing and talking to himself all the time, he got her out of her clothes, and then, as she huddled, naked, in the big, cold bed, hauled off his own and fell on top of her. 'Man and wife.' He was talking to himself now, not her. 'One flesh.' He kissed her suddenly, hard, leaving the taste of blood in her mouth. His hands moved down from her shoulders to her breasts, hurting them, and, with a kind of horror, she felt her body suddenly move against his as if it knew something she did not.

'Ah,' he said, an animal sound. His hands were doing something lower down and again she was aware of fierce, unexpected, disgusting pleasure, then of sharp, intimate pain, and then of nothing.

11

'MISS, MISS, ARE you all right, miss?' The frightened whisper gradually penetrated Caroline's consciousness, and she opened heavy eyes to see Tench bending over her. 'Shh,' Tench put finger to lips. 'He's still asleep. Very sound, he is. Oh, miss, is it too late? Did he? I did so hope...' As she uttered the broken sentences, she was looking down at the tumbled bed, and her young mistress, bare-shouldered, heavy-eyed and with an unmistakable bruise on her lip.

Caroline, too, had realised that she was naked in bed, and was beginning to feel the places where she hurt. She lay there, speechless, colour slowly flooding her face.

'I was afraid so, when he sent me away.' Tench had summed up the situation, and spared Caroline further questions, merely moving away to find her a négligé and helping her lovingly into it. 'Come through into his dressing room, miss,' she whispered, 'so we can talk. Jenkins says he'll likely sleep for hours. Oh, miss, I am *sorry* I didn't manage to tell you last night.' She closed the dressing-room door behind them. 'I should a' stood up to him, but how could I?'

'Told me what?' Caroline was glad to subside on to the chair Tench pulled forward for her.

'I knew something was up, the minute we got here.' Tench automatically began to brush out Caroline's hair. 'You could tell, the way they was looking... The servants... whispering behind their hands. But nobody come up here to me, miss, and I was that busy unpacking your things, and the girl that brought your hot water just giggled and said madam said to hurry, and by the time Jenkins told me over my bit of supper, it was too late.'

'Told you what?' Caroline asked again.

'They're broke, miss. Stony. That brother of madam's, the mill owner as killed himself. He had the handling of all their money, see. I don't rightly understand how, but it's gone,

128

miss.' She put a hand up to her mouth. 'I should be calling you madam,' she said. 'If only I could a' told you last night, you might a' got it annulled. Is that the word?'

'It doesn't matter,' Caroline said dully. 'Don't look so wretched, Tench dear. I don't think it would have made any difference. What could we have done, you and I?' She sat, staring at her own blanched face in the glass, seeing it all. No wonder Mrs. Tremadoc had received her with such surprising enthusiasm. Instead of being an incubus she was now their sole hope of support. Mrs. Tremadoc had doubtless already been in touch with the Duke—with her father, she reminded herself bitterly. Had they actually met? she wondered, and passionately hoped not. Last night, she had been too overwhelmed by the strangeness of her situation to formulate her impressions of Mrs. Tremadoc, but this morning, imagining her face to face with the Duke, she knew her for a vulgar, stupid woman. If I had known what she was like, she thought, I would never have married her son.

Too late now. 'I must dress, Tench. I need to talk to Mrs. Tremadoc.' The other thing she had recognised, half consciously, last night, was that Mrs. Tremadoc entirely dominated her weak son.

'Are you fit, miss—ma'am?' asked Tench doubtfully.

'I have to be. Mourning, Tench. The dress I had when the Duke's aunt died. Mrs. Tremadoc has just lost her brother, remember.' And, saying this, suddenly found herself actually sorry for her.

It made their meeting just slightly easier. Mrs. Tremadoc was drinking tea in the dining room whose over-bright colours seemed even more tawdry in the light of a fine morning.

'You're bright and early, my dear.' Mrs. Tremadoc rose to greet her. 'I thought you and dear Geraint would sleep till all hours today. But I hope it means that you slept well in your new home.' There was something about her tone that confirmed Caroline's suspicion that she had ordered her son to . . . to . . . she could not find even mental words for what had happened to her last night. Now, Mrs. Tremadoc longed to know if her son had made sure of her.

'Yes, thank you, ma'am,' she said. Tremadoc would tell his mother soon enough.

'Tea or coffee?' asked that lady now. 'The tea is fresh made, but I could send for coffee . . .'

'Tea will be just the thing, thank you.' She had been glad

to see that there was no servant in the dining room. 'I am afraid I am not much of a breakfast eater.' Food would have choked her this morning, but she noticed, with a kind of cold misery, that this was another lie she had found herself forced to tell in this house. Her new home. 'I am so sorry, ma'am.' She plunged into it. 'I was most remiss last night in not condoling with you on your brother's death.'

'Thank you.' Mrs. Tremadoc's hand shook as she poured Caroline's tea. 'It was good of you to put on mourning for him.'

'I am a member of the family now. It is only right.'

Mrs. Tremadoc gave a little sigh as if this had answered the question that had been exercising her. 'My dear,' she put a warm hand on Caroline's cold one, 'We must talk, you and I. This was a rash enough business, I am afraid, of yours and my dear Geraint's, but we are to let bygones be bygones and think of the future.'

'Yes, ma'am.' Caroline sipped hot tea, found it reviving, and wondered if she had done Mrs. Tremadoc an injustice.

'My poor, dear brother.' Mrs. Tremadoc put a lacy hand-kerchief to her eyes. 'Always so good to me. He managed everything for me . . . for Geraint and me. But—this cruel war. He never believed it would break out again after the Peace of Amiens. He thought . . . he said . . . Of course I trusted him! My own brother. He wrote me such a letter . . . Before . . . before he put a period to his existence. So kind, so loving, so sorry. It's all gone,' she concluded simply. 'I don't rightly understand, only that it's all gone. If it were not for the dear Duke there would be an execution in the house this instant.'

'The Duke?' But it was what Caroline had expected.

'Your kind father! Just fancy, when my Geraint was used to sing your praises—his Amoretta—and I'd keep telling him you were a little nobody and he should look higher! Little did I know whom you was.' Launched into her story, discretion and grammar were slipping together. 'You could have knocked me down with my fan when I got back to town and heard the talk. Cos, love, you've got to face it, talk there was, and no two ways about it. Lucky for you my Geraint's a real gent, and married you all right and tight and brought back your marriage lines, which I asked him last night, the very first thing.'

'Well,' Caroline could not help it. 'Lucky for you too.'

'What?' Mrs. Tremadoc looked momentarily taken aback,

then burst into a fit of giggles. 'Well, fancy that,' she said at last, wiping her eyes with the lacy handkerchief. 'So you're not just a little mouse after all. I believe we shall deal admirably, us two, and no roundaboutation needed. You must know by now that my Geraint's gentle as a lamb and innocent as a babe. If there's contriving to be done, you and I will have to do it; and, no two ways about it, dearie, contriving there's got to be. That father of yours is a hard man, and no mistake, but I'm sure you know the way to bring him round your thumb.'

'I? Mrs. Tremadoc, don't set any hopes in that, I beg you.' Every instinct told her that this must be made clear at once. 'I'm afraid the Duke does not even like me very much. Anything he does for me will be from a sense of duty only.'

'So? Well, that's a facer, and no mistake. We'll just have to think what's best to do to bring him about, won't we?' Mrs. Tremadoc drank a good swig of tea, put her elbows on the table and leaned forward to speak confidentially. 'You must know, dearie, better than anyone, what really happened that day in Richmond Park.'

'What happened?' Caroline flushed, then paled, remembering it all, remembering Blakeney.

'Ah.' It was a sigh of greedy satisfaction. 'You do know it all. I was positive you would. Lady Charlotte and that Gaston wa'nt it? Gave young ffether the slip and off on their own God knows where. Well, now, who's to know what happened between them two before they learned the truth about themselves. Lord!' She giggled again. 'Trust a man to make a mull of things. Fancy that ramrod of a Duke letting you all grow up together without knowing you was brothers and sisters, wrong side of the blanket. Serve him right if it was four bare legs in a bed with them and his daughter ruined. Oh, he's been mighty clever, so he thinks, putting it about that there was only one elopement, yours and my Geraint's, but you and I know better, don't we love? And so we shall tell the Duke if he don't see us right.'

'Mrs. Tremadoc, I do not understand you.' But Caroline was very much afraid that she did. What the woman was proposing was blackmail, pure and simple.

'Bless the child.' Mrs. Tremadoc rolled a roguish eye at her. 'I keep forgetting what a very newly married lady you are. But, look, dearie, all we have to do is convince that stiff-necked father of yours that you can spoil his fine story about

Lady Charlotte if you want to, and he'll pay anything to keep you quiet.'

'I was afraid that was what you meant.' Caroline's cup clicked in its saucer. She was paler than ever, and breathing fast. 'Let us have this clear between us, once and for all, ma'am. Whatever the Duke might have owed me, as my father, I forfeited when I ran off with your son. Anything he may do for me is more than I deserve. As to Lady Charlotte, I am able to tell you that her brother fetched her home that same evening, and Mr. Mattingley had found them even before that.'

'Ah,' said Mrs. Tremadoc, 'but was he in time, that's what I want to know? And what the world will, if the story gets out. Half-brother and sister. Not pretty, dearie, not pretty at all.'

'The story is not going to get out,' said Caroline. 'I'm more glad than I can say if they have really been able to use my wretched elopement as cover for Lady Charlotte's escapade, but escapade is all it was, and if I ever again hear you so much as suggest anything else, I shall leave this house at once, never to return. And take any allowance the Duke may choose to give me with me.'

'Ho, will you!' But Mrs. Tremadoc looked shaken. 'Now that's something you ain't going to be able to do, and the sooner you know it the better. I've got news for you, miss. All My Lord Duke chooses to offer his son-in-law is a family living down in the country, God knows where, paying some kind of miserable pittance.'

'A living? Mr. Tremadoc?' Caroline put a hand to her mouth to quell a spurt of astonished laughter. 'Never! But, surely, he's . . . he's not qualified.'

'In orders? No, of course he's not, but there's no problem about that. He did very well at Cambridge, did my Geraint. With the Duke behind him, he'll have no trouble.'

'No,' said Caroline thoughtfully. 'I suppose he won't.' She thought of Mr. Trentham, so truly good, a man of God. 'Mr. Tremadoc won't like it,' she said.

'Of course he don't. That's why it's up to you to do something about it, miss. After all, you lured him into marriage.'

'I did not!' And yet, she thought, there was horrible truth in the accusation. 'We were a pair of fools,' she said. 'And must face the consequences of our folly. And you and I must not quarrel, Mrs. Tremadoc.'

'*I'm* not quarrelling.' Mrs. Tremadoc bridled, something Caroline had read of but never seen before. 'I'm sitting here, listening to I don't know what kind of impertinence from my new daughter-in-law, when all I am trying to do is advise her for the best.'

'Good,' said Caroline. 'Then let us agree that there is nothing I can do to change the Duke's mind. You must believe me when I tell you that is true. He's a . . . an obstinate man.'

'Deaf as a post and stubborn as a mule, I've heard. Well then, what about that mother of yours, Mrs. Winterton. Can't she bring him about?'

'She's ill,' said Caroline. 'She and the Duchess have gone to Bath. And even if she wasn't, I doubt if she'd speak for me. What the Duke says is her law.'

'Well,' said Mrs. Tremadoc, 'Lord knows, I can understand that. How about the Duchess, then? Everyone says she's a right one.'

'She's always been good to me.' Looking back, Caroline knew how true this was. And then, quickly, before Mrs. Tremadoc should sprout a new crop of rash hopes. 'But I'd rather die than ask her. Mrs. Tremadoc, please accept that. And after all, might not a country living be the very thing for Mr. Tremadoc? I'm sure he has told me often enough that he finds the London life distracts him from his poetry. In the country he will have time . . .'

'Between marrying and buryings?' said his mother gloomily. 'Well, I tell you as I told him that it's no use your imagining I'm going to sink myself in a country grave along with you. I've got my jointure still, Brother Tom never got his grasping hands on that, and if you two decide to bury yourselves alive at Oldchurch, I'll just have to look about me here in Town. And you'll have to learn how to hold housekeeping, miss, which I warrant will come as a shock to you both. My Geraint's a difficult man to cater for, with a stomach like a princess. I'll like to see how you contrive for him on your £1,000 a year.'

'A thousand a year?' exclaimed Caroline. 'But, Mrs. Tremadoc, that's riches!' Mr. Trentham, she knew, had managed on £700. 'I'm glad you saved your jointure.' She longed to have Mrs. Tremadoc confirm again that she did not intend to live with them.

'The widow's mite,' sniffed Mrs. Tremadoc. 'The Duke's man, that Grant, actually had the gall to suggest I might put it towards paying off poor Geraint's debts, but I soon put him right about that.'

'You mean, the Duke is paying Mr. Tremadoc's debts as well as giving him the living?'

'Well, of course,' said Mrs. Tremadoc. 'He could hardly have a son-in-law in the debtors' prison, could he now? That Grant wants to see you, by the way. I said we'd send when you were safe home and rested.'

'Then let us send straight away.' Caroline rose. She longed to be alone, to consider everything she had learned from her mother-in-law, but where could she go?

'I've had a fire lit in the morning room,' said Mrs. Tremadoc. 'My Geraint's not to be disturbed when he sleeps late. I'll send directly for Mr. Grant, and do you be thinking hard, miss, about your position. I tell you to your head, Geraint will never forgive you if you don't find a way out of this mess.'

'It's not I who lost his money,' Caroline was goaded into replying.

'Tell that to Geraint,' said his mother.

Arriving half an hour later, the Duke's man of business was amazed at the change in Caroline. He had expected an awkward interview with a tearful child and was at once relieved and disconcerted to find himself confronting a very pale, very composed young woman in full mourning. 'It was good of you to come so soon,' she said, when the first, difficult greetings were over.

'Not at all. The Duke left strict instructions that I was to lose no time in letting you know exactly where you stood.'

'The Duke's not in town?'

'No. The whole family are in Bath. They mean to remain there until Mrs. Winterton is better.'

My mother, she thought. 'How is Mrs. Winterton?'

'Not at all well, I am afraid. The Duke instructed me to tell you that she must be spared any further nervous upsets.'

'I see.' A little glow of anger lit in Caroline's heart. Was she to be blamed for Mrs. Winterton's illness along with everything else? Her mother's illness. I shall never be able to think of her as my mother. A mother would have told her, warned her. She looked at the lawyer very straight. 'I would not dream of doing anything to worry Mrs. Winterton.'

'Of course not.' He was pleased that she had taken his point so quickly. 'In fact, the Duke thinks, all things considered, that the less communication there is between you and the family, the better. It is precisely on that understanding that he makes the offer to you about which, I have no doubt, Mrs. Tremadoc will have told you.'

'I would prefer to hear it direct from you,' she said.

'Understandable. Most understandable. And wise, too, if I may say so. I have had some dealings with Mrs. Tremadoc. It will be much better, if, after today, I deal direct with Mr. Tremadoc. I am surprised not to see him here today, but it is convenient enough, for this once, since I have a personal message for you from the Duke.'

'Yes?'

'He asks for your solemn promise that you will say nothing, to anyone, about the events of the day before your elopement.'

The little glow was a flame of anger now, but she controlled her voice. 'He does not need to ask.'

'I was sure of it,' said Grant heartily. 'I said as much to his Grace himself. "She's a member of the family," I told him. "She'll do nothing to injure it."'

'You were quite right.'

'Satisfactory. Most satisfactory. I will give his Grace your solemn assurance, and now we can get on to the pleasanter side of my visit. His Grace feels that all things considered it will save a deal of awkwardness if you and Mr. Tremadoc settle somewhere out of town. There is a living in his gift has just fallen vacant. Mrs. Tremadoc did not seem to think her son would wish to take Holy Orders, but I am sure you will be able to persuade him. It's a good living; £1,000 a year clear; he would be able to appoint a curate if he found the duty too onerous. Oldchurch is a thriving little town, you will find, and the vicarage a good one, I believe. Big but not too big, and a convenient distance from the church, not hanging over the graveyard the way some of them do. I am sure you will find it a most eligible situation, Mrs. Tremadoc.'

'You will think me very ignorant,' she said. 'But where is Oldchurch, Mr. Grant? I confess I never heard of it.'

'Why should you have?' He thought ignorance most suitable in a woman. 'It's on Romney Marsh, Mrs. Tremadoc, wool country, of course; you will find it similar to Cley in some ways.'

'Then the farming will have been hit by this endless war as it has been at Cley,' she said. 'And the £1,000 a year is presumably in tithes, Mr. Grant?'

'Why, yes.' He looked at her with surprised respect. He had raised this aspect of the case with the Duke, being a man

who liked to be prepared for every eventuality, and the Duke
had laughed it off. 'They'll never think of that,' he had said,
'but if they do, tell them I'll make the income up to £1,000 if
necessary.' He told Caroline this now, glad to be able to do
so.

'It's good of the Duke,' she said. 'And I understand from
Mrs. Tremadoc that he has paid my...' she boggled for a
moment. 'Mr. Tremadoc's debts. Please tell him how very
grateful I am. And that I will do my very best to persuade Mr.
Tremadoc that he should accept this kind offer.'

'Tell him there won't be another one,' said Grant. 'You
know the Duke, ma'am.'

She gave him a very straight look. 'I do indeed,' she said.

'For all the world like her father,' he told his clerk afterwards. 'Gave me a real turn, it did.' For the moment, he put
his hand in the capacious pocket of his coat and produced two
notes. 'For you, ma'am,' he told her. 'One of them got mislaid,
somehow, at Chevenham House, which explains the direction.'

From Blakeney? She took them eagerly, noticing that one
was addressed, in a hand she did not know, to Miss Thorpe.
The other, addressed to her as Mrs. Tremadoc, was in the
Duchess's well known, flowing hand. 'Thank you.' She con-
cealed her disappointment gallantly. 'Any messages, Mr. Grant?'
But how should there be?

'No ma'am.' Suddenly, to his own surprise, he felt un-
speakably sorry for her. 'But the Duchess...'

'Of course. Stupid of me. Thank you, Mr. Grant.' It was
dismissal, and he accepted it as such, rising to his feet.

'I shall hope to hear from your husband.'

'As soon as possible.' She was eagerly opening the Duchess's note as he took his leave.

It was short and to the point:

Dear Child,
   The Duke has told me what he intends to do for you,
and I hope you will feel, as I do, that he has been kindness
itself. But I would like to feel that you had a little independence of your own, and mean to allow you £50 a
year pin money out of my own funds. I do hope you will
accept this, and let it be a secret between you and me.
I have asked my friend Mr. Coutts to make the arrangements for me, and you should be hearing from him shortly.
Dear child, I wish you so very well.

A tear fell on the signature as Caroline opened the other letter. Dated the day after that disastrous outing to Richmond Park, it was even shorter than the Duchess's and quite as much to the point:

Dear Miss Thorpe,
I was sorry not to be able to see you this morning. You will forgive me if I speak plainly, as to a friend. It strikes me that you will find yourself awkwardly situated, just now, at Chevenham House. It would make me both proud and happy if you would consent to change your state by becoming my wife.
[And the bold signature] Charles Mattingley.

Mattingley. If she had only known. He would have helped her.
There was a postscript:

I must leave town for a couple of days. I will hope to hear from you on my return.

He must have come back to the news of her elopement with Tremadoc. But why had she not had his note at the time? The answer stared her in the face. Someone at Chevenham House had intercepted it. Had also intercepted her note to Blakeney? Of course. No wonder he had not come to her rescue. It is more than I can bear, she thought. And then, but I have to bear it.

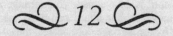

VISITING THE CINQUE PORTS, Queen Elizabeth the First had called Oldchurch the brightest jewel in her crown, and Caroline, seeing the little hill town for the first time in silhouette against the sunset, could understand why. It looked a fairy place, rising from the high flint walls that still defended its loop of river to

the bold outline of its church tower at the top of the hill. The
sea that had made it useful as a harbour to the Tudor fleet was
three miles away now, beyond the marsh that was so like and
yet so unlike her beloved marshes at Cley.

Tired from the journey, and from Tremadoc's constant,
habitual grumbling, she felt this darkening marsh as alien,
unfriendly, and could not suppress a superstitious shiver as the
carriage drove in through the Land Gate and up the steep hill
towards the church. Timber-framed houses overhung the street,
their upper storeys almost meeting, so that it was suddenly dark
in the carriage. Beside her, too close for comfort in the confined
space, Tremadoc shifted uneasily. 'The back of beyond,' he
exclaimed. 'It's too much! I shall die, and it will be entirely
your fault for making me come to this dreadful place. And
don't forget the income from the living will die with me, so
no use to be planning to set up as a merry widow when I am
gone. My mother wouldn't help you if you were starving, not
after the way you have behaved. Pretending you have no influence with the Duke! Making me take orders! Bringing me
down to this deadly hole to burn out my genius in the wilder-
ness. We poets need company, the interplay of lively minds.
What shall I do in this black hole?'

'We will find out soon enough,' she said as the carriage
emerged from the dark little street into what seemed almost a
Cathedral Close of pleasant brick-fronted houses set around a
well-kept green. It was still warmed by the last rays of the
setting sun striking almost horizontally past the looming shape
of the church. The windows of the house outside which the
carriage stopped reflected the sunset with a crimson glow that
made her shiver again, thinking of blood.

'I'm too ill to move,' said Tremadoc. 'Send Jenkins with
my cordial. He can help me into the house when you have
found if there is a room fit to receive me. If not, I shall go to
the Castle Inn until you have made your arrangements.' He did
not trouble to move his feet, and she climbed awkwardly across
him to emerge by the carriage door nearest the house. The front
door was open now, and Jenkins and Tench stood there, smiling
a welcome.

She hurried up the two shelving steps to greet them, warmed
and reassured by their friendly looks. 'All's ready for you,
ma'am.' Tench bobbed a curtsey. 'Mr. Jenkins and I have been
busy as can be and I hope you'll be pleased with what we've

done. And a fire ready for the master, like Jenkins says he always wants after a journey.'

'He wants his cordial too, Jenkins,' said Caroline. 'Before he even gets out of the carriage. The journey was too much for him, I am afraid.'

'Very good, ma'am. I'll see to it at once.' She thought the two servants exchanged some kind of understanding glance before Jenkins turned back into the house and Tench took Caroline's arm to urge her in.

'You look white as a sheet, ma'am. I hope the journey's not been too much for *you*.'

'I'm a little tired,' admitted Caroline. 'And so grateful to you, Tench, for coming on ahead and seeing to things for me.'

'I hope it's all as you'd like it.' She led Caroline across a surprisingly spacious hall and opened a panelled door. 'The drawing room. I had a fire lit here as well as in the master's study.'

'Oh, thank you, Tench.' She was glad to let her maid undo her bonnet strings and ease it off her aching head. 'I don't know how I'd manage without you.'

'You've got two of us now, miss...ma'am, I should say,' said Tench surprisingly. 'Mr. Jenkins has been at me and at me all the time we've been down here, and I don't know how it come about, but just this morning I up and heard myself saying yes. You won't mind it, ma'am?'

'Of course not! Why, Tench, I'm delighted. I've always thought Mr. Jenkins a kind, good man ever since that dreadful journey to Gretna.'

'And so he is,' said Tench, 'and that fond of you, ma'am. Only one thing. I hope you won't mind it, but he thinks best not to tell the master. Mr. Tremadoc don't like married servants, it seems.'

'Oh?' It seemed to her that she learned a disconcerting new thing about this husband of hers every day. 'But...he's the vicar, Tench, how can you marry?'

'We're Chapel, Mr. Jenkins and I. We've spoke to the minister already. He's agreeable; it's just to wait a bit, and that'll do Jenkins no harm, I reckon.'

'But how will you manage?' Caroline put a hand to her aching brow. Every instinct revolted at the idea of keeping secrets from her husband, but the fact remained that Jenkins knew him much better than she did.

'Oh, as to that, we've got it fixed up all right and tight.

You'll understand in the morning when I take you round the house. For tonight, what you need is your supper and your bed. I've contrived a dressing room for Mr. Tremadoc like he had in town. And a cot in it, too, like he had there. And here he comes now, ma'am.'

The warning note in Tench's voice and the arrangements she had made showed Caroline that her maid was under no illusions as to the state of her marriage. She reached up to press her hand. 'I'm so happy for *you*, Tench,' she said.

Tremadoc drank some more of his cordial with the light supper sent in by the new cook, and mellowed a little. 'The house don't look half bad now it's got some furnishings,' he told Caroline over dessert. 'I tell you, I quite despaired when I came down for my induction, but that woman of yours seems to have done pretty well. And the cook is quite out of the way; I wouldn't be surprised to find these pastries on a select London table.' He helped himself to another.

'The cook is a Frenchman,' said Caroline, who had made a point of visiting the kitchen as soon as she had changed her dress, and whose fluent French had made her instant friends with the fiery little refugee installed there. 'I think it best not to ask just how he got over here.'

'No, indeed. Let me warn you, Caroline, that there are many things here in Oldchurch about which one should not ask. It was all explained to me when I came down before and I have promised on both our parts that we will never interfere in what does not concern us.'

'And what, exactly, does that mean?'

He took another pastry. 'That's what I am saying to you, madam. That it does not concern you.'

The callers began next day. Luckily for Caroline, Tench had warned her of them and made her wear her second-best mourning dress. 'And an apron,' advised Tench. 'Then if one of the old tabbies should come early hoping to catch you out, she can't say you don't hold housekeeping. And I'm not your maid, ma'am, don't forget, but your housekeeper now.'

'Then I don't know what you are doing brushing my hair.' Caroline kept her voice low, remembering her husband asleep in the next room.

'That's between ourselves, ma'am. And because I love to do it. Besides it gives me a chance to talk to you, when none of those Oldchurch servants are on the listen. You want to be careful what you say in front of them, Miss Caroline. From what I can find out, they're all cousins, and all related to staff in the other houses. If you sneeze at breakfast, it will be all over town by dinner that you've taken cold.'

'Oh dear,' sighed Caroline.

'And their employers no better.' Tench changed the brush to her left hand and warmed to her theme. 'They're all kin, too, from what I can make out, all Tories, and all ready to be scandalised at anything you do.' Her eyes met Caroline's in the glass. 'I'm sorry, ma'am, I hate to worry you, but facts is best faced and there's no doubt but there has been talk.'

'Oh, no!' But she had been afraid of it.

'And Mr. Tremadoc not much help neither.' Tench lowered her voice with a quick glance at the door to the bedroom. 'By what Jenkins has heard in the tap at the Castle he talked pretty free when the Oldchurch Club dined him there. Jenkins come home mad as fire the first night we was here. He'd a' quit the post long since, he says, if it wan't for you—and me, ma'am. A proper nodcock, he reckons the master is, with his cordial and his travelsickness and his blabbermouth.'

'Tench, you are not to speak to me like that about my husband . . . That will be all, thank you, I will finish dressing myself.'

'I'm sure I beg your pardon, ma'am.' Tench dropped a quick curtsy and left her with one backward glance in which surprise and respect were equally mingled.

Left alone, Caroline sat for a moment, gazing forlornly at the white face in the glass. She had had to do it, but was afraid she might have lost a useful pair of allies, and very much wished she had been able to find out just what indiscretions Tremadoc had committed. Then, with a little sigh, she rose to her feet, finished dressing and went downstairs to drink tea in the sunny dining room at the back of the house.

To her relief, Tench was awaiting her there, now very much in her capacity as housekeeper and quite as eager as she was herself to pretend that the rebuke had neither been earned nor spoken. After breakfast, they toured the house together and Caroline was delighted with it. It was much larger than its narrow frontage on the green suggested. At the back, it was L-shaped. A wing thrown out on the north end sheltered the neglected garden lying between the house and the steep cliff that made a town wall unnecessary on this side of the hill. Since only a low wall ran along the cliff, the eastward facing garden was full of morning sunshine.

'You'll be quite private in it,' Tench told her. 'Servants' quarters are in the wing, see, looking the other way, and there's a very strange old gentleman lives in the house next door behind that high wall. Knows no one and goes nowhere. He won't trouble you, that's for sure, and Jenkins asked me to tell you he'd be happy to get the garden in order for you, if you'll just tell him what to do.'

'Oh, he is kind!' exclaimed Caroline. 'I do thank you both, Tench.'

The first caller was announced half an hour later. 'It's Mrs. Bowles, ma'am, the Mayor's lady,' Tench told her. 'There's cakes and wine ready in the drawing room.' She was untying Caroline's apron strings. 'There,' she gave her a loving little push. 'You look every inch the lady, and that's what counts.'

An enormous woman in purple satin and a turban, Mrs. Bowles looked Caroline up and down with frank curiosity.

'Well,' she said at last, 'you don't look like the scarlet woman to me.'

'I beg your pardon, ma'am?'

'My husband the Mayor gave me strict orders to be your first visitor.' Mrs. Bowles selected the largest chair and settled herself in it with a little sigh. 'I'm too big to stand. If you'd just give me a footstool, dearie, we could be cosy, you and I. The others won't be here for ten minutes, or I'll have something to say to them. That's right.' She lifted swollen ankles on to the stool Caroline pushed up. 'And then a glass of madeira, and one of those queen cakes, though I shouldn't, and you tell me all about it, dearie.'

'All about what, ma'am?' Caroline obediently filled the glass and passed the plate of cakes.

'About all this talk. If you don't speak up for yourself, who else will, that's what I want to know. Well, now,' she took a hearty sip of madeira, 'We know all about your father, that's of course, seeing as how it's his living, but this story of you and that half-brother with the French name, that's what we can't stomach, and, frankly, dearie, now I've seen you, what I find hard to believe.'

'Me and Gaston?' Caroline sat down rather suddenly on a straight chair. 'What story, ma'am?'

'Gastong. That's the name.' Mrs. Bowles ate half a queen cake at a mouthful. 'That's what I thought,' she said. 'The minute I clapped eyes on you, I thought, nohow will I believe it.'

'Believe what, ma'am? I beg you will take me with you.'

'Why, that you ran off with your half-brother and Mr. Tremadoc took you out of pity and to oblige the Duke. Well,' said Mrs. Bowles, daunted by Caroline's look of silent shock, 'it's what Mr. Tremadoc said himself, or as good as, that night at the Castle, only Mr. Bowles, he said the lad had drink taken and didn't rightly know what he was saying. Kind of in a daze he seemed to be, Bowles told me. Funny kind of clergyman, if you ask me. Now, dearie, if you're over the first shock of it, and I can see it *was* a shock, just you tell me the truth of the matter, once and for all, and I'll see it gets where it matters. If we women don't stick together, who's going to look out for us, that's what I want to know.'

'Thank you, ma'am.' Caroline said it from the heart. 'But as to telling you what really happened, that's what I can't do, because it concerns other people, but I beg you to believe that I have committed no greater folly than that of running off with Mr. Tremadoc.'

'Folly indeed, from all I hear about him,' said Mrs. Bowles robustly. 'What about that Gastong then?'

'We've never even been friends,' said Caroline. 'I wouldn't trust him across the street.'

'So it was one of the others, just like I thought,' said Mrs. Bowles. 'Lady Amelia or Lady Charlotte, and you left to bear the blame. Well, like mother like child, they do say, and we all know about the Duchess—and the Duke, come to that. Oh, I'm sorry, love, I didn't mean to put you to the blush, and you're not to start crying neither because if I'm not very much mistaken that's Mrs. Price's carriage now, and Mrs. Trumpler will be with her 'cos they always hunt in couples, so you just greet them like the lady you are and leave me to sort things for you.'

'Oh, thank you, Mrs. Bowles. You really believe me!'

'Course I believe you,' said that lady comfortably, 'your colour would show you up, soon enough, if you were to try any taradiddles on me. Mind you,' she gave Caroline a very shrewd look, 'I'm not so simple I can't see there's more to it than you've told, but that's your business.' She held out a fat hand encrusted with rings. 'Friends, then?'

'Friends, indeed.' Caroline bent to brush a swift kiss against the highly coloured cheek. 'I'm more grateful to you than I can say.' She straightened up to greet Mrs. Price and Mrs. Trumpler, who came through the wide doorway side by side and stood for a moment gazing a question at Mrs. Bowles, one tall, thin and curious, the other short, stout and censorious.

Mrs. Bowles rose or rather surged up to the occasion. 'Mrs. Tremadoc and I have had a good talk,' she told them, putting a warm arm round Caroline's shoulders. 'I know all about what the poor child has gone through and have promised her my countenance.'

'I'm so pleased.' A neat curtsy from Mrs. Price.

'I'm quite delighted.' A rather frigid little bob from Mrs. Trumpler.

'Those London papers,' sniffed Mrs. Price.

'Those London ladies,' suggested Mrs. Trumpler.

'I'm not a London lady at all,' Caroline seized her chance. 'I've only been there since the winter, and I don't care if I never go back. Your marshes here remind me a little of the country round Cley where I grew up.' She poured and passed madeira and cakes as she talked.

'Country bred, were you?' asked Mrs. Price.

'If you can call Cley the country,' suggested Mrs. Trumpler. 'Bigger than Bodiam Castle, I've heard tell. Without the moat of course. I don't rightly call that country living, Mrs. Tremadoc, nor yet a proper breeding for a clergyman's lady, by all one hears.'

'No,' agreed Caroline with unmistakable honesty. 'I am entirely of your mind, Mrs. Trumpler. Before I went to Cley I lived in a country vicarage in Herefordshire, not half so big and beautiful as this house, with a great big country parish that kept my father—my adopted father.' She felt her colour rise . . . 'Kept him busy from morning till night.'

'Fancy that!' said Mrs. Price.

'Only to think!' chimed in Mrs. Trumpler.

'You never told me that,' said Mrs. Bowles, but without any hint of reproach. 'So you do know something of what a parson's lady should do?'

'I should hope so,' said Caroline. 'But I expect the problems were different in Herefordshire from what they would be in a rich parish like this.' And she managed a couple of informed questions to the three ladies before the door opened again to admit a fresh batch of guests. Greeting in turn the wives of the Collector of Customs and the town's two leading lawyers, as Mrs. Bowles introduced them, she felt the tide of opinion set in her favour.

Mrs. Bowles, surging up to her presently to say goodbye,

confirmed her impression. 'I've over-stayed my time,' she said, 'but I've been enjoying myself. You'll do, dearie, you'll do nicely. I just hope that husband of yours does half so well.'

Tremadoc had been meeting his church wardens and when he returned for the light luncheon that had been set late for him his fretful look and tone suggested that Mrs. Bowles had been right to be doubtful.

'How did you get on with the tabbies?' He helped himself to a liberal glassful of his cordial. 'If they are anything like their husbands you must be as fatigued as I am. There's no pleasing them, I tell you! That Bowles fancies himself God Almighty because he's town Mayor. Of all the Jacks-in-Office. Imagine objecting to the idea that I should have a curate! I ask you, how am I to write my masterpiece if I don't have the help I need in the parish. Just because the old dodderer they had before managed without is no argument for me, and so I told them. Why, the Duke as good as suggested I have one!'

'But they don't seem to reckon much to the Duke down here.' Caroline wondered as she spoke when her husband had met her father and what kind of shabby bargain had been struck. Had Tremadoc actually agreed to let her be slandered by the story of the elopement with Gaston? And what had he got in exchange? 'They're all Tories, Tench says.'

'A parcel of nobodies. If they think they and their penny-pinching ideas are to come between me and the execution of my masterpiece they are fair and far off the mark and so I shall show them.'

'You are absolutely right, my dear,' she told him. 'And I had been meaning to offer you my services as an amanuensis for your great poem.'

'As a what?'

'As a secretary. To write it down for you. I know what an effort composition is to you, what a strain on all your powers. Do you not think if you were to come into the morning room, where there is a good fire burning, and sit in a comfortable chair, and dictate to me as your genius moves you, you might find your poem growing fast, and what could more effectively silence these local busybodies than to publish at least a few stanzas, a canto or two?'

'Why, Caroline, that's the deuce of a good idea.' He drained his glass of cordial and rose somewhat unsteadily to his feet. 'We will start at once.'

Sitting quiet beside him, pen in hand, Caroline had plenty

of time for the thoughts that would wander, always, to Blakeney. She had had no word from him, and though it had been impossible not to go on hoping for one, she had not really expected it. Not after she had understood that he must have received her note too late to save her from her disastrous marriage. Too honest to congratulate her on it, he must have decided, as she had herself, that only time, silence and absence could help them. How long? She dreamt of him, night after night, painful dreams that now, horribly, mixed him up with Tremadoc. She would love him until she died, but presently, she prayed, she would love him as a brother. In the meantime, she comforted herself a little by putting her heart into a series of sonnets he would never see.

She sighed and picked up her pen to take down a staggering iambic line and wonder if even Tremadoc could fail to see how bad it was. Her mind wandered again, this time to that surprising letter of Mattingley's. What would she have done if she had received it the day it was written? Too late to be thinking of that now. She had not even been able to thank him for his amazingly generous offer, having learned from a casual remark of Tremadoc's that he had surprised his friends by suddenly accepting a diplomatic posting to St. Petersburg, and had already left London when they returned from Gretna Green. Could her failure to answer him have had anything to do with this? He must have thought her discourteous beyond belief when he learned of her elopement.

But his acceptance of the dangerous post in war-torn Europe merely added to the feeling of admiration and respect that had grown in her since she had received his surprising offer. It was odd, she thought, dutifully copying down another halting line of verse, how sheltered from the realities of the war they had been at Chevenham House. The Duke and his friends had talked of the war as if it were an aspect of politics. There had been military reviews, of course, which the Duchess and Mrs. Winterton had attended in most becoming travesties of Hussar uniform, and Blakeney had done his duty with the Volunteers, but it had all seemed play acting, like the Duchess's uniform. Down here, on the threatened marsh, things were very different. Boulogne, with Bonaparte's army and invasion fleet, was just across the Channel. She wondered, looking back, if the same invasion fears had not run through the towns of Cley and Blakeney as she felt here at Oldchurch. They were on the Norfolk coast, after all, equally exposed to the French threat. Was it only in the great houses that one lived an artificial life, sheltered from the fact of war?

But Tremadoc was just as unaware as she had been, she thought, even if he was writing a poem about *The Downfall of Bonaparte*. With him, too, it was all talk, all play-acting...

'Enough for today.' His voice interrupted her thoughts, as he put a shaking hand to his brow. 'I am quite worn out with composition. Read me what I have done.'

She did so, and, reading, found how surprisingly easy it was to improve his stumbling lines as she went along.

'Excellent!' he said at last. 'Ring for Jenkins. I positively must have a glass of my cordial before I choose my sermon for Sunday.'

'You do not think you should write one of your own,' she ventured. 'Particularly for your first appearance?'

'Nonsense,' he told her. 'They'll never know the difference. Parcel of country bumpkins who can talk of nothing but war and the price of mutton.'

He was proved wrong when Mrs. Bowles paid Caroline a morning visit a few weeks later. 'It won't do.' She accepted chair, stool, and glass of madeira like the regular visitor she was. 'You must tell that husband of yours that it won't do. Mrs. Vail called on me yesterday and suggested I drop a word in your ear. She don't feel it quite her place, as relict of the late vicar, but she brought me the book Mr. Tremadoc took his sermon from, Sunday, and not even word perfect, neither. Said Samarian when he meant Samaritan, didn't he? Well, dearie, there's no two ways about it, it won't do. And, another thing, he don't seem to know we've got a war on. We need fighting sermons, something to keep folks' hearts up, down here where we know we're likely in for the worst of it. Did you see they're repairing the walls, down by the Water Gate? How do you fancy being besieged? I can't say I relish the idea, but I'm laying down an extra supply of food for the winter, just in case, and so should you, if you can see your way clear. I'd make your husband spend his money on that, if I were you, not on getting in some fancy curate to look down his nose at us commoners.'

'Oh, Mrs. Bowles—' Caroline put out a protesting hand.

'Not you, love,' said Mrs. Bowles, taking it and squeezing it warmly. 'You've no more airs than one of my own girls, bless you. Anyone would think it was Mr. Tremadoc was the Duke's child, not you, the way he goes on. And him nothing but a cit, when all's said and done, and would be a bankrupt one if it weren't for your pa.'

'Oh dear,' sighed Caroline, used by now to the fact that in Oldchurch everyone knew everything about everybody.

'Didn't that foster father of yours write sermons?' suggested Mrs. Bowles, realistic to her fingers' ends. 'If you chanced to have some of those in your commonplace book, no one here could possibly know they wasn't your husband's. If you could get him to put something in about the war, that is.'

'Goodness, I'm not sure.' Caroline knew very well that she had none of Mr. Trentham's sermons, but it had given her an idea. 'I'll take a look, Mrs. Bowles, and thank you a thousand times for suggesting it.'

Tremadoc finished dictating that afternoon and gave a little sigh of satisfaction when she had read his stanzas back to him. 'There!' he said, with justified pleasure. 'When that gets published those muttonheads in town will see what an unusual clergyman they have got, and stop fussing on about my sermons. As if I had time to be composing them too!'

It gave her exactly the opening she had wanted. 'Do you know, my dear?' She looked up from a correction she had been making. 'I had a thought about that. I found copies, just the other day, of a batch of sermons my foster father, Mr. Trentham, wrote for just this time of year. It must have been in one of the early years of the war. I was amazed at how appropriate they seem to the way things are now. Indeed, they struck me as a little out of the ordinary run, so I copied a few out for you in the hopes that you might just possibly find them of some use.'

'Oh?' Tremadoc thought about it. 'His own composition?'

'Why, yes. He always wrote his own.'

'Nothing else to do, I suppose, poor man. Well,' carelessly, 'let me have a look at them. It would certainly save the trouble of copying notes from one of those plaguey volumes.' And when she returned with them. 'Your handwriting? Why, of course, that fits. Dictated by me, just like my great poem.'

'Yes, dear,' said Caroline meekly.

Autumn broke over Oldchurch with a frenzy of equinoctial gales. A wild north-easter lashed across the marsh, tearing branches from stunted trees and rattling windows in their frames; torrential rain poured in rivulets down the steep streets, and people went about their business more contentedly than through the fine weeks of summer. Not even the staunch Oldchurch fishing smacks could go out in this. There might be no fish, but there was no chance of an invasion either, so long as the storm lasted.

Confined to the house by weather too bad even for her, Caroline missed the daily visits to the poor and sick that took her up and down the narrow lanes of Oldchurch. The fresh air and exercise had done her good after her confined London life, and so had the simple nourishing meals M. Japrisot sent in. 'She needs good food, the little madame,' he had explained to Tench. 'My sister had just such a blind little look, and I cured it for her with my cooking. I shall do the same for our little angel.'

Full of new energy, Caroline sent for Tench after breakfast one stormy morning. 'I've had it on my mind ever since I came that I have not been through the cellars,' she told her. 'Now that we have quite filled the larder and pantries with preserved goods against an emergency, we might find there was some space we could use belowstairs. Will you ask Barrett to come to me, with his keys? And I would like you to come too, of course.'

Tench was looking doubtful. 'Ma'am, do you not think you should speak to Mr. Tremadoc first? Mr. Barrett's that particular about his cellars! Why, Jenkins offered to go down and fetch up a couple of bottles for him when he had that feverish cold t'other day, and you'd a' thought he'd asked for the keys to the Tower of London. And him being the only servant that come with the house does make him a mite difficult about things. Like not being here when you arrived. The idea! Luckily my Jenkins is not one to take offence, so we manage well enough in the room, but it ain't easy, ma'am, and I'd be lying to you if I let you think it was.'

'You should have told me, Tench.' Caroline herself had never liked Barrett, who she suspected of listening at doors. But Tremadoc had agreed to keep him on when he had come down for his induction and when she had protested at it as an absurd extravagance for people in their position, he had flown into one of his frightening fits of rage and she had let the matter drop. It was a poor kind of consolation that Barrett behaved more like a pensioner than a servant, leaving Jenkins to perform all the other duties that usually belonged to a butler, while he was content with his absolute control of the cellar.

'It's ridiculous,' she said now. 'We pay that man good

wages to do nothing!' She had been shocked to find just how
much Tremadoc had agreed to pay Barrett, and now, with the
cost of living rising all the time, to get rid of him seemed an
obvious economy. 'I'll speak to Mr. Tremadoc,' she decided.
'You're quite right, the order would come best from him.'

'If he'll give it,' said Tench.

Caroline decided to raise the subject in what she had learned
was her husband's happiest time of day, the glowing moment
when she had just read back the verses he had composed, or
thought he had composed. It was amazing how easily they had
slipped into what was, in fact, hardly a collaboration. Tremadoc
had planned his poem on a grand, classical scale, with the
powers of good and evil acting both as chorus and as the
impulses behind the Allied Powers and Bonaparte. She was
genuinely impressed with the magnitude of the scheme, and
now that Tremadoc hardly seemed to notice the liberties she
took with his actual verses, it seemed to her to be going remarkably well. The first canto, which would end when Bonaparte became First Consul, would soon be finished, and
Tremadoc planned to seek a publisher for it as it stood, and
then go on with his great work, publishing it a canto at a time.

'There.' She finished reading aloud the Spirit of Evil's hymn
of triumph. 'I do congratulate you, my dear.' She meant it.

'It does read well,' he said, preening himself. 'Even you
managed to make it sound quite thrilling. Indeed,' he added,
'you read well enough, for a woman.'

'Thank you.' She kept her voice neutral. He had gone to
the Wednesday dinner of the Oldchurch Club the day before,
and she was beginning to wonder just what went on there. He
always came back from the dinners in a strange mood, both
drunk and, she thought, frightened. He tended to talk wildly
about equality and liberty, about the mastery of man and the
wickedness of women. She had learned to expect a bad night
with him, but last night had been worse than usual. It had
almost seemed as if he felt he must hurt and humiliate her.

Rain lashed the windows in the gathering dusk. Her spine
prickled cold. Down at the foot of the hill, the Land and Water
Gates would be being locked and barred as the city fathers had
ordered at the height of the invasion panic. It was not pleasant
to think that there was no way out now, until morning, from
this close-packed hill town. From her husband whose moods
she found increasingly frightening. Did other women in Oldchurch feel like this? Mrs. Bowles? She remembered her, that

first day, saying something about women standing up for each other. 'If we don't no one else will.' But it was not the kind of thing one could ask about.

'Your wits are wandering again.' Tremadoc's impatient voice recalled her to the present, the over-warm little room, and the faint, bittersweet smell of his cordial. 'I said, "Have you heard from the Duke?"'

'Not yet.' At Tremadoc's insistence, she had written to her father explaining how very badly the Oldchurch tithes fell short of the promised £1,000. 'I do feel,' she said now, 'that it would have been better if you had let me write to Mr. Grant. It's not the kind of thing with which the Duke concerns himself.'

'Then it's time he learned to,' said Tremadoc. 'Trust a woman to make foolish objections. Oh, dammit, you've brought on one of my spasms with your foolish cavilling. Ring for Barrett. I need a new bottle of my cordial.'

She had promised herself that she would speak about Barrett. The moment was not propitious, but she set her teeth and went ahead. 'Before I do so, my dear, there is something I had been meaning to say to you about Barrett. Surely with tithes so low and living so high it is time we faced the facts and got rid of him. Really he does nothing, except keep the key to the cellars, and I think it more than time I went down and made an inspection there. If they run right under the house there must be space and to spare. It is just to springclean, and then, if the farmers want to pay their tithe in kind, we will have somewhere to store their offerings.'

He slapped her face. 'There, woman! And there, and there! Let that teach you never to speak to me like that again.' And then, horribly, before she could speak, burst into a helpless flood of tears. 'You don't understand anything,' he moaned at last. 'Send for Jenkins. I must get to bed. I'm not well; not well at all.'

It was obviously true. Shock and rage at the blow gave way to anxiety as she waited for Jenkins. And when she went up to their room a little later, she found Tremadoc lying in the big bed, propped high on pillows, deeply asleep but breathing shallow and with difficulty. When she felt his forehead, it was clammy to her touch, and he twitched away from her hand, muttering something in his sleep. She went downstairs and found Jenkins. 'You must go at once for Dr. Martin. Ask him to come as soon as he can.'

Barrett was hovering in the hall as he so often did. 'The

Reverend Mr. Vail always sent for Dr. Peabody from Win-
chelsea,' he said in his soft, apologetic voice. 'He is a member
of the Oldchurch Club. The gentlefolks here don't think much
of young Dr. Martin.'

'But the poor worship him,' said Caroline. 'And I've seen
his work in their cottages. Fetch him, please, Jenkins.' For a
moment, she was tempted to continue her challenge to Barrett
by telling him to show her the cellars, but this was not the
time.

Back in the bedroom, she found her husband thrashing about
in the bed, muttering to himself, his breathing harsher and
more difficult than ever. Suddenly he sat bolt upright. 'They're
coming!' he exclaimed. 'Save me! They're coming!'

'Hush.' She took his hand, and pushed him gently back
against the pillows. 'You're quite safe here with me. I won't
let anyone get at you.'

He was crying now. '*A la lanterne*,' he muttered, and
then, 'Spare me! I did as I was bid.'

He must be dreaming about the Terror in France, the black
time when the mob dragged aristocrats to their death with cries
of '*À la lanterne*.' To the nearest street lamp, which would
serve as a gallows. They must have been working too hard at
his poem, and she was ashamed to remember her own almost
feverish enthusiasm as they wrote the stanzas about the revolu-
tionary chaos out of which Bonaparte's bid for power had
sprung.

She stroked Tremadoc's damp forehead soothingly and
wished Dr. Martin would come. Oddly enough, though she
had encountered him by many a parishioner's sickbed, she had
never met the doctor socially. He was unmarried, of course,
but it still seemed strange that he appeared at none of the formal
parties to which she and her husband had been invited. But the
town gentry did not like him, Barrett had said, and Barrett
would know.

The front door bell jangled and she hurried downstairs to
greet the small, dark-haired doctor. 'Good of you to come so
quickly.' She led the way upstairs. 'I'm anxious about my
husband. I hope it is nothing but over-work and over-strain,
but his condition puzzles me. It is quite unlike anything I have
seen before. Well,' she ushered him into the bedroom and held
a candle for him close to the bed, 'you can see for yourself.'

'You'd not rather your housekeeper helped me?' He was
washing his hands in the porcelain handbasin. 'Most of the

ladies . . .' He gave her a wry smile as she handed him a towel. 'Not that I come to many houses like yours. I'm obliged to you, ma'am.' He seemed to have accepted that she would stay, and moved back to the bed, leaning down to listen to the harsh breathing, then rolling back Tremadoc's eyelid to look closely at the sleeping eye. 'How long has he been like this?'

'Three hours, something like that.'

'And before?'

'Nothing like this. Oh, he has bad dreams sometimes, wakes himself screaming and sweating—well, clammy as he is now. Not a fever; I don't rightly understand it.'

'In that case,' the doctor seemed to make up his mind, 'I think we can safely let him sleep it off. If I could have a word with you downstairs, ma'am?'

'Of course.' She led the way downstairs, aware of Tench, waiting to take her place by the sickbed, and Barrett, hovering as usual. Once in the morning room, with the door shut, she turned to face the doctor. 'You said sleep it off?' Here, where the light was better, she was shocked by the fatigue lines on his thin brown face.

He was looking at her with something disconcertingly like sympathy. 'You did not know that your husband was addicted to opium, Mrs. Tremadoc?' And then, moving quickly, 'Here, sit down. Shall I ring for your maid? I'm a brute to put it to you so sharply, but I thought you must have known.'

'Opium?' Her hands on the arms of her chair. 'Impossible!' And then, 'Fool that I am! His cordial . . . His mother smelt the same.' How strange to find herself saying it to this stranger.

'Laudanum,' said the doctor. 'Many ladies take it, for pain, for comfort, and, if they are not lucky, for life. Your husband is a most interesting man, ma'am. Those sermons of his are something quite out of the common run; they have even made a churchgoer out of me. We must put our heads together to see how we can save him. He has been over-working, you say. Well, that is understandable enough. The cares of a new parish, though,' delicately, 'I have not heard of him as a very active pastor, aside from his remarkable sermons. It is you I have had the pleasure of meeting in the cottages. But those sermons . . . And then, I have heard talk of a magnum opus being composed. An epic poem? Something of the kind?' An indescribable something in his tone suggested that he had some doubts about this.

'Yes,' she said shortly. 'He is writing a poem about the downfall of Bonaparte.'

'A patriotic theme.' Drily. 'It goes well?'

'He has just finished the first canto.' She had almost said we.

'And he was at the Oldchurch Club yesterday,' said the doctor, confirming her view that everyone in Oldchurch knew everything. 'That, too, might be something of a strain, for a stranger, coming new into the town. I am not, myself, a member. In fact—' He paused. 'No; gossip. Well, ma'am, I can only urge that you prevail on Mr. Tremadoc to take more care of himself and to give up that cordial of his. Keep him contented, keep him happy, as I am sure you know how to do, and I am sure it will be possible for him to wean himself from it gradually. I'll call tomorrow, to discuss it with him, but I shall rely on you, who can, I am sure, do more for him than anyone. You do not know, I suppose, what strength it is?'

'What strength?'

'Laudanum's a tincture, ma'am,' he explained. 'Opium dissolved in alcohol. It is a question of how many grains. I am afraid, judging by your husband's condition, he must have been steadily increasing the dose.'

'You sent for Dr. Martin!' She should have anticipated Tremadoc's reaction. 'That ill-bred son of a farrier! I'll not have him in my house again, and so Barrett shall tell him when he calls in the morning. Of all the panics over nothing! Of course I take laudanum; it's the only thing for this delicate stomach of mine. Anyone but an idiot female like you would have known it for what it was. I certainly make no secret of it.' He laughed in her anxious face. 'Anyone would think, to look at you, that I was taking poison.'

'Dr. Martin seemed to think that that was just what it was.'

'Fool of a man. Mind you, I am touched by your wifely anxiety; quite the devoted little woman are you not? Oh, well,' tolerantly, 'if it will allay your fears we might as well send for Dr. Peabody in the morning. He will tell you, I am sure, that there is no need for you to be nagging away at me about my medicine.'

'But Dr. Martin . . .'

'Can go away with a flea in his ear. Send me Barrett, and I'll give him my instructions. No'—he anticipated her protest—'you are not to see Martin. I'll not have him cross the threshold of my house.'

'But why?'

'None of your business.' He turned impatiently away from her. 'I'll have no more of your interfering. Go down and send me Barrett and tell that lazy cook of yours I want a neat little supper, up here, right away. You may share it with me, if you promise to behave yourself, and then come to bed and show me that you have remembered your place.'

It was another horrible night. She was not sure whether he was trying to convince himself, or her, that there was nothing the matter with him. 'I'll be master in my own house,' he said at last and fell into the deep sleep of exhaustion, leaving her to lie, hour after hour, rigid and wakeful at his side, feeling where he had hurt her and wondering how she could face the future.

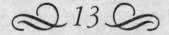

13

TREMADOC WAS NOT at all surprised when the first publisher they approached accepted *The Downfall of Bonaparte* with enthusiasm, 'I wish now I'd followed my first instinct and sent it to Murray,' he said. 'But this fellow Comfrey writes a civil enough letter. The £30 he offers will come in very handy since your father continues such a skinflint.'

'You do not think,' said Caroline hesitantly, deciding to ignore the reflection on the Duke, 'that it might be better to accept Mr. Comfrey's other offer, that we should share both the expenses and the profits? I really believe,' she hurried on before he could interrupt her, 'from the way he writes, that Mr. Comfrey is as confident of your poem's success as I am. Just think how maddening if it should become a popular success and you found yourself entitled to nothing beyond the first £30. Somebody told me [it had been Charles Mattingley] that Miss Burney sold her *Evelina* outright for £30 and never got another penny. Just think how much money the publisher must have made by it!'

'Oh?' Tremadoc thought about it. 'Yes, you might even have an idea there.' He picked up the letter and studied it again. 'He does seem very eager to know how I am getting on with the second canto . . . Yes.' He made up his mind. 'Write him for me—in your fairest hand, mind. Say I will share the risks and the profits, and tell him he shall have the second canto by Christmas.'

'So soon?' And then, aware of his darkening brow. 'I am afraid you will over-tire yourself, as you did in finishing the first canto.'

'Nonsense,' he said. 'I know you. You just grudge the time you spend taking down my immortal verse. I know you would rather be out on the gad about the town. And that reminds me of something. I will not have you gossiping with that upstart Martin. Yes, well may you blush ma'am. You forgot, did you not, that I have friends in Oldchurch who will let me know when my wife misbehaves herself. Taking his hand in public, whispering to him down by the quay! Well,' he sighed, 'like mother, like daughter, I suppose, and I should be grateful we live where there are eyes to see you.'

'Mr. Tremadoc!' She was on her feet, shaking with anger. 'That is enough. I do not know which of your drinking companions chose to tell you he had seen me talking with Dr. Martin, but it is perfectly true. And I shook him by the hand when I met him. I had been hoping to meet him ever since you had him turned from the door so rudely when you were ill, but I think he must have been avoiding me. If you really want to know, I was apologising to him on your behalf, and he was enquiring, most civilly, about your health. I was glad to be able to tell him that Dr. Peabody had persuaded you to cut down on your laudanum and that you were much better as a result. And now, if you will excuse me, I have your Sunday sermon to write, as well as this letter to Mr. Comfrey.'

It was a timely reminder. The sermons that she had pretended were by her father had run out just when their success had established him as a notable preacher. He had badgered her for days to write to Sophie in the hopes that she might have some more of Mr. Trentham's work, and in the end she had been reduced to telling him she had written the sermons herself. He had not believed her until she wrote him another one, for Harvest Festival, which reduced the congregation to patriotic tears, and then, of course, he had been angry, but in the end had forgiven her, saying that sermons were the kind of boring thing a woman might be good at. Since then, he had expected one a week, though he continued loud in his amazement at a mere woman's being able to do it. She sometimes wondered just what would happen if he should ever realise how much she contributed to *The Downfall of Bonaparte*.

She sat down tiredly to write to Mr. Comfrey. Tremadoc might not be suffering from over-work, but she most certainly was. The first batch of sermons had been easy enough. She had found herself brimful of ideas and been glad of the chance to express them, but now she felt herself drying up. Oldchurch was not a place that stimulated the mind. Week after week, she talked of housework with the servants and of the cost of living with the neighbours. It was only now, when she was exiled from it all for ever, that she recognised just how stimulating the life and talk at Cley and Chevenham House had been. Many of the ideas for the first set of sermons had come from remembered conversation; and it often amused her to sit, prim as a pin in her pew on a Sunday, and hear her husband unconsciously quote one of Charles Mattingley's more trenchant remarks.

If she had had access to a newspaper, it would have helped, but Tremadoc would not take one, pointing out that he could read them at Oldchurch's one coffee house. He could. She could not, and it was no use thinking he would remember and tell her what he had read. Worst of all, they had no books except her own small collection. She had drawn on the Duchess's £50 in order to subscribe to Oldchurch's small circulating library, and was sure of the latest novel or volume of sermons, but Mrs. Norman's little room behind the linen draper's in the High Street had no works of reference, no classical texts, none of the wealth of material that had been ready to her hand in the old Duke's library at Cley.

She finished the letter to Comfrey and began to look through her notes for Sunday's sermon. Monday was Guy Fawkes day, and a government edict had prohibited the lighting of bonfires for fear that they should be confused with the beacons that stood ready, all along the coast, to give warning of an enemy invasion. Surely there was something useful that could be said about this? There was a great deal of popular feeling, she knew, against this edict in Oldchurch where Guy Fawkes day seemed to be a very special occasion. She had seen signs of at least one illicit bonfire down on the quay below the garden where the new Martello Tower was being built. There was a quotation from *Kings* that would serve as a text: 'And after the earthquake a fire: but the Lord was not in the fire: and after the fire a still small voice.' Yes, that would do. She wrote away busily for half an hour or so, only stopping when Tremadoc looked in to ask impatiently if the letter to Comfrey was ready for his signature. 'I want it to catch today's post.'

'Yes, here it is.' She handed it over and he read it through, grunted approval and signed it. 'And this is the sermon?' He picked up the first sheet, looked it over idly then tore it across with an angry oath. 'Fool of a woman. Do you understand nothing? Guy Fawkes night is one of the great celebrations of the year, here in Oldchurch, and no government on earth is going to stop them from having their procession and their bonfires. And you expect me to preach against it!'

'I thought you might feel it a good opportunity,' she said mildly. 'From what I have heard from Mrs. Bowles and others of the women, it is a kind of saturnalia and often ends in violence and bloodshed. Surely, as a man of God, and a good citizen, it is your duty to speak out against it?'

'Duty be hanged, and I'll not have you preaching to me! Guy Fawkes night is a man's occasion, that's all. A little rough, perhaps, good honest high spirits and rugged Protestantism.'

'You mean the kind of Protestantism that led to the Gordon Riots?'

'Nonsense! The City Fathers of Oldchurch have everything well in hand, and no harm ever comes to anyone unless some idiotic woman ventures out and encounters the procession. I have been instructed to warn you that it is not a night for ladies to be abroad.'

'You do not mean that you will be joining the procession?' Who had 'instructed' him, she wondered.

'I shall be one of the leaders. Now, sit down and write me a sermon that will not make me ridiculous.'

To Caroline's regret, November the fifth dawned brilliantly fine. Jenkins had made her a flagged path down the garden, so that even when the grass was wet she could get down to the terrace by the low wall along the cliff edge and look out at the wide view of river, marsh and sea. Warmly dressed to go out shopping, she went down there first for a cold breath of morning air and saw that what had been merely the suggestion of a pile of sticks on the quay had developed overnight into a huge bonfire ready for the lighting. It seemed to her to be dangerously near to the foundations of the Martello Tower that grew so slowly. Parliament had urged the building of these defence towers almost a year before, but nothing seemed to go right with this one. Today, she could see the men who should have been busy on its walls idling on the quay with the other loungers who congregated round the Oldchurch Inn. She congratulated herself, as she had before, that the cliff was sheer to the river below their garden, with no means of access from the quay, which lay a little to the south.

It was too cold to stand. She went back through the house and down the steep hill to the High Street, which she found a scene of unusual activity. All along the street, shopkeepers were busy boarding up their windows. Visiting Mrs. Norman's little library to ask for the second volume of *Thaddeus of Warsaw*, she found that Mrs. Norman, too, had a man working at her small window.

'But you are not even on the High Street,' said Caroline. 'Is it really so bad as that?'

'I'm a woman in business, aren't I?' said Mrs. Norman. 'They don't like that. I shall spend the night with my good friend Mrs. Bowles, as I always do, just in case some rapscallion should decide to entertain himself by breaking my upstairs windows. I hope you've been warned to close your shutters tonight, Mrs. Tremadoc, and show no lights.'

'I can't believe it!'

'You will when you've heard them,' said Mrs. Norman.

Tremadoc had an extra glass of laudanum with his dinner and Caroline knew better than to protest. Soon afterwards, he put on his heavy greatcoat. 'Barrett will lock up after me,' he told her, 'and see to it that the shutters are closed along the front of the house. The procession forms up on the far side of the church and marches round the square before it starts through the town and so down to the quay. You will not watch it, ma'am.'

'I do not intend to,' she told him. 'I do not at all wish to see you involved in such a barbarous affair. Jenkins tells me that they actually burn the Pope in effigy, down on the quay. I should have thought if you were going to burn anyone, it would make more sense to burn Bonaparte.'

'You understand nothing of the matter. The Guy Fawkes day celebrations here are an ancient and honourable tradition, dating back to the end of the last century. The first bonfire was lit on the day Protestant William landed at Torbay. November the fifth, 1688.'

'Protestant William?'

'William the Third, gabey. The man who would not rule through his wife, nor yet be ruled by her. They had another special celebration, here in Oldchurch, the year she died and he ruled on alone.'

'I don't like it.'

'Nobody asked you to.' He pulled on his gloves. 'Barrett will wait up to let me in. I have told Jenkins that I shall not need him. I shall be very late. There is to be a select celebration at the Castle Inn after the festivities are over. No need for you to wait up for me, either.'

'I do not intend to,' she said.

By the time Barrett had closed the ground-floor shutters and retired to his snug little room off the hall, it was almost dark. Since she must not show a light on the square, Caroline retired to the small garden room she now used as a study. She had heard critical murmurs, in the High Street, about yesterday's dull sermon, knew they had been justified, and knew, too, that they were bound to get back to Tremadoc and very likely precipitate one of the rages that she found increasingly terrifying. But rack her brains as she would, she could not think of any words to put into his mouth, now, when she felt so totally out of sympathy with his ideas. Had she really hoped that being a clergyman would steady him, make him think? Well, she had her answer.

'Ma'am.' Tench was at the door, candle shaking in her hand. 'Ma'am, they're coming. You can hear them even from our windows. It's horrible, ma'am. Like animals.'

'I must see,' said Caroline. 'Come upstairs with me, Tench, to the guest bedchamber. Its windows look out over the square.'

'But the master said . . .'

'We'll leave the candle in the hall and shut the door. No one will see us, there in the dark. But don't come if you don't want to, Tench dear.'

'It's Jenkins, ma'am. He says he don't half like what he's heard at the Castle Inn. Back in London is where he want to be, and no two ways about it.'

'Oh, Tench, you wouldn't leave me?'

'No, ma'am. But I think I'd best not leave Jenkins tonight in case he gets too set in his ideas.'

'Very well.' She watched Tench go through the green-baize

door that cut off the servant's wing, then trod silently up the shallow stairs, candle in hand, grateful that Barrett had shut himself into his den, where she suspected, he kept a private supply of pipes and porter.

She put her candle down on the table in the upstairs hall and opened the heavy door of the guest room, then stopped dead, assaulted by a savage wave of sound. Feeling her way to the window she opened the shutter cautiously. The procession was just entering the square from the lane beside the church. Torchlight flared on masked faces as the leaders turned to their right, to go round the square widdershins, and she saw that as well as masks many of the torchbearers were wearing what looked like masquerade costumes. Some were merely enveloped in all-concealing dominos, but others appeared as red Indians, warpaint gleaming in the torchlight, or as animals, with masks resembling bears and wolves and foxes. Try as she would, she could not recognise Tremadoc among the leaders, but hoped he was in a domino rather than one of those sinister animal masks. At least, she comforted herself, if she could not recognise him by the fitful glare of the torches, no one else would be able to, either.

Now the insistent beat of a drum could be heard among the shouts and growls and war whoops with which the procession had entered the square. It was a ragged savage rhythm, a kind of undertone to violence, and she began to understand what Mrs. Norman had tried to tell her. Horrible to think of the women of the town, crouched in their houses, waiting while these beast-men passed their doors. The leaders had reached the house now, and a torch, lifted high, flared outside her window, making her shrink back in instinctive terror. The shouting grew to a savage roar as a cluster of torches appeared beside the church illuminating a seated figure, carried high on men's shoulders. The red robes told her that this was the effigy of the Pope that was to be burned presently, down on the quay, and now she saw, behind it, a huge placard, carried between two men, reading, 'No Popery.'

The procession stretched all round the square now, and still more torch-carrying figures were pouring in from the entrance by the church. Most of these were not in costume, but they all wore rough masks and slouch hats pulled well down on their heads. If any violence should be done tonight, it would be hard to find witnesses to it.

The leading torches moved, flaring and flickering, into the

graveyard that lay to the church's left and she shuddered at the thought of these barbarian, these pagan, figures trampling over the graves of their own dead. The drum was nearer, almost under her window, and she felt its barbaric rhythm stirring her blood, and was ashamed of herself, and afraid.

She sat down on a high chair by the window and watched as the last of the procession straggled round the square. She caught the gleam of bottles, passing from hand to hand, and understood why the shouting was becoming increasingly strident. It would be a miracle if no blood were shed before the night was over. And on the thought, she heard one shrill, desperate scream, mingling with the roar of the crowd, followed by a lull in the shouting, against which the second scream sounded loud, and clear, and blood-stopping. And, from the crowd, a growl of satisfaction.

A woman's voice? Her hands writhed in her lap. Nothing she could do, but she could not bear to listen. She picked up her candle and tiptoed silently back down the stairs. In the garden room, she tried to make herself concentrate on next Sunday's sermon. There must be some words she could put into Tremadoc's mouth that would suggest the horror of to-night's doings. Half an hour later, she looked at her series of false starts and admitted defeat. Tremadoc might be stupid, but he was quick enough where his own interests were concerned. Her best hope must be that the doings of the night would have horrified him as much as they had her. Perhaps, in the morning, they would be able to discuss it and he would agree that some-thing must be said next Sunday.

Now she thought she heard shouting from below the cliff. On an impulse, she put on a heavy cloak and opened the door that led into the garden. The night was cloudy, but not totally dark. She put the tinderbox ready and blew out the candle. Once her eyes had got used to the darkness, she would be able to find her way down the familiar path to the terrace wall. There was a glow of light in the direction of the quay. The mob must be down there already. Yes, as she picked her way carefully along the flagstones, she could hear the beat of the drum, the hoarse half-human shouting. She paused, longing to hurry back to the house, get into her bed, pull the covers over her ears.

Her husband was parson of the parish where this orgy was taking place. If she was to persuade him to speak out against it, she must see it through to the end. She set her teeth, and, surprisingly, found herself thinking of Blakeney, something she tried hard not to do. We are the children of a Duke, she thought. There are duties as well as privileges. And then, bitterly: what privileges? But her cloak was warm around her. She had given alms to a starving beggar woman in the High Street that morning, blessing the Duchess for the £50 that made such things possible.

I wish I was the Duchess's daughter, she thought, and moved quietly forward to lean her arms on the wall and look down. The quay was bright as day, with flambeaux fixed at intervals along it. The bonfire had only recently been lit and was just beginning to flare up. The crowd of men must have doused their torches, for they stood, a black mass, just outside the Water Gate, with the bonfire between them and the dark, irregular shape of the Martello Tower. The shouting had died down, and someone was speaking, or, perhaps, reciting. She could catch the sense of rhythm, like that of the drum, but not the words. As the speaker finished, the effigy of the Pope was brought forward and tossed on to the now raging fire. It went up with the flash and crash of an explosion, scattering the screaming crowd in all directions. Stunned for a moment, when she looked again, flames were licking around the scaffolding of the Martello Tower.

Another, closer sound made her look quickly down over the wall to the cliff below. Something was happening there. Impossible. A light glowed for a moment, showing a dark shape, apparently emerging from the cliff. A face gleamed white in the darkness, then the figure began to move slowly away, down the sheer face of the cliff. On a rope? On a rope ladder? Impossible to tell, but there could be no doubt that the figure had emerged from under where she stood. From an extension of their cellar. The cellar she had never been allowed to enter.

She watched, spellbound, as the figure disappeared slowly into the darkness below, which was made more absolute by the nearby flare of the bonfire on the quay, and the flames that were now mounting high from the Martello Tower.

Straining her eyes, she leaned forward to peer down to where the river lapped at the foot of the cliff, its water catching a glimmer of reflected light from the bonfire. Yes, there was the dark suggestion of a small boat and she either imagined or heard the soft plash of oars. Whoever had climbed down the cliff would be safe away and down to the sea before the fire burned out.

'Well,' said a man's voice out of the darkness. 'And what are you going to do about it?'

Who? Where? Her heart thudding, she peered about her in the darkness. It was not Barrett's voice, thank God, though for a moment it had seemed familiar. A Londoner's, of course, but she knew no one with such a deep bass. 'Who is it?' Her voice shook.

'Here.' A flicker of light to her right, where the dividing wall ran down between her garden and that of the recluse next door. She had never seen him. She must be seeing him now, looking round the end of the wall at her, illuminated by a dark lantern, its shutter swiftly opened and closed to let her see the white wig, the eyes bright above a grizzled forest of beard. 'Don't be afraid,' he said, invisible again, the lantern shuttered. 'Come a little nearer. We must talk, you and I.' And then, a reassuring hint of laughter in his voice. 'May I introduce myself? Your neighbour, John Gerard, and very much at your service. I have been wanting a chance to make myself known to you, and hope you will forgive me for frightening you just now.'

'What's one more fright on a night like this? But ought we not to be doing something about the man who went down the cliff? A smuggler, I suppose.'

'Report him to the authorities, you mean? My dear madam, surely you have lived in Oldchurch long enough to know that the authorities would be on his side. That is precisely why I made myself known to you. I was afraid you might feel it your duty to do something precipitate. Leave it to me to report the incident, and, Mrs. Tremadoc, I do urge you to show as little as possible of what I know you must feel about tonight's doings. If you had been planning to try to get your husband to preach against them, I beg you to think again. You will only endanger yourself and achieve nothing. I am afraid he is deeply involved already.'

'But what am I to do?'

'Get him away from here. Oldchurch is a dangerous town. Think of an excuse, persuade your father to find your husband another living.'

'He wouldn't do it,' she said. And then, a little bitterly, 'You know all about me, I can see.'

'Everybody knows all about everything here in Oldchurch.

Even a recluse such as I am has servants to be his ears. From what I have heard, I have felt anxious about you, and am ashamed to have been so slow in getting in touch, but it is difficult to break out of a character so well established as mine is as a recluse. Now, I think, we should put our heads together and contrive how we can meet from time to time. One idea did occur to me. My spies have told me what a regular patron you are of Mrs. Norman's inadequate little library. Might you not learn about mine and make a formal request to use it?'

'Oh, *yes!*' she exclaimed. 'But how would I find out about it?'

'Ask Mrs. Norman if there is not someone in town with a collection of books. It is odd enough to be generally known. And now it is high time you got back indoors.' They both looked down to where the bonfire had smouldered into a huge glowing pile and a rather lethargic chain of men were throwing buckets of water on to what remained of the scaffolding of the Martello Tower. 'I do trust no one knows you are here,' he said.

'No. Barrett is shut up in his front room. I take it you know about Barrett.'

'Enough to tell you to beware of him. Get yourself indoors and to bed without showing a light, Mrs. Tremadoc, and remember you know nothing about the explosion that set light to the tower. And I shall look forward to receiving your request to be allowed to use my library, though I warn you I shall cut up pretty rough before I allow it.'

'Oh, thank you,' she said. 'I feel . . . I feel safer for having met you.'

'Don't feel too safe, Mrs. Tremadoc.'

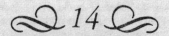

14

TREMADOC KEPT TO his bed next morning and Caroline thought him a badly frightened man. If it had not been for John Gerard's advice, she would have been tempted to seize the chance to try to persuade him to cut his connection with what seemed to be no better than a gang of smugglers, but in her heart she knew it would have been useless.

Instead, she put on cloak and bonnet, picked up the volume of *Thaddeus of Warsaw* that she had not even opened, and told Barrett that she was going out shopping. 'I take it the town will be quiet this morning?'

'Yes, madam, and tidy too. The bonfire boys are good citizens and always see to it that there is no unpleasantness after their night out. I trust you were not disturbed by the procession.' He gave her a sharp glance from watery eyes. 'You look a trifle fatigued this morning, if I may make bold to say so.'

'Well,' she picked up her basket. 'It was quite noisy, even at the back of the house.'

The square lay quiet in pale November sunshine. Barrett was right, aside from some trampled grass, there was no evidence of last night's riotous procession. It could all have been a dream—a nightmare. But the High Street, when she got to it, seemed unusually quiet this morning. She had planned this outing carefully, and began by a visit to the stationer's where she bought a quire of foolscap paper. 'My husband uses so much when he writes a sermon,' she explained, but the clerk was hardly listening. She had interrupted a whispered conversation at the back of the shop and thought he was eager to return to it.

She paused at the fishmonger's to ask if they had any fresh fish, and was met by a glum refusal. 'They don't go out on Guy Fawkes, ma'am. His Reverence will have to wait till tomorrow for his sand dabs.' Something a little shifty about the straight way he met her eyes as he said it?

She turned down the lane that led to Mrs. Norman's little shop and stopped, horrified. Mrs. Norman's precautions had not been enough. The door of the shop had been broken open and the interior looked as if it had been hit by a hurricane, with books and ravaged pieces of books lying everywhere. Mrs. Norman herself was standing in the middle of the chaos, wringing her hands. 'It's the end,' she said, over and over again on the same note. 'It's the end.'

'I am so very sorry.' Caroline put down her basket and took both the distracted woman's hands. 'You should not be here. Upstairs. Is it all right?'

'They looked there,' said Mrs. Norman dully. 'A little damage. Nothing to signify.'

'Then come upstairs,' said Caroline. 'You should be resting. Let me get you something to calm you. Sal volatile perhaps?' So much for Barrett's boast that the bonfire boys left all tidy behind them. 'I am sure my husband will be able to arrange to have things down here made straight for you.' She urged Mrs. Norman gently up the steep stair.

'But my stock. There's no replacing my stock! I shall be made bankrupt, Mrs. Tremadoc. I shall have to go on the parish.' She let Caroline push her down on to her stiff little sofa. 'I would rather die. I wish they had killed *me*!'

'What do you mean?' Caroline was startled by her emphasis on the last word.

'You did not know?' Mrs. Norman's face livened up a little at this chance to impart information. 'A poor girl from the back slums by the Water Gate went out last night, to look for Dr. Martin. Her child had the croup; she thought she could avoid the procession. She was unlucky.' She fell silent, staring into the smouldering fire.

'What happened?' Caroline remembered the screams she had heard.

'She was cutting through the back lanes; one of those beasts caught a glimpse of her. Then it was view halloo and tally ho. They chased her clear down the High Street, screaming, knocking on doors, asking people to open to her. She came here, thinking I might help, not knowing I always go to Mrs. Bowles. When she found the house shut up, she ran off down the Green Lane to the river. Water Gate's open, of course, Guy Fawkes night. She must have nearly got away; they spent some time here, as you can see, looking for her. But some of them caught her just the same. When they had finished with her, she jumped into the river. She's dead, Mrs. Tremadoc, drowned dead.'

'No!' She poured herself a glass of the sal volatile with a shaking hand.

'It will be hushed up, of course,' said Mrs. Norman. 'Given out as plain suicide. It's happened before.' She reached out a hand and took Caroline's. 'Don't mind it too much, my dear, it's the way things are here at Oldchurch, and at least it was the tag end of the procession. Mr. Tremadoc could have done nothing about it.'

'Thank you,' Caroline said mechanically. So much for her hope that her husband's presence in the procession might not

be known. It reminded her of the purpose of her visit. More
than ever, now, she felt the need to keep in touch with John
Gerard, who seemed the only sane person in this town of
madmen. 'What will you do?' she asked. 'About the library?'

'There's nothing I can do. It took all the little capital I
inherited from my husband. It means the workhouse; I'd rather
die.'

'No!' exclaimed Caroline. 'I won't have it. It's their doing,
those beasts last night. There's nothing they can do for that
poor girl, but at least they can make amends to you. I shall
take up a subscription for you, if you will let me, from all the
citizens of the town. After all, the library is a public service;
everybody uses it. Will you allow me to do this for you?'

'Oh, Mrs. Tremadoc . . . But do you dare? Will your husband let you do it?'

'I think he will be glad to let me. And I hope I can persuade
him to send his man Jenkins to help you with the clearing up
downstairs. I would urge you to go back to Mrs. Bowles in
the meanwhile, but I imagine you would prefer to stay here.'

'Yes,' said Mrs. Norman. 'There are men in this town who
do not much like the library. They think their wives waste
working time in reading. If they got the chance they might like
to finish what was begun last night.'

'And you'll stay to stop them? You're a brave woman, Mrs.
Norman.'

'It's my livelihood.'

Caroline went straight home and found Tremadoc still in
bed. 'I have been down to the town,' she told him.

'Oh have you?' His pitiful attempt at a casual note told her
that he knew what had happened the night before.

'Yes. I went to the library—what's left of it. Mrs. Norman
told me what happened last night. I suppose you heard all about
it at your "select gathering".'

'We broke up early,' he said. 'A most unfortunate accident.
I suppose the poor girl was frightened by the masks and slipped
and fell in the river. She should have known better than to be
out.'

'You really believe it was an accident?' But she could see
that he was trying to. 'We will have to discuss, when you are
feeling better, just what you are going to say in church on
Sunday, but for the moment I have two requests to make of
you. I would like to send Jenkins down to set things to rights

in Mrs. Norman's shop, and I intend to take up a subscription through the town to replace her stock of books.'

'You intend?' His head moved angrily against the pillow. 'Without so much as consulting me!'

'I am consulting you. And I think, if you pause to consider, you will see that it can do nothing but good. Word of what happened here last night is bound to get out. If you, as vicar of the parish, are seen to be taking the proper steps, it may lessen the talk. And I am sure if we take a lead, others will follow. You will want, I know, to find out what is happening to that poor girl's child and make sure it is provided for.'

'It's a bastard,' he said.

'That hardly diminishes my sympathy for it. Will you make the enquiries about it, or shall I?'

'Bowles said he would.' Angrily. 'You think you are the only one who can think of anything.'

'That's admirable. My plan is to go straight to Mrs. Bowles and propose the subscription to her. Now I know she will help me.'

'Women's work.' He turned away from her. 'Gossip and chatter and reading trashy books. I'm exhausted. Let me rest!'

Mrs. Bowles agreed enthusiastically to Caroline's proposal. 'My husband is a very unhappy man this morning, Mrs. Tremadoc, and I have no doubt yours is too. Oh, they give it out that that poor girl slipped and fell, but you and I know better. Mr. Bowles has already made arrangements for the child to be looked after, and I am positive he will agree to your plan. You intend to canvass for the subscriptions yourself?'

'Yes, indeed. I thought, if you agree, that I might call at the houses in the square, and then if you and your friends were to share out the rest of the town between you? You know better than I who should do each district.'

'I certainly should.' Mrs. Bowles, who had looked sick and wretched when Caroline arrived, was cheering up by the minute. 'We will all be the better for something to do. I'll put on my bonnet and call on Mrs. Price and Mrs. Trumpler right away. Leave all to me, my dear.'

'I shall start work on my way home,' said Caroline. 'By the way, tell me about the strange man who lives next door to us. I am sure he must be able to afford a subscription with a big house like that and all those servants.'

'If you dare call on him,' said Mrs. Bowles. 'The old curmudgeon. He sent Mr. Bowles away with a flea in his ear when he called, but maybe he will be less uncivil to a Duke's daughter. If you think it proper? You do not think perhaps your husband?' Her doubtful tone told Caroline that she too knew perfectly well that Tremadoc had joined in the procession the night before.

'Mr. Tremadoc is not well today,' said Caroline. 'I shall go myself. I look on it as my duty.'

'I'm proud of you, my dear.' Mrs. Bowles surprised Caroline with a hearty kiss. 'We all are. And glad to have you for our vicar's wife. Blood will out, that's what I said to Mrs. Price and Mrs. Trumpler just the other day and it's true, my dear, and I hope the Duke is as proud of you as we are.'

Caroline smiled ruefully. 'I am afraid he is still not best pleased about my marriage.'

'Well,' Mrs. Bowles began. And then, 'No, my dear, I can see you don't want me to say it, but we all think you're worth ten of him. A belted earl would not be good enough for you!'

'I wonder why earls are belted,' said Caroline and rose to take her leave.

She began her canvassing on her way home, starting anti-clockwise around the square as the procession had done. All the ladies in the square had called on her when she first arrived, and all of them welcomed her eagerly. Most subscribed at once, but one or two said they must consult their husbands. None of them talked much about the events of the night before and Caroline thought sadly that all their husbands must have taken part. Were they secretly wondering whether their own men might have been concerned in the poor girl's death? Thinking this, she realised what a debt of gratitude she owed to Mrs. Norman for her assurance that it had been the hangers-on at the end of the procession who had been responsible.

Reaching John Gerard's house at last, she pulled firmly at the rusty bell. The door was opened after some delay by a surprised-looking servant, whose jaw dropped when she stepped firmly inside and asked to see his master. 'It's about a subscription for Mrs. Norman,' she explained for the man's benefit. All the servants of Oldchurch are cousins, she remembered.

The man returned almost at once, looking more surprised than ever. 'The master asks if you will be so good as to join him in the library.'

It was a huge room, lined entirely with books. A man sat hunched up at a big desk with its back to the long windows. As he rose awkwardly to his feet she saw that one shoulder was higher than the other. He was older, too, than his voice had made him seem the night before, a tall man in an old-fashioned snuff-coloured suit and a full-bottomed wig. Dark eyes peered sharply at her from the forest of grizzled whiskers, but his voice was friendly as he greeted her. 'Clever of you to think of the subscription for Mrs. Norman,' he said, when the door had closed softly behind his servant. 'I am very glad indeed to have the chance of seeing you again so soon, and was at my wits' end as to how to arrange it. I wish I could persuade you and your husband to move away from Oldchurch, Mrs. Tremadoc.'

'I only wish we could. But I am afraid there is no chance of it, at least for the moment.' Sometimes, wildly building castles in the air, she dreamed of an instant, stunning success for *The Downfall of Bonaparte* that would make it possible for Tremadoc to quit the Church. But the poem would not even be published until the spring.

'You do not think that if the Duchess were to speak to the Duke?' he asked. And then, 'Forgive me, but the talk has been wide enough.'

'It has indeed,' she said wryly. 'I think when I arrived the good ladies of Oldchurch expected a scarlet woman at the least of it.'

'You lost no time in making a conquest of them. But it's your husband I am anxious about. He is such a strange mixture, by what I hear. Not two ideas to rub together in conversation, and then those brilliant sermons, which cut quite close to the bone, here in Oldchurch. If you have any influence on him, Mrs. Tremadoc, I think you should try to persuade him to tread a careful path for a while. Last night's disaster is bound to be reported in the national press and it would be unfortunate if any trenchant comments of your husband's should also receive general attention.'

'I don't understand.' She had had another dream about writing Tremadoc a sermon so powerful that it would gain him promotion.

'Of course you do not. That is precisely why I am delighted to have so early a chance to explain to you just how things stand here in Oldchurch. There is a very powerful gang indeed at work here and one against which it has been impossible to get evidence that would stand up in court. As you must have realised, they have a stranglehold on the town. Those who are not actually members have been frightened into cooperation.

It is like the Hawkhurst gang, years ago, only worse, much worse. That was no accident last night. Someone persuaded that poor girl that she could get safely up to the doctor's house. She must have known something that made her a danger to them. I wish to God I knew what. Let her fate be a warning to you. I do devoutly hope you got back into your house without Barrett's being aware that you had been out.'

'Yes. He's a member, of course.'

'A powerful one. I have long suspected that there was a means of access by way of your cellars to the cliff, but last night was the first time I had seen it used. The man got clear away, I am afraid. I had hoped he might be stopped by the preventive cutter down at the harbour, but they were called away on a fool's errand over to Hastings. It's a formidable gang, I do beg you always to remember that.'

'Horrible,' she said. 'Just for profit!' She looked down at her hands, folded in her lap. 'I feel . . . dirty. I suppose everything one buys, here in Oldchurch, is run goods.'

'I imagine so. Best not to think about it too much. The less you know, the safer you will be. I have wondered, a little, about those London servants of yours, the couple who have married without your husband's knowledge.'

'You are well informed, Mr. Gerard.'

'Forgive me! Don't you see, this is just what I am trying to tell you. There are no secrets here in Oldchurch, except from you women and from your husband.'

'And Dr. Martin?'

'Clever of you. I think he must have decided that the duty of healing comes first. He makes a policy of seeing nothing and saying nothing, and so far it has been respected. Lucky for him that poor girl did not get to him last night or he might have met with an "accident" too. And now'—his voice was friendly and she suspected a smile behind the forest of beard—'I have seen your eyes wandering to my books. Having become publicly acquainted over the very generous subscription I am about to give you for Mrs. Norman, you are going, are you not, to ask my permission to make use of my library? And, much to everyone's surprise, I am going to give it. Why, I wonder? Have I, perhaps, fallen a little in love with you, in my dotage? I might well have, and, indeed, we might let out just a hint of that, but, in the main, if you will bear with me, I think I must be thought to be attempting to curry favour with your powerful papa.'

'That will not make the world think you very well informed.'

'Just so. I am a simple creature, remember, a nonentity who retired down here after a moderately successful career in the law, and a disastrous marriage.'

'Then why would you want to curry favour with the Duke?'

'Why indeed?' Again the hint of a smile in his voice. 'You'll be an ally in a million, I can see. But, in fact, I have an answer to that one. It is for my nephew's sake, a young lawyer, who hopes for preferment through the Duke's good offices.' He reached down to open a drawer of his desk. 'And now for my lavish subscription. £20, I think. I shall look forward to your next visit, Mrs. Tremadoc.'

'Use the old lunatic's library?' Tremadoc had whistled at the size of Gerard's contribution. 'You used your charms to some purpose, I can see. Well, I see no harm in it. I can't have you turning out any more disasters like last Sunday's sermon. I had a call from old Bowles, by the way. He is pleased with your idea of the subscription for that Mrs. Norman. I suppose I had better contribute something myself.' He felt in his pocket and reluctantly produced a guinea.

'I shall give something too.' She had been forced, in the end, to tell him about the Duchess's allowance, and was always afraid he would appropriate it. 'Five guineas between us, perhaps?'

'If you want to throw your money away! And that reminds me, it's high time you wrote to your father again. So far as I can reckon, this living brings in little more than £600 a year. How is a man to live on that? No wonder if the County have not come calling, when they must know we cannot afford even to keep a carriage and return their calls. And no hope of a curate, either, though, thank God, we seem to brush along well enough without one.'

She smiled at him a little wryly. 'Have you any suggestions for next Sunday's sermon, my dear?'

'Only that the less you hint about last night's doings the better. Mr. Bowles had a word to say about that, too. The girl was Chapel, luckily, and not even from this parish. They have sent her body—and her bastard—back where she came from, and that's an end to that.'

Shockingly, it was. The events of that Guy Fawkes night were shrouded in a conspiracy of silence. If there was any mention of the girl's death in the national press, Caroline never heard of it. The only visible result was the burnt Martello Tower, and the bright new shop the men of the town were decorating for Mrs. Norman, which she was soon able to fill again with books from the generously subscribed collection. And for Caroline, her weekly visits to Mr. Gerard's library. To her relief, he had tactfully suggested a time when he would not be using it himself, so that she was free to pursue her researches alike for the poem and the sermons without his noticing what she was doing. When she was ready to leave, with a borrowed book under her arm, she would be summoned to the front parlour, where he awaited her with madeira and biscuits.

The conversations that followed were as helpful for her sermon writing as the library itself. His was a strong and well-stocked mind and she soon recognised that he was as starved for conversation as she was herself. It seemed to her extraordinary that he should stay in this dead little town beside the marsh when the world was presumably his to choose from. He was a Whig, too, totally out of place in such a Tory stronghold, and it was an enormous comfort to her to be able to talk freely about politics and the progress of the war again, to question him about the newspapers she was now able to read in his library. Her only fear was that he might recognise his own influence on Tremadoc's sermons, but this was unlikely as he only went to church very occasionally.

He appeared on Christmas Day, very upright in a front pew, and she was glad she had based the sermon on her memory of one that Mr. Trentham had preached the last year she was in Wales. She had cried as she wrote it, and remembered him, and Giles, whom she had loved in her childish way. What had become of Giles, she wondered, and almost wrote to Sophie in the hopes of learning something. But it was all too far away, too long ago.

Chevenham House, too, was remote as a dream. She did not even know if the family had spent their Christmas there or at Cley. Mr. Coutts had sent her a banker's draft for £10, 'With the compliments of the Duchess of Cley,' but there had been no word from either the Duchess or her mother. The Duke's ban on communication with her must still be in force, she thought, and tried not to hate him for it. Only Blakeney must have defied him. Her one Christmas parcel was a beautifully bound volume of Cowper's *Poems* inscribed from her loving brother, Blakeney. Writing to thank him was the most difficult thing she did that winter and gave rise to a new batch of sonnets.

It was a rough winter on the windy marsh, with little fear of invasion and the Martello Tower still growing at its snail's-pace. The town walls, on the other hand, had been completely repaired and the gates strengthened, and sometimes, lying in bed and listening to the wind howling round the windows, Caroline was almost glad to remember that somewhere, down in the cellars where she had never been allowed to penetrate, there was an escape route to the world outside.

February came with floods lying silver across the marshes, and the proofs of *The Downfall of Bonaparte* by special messenger from London. They were accompanied by an enthusiastic letter from Mr. Comfrey, who urged their speedy return, since he wished to publish as soon as possible. 'I hope you can arrange to return them to me by hand,' he concluded his letter.

Tremadoc brightened up at this. 'An excellent notion. I shall take them myself and so get a look at the kind of house the old man runs. And perhaps have a word with the man Grant at the same time, since your father does not choose to answer any of your letters. A fine take-in you were! My mother will be shocked when she hears how I have been treated.'

'You will stay with her?'

'I expect so.' Carelessly. 'A few days. I wonder.' A new thought struck him. 'A week perhaps? Tom Bowles was telling me just the other day of a young man over Hastings way who is prepared to do one's Sunday duty for a consideration. You'd like a week off your sermon writing, I expect.'

'I would indeed.' She put a tired hand to her brow and turned another sheet of the galleys. They were well into the third canto of the poem now and she was finding the cumulative strain of writing and her inevitable domestic and parish duties almost more than she could bear. Tench was a tower of strength, but she was the mistress and must take the lead and make the decisions. And then there were the duties to the old and sick of the parish, whom her husband neglected so shamefully. She had had to cry off an engagement to tea with Mrs. Bowles only the day before on grounds of sheer fatigue and had received a scolding from her husband in consequence.

'We can't afford your fine lady airs here,' he had told her. 'Bowles was offended, and told me so.'

'Mrs. Bowles was not.'

'What's that to say to anything?'

In the end, Tremadoc stayed two weeks in town and Caroline was appalled at the difference his absence made to her life. March was going out like a lamb and the garden full of unexpected pleasures. The snowdrops and crocuses that had come up in the flowerbeds she and Jenkins had cleared had given way to daffodils embroidered about the lawn, and a tree that leaned over the wall at the end had frothed into white cherry blossom. A sheltered bench under it commanded a wide view of marsh and sea and when the sun shone she could sit there in the middle of the day, hemming the sheets they needed so badly and planning the next canto of *The Downfall of Bonaparte*. It was a pity, she thought wryly, watching brown sails curving down the invisible river to the sea, that Napoleon showed so little sign of downfall. Planning his poem, Tremadoc had assumed that victory was near and would have happened by the time he brought the story of his villain/hero up to the present. But here they were, actually dealing with the events of the previous year, and victory seemed as far off, as unlikely as ever. They had discussed this problem before Tremadoc left for London, Caroline pointing out that Mr. Comfrey was bound to want to know his plans for the rest of the poem. 'We need a hero, on the side of the right,' she had suggested. 'Do you think, perhaps, Lord Nelson?'

'Not precisely my idea of a hero,' Tremadoc had objected. 'How would I manage about Lady Hamilton? He flaunts his passion for her more flagrantly every day, and there is even talk that she may have had a child by him. You may think an illegitimate child a great argument for heroism, but I cannot agree with you.'

She had hated him for the hint at her own birth, but been compelled to agree with his argument. Now, as the brown sails glided out to the open sea, she chewed her pencil and cast about for an alternative hero. A year ago, Pitt would have been the obvious choice, but his second administration had been dogged by scandal and disaster and his popularity was waning. Fox, too, was out of the question, an impossibly unromantic figure. The old King was tottering on the edge of insanity, and not even Tremadoc's habitual sycophancy could accept the bloated Prince of Wales for his hero. It's not an age of heroes, she thought sadly. Thinking this, she found her mind turn, as it still would, to Blakeney; felt a sonnet form itself almost complete in her head and wrote it down below her random jottings for the next canto.

Tremadoc returned the next day, exhausted from what had obviously been a steady round of dissipation. She thought he looked far from well and made no objection when he inisisted on going straight to bed without answering any of the questions that burned in her mind. Wise by experience, she did not ask them and it was only gradually that she learned about his trip. His mother had been shocked by what he had told her about their life, and disgusted to learn that there was as yet no sign that she was to have the grandchild and heir that she longed for. 'Her new house is well enough, but small. Crammed with furniture, of course.'

'I imagine so,' said Caroline drily. Mrs. Tremadoc had taken the lion's share of the furnishings of the old house. 'What did you think of Mr. Comfrey?' she ventured.

He laughed. 'What a take-in. I thought him a venerable old wiseacre and he's quite a young man. I just hope he knows his business, but he is quite properly appreciative of my poem. The second canto is to come out in the autumn, and the third, he thinks, in the spring, though he may bring it forward to Christmas if the first has the success he hopes for. He asked me when he could hope for more and I told him that if the muse was propitious the fourth canto should be completed some time this summer. We talked a little about my problem over the heroic figure and he was most sympathetic. He thinks nothing of your suggestion of Lord Nelson, by the way. A vain little man, he thinks him, for all his victories, and quite besotted with Lady Hamilton. Oh, I called on your mamma, by the way.' The connection was painfully obvious. 'She is much better, you will be glad to hear, looking quite the thing again. I told her how we were having to pinch and scrape down here and she promised to speak to the Duke on our behalf. He is as much her slave as ever, I am glad to say. Well, and no wonder! You should see the poor Duchess. Quite bloated and all her lovers vanished. When I saw her I quite understood why Mattingley suddenly plunged into the diplomatic service and showed a clean pair of heels to Moscow or Petersburg or wherever. He's sadly missed in the clubs. And so am I! You should just have seen the welcome I got at Watier's and the night we made of it. They hung on my words, I can tell you, when I told them about life in Oldchurch.'

'I hope you didn't tell them too much.'

'Too much! What a ridiculous notion.' But she thought he looked suddenly frightened. 'I've another piece of news for you.' He hurried to change the subject. 'What do you think of Amelia's being married before Charlotte? And you'll never guess to whom?'

'No? I don't suppose I will.' She must not ask for news of Blakeney.

He laughed. 'To ffether, of all people. There's one in the eye for Charlotte. I never did like that girl. Too high in the instep by a half. The Duke's little story about you and Gaston don't seem to have taken so well with the town as he hoped.'

'Is there any news of Gaston?'

'Not a word. Sunk without a trace. Do you think he's gone to France to look for his aristocratic connections?' He laughed coarsely. 'Aristocratic garbage, poor Gaston.' One of his quick, sharp looks. 'Dying to ask about Blakeney, ain't you? Your beloved brother. Well, I'm a good husband, I'll tell you. Had an almighty row with his father, by all reports, and has gone off to sulk and raise a regiment of militia at Cley. Quite the patriotic little nobleman. He'd have been in the regular army if his mother would let him, but he still listens to her.'

'You are well informed,' she said.

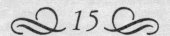

15

*T*HE *DOWNFALL OF BONAPARTE* came out at the end of April and was an instant and overwhelming success. Its publication almost coincided with the news that the French Admiral Villeneuve had eluded Nelson in the Mediterranean and slipped through the Straits of Gibraltar to join the Spanish fleet at Cadiz and vanish westwards. In London, fears for the British West Indies brought criticism of Nelson, who was accused of overprotecting his friends at the Court of Naples and thus allowing Villeneuve to escape.

It was just the moment for a rousingly patriotic poem that practically identified Napoleon with the powers of darkness.

'Your verses are on every lip,' wrote Comfrey enthusiastically from London, 'and copies walk out of the shops as soon as I can get them there. I am setting a reprint in train at once. May I venture one suggestion?' he went on in his elegant copperplate. "If your third canto is not yet finished, it might be well to think very hard how you are to treat Lord Nelson. If he fails to make good his initial error, this could be the end of his career. I do not need to emphasise to you, who live on the invasion coast, how appallingly Villeneuve's escape imperils this country as well as the West Indies.'

'That's all very fine,' said Caroline when Tremadoc's first exuberance had yielded to a more rational mood and they could discuss Comfrey's suggestion. 'But suppose you take Mr. Comfrey's advice and belittle Nelson, and then the canto comes out just when he has achieved one of his surprise victories? Can you imagine anything more disastrous?'

'There is something in what you say. I shall have to consult my muse. Ring for Barrett, I think this calls for celebration. Lord, what a blessing that I was wise enough to insist on a share of the profits, instead of meekly accepting the miserable £30 Comfrey offered. I should have been finely taken in if I had followed your advice.'

She knew him too well to think of pointing out that in fact their positions had been exactly the opposite, with him eager to take the cash. It was her day to work in John Gerard's library and she made her excuses and left her husband downing his second glass of laudanum and trying to work out how much he would make from the poem.

Unusually, Gerard was waiting for her in his library. 'I must congratulate you on the success of your husband's poem,' he said. 'I have sent for a copy from London, and long to read it. And congratulations, too, on the publisher's timing. The poem could not have come out at a happier moment, either for your husband or for the country. By everything I have heard of it, it should be just the stimulus that is needed at this anxious time.'

'Anxious indeed.' She had been hoping for a chance to discuss the political situation with him. 'Mr. Comfrey the publisher writes that Lord Nelson is being savagely criticised in town. He wants my husband to bear this in mind while completing his third canto.'

'Cry the man down, you mean? I wonder if that would be wise. Nelson has surprised us before, and may again, and, besides, from the patriotic point of view, surely he should be supported?'

'That is just my view. May I quote you to my husband? He does not set much store by my opinions.'

'Then he is not quite so wise a man as his sermons—and by the sound of it this poem—would seem to suggest. But no man is wise on every count. Now I must leave you to your studies. What is your commission today, I wonder?' She had decided some time before that she had better admit to doing what she described as a little work for her husband's sermons.

Now she laughed. 'Mr. Tremadoc is so elated with the good news about his poem that he has actually commissioned me to find him a text for Sunday's sermon.'

'He must certainly expect a crowded church. Really, Mrs. Tremadoc, I am inclined to suggest that he simply read us one of the powerful speeches of the Spirit of Good to which I have seen references in the public prints.'

'Oh, no,' she protested. 'He would never do that. My husband is a modest man, Mr. Gerard.'

'You surprise me.' Was there a hint of friendly mockery in his tone?

She did not pass on his suggestion to Tremadoc, for fear that he would yield to temptation and make a fool of himself. It was bad that he had never mastered the art of reading verse aloud, and worse that he had not recognised this. But Gerard's suggestion had given her an idea. She took her text for the sermon from the poem, two lines in which the Spirit of Good urged perseverance in the face of heavy odds, and then simply rendered the rest of the speech into prose.

'I had thought of doing that very thing myself,' said Tremadoc, when she showed it to him. 'As to Nelson, you say your mad old hermit advises against attacking him, and that is just what I have been thinking too. Better safe than sorry and all that, and who knows, the new man at the Admiralty, old Barham, may bring things to rights, even if he is over eighty. Now, sit down and write Comfrey to ask when I can expect to see the colour of his money. I've had a call from Bowles while you were out. Full of congratulations, all smiles, and the Oldchurch Club seem to expect to be given a dinner on the occasion of my success.'

'Good gracious. I must talk to M. Japrisot.' She had longed to try her French chef's hand at a dinner, but so far Tremadoc had refused, saying that if the County would not come to them, he did not propose to start entertaining the Town.

'Nonsense,' he said now. 'A dinner at the Castle, of course.'

That was an anxious summer at Oldchurch. On a clear day, one could see the cliffs of Boulogne, dangerously near across the Channel, and imagine Napoleon's invasion army drilling there. Rumours about Nelson, about Villeneuve and the other French admiral, Ganteaume, flew thick and fast. If Villeneuve and Ganteaume could unite and command the Channel for as much as twenty-four hours, with a favourable wind, Oldchurch would find itself in the front line of England's defences. And the Martello Tower down by the quay was still only half built.

'I've noticed that, too,' said Gerard, when Caroline remarked on it. 'It is not something to which I would refer in public if I were you. I had it in mind to suggest to you that it might be wise if you could persuade your husband not to mention it in his sermons.'

Curiously enough, Tremadoc had cut out a reference of hers to the Martello Tower just the week before. 'You mean to tell me that it is not only smuggling here in Oldchurch?' she asked now, anxiously.

'Smuggling and every kind of chicanery always go together. This is a dangerous place, Mrs. Tremadoc, as I have told you before. Surely now your husband has made such a name for himself he should be able to find another living?'

'We've no influence,' she said. But there was more to it than that. Something—success perhaps—had changed Tremadoc. He seemed, these days, almost contented with life in Oldchurch, and scouted a timid suggestion she had ventured about the possibility of moving away when the money for *The Downfall of Bonaparte* began to come through.

'Nonsense,' he turned on her. 'We are very well where we are. And, besides, when is this money going to come? Here it is August and I have no doubt that Comfrey is dining out very happily at my expense.'

'He says it takes a while to settle the books,' she said.

'Of course he says so, but should we believe him? That's the point. If you would just bestir yourself with your fair copying of the third canto, I would take it up to him myself and insist on my rights. I'm surprised he has not invited me before this. It is high time I began to move in the literary circles to which I now belong. I should be mixing with my equals, with that Coleridge you so fancy, with Wordsworth and Southey. Who knows? That old fool Pye, the Poet Laureate, might snuff it at any moment. He must be sixty if he's a day, and then I need to be in town, to be known.'

She thought his chances of the laureateship more than slender, but went to work with a will on her fair copying, his proposed visit to London a powerful incentive. They had been married over a year now and the future loomed dark before her, a life sentence. Her only remissions were the increasingly frequent evenings Tremadoc spent with the Oldchurch Club at the Castle Inn. And even these were paid for when he got home, sometimes euphoric, sometimes in a kind of inebriate despair, always wanting more of her than she could possibly give. And, always, afterwards, the sweating, nightmare-ridden sleep from which they both woke exhausted.

This time, Tremadoc talked of spending at least two weeks in town, and she hoped that in the end it would be longer. 'If that skinflint Comfrey has not settled his books yet, he will just have to give me an advance against my earnings. I do not propose to make my first appearance as author of *The Downfall of Bonaparte* looking the country parson, nor yet to arrive at the club in a hackney carriage like a Johnny Raw. My first call will be upon Weston for some clothes in which I am not ashamed to be seen, my second on Hatchett for a curricle and pair. You will enjoy being able to drive yourself about the marsh when I have brought it home. Then perhaps we will be able to mix in the society I deserve.'

'A curricle? You do not think a light carriage of some kind might be more useful? And where will you keep it?'

'Trust you to make nothing but objections! At the Castle, of course. It is all arranged with old Strudwick, the landlord. And as to a carriage, it might be more use to you but it certainly would not be to me, and it is, after all, I who have earned this fortune.'

She did not dare point out that whatever the first canto earned, it would hardly be a fortune, and resigned herself in advance to the fact that he would almost certainly spend the entire proceeds of the poem on his London trip. There was to be no let-up in the stringent course of economy which the steadily rising cost of living compelled her to practice. She sometimes wondered how Mrs. Bowles and the other married ladies of Oldchurch contrived to keep up their lavish standard of living. Widows like Mrs. Norman were now in visibly straightened circumstances, with tallow instead of wax candles, old dresses turned outside-in to pass as new, and old caps trimmed up with feathers. But Mr. Bowles had just bought his wife a fine new landaulet and the day Tremadoc left for town Mrs. Bowles invited Caroline to drive out on the marsh with her.

'I thought we would go and see what progress they are making with the Royal Military Canal,' she said as they drove out through the Water Gate on to the marsh. 'The air will do you good, child. I shall tell Bowles to speak to that husband of yours when he gets back, about the way he keeps you chained to your desk, copying that poem they make such a to-do about. You look properly peaked, and no two ways about it. Or— could it be that you are in an interesting condition?'

'No.' Caroline wondered if perhaps the question had been the true purpose of the trip, but once again she had had to send Mrs. Tremadoc news that would disappoint her. 'I am afraid I am a sad disappointment to my mother-in-law.'

'But not, I think, to your husband,' said Mrs. Bowles acutely. 'Don't you go fretting, my dear. Time enough to be thinking of setting up your nursery when Mr. Tremadoc has settled down a little. Are you not anxious about letting him go off to town on his own?'

'There is nothing I can do about it.'

'Of course not. We must obey our lords and masters, but mine seemed a trifle doubtful about the wisdom of Mr. Tremadoc's trip. He asked me to drop a word in your ear, suggesting you urge your good man to be careful how he talks at that London club of his. Something came back here to Oldchurch after his last visit that made Bowles quite angry. Oh, gossip and nonsense, I expect. A young man on the loose in town and finding us country bumpkins good for a jest. Perhaps when you write to Mr. Tremadoc you could drop him a hint?'

'I will certainly try.' Caroline remembered a moment of anxiety after her husband's previous trip. 'But I am afraid he is not likely to listen to me.'

'They don't, do they?' Mrs. Bowles was philosophical about it. 'Shall we have the landaulet open, my dear, and blow the cobwebs away? Such a fine day; it's hard to believe that Boney's across there, drilling his troops to invade us.' She pointed at a little church, crouched low on the marsh. 'Or that that church is full of pikes,—and muskets, I hope,—for the militia in case of a landing. Do you know why Bowles really bought me this little carriage? It is to get me safe inland when the beacons are lighted. And I mean you to come with me, and no two ways about it.'

'You are more than kind,' said Caroline. 'But in fact, Mr. Tremadoc spoke of buying a curricle while he is in town. I suppose he may have had very much the same idea . . .' It had not, in fact, occurred to her before, and did not seem entirely in character now.

'A curricle? You'd have to leave that housekeeper of yours behind, which would go against the grain with you, I know. Bowles thinks there will be no place for women and children in the town when once the French have landed. Now the walls are repaired at last, the militia mean to make a stand to the death in the hope of delaying the enemy's march on London. They will not want to be cumbered with us women. If I were you, my dear, I would write to Mr. Tremadoc and urge the virtues of a carriage like this one, that will take four people, maybe even more in a crisis.'

'My husband may plan to stay behind,' suggested Caroline. 'After all, as vicar of the parish it would surely be his duty.'

'It's his duty to visit the sick,' said Mrs. Bowles, unusually tart. 'But it seems to be you who do it. Anyway, Bowles and his aldermen have made a list of those they wish to stay. No extra mouths, you understand, in case of a siege.'

'It's hard to believe.' Caroline looked at white, newly sheared sheep, peacefully grazing the sunlit marsh. 'You don't think that that victory of Admiral Calder's may have altered the balance of things in the Channel?'

'Victory?' snorted Mrs. Bowles. 'Bowles says it sounds more like a defeat to him. What use is a scrambling kind of victory like that if you don't follow it up? Bowles says it is bound to have damaged the spirit of the men. If Nelson makes one more of those Mediterranean trips of his to visit his good friend the Queen of Naples, Bowles thinks we might even have another naval mutiny here, as in '97, and then what is to stop those flat-boats of Boney's from bringing over his army?'

'I don't believe it,' said Caroline roundly. 'And even if I did,' she went on, 'dear Mrs. Bowles, forgive me, but I would not say so.' A quick look indicated the coachman, all ears on his box.

Mrs. Bowles patted her hand patronisingly. 'All in the family, my love, all in the family. I look on you quite as one of my own.'

Caroline returned from that trip tired and a little frightened. If Mr. Bowles intended a gallant defence of Oldchurch, he was going a strange way about raising the spirits of the garrison. But Mrs. Bowles's remarks about Nelson had given her an idea. John Gerard still built his hopes on Nelson's genius for pulling victory out of defeat. If he should do so, she would need to write a eulogy of him by the Spirit of Good similar to the one about Lord St. Vincent in the second canto. She would spend her next visit to Gerard's library in finding out what she could about the fiery little admiral with the dubious reputation.

A few days later came the news that Nelson had landed at Spithead and been given a hero's welcome. 'I don't understand it,' said Mrs. Bowles, as always her husband's echo. 'Anyone would think he had scored a great victory instead of scurrying about the Atlantic achieving nothing.'

'I suppose we need a hero,' said Caroline thoughtfully.

Gerard agreed with her. 'Heaven help him if he fails us now. The mob will soon turn against him unless he produces the miracle the country longs for. Mob hysteria is a frightening thing, Mrs. Tremadoc, even when it is enthusiastic, as now. It's a bad indication of the spirit of the country. Dr. Martin would call it a malignant symptom, I think.'

'Well,' said Caroline. 'At least we don't seem to be suffering from it here in Oldchurch.'

'You've noticed that too? What does your friend Mrs. Bowles say?'

'Just what you did. That the mob will soon turn against Nelson unless he gives them the victory they long for.' She took a sip of wine. 'I think it is just as well that my husband is in town and not at present working on his poem. One would need to be a sorcerer to know what to say. He must be very grateful to you, Mr. Gerard, for your advice about Nelson. Whatever happens, the Admiral most certainly cannot be dismissed as negligible. He will go down in history either as a hero or a figure of tragedy.'

As she had hoped, Tremadoc prolonged his stay until early in September and surprised her by driving up to the house one windy morning in his spanking new curricle, with Jenkins up behind. 'Well,' he greeted her with a casual kiss and she thought he looked even more haggard than on his previous return. 'What's the news here in Oldchurch? London's humming with it,' he went on without giving her a chance to answer, 'Nelson's back on the *Victory*. Now we shall see some action. There's a hero for you. I met him, I'll have you know. An inconspicuous little figure of a man until you see the eyes . . . eye, I should say, but what a glance! An eagle, I thought I'd call him. England's eagle.'

> Now England's eagle stooping to his prey
> Puts end to fear and chases clouds away.

'I hope you are ready to go to work, Caroline, after your long holiday. Young Comfrey plans to publish my second and third cantos together before Christmas and wants the fourth for the spring. He promises better terms for it, too. Not a bad young man, that. Seems to have a head on his shoulders. Knows all about puffing—advertising, I mean. You wouldn't understand, but he knows his business, I am beginning to think. Sharp, though clutch-fisted. Do not be expecting a cloud of gold from London. The cost of living there is enough to frighten a man! And my mother not well and insisting she must see Sir Walter Farquahar. And I must pay, of course! Nothing the matter with her but old age and self indulgence, if you ask me, but Sir Walter had to pull a long face to earn his fee. Well, what of my dinner and the Oldchurch news.'

'I am sure Japrisot will send up just as soon as he can produce something worthy of your return.' Useless to point out that he had failed to warn them of his coming. 'As to the news here in town, there's not much. There was an accident to the Martello Tower the other day, the scaffolding gave way and a man was killed, I am sorry to say. Mrs. Bowles tells me her husband has been enquiring when I expected you.'

'Naturally I would be missed,' he said. 'A public figure such as I am now. Oh,'—carelessly,—'I called at Chevenham House and was pressed to stay to dinner. That is where I met Lord Nelson, as a matter of fact. The Duchess looks worse than ever but Mrs. Winterton is in fine fig. Seems she and that brass-faced Lady Hamilton are bosom friends; she was there too—Lady Hamilton—stout as the Duchess and loud-voiced as Mrs. Bowles. She treated us to her "attitudes"—I never saw such a take in. A fat woman in a shawl playing Venus! Young Blakeney looked sick as a horse and I could not blame him. And his sister Amelia—Lady ffether, I should say—all airs and graces and going in to dinner ahead of Charlotte. Not a happy family, that, if you ask me.'

She longed to ask him about Blakeney, but thought it better

to turn the conversation. 'Did Mr. Comfrey introduce you into
the literary world?' she asked. 'Coleridge and Wordsworth and
the men who write for the Reviews?'

'No.' He looked momentarily taken aback. 'Odd thing;
Comfrey didn't seem to wish it. Thought I ought to keep my
novelty value, something like that. Let the critics judge me by
my work only. Said I'd find the poet set a dead bore. Very
likely he was right and to tell truth I was so occupied with my
mother's illness and my old friends at the club, I'd hardly have
had the time. Probably all for the best. Mrs. Winterton said
I'd find them a pack of nobodies. Asked to be remembered to
you, by the way; wanted to know if you were breeding; I said
thank God no. And, thank God, there's dinner!'

He drank a great deal of his cordial both during and after
their late dinner and fell into an exhausted sleep the moment
his head touched the pillow. Looking at him for a moment
before she blew out the candle, she thought he looked more
than just exhausted, and she had noticed when he kissed her
on his arrival that he now had the same sweet, slightly corrupt
smell as his mother. His speech was different, too, hurried,
sometimes almost confused. She found herself wondering if
Mr. Comfrey had not perhaps avoided introducing him into the
literary world for fear of the impression he might make there.
The publisher must be a sensible man. She must get Dr. Martin
to see Tremadoc, but racked her brains in vain as to how to
do it.

She lay awake for a long time thinking it all over. Extraordinary to have her own mother ask to be remembered to her.
But why should it surprise her? It had been the Duchess, not
her mother, who wrote to her after her disastrous elopement,
and sent her the invaluable allowance. It had always been the
Duchess who thought, who cared, about her. The poor Duchess . . . She looked worse than ever, Tremadoc said. And no
wonder. With Charles Mattingley still abroad, she must lead
a sad life of it at Chevenham House. As always, Caroline came
back to the amazing fact of the continued friendship between
the Duchess and her mother. But then, she remembered, sigh-
ing, Frances Winterton could be a great charmer when she
wanted to. It was just that with her daughter she never bothered.
If the Duke had only liked me, Caroline thought, everything
would have been different. And then, with her usual realism,
but I don't like the Duke. Why should he me?

This time, Tremadoc stayed in bed for two days to recuperate from the fatigues of town, but arose on the third looking very much better and announcing his intention of going to the Oldchurch Club dinner that night. 'They will be all agog to hear the news from town. I shall have so much to tell them. To have actually met Lord Nelson! I expect to be quite late. No doubt there will be a million questions to be answered.'

He did indeed return late, but she was still awake when he returned, and lay, feigning sleep, as he made his befuddled preparations for bed. Climbing in beside her at last, he was muttering to himself. 'Not a hero,' he said. 'Flash in the pan . . . flash in the pan . . . flash in the . . .' He was asleep, but she lay awake for a long time, wondering what it meant.

She found out when they began work next day. 'I have been thinking a great deal,' he announced. 'I could not sleep for it.'

'Oh?'

'Yes. About my poem. Very important to get it right. Have to remember, cup and lip, all that. However hard I work, can't be published before spring. Well, Nelson's the rocket now, but may be an *ignus fatuus* by spring. Yes, *ignus fatuus*,' he repeated the words, which she had never heard him use before. 'I am going to have to be very careful indeed what I say,' he told her portentously. 'Crowd hysteria is one thing, but what of the voice of posterity? What of the future? That is what I ask you.'

'It's a good question.' She wondered who had put it into his head.

16

ALL THAT SEPTEMBER and into early October, as Nelson searched for the enemy fleet, and rumour and counter-rumour flew around England, Caroline and Tremadoc argued about the fourth canto of *The Downfall of Bonaparte*. It was the first time she had felt the need to oppose him openly on a point of this importance, and the results were unpleasant. His temper, never good, was now on a hair trigger. When she suggested at last that they simply abandon work until after the expected naval battle, it exploded.

'Idiot!' He was white and sweating, and a nerve twitched under his left eye. 'Comfrey must have the canto by the end of the month if it's to be out when he intends. What use will it be months after the event! I tell you, Nelson's fleet's rotten with mutiny; the men know him for the petty little womaniser he is. Let him just meet Villeneuve, and he's pricked, like a fool's bladder.'

'I don't believe it!' She fell back as he struck her on the side of the face, hard. 'If you do that again,' she faced him steadily, 'I will leave you, Mr. Tremadoc. And tell the whole world why.'

'You'd never dare!'

'I would, you know. What have I to lose? You hit me once before. I have thought about it since. You were ill then; I let it pass. I shall not do so again, and you had better remember. I married you for better or worse, and I mean to make the best of it, but there are limits.' He was very near to hitting her again. Their eyes met and held. Where would she go if he did? To John Gerard?

'Mrs. Bowles to see you, ma'am.' If Barrett saw anything odd about the tableau they presented, he did not show it. 'I've told her you were working, but she asks most particularly to speak to you.'

'Tell her I will be with her directly.' She moved past Tremadoc to the door, glad to have the moment of confrontation safely resolved.

In the hall, she paused for a moment, her face throbbing. It had been a savage blow. The temptation to take flight to her room, Tench, and comfort, was strong, but she resisted it. If her husband was really going out of his mind, as she horribly feared, she must have help. Confide in Mrs. Bowles? The thought was abhorrent, but who else was there? John Gerard was a last resource, for the moment she needed the help of Tremadoc's friends, of the members of the Oldchurch Club, much though she disliked the idea. She looked at her reflection in the big gold-framed glass and saw that her right cheek was slightly reddened, but not, she thought, noticeably so. She opened the drawingroom door and found Mrs. Bowles standing by the window.

'Thank you for seeing me, my dear. I trust your good man will forgive the interruption, but Mr. Bowles most particularly told me to visit you this morning. He was . . . he and the others were a little anxious about Mr. Tremadoc last night. Has he been working a trifle too hard, my dear, on that poem of his?'

'I am afraid he has.' Caroline snatched at the suggestion. 'I'm worried about him too, Mrs. Bowles, but what can I do?' She flushed, aware of sharp eyes studying her face.

'Bowles said he talked quite wild last night. About . . . I'm sorry to tell you, but about despair, and death and even about putting a period to his existence. Bowles thought it his duty as your husband's friend and yours to have me give you the warning. And to tell you that he has sent to ask Dr. Peabody to pay you a friendly call today. Just in passing as it were, to congratulate Mr. Tremadoc on his poem and take a quick look at him at the same time.'

'It's very good of Mr. Bowles to take so much trouble.' She could not help wishing he had sent for Dr. Martin, but even garrulous old Dr. Peabody was better than nothing.

'Nothing of the kind,' said Mrs. Bowles. 'We value our famous vicar and we *love* you, my dear.' She surged towards the door. 'And if you'll take my advice, you'll have a bit of steak to that face of yours without more delay, and a dusting of powder after, or Dr. Peabody may be drawing more conclusions than you may quite like. I'm sorry,' she concluded awkwardly. 'Send for me, my dear, if you need me.'

'Thank you.' She was very near to tears. 'It was my fault,' she managed. 'I ventured to make a suggestion about his poem.'

'They don't like to be crossed.' Mrs. Bowles summed it up and took her leave.

In the kitchen, M. Japrisot accepted Caroline's story of a collision with a door without comment and produced an admirably bloody bit of steak. Retreating with it to her room, Caroline was joined there by Tench, in tears.

'Oh my lamb,' she said. 'My poor precious lamb! And don't you be troubling yourself to lie to me, because there's no need. But how I can break my bad news to you is more than I can think.'

'Your bad news?'

'Some gossiping fool here in town has leaked to the master about me and Jenkins being married. Had Jenkins in this morning, the master did, made him a fine scene and gave us our notice. Ma'am my dear, what are you going to do without us?'

'Oh, Tench!'

'I'd stay by myself, ma'am, honest to God I would, if the

master would let me, but he won't and that's all there is to it. Told Jenkins he wanted the both of us out of the house tomorrow morning. A month's money and our fares paid back to London, to give the devil his due. And devil's the word, ma'am, so don't you go making faces at me. For two pins I'd go to Chevenham House and tell how you're being used down here.'

'They wouldn't care,' said Caroline wearily.

'The Duchess would. Right down fond of you, the Duchess is. Well, you was always a better daughter to her than those girls of hers. Who read aloud to her when her eyes were bad, that's what I want to know?'

'I enjoyed it,' said Caroline with truth. 'But, please, Tench, don't go plaguing the Duchess with my troubles. I am afraid from what Mr. Tremadoc tells me she has enough of her own.'

'In debt again, is she? Poor lady, I never saw anyone so took advantage of!'

Dr. Peabody called that afternoon, and was closeted with Tremadoc for some time in the small front parlour he used as his study. Emerging at last, he had Barrett show him into the garden room where Caroline was sitting, trying to work. 'I've been trying to talk sense to that brilliant husband of yours, Mrs. Tremadoc. Had you not noticed how he has been overworking himself?' His tone made it a reproach.

'I am afraid he overtired himself on his trip to London.' She was sitting with the light on the good side of her face. 'And of course his poem does present great problems, now that he has almost reached the present day.'

'A grave responsibility,' said the doctor. 'Combined with the masterful sermons I hear about it is enough to burn any man to the socket. You must take better care of him, ma'am, a great deal better care. We cannot afford to lose our men of genius. He is talking wildly, I should tell you, quite wildly. I have prescribed a sedative, which I urge you to make him take.'

'A sedative? Not, I hope, containing laudanum.'

'Oh, very mild, very mild indeed.' It was not quite an answer. 'And I have urged him to let that pushing publisher of his go hang for his next canto. He must take a little holiday, ma'am, a little rest, a little relaxation. You will know best how to persuade him of this. I leave it all in your capable hands.'

'Thank you,' she said dully.

To her relief, Tremadoc seemed to have taken the doctor's warnings very seriously indeed. In fact, she found herself wondering just what Peabody had said that left him looking almost frightened.

'Absolute rest,' he told her. 'The doctor says I am to have absolute rest. He is shocked that things have come to such a pass with me. I said that you and Comfrey between you are pressing me too hard about my magnum opus. There is to be no work on it until Peabody has seen me again and given permission. I do not propose even to tell you which way my thoughts are turning. Oh—and another thing.' Carelessly. 'Peabody is anxious about my nightmares. My sleep is not to be disturbed. You will be so good as to remove your effects to the guest chamber until I am better. I hope you will not mind it too much. I am to keep my room for a week at least; no guests; no distractions. Oh, the pains and penalties of genius!'

Concealing her relief at this edict, Caroline tried in vain to persuade him that if he was to be nursed in his room she would need Tench to help her. His banishment of Tench and Jenkins was irrevocable. 'I'll not have servants about me I cannot trust.'

Tench was in tears again when the couple left next day. 'We are going straight to Chevenham House,' she told Caroline. 'In hopes of work there.'

'I'll give you a note for the Duchess, Tench, but, mind, you are to say nothing more than that Mr. Tremadoc has overworked himself and is resting under the doctor's orders.'

'As if he ever did anything else,' said Tench. 'You take care of yourself, ma'am, my love, and look after that eye of yours.'

Caroline smiled ruefully. 'No gadding for me for a while. You will not mention my accident at Chevenham House, Tench.'

The Hastings curate was to do Tremadoc's Sunday duty so she could put away the sermon about steadfastness in face of danger that she had been trying to write, and let herself rest while Tremadoc did. He had given strict orders to Barrett that no guests whatever were to be admitted and at first this was a relief to her, since she did not wish to have to keep explaining about the 'accident' to her eye.

A week later, with the bruise almost gone, she decided that the time had come to face the world again. It was a bright October morning with dewdrops sparkling on cobwebs in the garden where she walked every day. But today, it would be good to get out of this house that now seemed to smell of sickness, and to tell Mrs. Bowles about her anxiety for

Tremadoc, who seemed to get worse instead of better. She put on her bonnet and warm pelisse and picked up a shopping basket. Perhaps some fresh fish from Oldchurch Bay would tempt Tremadoc's dwindling appetite.

'Ma'am?' Barrett emerged from his cubbyhole by the front door and stood in her way. 'The master said there was to be no going and coming.'

'I beg your pardon?' She looked at the little man in amazement.

'No going out, he said.' Barrett took a step forward as if to intercept her bodily.

'I never heard such nonsense in my life. You have misinterpreted your orders, Barrett. Don't let it happen again.' For a moment their eyes met and locked, then he took a step backwards.

'I'm sorry, I'm sure.' It was the Duke's daughter, she thought, before whom his eyes fell.

Outside in the street, she made herself walk slowly, taking deep breaths of crisp autumn air, angrily aware of an accelerated heartbeat. Absurd to have let the little man actually frighten her with his obstructiveness. Absurd? Looking back on the odd little scene, she felt an extra dimension to it. Was it her overheated imagination, or had the whole house been somehow listening, waiting for the outcome of the strange moment of conflict? If Barrett had actually obstructed her, would Japrisot have emerged from the kitchen? And taken her side? How very strange, how frightening to be thinking like this.

Mrs. Bowles greeted her enthusiastically but, she thought, or was this her imagination at work again, with a touch of surprise. 'I'm so very glad to see you feel able to leave your husband, my dear, and sorry to hear he is no better. What is the matter, do you think?'

'Dr. Peabody says it is overwork.' She managed to keep her voice neutral.

'That's just what Bowles thinks. Too brilliant by a half, and doesn't know his own strength. So you'll just have to be wise for two, my dear. Now, have a glass of my elderberry wine and tell me what you think of the news.'

'News?' Caroline was glad to sip the sweet, strong wine. 'Do you know, Mrs. Bowles, I have hardly thought of it all week.' She had missed her usual visit to John Gerard's library, unwilling to let him see her bruised face.

'Of course not,' said Mrs. Bowles approvingly. 'And all the better for it. No use crying before the milk's spilt. But I can tell you, Bowles has the darkest fears for our safety. He thinks Nelson a beaten man already and expects daily to have news of either a victory for Villeneuve, or, what might be even worse, a new mutiny in our fleet. It is no wonder your husband does not feel able to go on with that brave poem of his. I understand that he is resting absolutely?'

'Oh, yes.' Had Mr. Bowles told his wife to ask the question? Why was her mind running away with her so today? She thought she would call at Gerard's house on the way home and ask if she might borrow his most recent newspaper.

He welcomed her with obvious relief. 'I was really beginning to think of taking Mahomet to the mountain and paying a call on you. Your husband is not well, I understand, and, if I may say so, you look fagged to death.'

'I am a little tired. And, yes, my husband is not well. I must not stay more than a minute.' She was oddly tempted to tell him about that curious little moment of confrontation with Barrett. Absurd. A wailing woman talking of imagined troubles. 'But I long to hear what you think of Lord Nelson's chances,' she went on. 'I have been calling on Mrs. Bowles and her husband is very gloomy indeed. He seems to expect either defeat for Nelson's fleet or mutiny.'

'Does he so?' He thought for a moment, then: 'Mrs. Tremadoc, I wish you would take your husband to London. To consult a doctor there, perhaps? To visit your family? Entirely between ourselves, I do not place much confidence in Dr. Peabody's ministrations.'

'No more do I.' She was glad he had brought the matter up. 'In fact, I have been wondering if the sedative he left for my husband has not actually been making him worse.' Oddly enough, she had hardly formulated this thought even to herself before, but here it was, sharp and clear in her mind.

'Have you indeed? Well, if I were you, I would most certainly wish to get another opinion. And in the meanwhile, I would almost be inclined to discontinue the draft. Dr. Peabody is an elderly man. I would not wish to take medicines he prescribed.'

'My husband would never agree.'

'Need he know? How does he take the draft?'

'With quassia bitters. You mean?'

'I suggest a substitution. Excuse me a moment?' He left the

room and returned after a short interval with a medicine bottle that looked exactly like the one she had at home. 'You will need to arrange an accident to the label,' he told her. 'But that should be easy enough. It is quite harmless, of course. A placebo, merely. But I wish you would persuade Mr. Tremadoc that a trip to town would do him more good than anything.'

'I'll try.'

The 'accident' to the label, and substitution of the bottles was easy, but her suggestion of a trip to London met with a petulant negative. 'You wish me to brand myself a public coward? To run away from the invasion coast in the hour of crisis? Never! And you're not going, either! Your place is at my side, to nurse me back to health. Dr. Peabody called while you were out on the gad in town. He was shocked not to find you at my side, and not best pleased with my condition. You are to double the dose of my medicine, if you please.'

She did so, breathing a sigh of relief for the successful substitution, and was delighted to see his condition begin a steady improvement as the second week of October dragged by and the town of Oldchurch bent before rumour and counterrumour like a cornfield in an uncertain wind.

It was extraordinary, she thought, cutting across the graveyard on her way home from Mrs. Norman's library, that all the rumours in town seemed to be bad. It was not a question of defeat or victory, but of defeat or mutiny. If things were the same all over the country, England was in dire straits indeed, but the newspapers Gerard now sent in to her when he had finished with them did not suggest this. The King had gone to town for the first time since his return from taking the waters at Weymouth, held a council at the Queen's House and prorogued Parliament, which hardly seemed the action of a monarch threatened with imminent invasion. And, besides, it seemed increasingly probable that much of Napoleon's invasion army really had marched east from Boulogne in August to go into action against the new coalition of Austria and Russia, backed by British funds.

'So how can they invade?' Caroline asked Mrs. Bowles. 'Even if our fleet were out of action, they would need an overwhelming superiority of numbers in order to make a landing good in the face of our defences.'

'So long as those were manned,' said Mrs. Bowles gloomily, pouring more elderberry wine. 'It is not only in the fleet that there is talk of mutiny, my dear. But enough of that. How is your husband, love? Does his improvement continue? Mr. Bowles was asking about him only this morning.'

'He is much better, I am glad to say. The nightmares have almost ceased, and he is eating again. He even talks of attending the Oldchurch Club next week, though I hope I will be able to persuade him not to do so.'

'The meeting before the Guy Fawkes day procession is always a lively one,' agreed Mrs. Bowles. 'Not perhaps the ideal function for a convalescent's first appearance in society, though I know Mr. Bowles is hoping your husband will be able to attend.'

Tremadoc insisted on going to the dinner, and in fact he was so much better since he had unknowingly stopped taking Dr. Peabody's medicine that she did not think the outing could do him much harm. Lying awake in the guest room at the front of the house, she heard him return very late indeed in company with Bowles who, by the sound of things, was having to support his staggering steps. They paused under her window, and she heard Bowles speak, low and with emphasis. 'Remember, not a word to anyone . . . and most particularly not to Mrs. Tremadoc. It is to be complete surprise, mind you. A complete surprise.'

'Surprise,' Tremadoc giggled. 'She'll be surprised, I promise you. Never did value me as she should. I'll surprise her, don't you doubt it.' His words were slurred, and she was relieved to hear the front door open below and know that Barrett had waited up for him. Presently, she heard Barrett help him laboriously upstairs and into bed and lay in her own, grateful to be spared the struggle of getting him undressed.

Guy Fawkes day dawned with more than a hint of fog in the air and Caroline, leaning over the garden wall to probe the grey mystery that was usually her view of marsh and sea, hoped very much that the fog would hold and cast a damper on the procession. She shivered, chilled by the damp air and memories of last year and the girl who had plunged to her death in the river. Visiting Mrs. Norman later in the morning, she found her making preparations almost as if for a siege. 'I'm staying at home this year,' she said. 'My nephew's coming to be with me. He's my heir; lives in Hastings and thinks nothing of our Guy Fawkes doings.'

'I'm glad.' Caroline suppressed a pang of envy. It was odd how much she disliked the idea of spending Guy Fawkes night alone in the house with Barrett, the rest of the servants out of earshot in their wing beyond the green-baize door. Over their early dinner she tried in vain to persuade Tremadoc not to join the procession and recognised with a touch of self scorn that she actually wanted him to stay at home for her own sake. But he was adamant, and, when she pressed him, angry. 'This year I have a duty to go.' He was important about it. 'I must leave you.' The clock in the hall struck the hour. ''I'm to join Bowles and the others at half past.' He left the table and a few minutes later she heard his voice raised in fury upstairs and hurried to see what was the matter. He was in the big bedroom, all the drawers of the tallboy pulled open. 'My surplice!' He turned on her in a fury of haste. 'What has happened to my surplices?'

'You intend to go in your vestments?' She looked in amazement at the black clothes that lay ready on the bed. 'But you'll be known!'

'I am to lead the procession! I remember how you grumbled last year that it was a pagan survival. Well! This time the Church Militant will be in the lead. I am to throw the figure of the Pope on the fire. I am to represent the Church Triumphant. And here I am likely to be late because you cannot even keep my linen in proper order!'

'I suppose Jenkins . . .' she began, aware of Barrett hovering behind her.

'Of course! Fool of a man. Where would he have put them?' He was pulling everything out of the drawers, throwing it on the floor in his feverish haste.

'If I might be of assistance?' Barrett glided past her and opened the hanging part of the closet, to reveal the surplices hanging there like ghosts in the fog-laden air. 'Let me help you dress, sir? You will not wish to keep the procession waiting . . .'

'No indeed! Thank you, Barrett. That will be all, Caroline.'

Thus dismissed, almost as if she were the servant, Caroline retreated to the garden room and was surprised to find Japrisot awaiting her there.

'There is talk in the town, madame,' said the Frenchman. 'Talk of disaster to Milord Nelson. Wild talk. It will be a very bad night, I think. You should persuade Monsieur not to march with the procession.'

'I only wish I could,' she said wearily. 'I've done my best . . .'

'What the devil's all this?' Tremadoc must have finished his dressing at lightning speed. 'Get back to your quarters at once, you rascal, and, you, Barrett, make sure that there's no more tittle-tattle going and coming tonight.'

'I'll do that, sir.' Barrett ushered Japrisot out of the room and returned a few minutes later carrying the key to the servants' wing.

'That's right!' Tremadoc snatched it from him and pocketed it. 'That takes care of them. Now you!' He turned to Caroline as if she were an intruding stranger. 'I want to see you safe in your room before I go.'

'I wish you would reconsider,' she said. 'Japrisot says there are alarming rumours going about town. About a disaster to Lord Nelson.'

'What did I tell you? But if he has been defeated, as I have no doubt he has, all the more reason for a show of patriotism here in Oldchurch.' He pulled himself upright. 'I go to do my duty. Out of my way, woman!'

17

THE KEY HAD been removed from the lock of her bedroom door, and the bolt did not work. How long had this been the case? Absurd not to be sure, but she had never had cause to check on them before. Tonight, with the door to the servants' wing locked and its key in Tremadoc's pocket, she would have liked to be able to lock herself in.

Ridiculous, of course. Her imagination was overworking itself again. But she propped a chair against the door before she moved over to open the shutters a crack and peer out into the heavy darkness of the square. The fog had thickened again at dusk, and the lamp over the passage by the church showed only as a remote blur of light. No wonder neither Tremadoc nor Barrett had troubled about the fact that tonight she was sleeping at the front of the house. But it was odd, just the same. Frightening? As if what she saw no longer mattered? More than ever she wished that John Gerard had been at home when she called at his house on her way back from Mrs.

Norman's, ostensibly to ask if there was any news of Nelson's fleet. But his man had told her that his master had received an urgent summons to town, and left at once. 'He said he would be back tomorrow, ma'am. And to give you this, if you was to call.'

Gazing across the foggy, silent square at the one blur of light, Caroline thought tomorrow seemed a lifetime away. A deathtime? Nonsense. And absurd to have let herself be so out of proportionally disappointed at Gerard's absence. But he's the only friend I've got, she told herself. It's natural I should miss him. She unfolded his note and re-read it by the light of her candle:

> I am sure you will call, and more sorry than I can say not to be there to see you, but am summoned urgently to town. There are grim rumours afoot. Believe nothing rashly. Try to persuade your husband not to march tonight. And, above all, do not you go out for any reason whatsoever.

The last words were heavily underscored and followed simply by a scrawled: *In haste, J.G.*

The handwriting reminded her of someone's, but she could not think whose. Absurd even to suggest that she might consider going out anywhere tonight, considering what she remembered of last year. Were those Barrett's soft steps on the stairs? She was not sure, but closed the shutters quietly and removed the chair from the door. And that was absurd, too. Alone in the house with Barrett, whom else could she fear?

A gentle knock. 'Madam?' Barrett's voice. 'If I might speak to you for a moment?'

'Yes?' She opened the door a little and stood in the crack. 'What is it, Barrett?'

'A message for you, ma'am. Come by hand. Urgent.' He held out a folded note. 'It's Mr. Gerard, ma'am, the servant said. In trouble. Asks you to go to him, quick, before the procession starts.'

'Oh?' Suspending judgment, she took the note and moved over to the candle, glad to notice that Barrett came no farther into the room. She read quickly:

Dear Mrs. Tremadoc,
I need your help most urgent. I have got safe away to

Mrs. Norman's. Bring bandages, a heavy cloak, quick, before the procession starts.

It was signed, after an illegible squiggle of a greeting, *John Gerard*.

If it had not been for the previous note, it might have convinced her. The writing was a gentleman's. The grammatical error might have been the result of haste. She would not have known that Gerard signed himself only with initials. She looked at Barrett, thinking fast. 'It's too late,' she said. 'Was the messenger delayed?'

'That's what he said. But the procession's not started yet. He came past the church and says they're still assembling. If you was to go through the churchyard and take the lane behind the Crown you could get to Mrs. Norman's easy.'

So he knew what the note said. How? Who would be waiting for her in the dark graveyard? 'Would you come with me?' she asked.

'I wish I could, ma'am, but I must mind the house. The procession passes right by, remember. You'll be safe enough at Mrs. Norman's. Like a fortress her house is, they tell me.'

Yes, Caroline thought, a fortress that would be closed against me. And yet, if she had not had Gerard's previous note, she might well have gone. She moved over to open the shutters. 'Listen. It's too late already.' The dull thud of a drum sounded hollow through the blanketing fog.

'That's just the assembly, ma'am.' Barrett's face showed blanched in the dubious light. 'They always take an age getting marshalled. You could do it yet. The man who brought the note says he will go with you. He's waiting.'

'One of Gerard's servants?'

'He says Gerard's hurt bad. No one else will help him on this night of all nights. I thought you was a good friend of his, ma'am.'

'So I am,' she said. 'But . . . think of me a coward, if you like, Barrett, but tell the man to go for Dr. Martin. He can give Mr. Gerard better help than I can. I am not going out tonight. I have my husband's orders.'

For an instant, she thought a look of frightened fury flashed across Barrett's face. 'I'll tell him.' He picked up the lantern he had placed on the chest in the hall. 'But I doubt he'll go. Martin's house is clear the other side of town.'

'He's not to stay here,' she said. 'I want to hear him leave at once, Barrett.' And realised, as she said it, that she had not heard the man come. Was he an invention of Barrett's? She stood in the doorway, watching the flickering light of his candle dwindle away down the curve of the stairs, then closed the door and replaced the chair, feeling a fool again as she did so. Moving back to the window, she re-opened the shutters and stood behind them, listening to the murmur of voices below. Barrett was indeed seeing someone away from the house, but they had most certainly not come to it since she had been up here, listening. It only confirmed her previous certainty that the note had been a lure to get her out into danger, but now she began to wish that she had pretended compliance, got out into the square, then called at one of the neighbours' houses for help. But would help have been available? John Gerard was away; the other neighbours might well hesitate to open up on Guy Fawkes night. Straining eyes and ears, she could not be sure that the man Barrett had let out had actually left the square. Was he perhaps lurking there, in the heavy darkness, just in case she should try to escape?

Escape? Her candle was burning low and she moved across the room to where a double-branched stick always stood on the dressing table in case she wanted to read in the night. It was not there. Crazy not to have noticed this sooner. The tinderbox that stood beside it was gone, too. In the morning, if she complained, Barrett would produce an apologetic maid who had taken it down to clean and 'forgotten' to bring it back. In the morning? Would she still be alive to make the complaint?

How much more light had she? Half an hour perhaps, and no way of relighting the candle; she must just make the most of it while it lasted. She moved round the room, searching for a possible weapon, and settled on the fire tongs as heavier than the small poker. If it was only Barrett? If she took him by surprise as he entered the room? There might be a chance, particularly if he had dismissed her as a coward. So . . . she arranged the pillows in the bed to look like her own sleeping figure. No one would come, she thought, until the procession had passed and she was likely to be asleep. For the time being, she left the chair against the door, to guard against surprise, and went back to the half-shuttered window, alerted by the louder sound of that insistent drum. Now it was joined by the squeal of fifes. The procession must be starting from the other side of the church.

As she had the year before, she watched the sinister masked

figures erupt into the square, flaring torches in their hands casting strange light and shadow on mask, and plume, and barbaric headdress. Only, this time, one unmistakable figure came first. Tremadoc's white surplice was illuminated by two torchbearers who walked on either side of him, but just a step behind, so that he did indeed lead the procession, a book, presumably the Bible, in his hand. As he approached across the square, she could see his white face and see that he was smiling with what looked like pure happiness. He is having his day, she thought, and felt suddenly happy for him, despite her own terrors.

Behind him, riding high on the shoulders of two masked savages, came the figure of the Pope, the three-crowned hat rising out of the open sedan chair in which the effigy was carried. Effigy? It was extraordinarily lifelike, she thought, as it passed under her window, and she drew back a little to make sure she could not be noticed.

The procession seemed even longer than last year's and it was an age before the last capering figure had vanished into the dark of the graveyard, and the throb of the drum had dwindled to a mere pulse in the head. No screams this year, thank God, and she was most certainly not going to venture out into the foggy garden to watch the huge bonfire from over the wall. The house was quiet. Waiting?

The candle end was beginning to flicker. Five minutes more and it would be out. Now she wished that she had asked Barrett for a new one when he brought the note that was not, she was sure, from Gerard. Was this evening to be one long tale of lost opportunity?

A sudden sound from downstairs took her to the door, heart wildly beating. What was Barrett doing? It almost sounded as if he had fallen over a bit of furniture.

'Mrs. Tremadoc?' A voice, low, urgent from the landing outside. Not Barrett's.

'Who is it?' She had the fire tongs ready in her hand.

'Charles Mattingley,' came the amazing answer as the candle flickered and went out. 'I've dealt with the man, Barrett, but we must get you out of here. Will you trust me.'

'Mattingley?' It did indeed sound like his voice, but after all this time how could she be sure? And, besides, what in the world could he be doing here?

'Yes. The Duchess's friend. Yours. Let me in; there's not much time. They're waiting outside in the square. To kill you.

When Barrett does not open to them they'll force a way in. Surely you know my voice?' And then, while she argued it with herself: 'Why did you never reply to my proposal of marriage, Caroline?'

'It *is* you!' No one else could have known about that. She pulled away the chair and opened the door. 'Thank God you're here. But how?' She would not have known him, wrapped as he was in an all-enveloping cloak.

'No time for that.' He picked up his lantern from the table outside her door. 'Trust me, Caroline, and do just what I say. A warm dark cloak; quickly; bring nothing; there's no time.'

'You're taking me away?' She was pulling on the heavy cloak that hung behind her door as she spoke. 'But Mr. Tre madoc?'

'Pray for him,' he told her. 'And come.'

In the downstairs hall a lamp hanging from a hook revealed Barrett tied into a big chair, loose in his bonds, apparently unconscious. Mattingley bent over him for a moment. 'He'll live,' he whispered, 'though whether he deserves to... This way.' The cellar door stood ajar. 'Keep close behind me. The steps are steep.'

Did he know she had never been down them? At the bottom of the dark, narrow flight he paused to let her past. 'Wait here. I must lock the door behind us. God knows how long they will wait, but not long, I think.'

It was ice cold in the cellar, and the air musty. She breathed a sigh of relief when Mattingley rejoined her, tucking the key into a pocket under his cloak. 'It's a heavy door. It should hold them for a little while. You do know me?' He pushed back the muffling cloak.

'I hardly would have.' He looked different, somehow, formidable.

'You've had a bad time.' It was not a question. 'But that's for later. This way, and watch your footing.' The lantern he carried illuminated racks of dusty bottles... casks... a pile of boxes. 'We're out of earshot now.' His voice, at normal pitch, echoed strangely in the low vault. 'I take it you did not know you lived over a smuggler's storehouse.'

'I most certainly did not.' But it explained a great deal.

'We're going to leave by their back way,' he told her. 'Careful now. This flight of steps is worse. Take my hand.' His was cold on hers. 'Not much farther.' They felt their way down something between a flight of steps and a rocky slope,

very narrow and slightly slippery, so that she was glad to be
able to steady herself with her free hand on the cold rock wall.
In front, he picked his steps like a cat, one hand holding the
lantern, the other encouraging hers. 'That's the worst of it
over.' They had reached a wider passage that sloped away
gently in front of them, and she began to smell salt air and
fog, and hear, once again, the threatening throb of the drum.

'The procession?' she asked.

'They must be almost down to the quay by now. When the
bonfire is lit is our time to get away.'

'We're going down the cliff?' She remembered what she
had seen last year.

'It's the only way. Lucky I know you for a girl who fears
nothing.'

'What in the world makes you think that?'

'I don't think it, I know it. Here we are.' The lantern light
showed nothing but fog, but she could tell that they were in a
larger cavern and, she thought, one that was open to the air.
'Over here's the opening,' he said, confirming this. 'Stand
still, while I make sure they are ready below before I rope you
up. Don't move a step,' he warned. 'The opening is sheer.
Hold this.' He gave her the lantern. 'They won't be able to
see a signal in this fog. I just hope I don't hit one of them.'
He picked up a stone from the cavern floor and moved cautiously away into the darkness. She felt the movement as he
threw, then thought she heard, far down, the sound of a muffled
splash. 'Just in time,' he said. 'Here they come.' There was a
roar of sound as the head of the procession must have emerged
from the Water Gate, and she had a vision of Tremadoc, leading
it, that look of pure happiness on his face. Pray for him, Mattingley had said.

'They're waiting.' He moved back towards her. 'There's a
harness here. You're not the first who's gone down. I'm going
to tie you into it and let you down to them. The cliff's sheer,
smoothed by generations of smugglers. Take off your cloak;
you'll be safer without it, though cold, I'm afraid.'

'Cold! As if that was the worst of it.' But there was almost
a hint of laughter in her voice as she obediently took off the
heavy cloak and dropped it on the ground, then fought down
a strange involuntary shiver as his quick, firm hands adjusted
the harness around her.

'You face the cliff.' His voice was matter of fact. 'If you
can, steady yourself with your hands and feet. I'll lower you

as slowly as I dare. They've lit the fire. We must hurry.' His hands checked the rope and again that shiver went through her.

'Now.' He urged her gently forward to where darkness, less absolute, showed the open front of the cave. The noise of the procession was louder, and as he halted and steadied her at the very edge of the cliff she could see the fire surging savagely upwards, the dark crowd leaping and shouting around it. 'Don't look,' he said. 'Over the edge with you, let yourself down by your hands, then, trust me, and let go.'

'And you?' She hesitated for a moment.

'Will follow you down the rope once you're safe. The sooner the better.'

'Yes.' The wildly blazing fire would not last long. As she lowered herself over the edge the insistent drumming stopped, the crowd hushed, someone was beginning to speak. Trema-doc?

'Let go.' Mattingley's voice from above, steady, commanding.

Her feet in their soft slippers felt the gritty sandstone of the cliff. The harness was firm under her arms. She took a deep breath, let go, swung dizzily for a moment, then felt her hands scrape against rough rock as she plunged steadily downwards. It was an eternity; it was an instant. She had never been so frightened in her life. And she had not even asked who was waiting below. She could hear voices now, the muffled splash of oars. They were drowned suddenly by a wild burst of music and shouting from the quay and then a scream so horrible that her hands and feet stopped obeying her and she plunged for a few moments, helpless, banging against an outcrop of the cliff, then, mercifully, was grasped by steadying hands, pulled side-ways, deposited in the rocking bottom of a small boat and, half fainting, felt the rope roughly removed.

'He's coming now.' A man's voice.

'And not a moment too soon.'

'What's happening over there? Can you see?'

'No, thank God, but I can guess.'

'Nothing we can do, but pray God it's quick...'

'He's still screaming.'

'Yes. Hold the rope steady. Ah!' The screaming had risen to a half-human pitch, then stopped. 'God rest his soul.'

Whose? She was afraid she knew. Pray for him, Mattingley had said. She lay where they had dropped her, every joint aching, hands and feet bleeding, trying with a numb mind to make sense of what they were saying.

'Christ!' said the first voice. 'I can smell it.'

Caroline could, too, and fainted.

She ached all over. The hand she put up to her brow was bandaged. There was light; the crackle of a fire; somewhere a bird was singing. Daytime? She turned awkwardly in the bed and tried to sit up.

'Don't.' A woman's voice; a gentle hand on her forehead. 'The doctor says you must rest.'

'Dr. Martin?'

'No dear. You're safe away from Oldchurch. At Denton Hall. Charles Mattingley brought you to us. We're your kin, child, cousins of your mother's.'

'Cousins?' It was an effort to open her eyes, but she made it and saw a plain, kind-looking woman sitting by the bed.

'Call it that.' Unbecoming colour flooded the tired face. 'Dick—my husband—don't much like it talked about. Well, you can't blame him. He thinks what his sister did killed his first wife. Poor Ruth, she died in childbirth and the little boy with her. A long time ago, my dear, and no blame of yours, but if it's all the same to you, we'll just call you a distant cousin, and save explaining to the children.'

'Children?' The woman was talking in riddles that her tired brain would not follow. There was something else, something lurking at the back of it, waiting to spring. 'You have children?' she asked.

'Yes.' The plain face became beautiful. 'Two boys and a girl. Francis and Richard and my little Jennifer. You'll meet them all when you are strong enough to come downstairs. Francis and Richard came home from Cambridge to protect us from invasion, bless the boys. They are both army mad, of course, but their father says they must get their education first. I'm tiring you with my chatter.' She looked conscience-stricken. 'Mr. Mattingley said you must rest. He'll be angry if he gets back and finds I've been letting you tire yourself.'

When Caroline next woke a small girl was sitting by the bed looking at her with large, interested eyes. 'Cousin Caroline!' She jumped to her feet. 'I'm Jennifer, and mamma said I was to call her the instant you waked.' She patted Caroline's hand. 'Now stay good and quiet until I come back with mamma.'

'You look much better,' said her mother, a few minutes later.

'I feel it, Mrs . . .' She hesitated.

'Purchas. This is my little Jennifer who has been watching by your bed. And Charles Mattingley is back and asks if he may see you for a moment.'

'Here?' She was surprised to feel herself blush.

'He says he must return to Oldchurch at once. Things are all at sixes and sevens there. He thought there might be something you needed.'

'I'd like to see him. To thank him. He saved my life, I think. And, besides . . .' There was something else; something terrible she had to face. 'I need to know what happened . . . I can't remember . . .'

'Yes.' A shadow crossed the tell-tale face. 'Jennifer, fetch Cousin Caroline mamma's best dressing gown, the one with the swansdown trimming. And my brush and comb. If you won't mind me making you a little tidy, my dear? I'm afraid . . . Your poor hands. But I think you should see Charles Mattingley.'

'Please.' The shadow still loomed at the back of her mind. 'Was it last night?' she asked.

'No, the night before. You slept all day yesterday. There's glorious news, my dear, a great victory for our fleet.' But her hand flickered to the knot of black ribbon pinned at her breast.

'A victory? But you're in mourning?'

'Nelson's killed,' said Mrs. Purchas. 'The whole country is in mourning.'

Caroline's bandaged hands shook so much that she was glad to let Mrs. Purchas comb out the tangles in her hair and adjust the swansdown-trimmed gown round her shoulders. 'There,' she said at last. 'You'll do, child. I'll send Mr. Mattingley in, and Jennifer shall stay with you for company.'

'Thank you.' Quick tears sprang to her eyes at this instinctive kindness. 'I'd like that.'

'Nelson's dead.' She had seen the black band on Mattingley's sleeve. 'And I owe you my life. I do thank you.' She held out her hand to him and he surprised her by kissing it, gently, through the bandages.

'Your poor little hands,' he said. And then, 'Yes, a glorious death, at the moment of victory. Just what he would have wished. But it was the news of that victory that set things aflame at Oldchurch. Word came up Channel in a fishing smack.

Bowles and his gang suppressed it, set it about that Nelson was beaten. It was their last chance, and they knew it.'

'Chance?' she asked. 'Gang? The smugglers, you mean?'

'Worse,' he said. 'Much worse. Traitors. They had committed themselves so far to Bonaparte that there was no turning back for them. Had you not wondered why the walls were strengthened but the Martello Tower neglected? Oldchurch was to have been the rallying point for the French army of invasion, the base for its march on London. When they heard of the French fleet's defeat, the conspirators decided to seize the town, hold it, and hope for a rescue from France. I doubt it would have come, but it would have been a terrible blow to British morale, and a bad time for the women and children of Oldchurch.'

'That's why Mr. Bowles bought the carriage,' Caroline said. 'He meant to send Mrs. Bowles away.'

'Very likely, but it all happened too fast. Too fast for him, too fast for us. The news only came on the evening of Guy Fawkes day. And the traitors had it first. It was all improvisation . . . panic. On our part too, I am afraid.' He was leading up to something.

'My husband,' she said. 'What happened to him?'

'I am so very sorry.' He put a hand on her bandaged one. 'He is dead. The soldiers arrived just too late to save him. I am so sorry, Caroline.'

The memory she had been fighting had leapt on her, whole and horrible. 'I knew it. It was him I heard . . . that scream . . . that . . .'

'Don't . . . Try not to think of it. He had been happy; think about that. They let him lead the procession, make the speech. I had a man there, he could do nothing, but he told me your husband had no inkling of danger, not until the very last moment, when he was to throw the effigy of the Pope on the fire, and they surrounded him. Then he knew . . . then he screamed . . . He was excited, my man said, enjoying himself. Until then . . . You must think of it as a hero's death, a martyr's. He died because of his fame, because of his poetry . . . They could not afford to let him live, a witness against them.'

'I killed him,' she said dully.

'Nonsense. You must not think like that. You had saved his life once already, as a matter of fact. That sedative draft old Peabody gave him was poison, you know. I think they must have let out too much of their plans at one of those drunken gangsters' dinners of theirs . . . They tried to frighten him into secrecy, then decided he was not to be trusted. I think so long as he was in Oldchurch, aware of them all around him, he kept mum enough, but when he went to London he felt safer.'

How much he knew. 'At the club,' she said. 'I remember Mrs. Bowles saying something . . . Oh, poor Mrs. Bowles, what has happened to her?'

'Oldchurch is a sad town this morning. I'm not sure which I pity more, women like Mrs. Bowles, whose husbands were killed, clean and quick in the fighting, or those whose men survive to stand trial for treason.'

'Can I go back there? Perhaps I could help . . .'

'No,' he said. 'It's like you to want to, but you've done enough. You're to stay here, to rest and recover with these kind cousins of yours.'

'I wish you would explain about them,' she said. 'Mrs. Purchas talks in riddles.' She looked quickly at Jennifer, but the child had lost interest in the conversation and drifted away to gaze out of the window.

Mattingley laughed, and she thought it a marvellously reassuring sound. 'I expect she finds it awkward enough in all conscience,' he said. 'She was a Miss Gurning, you know, one of the Quaker banking family. Dick Purchas married her as his second wife . . . Oh, twenty years ago, something like that, but they have lived very retired down here. I don't suppose she has ever got used—as you and I have—to the wicked ways of the *ton*.'

'I've not had much choice, have I?' said Caroline bleakly. 'You're telling me, Mr. Mattingley, that I am related to Mr. Purchas through my mother?'

'She is his niece, his sister Julia's child. She was a wild one, Julia Purchas. I remember the stories from when I was a boy. She fell in love with an American cousin, also called Purchas, though I think he spelled it differently, who rescued her from the mob during the Gordon Riots. Her family had him thrown into the Tower, tried to make him marry her, but he was married already. A romantic tale . . .'

'And she was my grandmother?'

'Well, yes. A very great beauty.' His tone was apologetic.

'And my grandfather?'

If he had looked unhappy before he looked wretched now. 'Are you sure you really want to know?'

'Yes. I have wanted to all my life.'

'I can understand that. Well, your grandfather... It turned out that Julia Purchas had had an affair when she was very young, with another American, a connection of the American Purchases, Francis Mayfield. She hoped to marry him. I'm afraid he behaved very badly.'

'Frances,' she said. 'My mother.'

'Poor child. She had a sad enough time of it, by all one hears. Born and brought up in secret, any old how, then planted in her uncle's household just when he was marrying his American love. No wonder if she has not always kept the line. It's an old, sad story, and Purchas asks me to tell you that he would as soon forget it, and your grandmother, who died abroad, many years ago. You are to forget the past and be his cherished cousin, if you will.'

'I can hardly forget my mother.' Caroline glanced at the child by the window and thought sadly that she must not stay long in this kind household. There was so much to be faced, so horribly much. 'And poor Geraint.' How seldom she had called him that. 'Your man is sure he did not know what was happening until the last moment?'

'Quite sure. He was enjoying himself, leading the procession. Happy. Hold on to that. In fact,' he hesitated. Then, 'I think I will tell you. My man thought Mr. Tremadoc had been given something... a sedative perhaps? His speech hardly made sense. Just a lot of rambling exclamations. A sad end for that remarkable man.'

Oh, poor Geraint, she thought. His last speech, and he had nothing to say because I was not there to write it for him. She would write a canto of *The Downfall of Bonaparte*. About Nelson's death. It would serve instead of the last speech he could not make. Death and victory. She would have to pretend it had been written before, of course. There was going to be a great deal of pretending... A tear gathered in each eye. 'Ah, poor Geraint,' she said. 'I am afraid I did him nothing but harm.'

'You made a man of him. I'd never have believed the man I knew in town could write that powerful poetry, those remarkable sermons.'

'You heard him preach? Mr. Mattingley, I understand nothing. I thought you were on a mission to St. Petersburg.'

'So did the world, as it was meant to.' He laughed. 'You can have no idea of how I sweated over my letters home. If you had been in town, you would have heard how the Duchess complained of my long silences and unsatisfactory dabs when they came.' A hint of colour along his cheekbones told her that this was an uncomfortable subject for him. And no wonder.

'She does not know?'

'Indeed not. You know as well as I do that what Chevenham House knows today, the world knows tomorrow. Of course, it will all come out now, and my usefulness is ended. But I'll never regret having exposed that nest of perverted traitors in Oldchurch.'

'Perverted?' But it was what she had felt.

'An ingrown community of petty tyrants. Little men who would be masters in their own houses, who got together at the Oldchurch Club and encouraged each other in their mean little cruelties. And boasted to each other when once the drink had gone round a few times. If their wives could have heard them, I think every woman in Oldchurch would have packed up and left. A set of dirty, grown-up schoolboys, telling tales. My man used to come home sick from those meetings. Sick with disgust.'

'Your man?'

'We had to have a man in the club, but he never reached its secret councils as your unfortunate husband did. Lucky for him. He is alive to tell the tale. He saw the perversion, but only had hints of the traitors who were using the men of Oldchurch.'

'Bowles?'

'I am afraid so. And that he must have given himself away to your husband in one of their drunken sessions. And of course the fact that Mr. Tremadoc was becoming such a public figure made him doubly dangerous. To begin with, Bowles thought he could frighten him into silence, but, forgive me, he must have decided that there was no relying on Tremadoc. So first he tried slow poison at the hands of Dr. Peabody, which you and I foiled between us, and, when that failed, set up the "accident" in the procession. And planned to kill you that night, too, for fear of what you might have learned. I wonder how he meant to make your death seem an accident.'

'I was to have been caught up in the procession, like that poor girl last year.' She told him about the forged note.

'Thank God you saw through it, Caroline.' He rose to his feet. 'I must go back to Oldchurch, but before I go, tell me you forgive me for failing to save your husband. It will be on my conscience to my dying day, but saving Oldchurch had to

come first. I do beg you to see that. If Bowles and his gang
had been alerted by Tremadoc's absence, by any kind of alarm,
they would have cancelled the procession and closed the town
gates at nightfall as usual. Long before the soldiers could get
there. It would have meant the full horrors of a siege and the
whole consequent shock to public opinion. As it is, the whole
business is to be hushed up. No one will ever know how nearly
Oldchurch came to yielding itself to Napoleon. If only the
troops had been quicker, riding from Hastings . . . I had thought
they would arrive before the procession reached the quay, but
the fog delayed them. Can you forgive me, Caroline?'

'If I can forgive myself,' she said. 'I can most certainly
forgive you. After all, you did save my life, though I still do
not understand how you came to do so.'

'You still don't see it, do you?' His smile stirred something
that might have been her heart. 'I hope you will forgive me
for this too.' And, as she watched in amazement, he seemed
to bend forward and crumple in on himself. One hand went
out to grasp a chair as if for support; the other shoulder was
hunched up. 'You have to imagine the wig and the concealing
forest of grey whiskers,' said John Gerard's deep voice.

'Dear God! It was you all the time!'

'And very happy your visits made me.'

'But it's impossible,' she exclaimed. 'John Gerard had been
living in Oldchurch for years. He was an established figure
when I got there.'

'And very scared I was that you would see through me at
once with those clear eyes of yours. But think a little, Caroline.
Think how often, before, I was out of town on one party of
pleasure or another.'

'Yes, the Duchess always used to say . . .' Caroline stopped,
blushing crimson.

'That I kept a country mistress. Of course she did. And, on
the other hand, my character as a recluse protected me in
Oldchurch. An occasional crusty appearance at church was
enough to keep it up. My man turned away callers. In fact, I
had only been John Gerard for two years or so when you came
there. The Preventive men reported some very odd goings on
around there after the Peace of Amiens. It had always been
known as a smuggling port. Used to be one of the favourite
haunts of the notorious Hawkhurst Gang. But this was more.
This smacked of treason. When the war broke out again, I
happened to mention to a friend that I meant to enlist. It was

no time to be playing the fop in London. And, besides, I wanted to get away . . . and yet, there were reasons why it was difficult.'

The Duchess, she thought. Or had he half wanted to get away from her?

'In the end,' he went on, 'before I could enlist, I was approached very secretly on behalf of the Home Secretary. Asked to go down to Oldchurch and find the traitor. I found a whole nest of them, and no proof . . . I only wish I had been in town when the Duke decided to give your husband the living there. If I could have put in a word with the Duchess before he had settled on it . . . But you know what he is like when once his mind is made up. That was a bad, unchancy time. When did you get my letter, Caroline?'

'Too late,' she told him. 'But I'll always be grateful.'

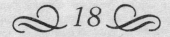

CAROLINE INSISTED ON getting up next morning. Anything was better than lying in bed, alone with her thoughts. Tremadoc had died horribly; her fault. Her friend John Gerard was Mattingley, the Duchess's lover. She had lost both her husband and her friend. It was disgusting to find herself thinking that Tremadoc's death had left her blessedly free, though without either home or income, but it was a fact, and must be faced. And so must her mother's history. Her host, bluff Dick Purchas, had greeted her with great kindness and urged her to make her home with them as long as she wished, but she sensed that he did so against his real wishes, or perhaps his wife's.

She understood this better when she met their sons. Francis and Richard were fair-haired giants in their late teens, chafing at the restraints of university life, and longing for action and military glory. Failing that, they were more than ready to plunge into love with the romantic figure she presented, and she could almost see them doing so. It would have been comic if it had not been so inconvenient. She would have liked to stay and rest in this friendly house, with its garden looking out over the downs, and with little Jennifer for her devoted companion and slave. But she knew that the house was not really friendly to her, and since Mattingley had told her about her grandmother, she could, sadly, understand why not. She thought a great deal about her mother these days as she rested and grew stronger. What a forlorn childhood it must have been. Thinking of her own happy one at Llanfryn, she felt suddenly grateful to her mother for arranging for her. And then, inevitably, wondered if it had really been Frances Winterton or her kind friend, the Duchess. Mattingley's kind friend the Duchess.

She wrenched her thoughts away to Jennifer, to whom she felt truly a cousin. She could have done so much for her. The child was bursting with ideas and instincts that were quite alien to her kind, busy, houseproud mother. If only she could stay, become her friend . . . But in this happy house she felt the shadow of her mother and grandmother lying over her darkly. Her hosts would be glad to see her go. And anyway, she told herself, she must get back to work on *The Downfall of Bonaparte*, which she meant to finish as Tremadoc's memorial. And this was not a house where women were expected to spend their time reading or writing. Now that she was better, there was no fire in her bedroom, and composition was impossible in the public rooms, with Mrs. Purchas bustling about, with Jennifer eager to sit at her feet, and Francis and Richard always on the look-out for ways to serve her.

She had promised Mattingley that she would stay where she was for the moment. Indeed, there was not much else she could do, and she was deeply grateful to him for finding her this asylum, where she felt herself growing stronger every day. He had undertaken to write to Chevenham House about her plight, explaining that he would in fact prefer to do so, granted the complete secrecy that must cover the disaster at Oldchurch. She was grateful for this, too, though she did not share his conviction that the Duke would instantly make provision for her. How had she made the Duke so completely her enemy?

Francis brought her first letters to her a week later, having met Charles Mattingley's messenger in the village. 'His master sends his kind regards, and hopes to call on you shortly.' He repeated the man's message. 'They are all to pieces in Oldchurch still, by what the man says. Oh, Mrs. Tremadoc, he told me about your husband! What a man! What a hero! We did not understand that he had been killed in trying to save his friend Mr. Bowles who had slipped and fallen into the fire. I am afraid those processions at Oldchurch are little better than drunken orgies.' He sounded suddenly like his mother. 'But your husband; what a hero! What a loss to his country:

> He is a man whom all the world must mourn,
> A vanished hero, never to return.'

It was a couplet Tremadoc had insisted on inserting into their stanzas about the death of Burke. It made, Caroline thought sadly, a very suitable epitaph for him.

'Thank you.' She smiled a kind dismissal to Francis, who was hopefully lingering beside her, and turned eagerly to the letters.

Nothing from Chevenham House. One was in Comfrey's small, neat hand. It was addressed to her, not to Tremadoc, so he must have heard the news. Her hand shook as she opened it.

He wrote with great kindness and sympathy to the woman he imagined desolate for her genius husband. Every word of praise for the lost poet made her feel worse, more of a hypocrite, more of a murderess. If she had not turned Tremadoc into something he was not, Bowles and his gang would probably not have killed him. It was knowledge she must keep to herself and learn to live with. She turned the closely written sheet and came to the nub of the letter. 'Is it too much to hope,' wrote Comfrey, 'that our lost genius has left some publishable fragments of his great poem? He spoke, when he was last in town, of a canto devoted to Lord Nelson, but we differed about the line he intended to take. He was critical of our hero then. If he did some work on the new canto, I devoutly hope he allowed his genius to be over-ruled by my caution. If anything does remain, flattering to Nelson, and worthy of your husband, I would wish to publish it with as little delay as possible, however imperfect. We must catch the moment, Mrs. Tremadoc.'

He turned to kind enquiries about her own health, and asked if he might give himself the pleasure of visiting her, as soon as she felt equal to it, to look over and discuss any fragments Tremadoc might have left. He would also, he said, like to consider publishing a collection of Tremadoc's sermons, which he had heard highly praised. 'I only wish I had heard him give one of them.'

From the tone of the letter, she was sure that Comfrey expected a runaway success for both poem and sermons if he could only publish them while the news of Tremadoc's 'heroic' death was still fresh. She must lose no time in finding somewhere to write the new canto she planned. But where? She opened the next letter, belatedly recognising the hand as Amelia's. Dated from the ffether country house near Cley, it was short and to the point.

'Mamma has sent me your news. Fancy Tremadoc a hero! Fancy you a widow! I don't know which I find harder to credit. Mamma thinks I should ask you to stay, and really it seems an uncommon good notion. I'm breeding, of course, and bored to distraction here on the cold fens. I asked Skinny, but she won't leave that brother of hers and his puling infant, so do come and cheer me up. I'll even let you read to me, as you used to do to mamma. See how low I'm sunk.'

And then, a postscript: 'We're all to pieces here since that fool of a housekeeper left.'

Caroline sat for a moment, looking sadly down at the letter. So that was the plan for her future. Unpaid housekeeper, companion and whipping boy to whichever member of the family chanced to need her. The reference to Miss Skinner gave it all away. But of course she would not leave her brother and his motherless child. If only there was more room in the little Cambridge house, but by what rights would she ask asylum there? She turned to the last letter, her heart sinking as she saw that it was from Tremadoc's mother. She had written to her as soon as her hand could manage a pen, making the most of Mattingley's story about Tremadoc's gallant death, but Mrs. Tremadoc had not had the letter when she wrote. Her letter was one long, bitter accusation. Caroline was an adventuress, a seductress, a murderess. She had turned son against mother. She would reap her reward now: 'Expect no help from me.'

It was all true. Caroline stared at the letter with unseeing eyes. Every word of it was true. She had trapped Tremadoc into a loveless marriage. She had made him famous, and, by doing so, had condemned him to death. And she was indeed reaping her reward now. No help from anyone. She could not stay here. She would not go to the ffethers. Chevenham House and Mrs. Tremadoc's seemed equally closed to her. She turned back to Comfrey's letter, so kind, so friendly . . . He said nothing about terms for publication, doubtless feeling that this would be out of place in a letter of condolence, but she thought him a fair man. If she were to write and ask him to advance the money for her to live on while she 'prepared' the sermons and the next canto of *The Downfall of Bonaparte* for the press, she was sure he would send it to her.

Live by herself? Where? Not in Oldchurch. Mattingley was right about that. Suddenly, overwhelmingly, she was filled with longing for the old vicarage at Llanfryn, the lost, fragrant garden of her childhood. Go there? But Mr. Trentham was dead and a new clergyman installed in the old house. Sophie was doubtless mistress of the Thornton household now, but to write to her was merely to apply for another post as unpaid companion. And, besides, she and Sophie had never really been friends. She wondered, as she often did, what had happened to Giles. Had he made his fortune in India, or had he just sunk there without trace? She would probably never know. Poor Giles. Sometimes, thinking of that distant past, she had wondered if her own coming, their adoption of her, had not done something to destroy that happy family. Am I a Jonah? Do I harm whomever befriends me? Blakeney was in the regular army now, serving under General Moore. If he was killed, it would be her fault too.

Calling on her two days later, Mattingley was troubled by her drawn look. 'What have you been doing with yourself?' he asked. 'You are supposed to be resting and getting better.'

'I'm being shamefully indulged.' She could not tell him that she now sat up to all hours in her cold bedroom, wrapped in a heavy cloak, writing her elegy for Lord Nelson until the candle failed her. 'But I must leave here, Mr. Mattingley. They have been kindness itself to me, but for that very reason I must go.'

'The boys, is it? I noticed that they had not gone back to Cambridge.' He did not add that he had come on them quarrelling in the stable yard and guessed she was the cause. 'You've heard from Chevenham House?' He had written to the Duchess urging that Caroline be invited back there, and, wise though he was in the ways of women, it had not struck him that his very urgency might defeat its own end.

'Indirectly.' He had never heard her so very nearly bitter. 'Amelia writes to invite me to stay with them. Indefinitely. I am to be something, I think, between housekeeper and companion.'

'You'll go?' Did he hope she would?

'No. I have written to Mr. Comfrey, the publisher, asking for an advance payment that will let me take lodgings in London and get my husband's papers in order for publication.'

'Lodgings in London? By yourself? Impossible. It would be social ruin.'

'I see no alternative.' Cold comfort that she knew he was right.

'You must go to Chevenham House! Of course they will take you in if you present yourself there.' And then, seeing her mutely shake her head, 'Well, that settles it! Caroline, marry me.' He knew it for a mistake before the words were out. 'I know it's too soon...'

'You are a very gallant gentleman, Mr. Mattingley, and I thank you.' She was on her feet, paler than ever. 'But I'll spoil no more lives. Besides, what would the Duchess say?' She turned with a quick breath of relief as Jennifer bounced into the room, her arms full of black crêpe. 'Jennifer and I are very busy,' she told him, 'making favours for the day of Nelson's funeral.'

He retired, cursing himself, and when he called again, a few days later, was amazed to learn that Caroline had left for London.

'She received an urgent summons from her mother-in-law's housekeeper,' Dick Purchas told him. 'It seems the old lady's been ill for some time; thought her daughter-in-law knew, but young Tremadoc never troubled to tell her it was serious. His death brought on a paralytic stroke. They need young Mrs. Tremadoc to see to things. I'm sad, but I can't say I'm not relieved. Sometimes I think there was—oh, it sounds crazy— not a curse exactly, but my poor sister Julia brought bad luck wherever she went. The boys have gone back to Cambridge.' It was very far from being a non sequitur.

'Mrs. Tremadoc left no letter for me?'

'A message. Her kindest thanks. She went off in a great rush; the carriage was waiting. My little Jennifer's quite broken-hearted.'

And so am I, thought Mattingley. How strange. How very strange. The first time he had asked Caroline to marry him, it had been merely a quixotic gesture... Or had it? Had he always felt more about the Duchess's protégé than he quite understood? At all events, the long, friendly association in Oldchurch, when she treated him as the wise counsellor and older friend she thought him, had done his business for him. Idiot to have spoken so absurdly too soon. What madness had made him do it? It was not just the thought that at all costs his future wife must be prevented from the social ruin of setting up house alone in London. It had been something else... something about the feel of her in his arms that night in the cellars. Surely the spark that had lit in him when he roped her up for the dangerous plunge must glow in her too? Or was it all his imagination? What did he know about a young thing like her? Suddenly, passionately, he found himself regretting his long affair with the Duchess. If only they had remained the good friends they could have been... But she had needed more than that, and he had been young and under her spell.

Caroline had spoken of the Duchess, just before Jennifer's disastrous interruption. He had hoped she did not know of that long-standing affair, but it had probably been absurd to do so. Just as well that she was not going to be living in Chevenham House. He could not have visited her there without seeing the Duchess too, risking re-involvement in the relationship he had hoped to end when pique at Caroline's failure even to answer his proposal had combined with anxiety about her move to Oldchurch to send him down to live there all the time. Caroline had transformed him from the dilettante part-time spy who left his servants to keep the watch he had undertaken in Oldchurch while he played his outworn part as the Duchess's devoted slave in London. It was a mercy he had gone down to Oldchurch. If he had not been there, events on that Guy Fawkes day might have worked out very differently. The little town might now be a bastion for Napoleon's army of invasion, and Caroline dead as well as her husband.

He would follow her to London, just as soon as he could, but for the moment duty kept him in Oldchurch where the government's agents were having a hard time of it trying to combine punishment for the surviving conspirators with secrecy about what they had actually planned. It would be a while before he could abandon his part as John Gerard, and he told himself that was probably a good thing. Respectably established in her mother-in-law's house, Caroline would have time to get over the shock of her husband's death. He had known hers, always, for a marriage without love. After all, he had seen her and Blakeney together on that fatal day in Richmond Park, and known that in marrying Tremadoc she had consciously taken second best. He had sometimes been surprised that she did not show more respect for the brilliant figure her husband had become, but then, he told himself, no man is really a hero to his wife. Would he be? What a strange question. First I must persuade her to marry me, he thought, and returned to Old-church to plunge back into John Gerard's business, to get it finished.

Reaching London, Caroline was appalled by Mrs. Tremadoc's condition. She knew the servants, since Mrs. Tremadoc had taken them with her from the house in Grosvenor Square, and they were silently reproachful at first, until she explained that Tremadoc had given her only the most casual hint that all was not well with his mother.

'I should have thought of that,' said Mrs. Jones, the house-keeper. 'He never did take the poor Mistress's trouble seriously. And of course she did her best to put on a brave face for him when he came to stay. She's past that now, poor lady. The news of his death did for her, I think. She wrote to you, and sent for her lawyer, Mr. James, but the spasm took her before he got here. She's been as you see ever since.'

'What does the doctor say?' Caroline looked down at the motionless figure in the big bed.

'That it's a matter of time. Anything from days to years, he reckons. I'm glad you're come, ma'am. We all are. We was afraid it might be the mistress's nephew, son of her brother that lost all that money for her. Worried her to death, he has, with his begging letters. You must look for a visit from him, just as soon as he hears the news.'

'He's not been told?'

'We sent to *you*, ma'am.'

The lawyer and doctor both called that afternoon, the doctor to confirm what Mrs. Jones had said, and Mr. James to expand on it.

'I've never been gladder to have been out of town,' he told her. 'From Mrs. Tremadoc's note, I think there was no question but she meant to change her will. As it stands, everything goes to her son, and therefore to you. She is in no state to change it now, and I'm glad of it. That nephew of hers did his best to suck her dry. If you'll be advised by me, Mrs. Tremadoc, you'll have no dealings with him. Send him to me, if he proves importunate. You'll have little enough as it is, I am afraid. Don't go thinking it a fortune. But I suppose Mr. Tremadoc's poetry may bring you in something?'

'I hope so,' she told him. 'I am seeing his publisher to-morrow.'

'A sad loss, Mrs. Tremadoc.' He rose to his feet. 'A most surprising and brilliant young man, your husband. A very sad loss to the world.'

She was getting used to these curiously painful, ill-founded condolences. If she could bear them from Charles Mattingley, she thought she could bear them from anyone. She pushed the idea of Mattingley resolutely to the back of her mind, but it would keep recurring. It was so hard to get used to the idea that he was her wise old friend, John Gerard. She blushed angrily as she remembered how she had confided in him, admitted her ignorance, asked his advice as one might of a father if one had ever had a proper one. And all the time, her grey-bearded friend had been Charles Mattingley, the Duchess's lover, playing at spies.

He had saved her life by his spy-playing. No getting away from that. And impossible not to remember that moment of helpless ecstasy when he tied the harness around her. Doubtless that was the way he affected all women. Doubtless, too, he knew it was, and had taken it for granted that she would leap at marriage. Well, thank God, her instinctive reaction had been the right one. She had shown him his mistake, and next time they met he would be the Duchess's devoted slave again.

She would not call at Chevenham House for a while. They obviously did not want her there, and she very much did not want to see her good friend John Gerard transformed into Mattingley and dangling after the Duchess. She hated to think of them together, could not help it, and found her thoughts flash back to a day long ago, when she was a terrified child, new to Cley, and Gaston had sent her to burst into the Duke's private apartments. It had been a long time before she realised that it must have been Frances Winterton, not the Duchess, concealed in the huge four poster. Her mother. And her father. And he had never forgiven her. Of course it was he who had closed the doors of Chevenham House to her now. The Duchess had done her best for her by arranging Amelia's invitation. Impossible not to love the Duchess, who had always been more of a mother to her than Frances Winterton. She must never know of Charles Mattingley's brief defection. Well, why should she? He would be regretting his moment of madness by now. All over, all past, all done with.

She moved over to a window to look out at the house's

small, winter-bare town garden and think about fathers. The Duke was still in town, she knew, although parliament had been prorogued until January. A little shrimp, he had called her, all those years ago. Often and often, remembering this, she had imagined scenes in which he changed his tune. She was dressed for her presentation at court, for her wedding, for some state occasion . . . plumes and diamonds and a great sweep of crinoline, and he was looking at her in amazement. 'My beautiful daughter!'

Tears came suddenly to her eyes. Forgetting the Duke, she remembered Mr. Trentham. Suddenly, clearly, she saw his face as the Duke said those slighting words, years ago, his loving father's face, feeling with her, feeling for her, knowing it all, loving her. What friends they had been, working together in his study, what wonderfully good friends. Had he, she wondered, looking back, had he perhaps favoured her at the expense of his own children? Had she really been a disaster to that family?

A disaster everywhere? She turned impatiently away from the window and pulled out the sheet of paper she had hidden when the lawyer was announced. She was a good halfway through the canto on Lord Nelson now, and must make up her mind just what she was going to say to Mr. Comfrey when he called next day. What would the publisher be like? Tremadoc had never given her any kind of a picture of him, but then, describing people was hardly Tremadoc's long suit. Deep in self love, he hardly even saw them. She was going to have to be very careful how she talked to Comfrey. He said nothing about himself in his letters, but he was most evidently no fool. He had spent a good deal of time with Tremadoc, had refused to introduce him into the literary world, must therefore have seen the discrepancy between the man and the work. How would he have explained it to himself? If he had imagined the possibility of a collaborator, she would have to be cautious indeed. Unless she confessed it all? Could she perhaps tell him the whole story, and would he advise her what to do?

Deep mourning did not suit her. Eyeing the quenched, slight figure in the glass next day, she dismissed those fantasies about confiding in Mr. Comfrey. Nobody would believe that this inconspicuous figure was the real author of *The Downfall of Bonaparte*. She would show him what she had written, and tell him with timid, apologetic blushes, if she could manage them, that the rest had been taken down verbatim, in such a scrawl that nobody but she could understand it. She would be every inch the incapable young female and explain that she could only transcribe a little a day. That would give her time to finish.

That decided, and her sad morning visit paid to the sickroom where Mrs. Tremadoc lay inert as ever, she settled herself to await her caller in the neat, dull front parlour. The sound of a curricle, driven fast, drew her to the window because it was so unusual in this quiet, unfashionable street. To her amazement, it drew up smartly outside the house and the driver threw the reins to the smart boy who sat up behind, jumped down and strode up the two steps to the front door.

A moment later, he was being shown into the room, where she had hurriedly composed herself on one of the uncomfortable chairs.

'Mr. Comfrey, ma'am,' said Mrs. Jones.

'I'm early. Forgive me.' Bowing over her hand, the publisher looked as surprised as she felt. Tremadoc had spoken of his youth, but had said nothing about his good looks. He had very likely been jealous, she thought sadly. She herself had expected some drab young city-looking man, but this handsome stranger was fashionable from artfully dishevelled golden curls and whiskers to narrow grey trousers. He was thin, and very brown, and his hand, as he took hers, felt full of life as if he were charged with one of Mr. Mesmer's electric currents.

'You *are* Mrs. Tremadoc?' He looked about the room as if he half expected to see someone else.

'I am not what you expected?' She motioned him to a seat, sadly dismissing that dream of a confidant.

'Forgive me,' he said again, moving with controlled grace to hold her chair for her. 'I had . . . I had quite the wrong idea.' Looking momentarily out of countenance, he seemed younger still. 'Absurd of me.'

What in the world could Tremadoc have said about her? Or was it the voice of scandal Comfrey had listened to? What did the world say about the products of Chevenham House? She would rather not know. 'I was quite wrong about you, too,' she told him. 'I had expected an experienced publisher whose advice I would revere.'

'Which you will not mine?' Now he was laughing at her. 'Dear Mrs. Tremadoc, I do hope I can persuade you otherwise. I mean to be frank with you, as I was with your husband.' He paused, looking abashed. 'I beg a thousand pardons; there are so many things I should be saying.'

'You said them, Mr. Comfrey, most gracefully in your letter. Now we are to talk business, you and I. Let us, please, be frank with each other. I am a widow, and poor. I think you mean to make money from the work my husband has left. I hope you do. I need it. I mean to help you, and share it.'

'Help me?' Now she had indeed surprised him.

'Yes. I should explain. My husband came back from his last visit to London much impressed with what you had said to him in praise of Lord Nelson. He started at once to work on a whole new canto, devoted to him. He worked fast, when the spirit moved him. I was his amanuensis, Mr. Comfrey, but he was too quick for me. He was ... impatient when he was composing. I took it down as best I might; there are alterations, interpolations, he even left passages open, or wrote alternative passages ... In case of victory, in case of defeat ... Even in case of death. He said you might be wrong about Nelson— forgive me? I have it all, in my notes, but it will take me some time to transcribe it, to set it to rights. Don't look so doubtful! It's what I always did for him. You met him several times, Mr. Comfrey, you must have seen that he was an impatient man. He threw off his work at white heat, then left the shaping to me.'

'I see.' He thought about it for a moment. 'It's wonderful news, Mrs. Tremadoc. Tell me, how much? How soon?'

'A whole canto, I think. Early in the new year? It depends a little on the condition of my mother-in-law. She is gravely ill.'

'I'm sorry.' It was merely an automatic response. 'But publication must not depend on anything, Mrs. Tremadoc. Lord Nelson's funeral is on January the ninth. Hire nurses! Hire as many as you please and let me stand the expense. I must have the poem, sheet by sheet if necessary, so that it can come out in January at the latest. I am a man of business, and I tell you, speed is of the essence here. The volume of sermons can wait ... should wait until we have hit the public with the poem. I beg that you will bend every nerve to the transcription. Is there any way that I can help you?'

'I am afraid not. But there are a few pages I have already transcribed. I thought you would like to see them.' She was both amused and irritated that he had not asked her what she thought of the new canto. 'I copied them for you last night.'

She picked up the neatly written sheets and handed them to him.

He took them reverently. 'Excuse me?' He read fast, as she had written, totally absorbed, and she watched with equal intensity. Suppose, just suppose, she had written too fast, had deceived herself when she thought this the best of all . . . How strange to think that he held her future in his hands, this curly-haired young Adonis.

He put down the last sheet, and sighed. 'Magnificent. It will bring tears to every eye. Good God, Mrs. Tremadoc, what a tragedy, what a loss! And you have the whole canto?' He came to his feet and strode to the window as if the room was too small for him, then back to loom over her chair. 'I'm a selfish man, Mrs. Tremadoc. When I heard of your husband's death, I thought it meant my ruin. Mine's a small publishing house, a new one. When I received the first canto of *The Downfall of Bonaparte* I thought my chance of establishing myself had come. I have poured everything I had into promotion of your husband's work.' He laughed. 'More than everything! I thought the risk was justified. Now I know it was. May I send you a copyist, and may I call on your man of business to discuss terms?'

She smiled up at him. 'I'm sorry, but no to both, Mr. Comfrey. I have always fair-copied my husband's work; he liked me to do so. He was grateful for the small changes I made in it. His was the grand design, mine the attention to detail. I do not propose to change that. But I will hire nurses, if you wish to pay for them. My poor mother-in-law knows no one; it can make no difference to her, and I have as great an interest as you in the poem's success. We should publish it on the day of the funeral, I collect?'

'If you can do it.'

'If I can, I must. I shall be glad to have an excuse to keep to the house and see no one.'

'Very well. But the argeement, Mrs. Tremadoc. We must have a new agreement. Surely your man of business?'

'I would much rather settle it with you here and now, Mr. Comfrey.' She had thought about this and had her proposal for improved terms ready. He listened to it with surprised respect, agreed at once, and promised to have it drawn up for signature that same day.

'You are a very surprising young lady, Mrs. Tremadoc, if you will not mind my saying so.' He was on his feet, ready to go, but looked down at her thoughtfully for a moment, studying her face. 'It's a strange thing. You remind me of someone . . . No, that's not it. I feel as if I had met you before, but that is impossible. I have never been to Sussex in my life.'

'Sussex?' She realised, with wry amusement, that Tremadoc must have told his publisher nothing about her. Well, why should he have. But, curiously enough, she, too, had begun to feel the faint stirrings of an old memory. What exactly was it? Something about the way he moved? 'Quite impossible.' She was answering herself as much as him. 'We have most certainly never been introduced. Your charming name is not one I would have forgotten.'

'Oh, that!' He had a fine, carefree laugh. 'Just right for a publisher, don't you think? Memorable, I hope. But all my own invention, Mrs. Tremadoc. My own name's disgraced. I thought, when I returned to England, that I would make it good again, for my father's sake, my mother's. We were all to be happy together. A boy's plans, forgive me for boring you with them.'

'You're not boring me. I am so sorry. Do please go on.'

'They were dead, of course, when I got back. Both of them. And my sister had doubled the shame I brought on the family. An unlucky name, Mrs. Tremadoc, best forgotten. Giles Comfrey does very well.'

'Giles?' He had always signed with the initial only. 'Good God! You're *Giles*!' She was on her feet, holding out both hands. 'No wonder we remembered each other! Oh, dear Giles, I am Caroline, your sister.' And then, remembering what he had just said. 'Disgraced? Sophie? What do you mean?'

'Little Carrie?' He bent to kiss the hands swallowed in his, and once again, endearingly, he blushed. 'You did not like to be called that! Did you get in a great deal of trouble about those pearls?'

'No—well, yes.' She must not tell him that that had been the moment when everything began to go wrong between her and the Trenthams. 'It's all over now, best forgotten. But Sophie?'

'Ran off with young Staines. Just after my father died. She's living with him still. No marriage, of course. Dr. Thornton could not afford to divorce her, and if he could it would mean professional ruin. She writes boldly enough, but there are two children, poor little things.'

'You've not seen her?'

'No. Her letter was enough. I would rather not. Caroline.'
His colour deepened under the dark skin. 'Were they lies, the
things she said about you? I think they were the hardest to
bear. I had thought about you so much, all that time in India.
I have a string of pearls at home, bought for you, Carrie. Tell
me they were lies!'

'What did she say?'

'Not much. Enough. That we must forget you. She named
no names. Just said you had gone to your real mother, and—
forgive me—gone the same way she had. That it killed our
mother.'

'How could she!' Anger was warming. 'If you had thought
for a moment, Giles, you would have known that could not be
true. Your mother died when I was still a child. Just before
Sophie's own marriage. And—' It was her turn to blush. 'She's
wrong about my mother, too. Well, you live in the world, you
must know about her. She's Frances Winterton.'

'Good God!' He obviously did know about Frances, and
was taken all aback. 'Caroline, forgive me.'

'No need. There *was* a scandal about me. I do not propose
to tell you about it. But I was innocent, except for a foolish
elopement with poor Mr. Tremadoc.'

'I should not have believed her,' he said. 'I should have
sought you out, Caroline, but I have been so busy, setting up
my publishing house. I only got home a year and half ago.
That's why *The Downfall of Bonaparte* is so important to me.
Lord, Carrie?'

'Yes?'

'You used to write poetry. Reams and reams of it. And read
it aloud to me. Did you perhaps help your husband a little? I
never could quite understand about him . . . You really worked
with him on his great poem?'

'Why, yes, you could say I did.' But this was dangerous
ground and she shifted it. 'I am beginning to recognise you
now,' she said. 'But you look so much older. And your hair,
Giles . . . It used to be dark.'

He laughed, a little self consciously. 'The Indian sun. A
fortunate thing we men do not care about our complexions the
way you ladies do.' He had been thinking about what she had
told him. 'But, Carrie, if Mrs. Winterton is your mother, your
father must be . . .'

'The Duke of Cley.' She confirmed it without pleasure.

೨ 19 ೮

Even through the warm happiness of rediscovering Giles, Caroline kept her head, and her secret. She admitted to a closer collaboration with Tremadoc than she had previously suggested, but that was as far as she went. Every instinct warned her that she must not tell Giles that she was in fact writing the new canto and sending it to him, sheet by sheet, as she went along. If the poem was the success he confidently predicted, it would be time enough to confess to her authorship. Then, she thought, she might even risk showing him some of her own work, the sequence of sonnets she had written to Blakeney, which could easily be passed off as a young girl's first love poetry, to an imagined hero, and which she continued to think well of.

London was an anxious place that winter. The tragedy of Nelson's death had cast a shadow over his victory, and soon Trafalgar was almost forgotten in the grim news of allied defeats at Ulm and Austerlitz. But for Caroline it was a peaceful, preoccupied time. Her mother-in-law's illness combined with her own deep mourning to give her a complete excuse for keeping out of society. What could a young widow do more suitable than sit at home and copy out her dead husband's work? Busy writing his memorial, she was able to keep at bay her nagging sense of guilt over Tremadoc's death.

She was not at home to any visitors except the doctor, Mr. James the lawyer, and Giles. Mrs. Jones, turned dragon in her defence, effectively routed even Mrs. Tremadoc's nephew, who went grumbling off to Mr. James, got no good there either, and returned to Manchester. Giles visited her every other day to collect the sheets she had 'copied', and would have come daily if she had let him. But she was having a little trouble with Giles, who thought that if she could amend her dead husband's work, so could he, a delusion of which she had gently but firmly to dispossess him.

228

But they were wonderfully good friends and she had even accepted the exquisite string of pearls he had brought home from India for her, because it would have seemed churlish not to do so. He had wanted to write and quarrel with Sophie on her account, but she had been able to persuade him not to do so.

'Poor Sophie, she must have troubles enough of her own.' They had finished reading through the batch of verses she had produced for him and were sitting comfortably together in front of the fire in the little front room she had gradually turned into a study.

'I suppose so. But it makes me angry, just the same, to think how she slandered you. Caroline, I have been thinking . . . I would like . . . I would very much like to be presented to your mother.'

'My mother?' It was amazing how, here on the wrong side of the Park, it had been possible almost to forget about Chevenham House. She had, in the end, had kind notes from both the Duchess and her mother, who appeared to have accepted the fact that she was, for the moment, self supporting, but she had ignored their invitations to call at Chevenham House. There had been no word from the Duke, but then, as the Duchess had remarked, he was involved in the ceremonial arrangements for Nelson's State Funeral, and very busy indeed. Reading between the lines of the two notes, Caroline thought that the Duke must have been persuaded by his two ladies that however much he disliked her he could not absolutely cut the connection with his daughter. But she was sure he would be relieved not to see her at Chevenham House.

Giles was repeating his request: 'Yes, your mother. And . . .' he blushed his engaging blush. 'Your father, if you think it appropriate.'

'Which I do not. I'm sorry, Giles, but I prefer not to go to Chevenham House at the moment.' She had still heard nothing from Charles Mattingley, and did not even know whether he was down at Oldchurch, or whether he was once again an habitué of Chevenham House. She most certainly did not intend to risk meeting him there, seeing him once again the Duchess's faithful slave. It's all wrong for him, she thought angrily, that's why I dislike the idea so. If only her imagination would leave it alone.

Giles was looking disappointed. 'Your family, Carrie?'

'I look on you as quite as much my family as they are.'

She had explained their relationship to Mrs. Jones, who had begun to look a little askance at his frequent visits, and had no doubt that that lady was busily putting it about in the close-knit servants' underworld that her mistress had found a long-lost brother. The news would doubtless get back to Chevenham House soon enough.

'Thank you for saying that, dear Carrie.' He was on his feet now, making ready to go. 'I mean to be.'

Left alone, she sighed, and shrugged, and went back to work. She thought she had never worked so hard in her life. Since the poem was being set as she wrote it, there was no way, without extreme inconvenience and expense, that she could change anything. It made her task doubly difficult, and so did the lack both of a library and of the reliable advice about matters of fact that she had been able to get from 'John Gerard' when she worked in his. It was no use asking Giles in what year Nelson became an admiral or when Bonaparte had made himself Emperor. Giles would merely shrug, and smile and point out that he had most likely been in India at the time, busy making a fortune. And even on the events that had taken place since he returned to England he proved a disappointing source of information. 'I'm sorry, Carrie dear.' He shrugged off her questions. 'I'm a working man, you know. No time for politics and the papers.'

She bit back a sharp reply. After all, she hoped he was engaged in making both their fortunes, but she wished she could make him see that just for that reason it was important that she get her facts right.

'But if Mr. Tremadoc did not mind, why should you?' asked Giles unanswerably when she tried to explain this. He left her still distractedly wondering just exactly what had been so masterly about Nelson's battle plan for Aboukir Bay.

She was interrupted by Mrs. Jones, to ask, doubtfully, whether she would see Mr. Mattingley. 'I told him you were not at home, ma'am, but he said you'd be at home to him. A very masterful gentleman.'

'An old friend. Yes, I'll see him.' She jumped to her feet to study the flushed reflection in the glass. Of course her heart was beating faster. The last time they had met he had asked her to marry him.

Forget that. But she could not conceal her pleasure when he appeared. 'You have come in the nick of time.' The touch of his warm hand sent the blood racing through her, and she found herself babbling. 'I need your help. John Gerard's help. I am engaged in copying poor Tremadoc's poem for the publisher, and I cannot make sense of what he says about Nelson's battle plan. My notes are almost indecipherable, I'm afraid.'

'Unlike you.' He took the seat she had indicated. 'I'm glad to see you so well occupied, but you look tired. Are you working yourself too hard? The poem is to be published on the day of the funeral, I understand. It is being puffed everywhere by that busy publisher of yours.' Was there an implied question in the statement?

'The most romantic thing,' she plunged into it. 'Only imagine his turning out to be my foster-brother, Giles Trentham, with a new name.'

'Romantic indeed,' his tone was dry. 'But do not let him overwork you just the same. As to the plan Nelson made with his captains, fetch me pen and paper, and I will do my best to explain.'

'Oh, I do thank you,' she said at last. 'Now I see just what poor Tremadoc meant.'

'Have you your notes here? Perhaps if I were to look at them, I might be able to help?'

'Oh, no, thank you! I keep them upstairs in my room, and they are quite illegible, I am afraid. He composed in such haste; it was all I could do to keep up with him.'

'A remarkable man. There is to be a volume of sermons too, by what I hear.'

'Yes, I hope so.' This was all dangerous ground. She had always been afraid that he might recognise his own thoughts behind the words she had put into Tremadoc's mouth. The longer publication of the sermons was put off, the happier she would be. She changed the subject. 'Have you been in town long? What is the news from Oldchurch?'

'Only since yesterday. It's been a sad business down at Oldchurch. It will be a long day, I am afraid, before the poor women there realise how much better off they are without those sordid husbands of theirs. The more I have learned of the Oldchurch Club, the more I detest it. You must always remember, Mrs. Tremadoc, that those men's murdering your husband was in its way a very positive tribute to him.'

'Cold comfort,' she said.

'But truth.' He rose to his feet. 'I know how you value the truth. I learned that as John Gerard. That was a happy time. I hope you have forgiven me the deception.'

'I'd be an ingrate if I hadn't, considering that it saved my life.' She remembered those moments in the vault, felt uncontrollable colour rise in her face, and looked down at her notes to conceal it. 'I shall never be able to thank you enough.'

'The fact that you are alive will do! Caroline . . .' He stopped, her weeds reminding him that it was still grossly too soon. 'I think you should call at Chevenham House.' It was his turn to change the subject. 'The Duchess is very far from well. She misses you, I think.'

So he had gone there first. 'I am not going out yet,' she said coldly, and rose to her feet. 'I must not keep you, Mr. Mattingley. You will have a million friends to see, now that you are back in town.'

'I am keeping you from your labours. Forgive me.' He turned towards the door, turned back again. 'You do look tired. I wish you would let me take you for a drive, or better still a ride in the Park. I have a filly would suit you to a nicety, and it's not too cold, if you dress warmly . . . Today? Tomorrow? I am at your service. It would put some colour in your cheeks.'

'I'm sorry you find me so hag-ridden. It's a bad time with me, and, I thank you, Mr. Mattingley, but I am not going out at the moment.'

'Of course not.' He knew it for an absurd suggestion. 'But let me send the filly, and a groom to escort you. There could be no impropriety in that. Please?'

'I must be the judge of my own proprieties.' She held out her hand. 'Goodbye, Mr. Mattingley, and thank you.'

Left alone, she would not let herself think about him, but went to work with a will while his elucidation of Aboukir Bay was fresh in her mind. Writing steadily for a couple of hours, she forgot everything else as she always did in the absorbed happiness of composition. And yet, this canto, supposedly by Tremadoc, really was extraordinarily difficult to write. She had been reduced to what she knew was shameless padding and had dragged in a description of a wild garden at Nelson's house at Merton that was, in fact, her own beloved garden at Llanfryn. Writing it had given her the same pleasure and release she had had from the sonnets to Blakeney, and, to her relief, Giles had shown no signs of recognising the garden where he had grown up.

At last she stopped, tears in her eyes, and inspiration failing her. She put down the pen and leaned her head tiredly in her hands. Mattingley was right. She was exhausted. Only the need to finish the poem kept her going. Another few days and it would be done. What would she do then?

My occupation will be gone, she thought. The poem was a debt she owed Tremadoc. With it done, she would have to face her own bleak future. She must be some use in the world. Go to Amelia after all? Amelia was apparently the only person who needed her. No, for the moment Mrs. Tremadoc did. And, besides, more than ever she was reluctant to have any dealings with Chevenham House. Mattingley had gone there first. He must be dangling after the Duchess again. What a sigh of relief he must have breathed when she refused his second offer of marriage; Mattingley the unmarrying man.

She rang for Mrs. Jones and spent the rest of the day very busily checking stores in Mrs. Tremadoc's disorganised household. From the evidence of domestic chaos, she could tell that the old lady must have been much iller than anyone realised. If Tremadoc had only told her his mother was not well, she might have gone to London to look after her. Everything would have been quite different.

Foolish to think like that. A waste of time. Everything seemed a waste of time just now. Everything except the poem. 'I'm tired, Mrs. Jones,' she said suddenly. 'I think perhaps I will go to bed early and have a tray there. Just some broth?'

'You don't eat enough to keep a sparrow alive,' protested Mrs. Jones. 'You get to bed, Mrs. Tremadoc, my dear, and let me and cook alone to send up something that will do you good.'

'Why, thank you.' The unexpected endearment had brought tears to her eyes. 'You're all very good to me.'

'We love you,' said Mrs. Jones, surprising her.

Giles was to call next morning and Caroline refused breakfast in bed and was in her study early to copy out yesterday's stanzas. To her relief, they read well and she was able to greet Giles with confidence when he arrived: 'Not much longer now. I think you are safe for publication on the ninth. There is only the death of Nelson and then the lament for him by the Spirit of History. I think I should be able to have them copied in a week or so.'

'You will be stopping work for Christmas, surely?'

'Christmas?' She looked at him vaguely. 'Why?'

'Caroline, I'm ashamed. I have been letting you overwork yourself shockingly. You look exhausted this morning. You must give yourself a little holiday over Christmas, even if it

might mean we are a day or two late with the poem. What is
that compared to your health? In fact,' he coloured, 'I have an
invitation for you.'

'An invitation?'

'Yes, to dine at Chevenham House, quite in a family way,
on Boxing Night. You will enjoy the celebrations there, I am
sure, though of course it must be quiet this year because of
Nelson's death. All the more suitable for your first venture into
society. There can be nothing improper in your going to what
is in effect your home, Carrie.'

'I do not quite understand,' she said. 'How does it come
about that you bring this invitation, Giles?' She had fallen
without thinking into the old habit of christian names and now
sometimes wished she had not.

'Why,'—his colour was higher than ever—'I took the liberty of calling on your mother yesterday. I felt it only right
that I should, in all the circumstances. Did you know that that
husband of hers has died at last? In debt, of course, at Pau. I
felt it the least I could do to go and pay her my condolences.'
He laughed. 'If they were in order, which I doubt! But she
received me more than kindly, Carrie, and sent all sorts of
messages to you. What a delightful woman she is! I am surprised you have not spoken of her more. And beautiful! She
quite outshines that poor, bloated Duchess, and the cross-
tempered daughter. It's no wonder there are odds being laid in
the clubs now as to what might happen if the Duchess should
die.'

'Die? The Duchess? What do you mean?' Mattingley had
said the Duchess was not well, but she had assumed that it was
another of the migraine headaches that had always plagued her.

'She don't look a bit well,' said Giles. 'Oh, merry as a grig
on the surface, but hag-ridden underneath, if you understand
me.'

Caroline did, only too well. It was the way she felt herself.
'I must go to see her,' she said. 'As to Boxing Night, I will
think about it. You are invited too, I collect?'

'Why, yes, Mrs. Winterton was so kind as to do so when
she made me the bearer of her message. The Duke will be at
home for Christmas, she tells me, and young Blakeney hopes
to get leave. It will be quite a family reunion. Mrs. Winterton
urges that you come, Carrie. She wants you and the Duke
reconciled, she says.'

'Reconciled? You two have been mighty confidential.'

'She was kindness itself and treated me like the old friend that I am.' A look of self satisfaction made him suddenly a stranger. 'We have been plotting together for your good, Carrie. She quite understands how important the success of your husband's poem must be to your prospects, and undertakes to do all she can to promote it.'

'That's why you wanted to meet her!'

'That, Carrie, and other things which we will not discuss for the present. Now, I must leave you to your invaluable labours. May I carry your acceptance to Chevenham House?'

'I mean to call there myself, thank you.'

'I am delighted to hear it.' He was full of irrepressible good humour.

Left alone, she thought for a few angry moments, then rang for Mrs. Jones, ordered the carriage and hurried upstairs for bonnet and pelisse.

At Chevenham House, nothing had changed except the Duchess's looks, which horrified her. Frances Winterton, who had been ailing when she last saw her, almost a year and a half before, was in blooming health now, but the Duchess was grey beneath an unsuccessful camouflage of powder and rouge. There was something almost indecent about seeing the two of them together, and it was disconcerting, too, to notice that the servants seemed to turn for their orders rather to Mrs. Winterton than to their mistress. Was control of Chevenham House slipping into those grasping little hands before its mistress had even died?

'I thought my emissary would be successful,' said Mrs. Winterton when the first greetings were over. 'What a sly creature you are, and what a good mother I am to forgive you for letting me learn your romantic tale from servants' gossip and the romantic hero himself.'

'Romantic hero?'

'Your long-lost brother. If that is what you call him.' She laughed her knowing little laugh. 'And for so long as you wish to.' She patted the sofa beside her. 'Come and sit beside me, and tell me all about this marvellous poem of poor Tremadoc's. To tell truth, I never thought he had it in him. You must be a remarkable influence, child. I have commissioned your Giles Comfrey to bind me up a complete copy the minute the new canto is ready.'

'It's very good,' the Duchess leaned forward on the chaise-longue. 'I most particularly like the Spirits of Good and Evil, and the elegy for Mr. Burke. That was a master-stroke. I hope there is to be an elegy for our poor lost Nelson by the Spirit of Good.'

'There is indeed. I am...' She had almost said writing it. 'Transcribing it now. I am glad you liked the elegy, ma'am. Mr. Tremadoc was pleased with it, too.' This was entirely true.

'The poor man. I was so very sorry, Caroline.' She held out her hand and Caroline, who had so far stood awkwardly enough between the two of them, went straight to her, subsided on the floor beside her, and burst into tears.

'That's good. That's what you need.' The Duchess was stroking her hair. 'Cry it out, Caroline. You were always too proud for your own good. Let the tears come now; they will help.'

'What a scene of high tragedy!' said Frances Winterton impatiently. 'Anyone would think you had lost the man you loved, Carrie, rather than the one you had to marry.'

'That will do, Frances.' The Duchess spoke with sudden authority. 'We have all lost a man of genius and must mourn him as such.' She turned the conversation. 'How is your poor mother-in-law, Caroline? I was sorry to hear about that too.'

'Quite helpless,' Caroline looked up at her and fought to control the tears. 'It is only a question of time, I am afraid.'

'And you are looking after her. That is as it should be. Afterwards, it will be time to think about your future.'

'I have a crystal ball that shows it,' said Frances Winterton. 'We were always a romantic family.' She laughed. 'Now, Carrie, dry those ridiculous tears and tell me all about the pious Purchases of Denton Hall. How I laughed when Mattingley told us he had taken you there! I should just have liked to see poor old Uncle Dick's face when he found himself lumbered with my daughter. And that puritanical cit of a wife he married! I wager she wasn't best pleased to see you.'

'They were kindness itself!' said Caroline, wishing her mother would not use the nickname she hated.

'And you came away just as soon as you could. No need to tell me! No need of a crystal ball either. Those gawking boys fell in love with you, of course, and poor Uncle Dick was neither to hold nor to bind. Oh, I wish I could have been there to see the havoc you wreaked among them. I almost begin to think you are my daughter after all. I must tell the Duke how our little shrimp is coming out. You're coming on Boxing Night, of course, to draw the King with us and make that handsome cavalier of yours known to the Duke. And to Blakeney!'

Caroline kissed the Duchess and rose to her feet. 'Mr. Comfrey will most certainly come,' she said. 'But you must forgive me if I do not commit myself until the day. It must depend on how Mrs. Tremadoc is.'

'Quite right,' said the Duchess. 'But we will hope to see you, Caroline.'

20

GILES CALLED ON Christmas Day. 'Sweets to the sweet.' He handed Caroline a huge bouquet of showy, scentless hothouse flowers. 'I knew you would not allow me to give you the kind of gift I would wish to. These are merely a token of my . . . what shall I call it? My devotion! But you still look tired, Carrie. Perhaps a touch of colour for Chevenham House tomorrow? The Duke is a great connoisseur of beauty, from what I have heard.' He seated himself comfortably while she rang for a maid to put the flowers in water. 'Do you remember that time he came to Llanfryn, and how he called you a little shrimp? Lord, I was angry.'

'You said I was the wisest shrimp in Christendom.' It was heart-warming to remember it.

'Only after he had gone, thank God. I must have had some sense, even then. Enough to be civil to a Duke! I still can't quite believe he's your father, Carrie.'

'He hardly behaves as if he were!'

'Now, Carrie.' He shook a warning finger at her. 'That is no way to speak of your father. I think I begin to understand what your mother means about this little critical way of yours. Your father is a great man, with a great man's responsibilities.'

'Great?'

'A Duke. And that reminds me, do you not think, since it is Christmas, and a little for the Duchess's sake, that you should abandon those unbecoming blacks of yours just for tomorrow?'

'I am not at all sure that I shall go tomorrow.'

'Not go? I never heard such nonsense in my life. Not go to meet the Duke and his heir?' His voice was rising and she turned with relief as the maid announced, 'Mr. Mattingley.'

He, too, carried flowers, a fragrant little bunch of violets. 'I am come to wish you the happiest possible Christmas, to give you these, and to bring all kinds of loving messages from the ladies at Chevenham House.' He had been looking Giles up and down, now held out his hand. 'You must be the long-lost brother. How do you do, Mr. Comfrey? I hear great things of your new publishing house. I'm Mattingley.' His tone suggested an 'of course'.

'Thank you. Yes, I am hoping to make Mrs. Tremadoc's fortune for her.'

'And your own?'

'Well.' Giles laughed, not quite happily. 'It goes together. I am to thank you, Mr. Mattingley, for your kindness to my little sister Carrie. A highly romantic story.'

'I have thanked Mr. Mattingley myself.' Caroline sat down and gestured them to do likewise. How strange it was that when confronted with Mattingley, Giles's careful elegance looked just slightly wrong. 'And I wish you would not call me Carrie, Giles.' It had annoyed her more than she had recognised at the time to have her mother pick up the nickname from Giles.

'Brother and sister indeed.' There was a laugh in Mattingley's voice. 'I am come to take my leave of you, Mrs. Tremadoc.' His entire attention was centred on her now. 'I have received an urgent summons home to Hallam.'

'How pleasant to have a country seat,' said Giles.

'I find it a responsibility, Mr. Comfrey.'

'You will not be at Chevenham House tomorrow?' asked Caroline.

'Alas, no. But I hope you will. I know how much they look forward to seeing you.'

The Duchess? Once again, he had been to Chevenham House first. What had he given the Duchess for Christmas? 'I was telling Mr. Comfrey,' she said, 'that I will have to see how my mother-in-law is before I decide whether to go. I think there is a change in her condition.'

'I am sorry.' He thought about it. 'Or should I be glad for her?'

'You should be glad for Carrie,' said Giles. 'Tied by the leg as she has been.'

'Doing her duty, Mr. Comfrey?' Mattingley rose to his feet and Caroline was aware as always of the controlled strength that had helped to save her life. 'Do you know, I find myself in agreement with Mrs. Tremadoc. Caroline is a very much prettier name than Carrie.'

'You think so?' Giles had remained seated, now rose reluctantly as Caroline did. 'I like to remember that we are family, Carrie and I.' He sat down again after Mattingley had left. 'Your mother's right about him. Proud as be-damned! No wonder they call him "Mattingley the unmarrying man" in the clubs. I suppose if Princess Charlotte were a little older he might consider her, but I doubt he could bring himself to bear her tomboy manners, even with the reversion of a throne. He probably thinks a Mattingley worth ten of the House of Hanover anyway. I hope you've not let yourself be bamboozled by those grand airs of his, Carrie.'

'He saved my life.' Caroline was surprised how much she disliked the idea of Giles discussing her affairs with her mother. She picked up a sheaf of paper from the table beside her and changed the subject. 'I have got halfway through copying out Nelson's elegy by the Spirit of History. But the Duchess reminded me the other day that at the beginning of the poem, Mr. Tremadoc used the Spirits of Good and Evil for his chorus. He must have forgotten in the heat of composition. I think we should change it. It means correcting the last few pages I gave you, I am afraid.'

'Expensive.' His brow darkened. 'And hardly necessary. We'll leave it, I think.'

'No, Giles, we will change it, if you please.' And then, seeing him look mulish. 'I am sure I do not need to remind you that you undertook, in the agreement we signed, to make any changes I thought absolutely necessary. This is such a one.'

'Have a little sense, Carrie, do! I am publisher and printer of this poem, you merely the copyist. I must be judge of what is important. Spirit of Good, Spirit of History, it is all one.'

'If you felt like that,' she said, 'you should not have let me put that proviso into our agreement. I am afraid that I must insist. There are another ten or fifteen pages, I think, to be copied. I shall not start until I know the change has been made.'

He rose to his feet with a forced laugh. 'Determined little puss, ain't you? Very well then, I'll make the change just as soon as the holiday is over. The expense will come out of your share of the profits, of course, not that it makes much difference.'

'If you wish.' She felt suddenly tired. Did any of it matter?

She had been right in sensing a change for the worse in Mrs. Tremadoc's condition. Next day the old lady was visibly weaker, and the doctor arriving at last late in the morning, took one look at her and shook his head. 'Not long now.'

'Is there any chance that she may regain consciousness before she dies?'

'It's possible, I suppose. In a case like this, anything can happen. But if you are thinking of alterations to her will, Mrs. Tremadoc, there is no need to be troubling yourself. Neither I nor the lawyer would consider her in a fit state.'

'That was not at all what I had in mind.' She was glad to see him go. He and Mr. James must have put their heads together and decided she was looking after Mrs. Tremadoc merely to ensure she made no change in her will. Disgusting. But it made up her mind for her. She must stay by Mrs. Tremadoc in case she should come to herself and say what she wanted done with her property. A will might not be valid, but no one could stop her from making the appropriate arrangements after the old lady's death.

She wrote a quick note of explanation and apology to the Duchess and went up to relieve Mrs. Jones in the sickroom.

'Not long now, I fancy.' Mrs. Jones echoed the doctor. 'She's been restless for a while, almost as if she were coming back. It does happen, sometimes. You ring at once, dearie, if you want me. Promise.'

'Thank you.' She had brought her notes for the last canto and sat down to work by candlelight in the shuttered room. On the bed the old lady breathed heavily, her head moving restlessly on the pillow. Caroline had never seen death, but now felt it very near. Suddenly, she knew what the Spirit of History should say about Nelson's death. 'Death be not proud.' It was a quotation, she knew, but it gave her the theme she needed. She wrote away hard for a timeless while, then stopped, aware of a change in the room.

'Bitch,' said Mrs. Tremadoc.

'You're awake!' Caroline picked up the candle and moved over to the bed. 'Mrs. Tremadoc, can you hear me?'

'Murderess,' she said. 'My son. Me. My grandchild.'

'There was no grandchild, Mrs. Tremadoc.'

'Liar! You're not killing me either, I suppose.' She spoke with increasing difficulty. 'Brandy, give me some brandy!'

'Here.' Caroline poured a liberal glass and managed to help the old lady take a little.

'Not poisoned?' she said. 'Done my business already, ain't you? But murderess or no, you're not to let that nephew of mine touch penny. I'd rather you had it than he. For the child!'

'There is no child, Mrs. Tremadoc.'

'There will be. Geraint. Little Geraint. So beautiful. So good. And you killed him! Bitch. Lying, scheming, murdering bitch!'

Caroline's hand went out to the bell pull. Stopped. Let Mrs. Jones hear the old woman's malignant ramblings? Much better not, for everyone's sake. She gave her a little more brandy and sat down by the bed to listen to a stream of increasingly foul language. Mrs. Tremadoc was back in the far past now, a slum child growing up in the sordid back streets of Manchester. Hatred was her theme, and a longing to escape. She seemed to have hated everyone, but her brother most of all. Over and over again, she came back to him and his son. 'Not a penny; he's not to touch a penny. All for the child. All for Geraint. My little Geraint. You'll see to it! You! Caroline! Bitch, you. You'll see to it.' The words were slurring now, the eyes blinking shut.

Caroline turned at a scratching on the door. 'Come in, Mrs. Jones.'

'Mr. Comfrey's below, ma'am. Come to fetch you to Chevenham House, he says. Oh, dear God, look!'

There was no mistaking it. This was death.

So much to do. So much to arrange. So much to think of. She had refused to see Giles, who wanted to do everything for her. Mr. James would arrange the funeral. She saw him next day. 'Mrs. Tremadoc came to herself for a few moments before she died,' she told him. 'She talked about her money. And her nephew. I don't quite know what to do. She doesn't want him to touch a penny.'

'Good,' said the lawyer. 'Just as I hoped. So you inherit, as is entirely right and proper.'

'Not what she wanted. She thought there was a child . . . was to be a child. A new Geraint.' She felt her colour rise. 'There is not, of course.'

'Pity. What did she say precisely?'

'"All for Geraint. For little Geraint."' She felt her colour higher than ever. 'And other things.'

'Best forgotten? I've had the rough side of her tongue, too, Mrs. Tremadoc. No need to tell me. In fact much better not. As I see it, your position as heiress is unassailable, but if it makes you feel happier about it, you could always consider it as a trust for your first child. Call him Geraint.'

'But I have no intention of marrying.'

He rose to his feet. 'Life is full of surprises, Mrs. Tremadoc. Now you should rest. Leave all to me."

'Thank you.' If she had thought herself tired before, what was she now?

And the poem still not finished. Tremadoc's memorial. That was far more important than the pittance his mother had left. A whisper of remembered puzzlement ruffled the surface of her mind. 'Your position as heiress,' the lawyer had said. A grand lawyer's word for what was left of Mrs. Tremadoc's jointure. It was only because her business was with words that it had struck her. She rang for working candles and got a scolding from Mrs. Jones instead.

'You should be resting, not working,' she concluded.

'Dear Mrs. Jones, I must finish this. Only a little more now. When I have done, I shall be able to rest. Please, Mrs. Jones? I'll feel better when it is done. Just leave me alone?'

It was very quiet in the house. Upstairs, Mrs. Tremadoc lay still in her big bed. Outside, the watchman called the hour, 'and a fine night'. Caroline's hand was stiff when she put down the pen at last. It would do. She thought it would do. Her eyes were blurring strangely. She picked up the pen again to write 'Finis' at the bottom of the page. Finish? Her hand seemed to be shaking. She put it to her head. Murderess, the old woman had called her. True? She had often thought so herself.

So tired. She reached out for the bell pull; could not find it; felt the world go black.

'A proper fright.' Mrs. Jones's voice. 'Lying there by the hearth. Dead as a doornail we thought her at first. She would finish copying that poem, sir, there was no way we could stop her.'

'A very determined young lady.' The doctor's voice now. His hand on her wrist. 'No fault of yours, Mrs. Jones. Just exhaustion, I think, and no wonder. Best let her sleep it off.'

'I'm awake.' An effort to open her eyes, but she made it.

'Good. You gave poor Mrs. Jones the fright of her life, Mrs. Tremadoc. Now you will do exactly as I tell you. Rest, and nourishing food, and no disturbances whatsoever. No visitors, Mrs. Jones, until I give the word.'

'But my . . . but the poem. What happened to it? I had just finished. I remember writing "finis".'

'And nearly finished yourself falling into the fire,' said Mrs. Jones. 'But don't you go worriting, love. I gave what you'd written to Mr. Comfrey when he came next day.'

'Next day? How long?'

'Only two days,' said the doctor. 'And I'm sure you needed it. When you have had something to eat you will find yourself the better for the rest. But absolute quiet, Mrs. Jones. No word from the outside world. I'll not have her troubling herself with that poem of her husband's or anything else for the matter of that. I'll come again tomorrow.'

'Thank you.' Caroline was drifting off to sleep again.

She was waked by Mrs. Jones with a cup of hot broth, and lay listlessly letting the housekeeper feed it to her a spoonful at a time. 'Thank you,' she said at last. 'I could sleep forever. But, Mrs. Jones, the funeral?'

'Don't fret, love,' said Mrs. Jones. 'Everything's taken care of.'

She slept and waked, and ate what was given her, and slept again. The doctor's visits gave her a framework of days, but she let them drift past, uncounted.

His tone was beginning to change. Instead of 'Absolute rest,' he now urged, 'A little effort, Mrs. Tremadoc.'

'Why?' She fell asleep again.

'Don't let him fret you.' Mrs. Jones was feeding her savoury mince. 'I reckon you need all the rest you can get.'

'Must make an effort.' The doctor's voice was impatient. 'Mr. Comfrey is anxious to see you. I told him you would be up and about any day now. You wouldn't want to make a liar of me, Mrs. Tremadoc.'

'No?' Talking was too hard work.

Mrs. Jones, looking anxious. 'That Mr. Comfrey has called again. 'He's very urgent to see you. Do you think, just for a moment?'

'Here?'

'He is very pressing, very pressing indeed. Says he feels responsible. Remember he's your brother, he says. And surely you want to hear the news about the poem?'

'Oh, yes?' Strange that it seemed so unimportant.

'It's a great success, you know. Everyone's talking about it.'

'It's out?'

'Lord, yes. It came out the day of Lord Nelson's funeral. More than a week ago. It's been a long time, Mrs. Tremadoc. We're all worried. If you could just make the effort?'

'Oh, very well.' What did anything matter? 'If you'd get me a wrap, and my hairbrush...'

'I'll do it for you.' Mrs. Jones was shocked at Caroline's lack of interest in her appearance. 'You don't even want to see the hand glass?' she asked at last.

'For a brother? You may bring him up, Mrs. Jones, and you will stay, of course.'

'Very good, ma'am.'

Giles, too, looked anxious. 'We've all been fretted to death about you, Carrie. It's not like you to give way. And it's deuced inconvenient, too. The last canto's hailed as the cream of all. You're the talk of the town, Carrie. The world wants to meet the poet's widow.'

'Even though I am still in full mourning for him?'

'There is a time and a fitness for all things, and this is the time when we should be pushing *The Downfall of Bonaparte* for all it is worth. Everyone wants to know about that amazing husband of yours, and who better to tell about him than you? I have promised several people that you will see them.'

'Without my permission?'

'Well, Carrie, you were hardly in a state to give it, were you?' He had been looking her over with a considering eye. 'You are pale, and no wonder, lying here doing nothing all day. The doctor says there is nothing wrong with you that fresh air and exercise will not cure. I will come again tomorrow with my curricle and take you for a turn in the Park.'

'I'm too tired...' But was it more effort to resist than to give in to his friendly bullying?

'Nonsense. I'm surprised at you. What has become of your sense of duty? If you will not pull yourself together for my sake, and the poem's, perhaps you will for your mother.'

'My mother?'

'The Duchess is very ill. Dying, Sir Walter Farquahar thinks. Mrs. Winterton badly needs your support at Chevenham House. Imagine what her position will be if the Duchess should actually

die, though I personally think it merely another of her bouts
of nervous illness.'

'The Duchess? Dying? Why didn't you tell me? I must go
to her. Will you wait downstairs and drive me there?'

'At once? Today? Now you are being over-hasty.'

'Sir Walter knows the Duchess's constitution. If he says she
is dying... Mrs. Jones, will you order the carriage and then
come back and help me dress? On second thoughts, it is too
cold for your curricle, Giles. I'll not trouble you.'

'No trouble.' But he sounded relieved, and she thought he
must have another engagement. 'It is true, you will be better
in the carriage for your first outing. I am delighted to see you
pulling yourself together at last. I knew you could do it once
you decided to try. I will call again tomorrow to arrange when
you can see my friends from the press.'

'The press?'

'Well, of course. Who else would want to know about
Tremadoc?'

Her eighteen-inch waist had shrunk to nearer sixteen and
Mrs. Jones had to pull her dress together with a black ribbon.
Dressing was harder work than she had expected and she had
to sit down for a few moments after she had finished, the world
suddenly remote, as if she were viewing it through heavy glass.

'A little of the master's cordial, perhaps?' suggested Mrs.
Jones, anxious at her suddenly increased pallor.

'*No!*' She put her hand to her whirling head.
'But... something? A glass of port, I think.'

The sweet wine was comforting, but she still needed Mrs.
Jones's supporting arm on the stairs, and was glad to yield to
her urging that she come too.

The cold winter air had its inevitable tang of London fog
but breathing it steadied the world around her. She felt it become just slightly more real in the course of the short drive
across the Park to Chevenham House. There was straw in the
street outside, muffling sound. 'She is dying.' Caroline leaned
heavily on Mrs. Jones's arm as they climbed the shelving steps.
'I do pray I'm not too late.'

The big house was in a state of quiet, desperate bustle. They
had to wait for a moment for the groom of the chambers and
Caroline saw that here and there a servant's face showed signs
of tears. 'Everybody loves the Duchess,' she told Mrs. Jones,
who was looking about her with awe at the huge house and its
ranks of footmen.

'Mrs. Tremadoc!' The groom of the chambers was an old friend. 'I am glad you are come. Her Grace has been asking for you. If you will go up to the private apartments and wait in the small saloon, I will let her attendants know that you are here.'

She should have expected to find Blakeney and Charlotte in the small saloon. 'Charlotte . . . Blakeney . . .' She had not met Blakeney since that disastrous day in Richmond Park. 'I am so sorry.' Blakeney was in uniform, looked older, looked wretched, but that was no wonder. Charlotte, offering a cold cheek to be kissed, said she was glad Caroline had come at last. 'Mamma has been asking for you ever since she got ill. She can't understand why you do not read to her as you used to.'

'I am so sorry,' Caroline said again.

'I can see you've been ill.' Blakeney had taken her hand. How strange to feel nothing when he did so. It was not his hand now that made her tremble. 'You have had a hard time of it, I am afraid.'

'Thank you.' She looked up eagerly as the door opened and the Duchess's maid looked in. 'Miss Caroline, she will see you now. Be prepared for a shock, and not to show it. It's not long now, I'm afraid, my lord.'

'Thank God for that,' said Blakeney.

Caroline understood why when she saw the Duchess. Worn out with pain, she lay inert in Frances Winterton's arms, only her eyes alive. But they lit up at sight of her.

'Dear child, you are come at last!' Caroline just made out the words as she bent to kiss the Duchess's raddled cheek and smell the too familiar smell of death. 'God bless you,' managed the Duchess. 'Read to me? Read your husband's poem!'

'Should I?' Caroline looked the question at her mother.

'Why not?' Frances Winterton handed her the volume and she opened it with a little shock of surprise. It was the first time she had seen the complete poem. Giles had been as good as his word and had had a set bound up for her mother. She opened at the last canto and began to read, forgetting everything else in the effort to make the best of her poem for this good friend.

And slowly, slowly ebbed his life away
Lord Nelson's life on that victorious day.

She paused at the end of the stanza about Nelson's death and looked a question at her mother.

'It's good.' The Duchess's voice was a mere thread now. 'My clever little Caroline. Bless you, child.' The red-rimmed eyes fell shut and Frances Winterton rose and silently led Caroline out of the room. 'You'll come to me when it is all over,' she said. 'You must, Caroline. Charlotte means to leave me, I know it. I cannot remain here alone with the Duke. It's what the Duchess would wish.'

Caroline thought this was true. 'If Charlotte does go, I'll come,' she said.

'She'll go. Thank you.' Frances kissed her on a great wave of patchouli. 'The Duke will be grateful too.' If there was an implied promise in this, Caroline preferred to ignore it.

'I must go back to her.' Frances turned away. 'Take care of yourself, child. You look like Black Monday.'

At the little house that began surprisingly to feel like home, Caroline yielded readily to Mrs. Jones's suggestion of supper in bed. Reading to the Duchess, she had felt somehow alive again, occupied, needed... Now that strange, invisible wall of glass was back, dividing her from the rest of the world. She slept heavily, dreamlessly and woke again to the feeling that nothing mattered. She got up and dressed, because Mrs. Jones seemed to expect her to do so, ate a piece of toast, drank some tea, then sat with her elbows on the table, staring at nothing. 'I beg your pardon?' She looked up and saw the maid standing in the doorway, looking frightened.

'Please, mum, I said, might I clear?'

'Yes, of course.' Rising to move into the room that had become her study, she felt her head swim for a moment and wondered if she was going to faint. She sat down by the fire and stared into it vacantly. She ought to be doing something. What? The poem was finished. Tremadoc had his memorial. Murderess, his mother had called her. Murdering bitch.

She was still sitting there when Giles was announced some time later. 'I've just been to Chevenham House,' he told her. 'There is no change, or not much. No need for you to go today, your mother says. The Duchess is not really conscious now. She liked the poem, I hear. Clever of you to read it to her, Carrie.'

'Not clever,' said Caroline. 'No, not clever, Giles.'

'What's the matter?' He gave her a sharp look. 'What's got into you, Carrie? You don't look yourself today.'

'I don't feel myself. I don't feel anything, Giles.'

'Nonsense. You've overdone yourself, that's all, shut up here on your own. My curricle's outside. Put on your bonnet and a warm cloak and we'll take a turn in the Park. Air is what you need.'

It was good to have her mind made up for her. She rose obediently and went upstairs to get ready. A keen wind had blown away London's winter fog and he wrapped a fur rug warmly round her as she sniffed gratefully at the cold, clear air. 'Thank you, Giles,' she said meekly and he gave her a look of surprised pleasure as his horses moved forward.

It was earlier than the fashionable hour, but Caroline was still pleased when she saw that he was heading for the less crowded area of the Green Park. The last thing she wanted today was to meet any of her London acquaintance, and he must be aware of this. But then they turned up Constitution Hill she saw a little group of horsemen apparently waiting for them. 'Ah,' he said. 'A few friends of mine, Carrie. I told them we might just possibly come this way. You will enjoy hearing their praises of your husband's poem.'

'Oh, no!' She shrank in on herself.

'Oh, yes, Carrie. You are to be ruled by me in this. Don't you see, child, that any moment now you will be plunged even deeper into mourning by the Duchess's death? What could be more unlucky? If you are to talk to my friends of the press, it must be now. I explained to them that you could hardly receive them at home, so here they are freezing to death in hopes of a word with you. I hope you recognise it for the compliment it is.'

'I don't want compliments. I don't want to talk to anyone. I tell you, Giles, I am not fit.' Her brain felt numb. 'I feel a little faint.'

'Nonsense. You're not the fainting kind. I know you too well to be put off with your woman's excuses. Anyway, here we are. Just a few minutes with each of them, and we'll be able to go for another edition.' He raised his voice, became every tone the hearty English gentleman. 'Good morning, my friends. I must apologise if we have kept you waiting, but Mrs. Tremadoc was not feeling quite the thing. She was at Chevenham House all yesterday afternoon, reading *The Downfall of Bonaparte* to the poor Duchess. Who praised it highly, I can tell you.'

Disgusting, thought Caroline, wanting to protest, but it was easier to smile, return their civil greetings, and answer the questions that began to pour in on her from every side. Yes, indeed she missed her husband. Yes, she had had to copy out the last part of his poem from her own notes. 'A dark horse?' She looked at the man who had said this. 'What do you mean, sir?'

'I met him last summer, ma'am. For a genius, he had remarkably little to say for himself.'

'Unlike you gentlemen.' She smiled impartially at them all and felt she had scored a point. Then the curious fog in which she seemed to be moving closed in again, and she was back to the meek answering of questions. Yes, Mr. Tremadoc had written his own sermons ... Had been a member of the Old-church Club ...

'What about that club?' asked a small man with sharp eyes and an old-fashioned wig. 'Something a trifle havey cavey about it, if you ask me. Not just what you'd expect a clergyman to belong to.'

To her relief, Giles intervened. 'As I understand it, all the men in Oldchurch belonged. Just a men's dining club. Is that not correct, Mrs. Tremadoc?'

'Most of them.' Caroline remembered Dr. Martin and wondered what had happened to him. 'I would very much rather we talked of my husband's poetry.'

'Just so,' said Giles. 'The poetry is the thing, after all.'

'And an odd thing about that,' said the man who had called Tremadoc a dark horse. 'I remember Mr. Tremadoc saying last summer that Nelson had shot his bolt. Quite humorous he was about Nelson and Lady Hamilton as I remember it. Something happened to make him change his mind?'

'Something must have.' Caroline felt the fog closing in, but made a great effort. 'Well, he was right to do so, was he not?'

'He was indeed.' A burly man pushed forward from the back of the little group. 'A tragic end, ma'am. Can you tell us a little of how you felt when you heard that he had been burnt to death?'

'Sir!' She looked at him for a long moment of speechless indignation, then answered from a full heart. 'I felt a murderess,' she said.

'Carrie!' She must have swayed where she sat for Giles had his arm around her, holding her up. 'You don't know what you're saying. You will excuse us, gentlemen. Mrs. Tremadoc is not well.'

He scolded her all the way home and she listened with the

new meekness he liked so well, but sighed with inward relief when he left her at the door, explaining that he must make sure that none of the interviewers printed what he called her idiotic words.

He might have spared his pains. She figured, lightly disguised, in all the gossip columns next day, but as her words were dismissed as obvious nonsense, they merely served as a scandalous fillip to the poem's sales, and Giles soon forgave her. As for her, she did not care; she did not care about anything.

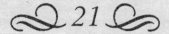

THE DUCHESS DIED on the same late January day as William Pitt, and Caroline's summons to Chevenham House came next afternoon. 'Charlotte leaves today,' wrote Frances Winterton. 'Come to me at once, child, I count on you.'

Mrs. Jones was relieved when the new, lifeless Caroline meekly packed her trunk and prepared to go. 'It will do you a power of good to be with your mother.' She surprised her mistress with a warm goodbye kiss. 'Don't fret yourself about a thing here. I'll see to it all for you, and look forward to having you home again soon.

'Though mark my words,' she said later to her friend the cook. 'There's death in that child's face, if ever I saw it. Or a nervous collapse at the very least. The life's gone out of her somehow. I wish I could have gone with her, and that's the truth.'

'She'll be among friends there,' said the cook. 'It's her mother, after all.'

'Never came to see her when she was ill. What kind of a mother is that?'

Settling back into the familiar routine of Chevenham House, Caroline felt that its heart was gone. On the surface, surprisingly little had changed. Frances Winterton sat in the Duchess's place, and gave her orders. The great domestic machine moved as smoothly as ever, ensuring the Duke's comfort, but something was missing just the same. Or was the lack in herself? Life was weary, stale, flat and unprofitable, and she went through its motions like a puppet, glad to have her strings pulled, along with the rest of the household, by Frances Winterton.

Pitt's death, following on Napoleon's victories or even caused by them, had cast a profound gloom over London society. But it also meant a new government, and Whig hopes were high. Charles Fox and his friends went to and fro through the hatchment-decked gates of Chevenham House to confer with the Duke, and Frances Winterton was very busy as the power behind the scenes.

But though men came, their wives did not. 'I wish you would persuade your mother to stay with you at the Tremadoc house for a while,' said Giles one morning when he had found Caroline sitting alone, doing nothing.

'Come to my house? But, Giles . . .' Impossible to imagine Frances Winterton in the little house on the wrong side of the Park.

'Or persuade Charlotte to come back here,' said Giles. 'It's true that your house is hardly what Mrs. Winterton is used to, but she must see that even Blakeney hardly comes now except when his father sends for him. I am afraid you are too much of a child to carry weight as a chaperone in the public eye. A pity that your mourning is still so new. As a bride you would be very much more the thing, but as it is I do beg that you will try to persuade your mother to come to you for a while. Carrie!' His voice sharpened. 'Are you paying attention to what I say?'

'About my mother?' She had indeed retreated into the strange, resounding vacancy where she seemed to spend so much of her time. 'Yes, but Giles, she'd never come.' He had said something else. What was it?

'Have you seen the Tremadocs' lawyer?' He held her unwilling attention with another question.

'Mr. James? No. He called the other day, but I did not feel like seeing him. I'm tired, Giles. Will you forgive me?'

'Poor little Carrie.' She had been afraid he would scold her, as he increasingly seemed to these days, for refusing to see the lawyer, but instead he rose to his feet, urged her to take care of herself, and her mother, and took his leave.

When he had gone, she sat for a long time, staring at nothing, unhappily aware that there was something she should be thinking of, something she should be deciding... But she was so tired... so very tired.

Her mother sent for her later that afternoon. 'Dear child.' Frances Winterton was marvellously elegant in her deep blacks. 'Giles Comfrey and I are anxious about you. It is time you stopped mourning that unlucky husband of yours and gave your thoughts a new direction.'

'Oh?'

'The future, child. The future! See how promising it lies before you! It is but to wait out the months of your mourning, and everything will be right again. How well I managed for you, after all. I declare, it's quite a fairy story. I always did love a happy ending.' She looked conscious, and Caroline wondered if perhaps the Duke had committed himself at last. 'The Duke's at Devonshire House.' Frances Winterton must have been thinking along the same lines. 'He practically lives there these days. I'll be glad when they have settled this cabinet crisis among them. I begin to find their politics a dead bore, and quite long for a breath of country air. I think when the new government is safely sworn in, you and I must set to work to persuade your father that we all need a little holiday down at Cley. You'd like that, wouldn't you? Carrie!' Her voice sharpened.

'I'm sorry.' Caroline's mind had wandered again. 'Cley, did you say?' A great tide of homesickness washed over her. Browngreen marsh, wide sky, blue sea. 'Yes, I'd like that.'

'Then speak to your father, child. He's full of starched notions these days. But he seems to find you vastly improved.'

'Does he?' Once upon a time, this would have pleased her. 'But he still never listens to what I say.' She thought of the library at Cley. 'You and I could go to Cley together, just the two of us,' she suggested.

'Nonsense,' said Frances Winterton.

The slow days ebbed past. Lord Grenville and Mr. Fox were said to be close to agreement on the composition of the new government. 'It's just a question of bringing the King round to having Mr. Fox,' Frances Winterton told Caroline. 'If I were a magician, I'd wave my wand and arrange a short sharp bout of his old madness for our Sovereign Lord, and we'd have a real Whig government tomorrow, with the Prince, God bless him, for Regent. I wish I was!'

'Was what?' Caroline had been wondering, as she often did, if it would be possible to persuade Giles to let her try her hand at a new canto of *The Downfall of Bonaparte*. Would he believe her if she told him that Tremadoc had outlined it to her?

'A magician, child! I'd wave my wand over you fast enough and banish those blue devils of yours. Anyone would think yours had been a love match, the way you peak and pine for that young man. Try for a little conduct, Caroline. Look at me! I have lost my dearest friend, and my husband, but do I mope and peer around the house, doing nothing and saying less? No, I try to be of some use in the world.'

'But what use can I be?' asked Caroline. She had sent her Blakeney sonnets to Giles, hoping that they would convince him she was capable of continuing the poem he thought was Tremadoc's. Several days had passed, and there had been no word from him. He must not have liked them. She tried to make a start on the new canto just the same, but the words would not come, and she found herself crying the helpless tears of complete frustration. Giles, coming down to her from Mrs. Winterton's apartments, found her sitting over her writing desk, tear-drenched handkerchief in her hand, her eyes still large with tears.

'Carrie, this has to stop!' He took the handkerchief from her and dried two lingering tears. 'Your mother is anxious about you, and so am I. You will make yourself ill if you go on like this.'

'I think I am ill.'

'Nonsense! You need a new direction for your thoughts, that's all. Stop maundering over Tremadoc and that poem of his. That's the past, Carrie; all over, done with. We have the future to think of. Our future, yours and mine.'

'Ours?' He had her full attention at last.

'What else? It's written in heaven, Carrie, in our stars. I knew it from the very first moment I recognised you. My little Carrie, my sister, my helpmeet. Waiting for me all this time. Making yourself ready to be just the wife I need. Don't look so startled, child! I have your mother's permission to speak, and she has spoken to the Duke. He gives his blessing. What a happy day it was for us both when you lent me those pearls of yours and started me on my way to India and my fortune. I shall repay you with long years of happy marriage.' He bent over her, his hands warm on her shoulders. 'Just think how delighted my parents would be!'

'Would they?' She had long suspected that it was the shock discovery about the pearls that had made Mrs. Trentham ill.

'Of course they would! They loved you, Carrie, as I do. As I need to, little tease!'

'Tease?'

'I should just about think so! Sending me this batch of nonsense you wrote for Tremadoc!' He removed his right hand from her shoulder and produced a crumpled bundle of papers from his pocket. 'Sonnets! Ambling scambling sonnets! Love and prove, dove and move! My poor little Carrie, I hope they pleased Tremadoc more than they do me! But at least it shows how hard you try to please a husband, and there's comfort in that for me. Don't look so flustered, my precious, I forgive you it all! I know just how it was: you were getting impatient, but how could I speak sooner? As it is, I am afraid our engagement must be a secret for the moment. There's scandal enough being talked about this house without our doing anything to add to it. How I wish I could marry you tomorrow, my little Carrie, and take you home to Bloomsbury Square, but it shall be soon, I promise you, just as soon as convention permits.' He laughed. 'I know someone who hopes for a double wedding, but the betting is against it at Brooks's. I think they are wrong, mind you, but the Duke will wait longer than we need to. In fact, I have half promised your mother that we will move in here when we return from our honeymoon. How I wish I could take you abroad, show you something of the world! Plague take this endless war! But we could go down to the west country, if you would like it. Perhaps take a look in at that garden of yours you set such store by, funny little shrimp that you were. Or would you rather go home to Cley? The Duke offers it, and in many ways I think that would be best. Sophie's still living bold as brass with that man of hers at Llanfryn, and I most certainly do not intend to take notice of her. I think you are right, Cley will be best.'

'But, Giles, I have not said yes!' This was all unreal. A scene from a play.

He laughed. 'Bless the child! Do you mean to hold out for a proposal in form! I thought we were beyond such things, you and I. But if you insist on your woman's privilege.' He dropped on one knee before her and allowed the faintest touch of amusement to colour his voice: 'Dear little Carrie, will you be my wife?'

'I don't know, Giles.' The words came out slowly. Looking

down at his carefully trained golden curls she had a quick, sharp vision of an unruly head of close-cropped dark hair and a sallow, sardonic face. There had been no word from Mattingley since he went down to the country. Not even the political crisis, not even the Duchess's funeral had brought him back to town. But wherever he was, he must be mourning the Duchess.

'I never heard such nonsense.' Giles was on his feet again, pulling her up from her chair. 'Of course you know! We have known from the first moment, you and I! Meant for each other! Made for each other! I have no doubt my father planned it from the day he took you on—poor little waif that you were. Not that I'm blaming your mother for a moment, mind you. Just see how well things have worked out for us all. A Duke's daughter! Never in my wildest dreams, sweating it out, off there in India, did I imagine that I would end up marrying a Duke's daughter.'

'Is that why you want to marry me?' Why could she not feel anything?

'Nonsense.' What a favourite word this had become. 'I'm not one for pretty speeches, Carrie, never was, but I can tell you this, I need you! I mean to get on in the world; to make a name for myself as a gentleman publisher. Who knows, perhaps Parliament in the end? The Whig interest, of course, granted your connection! With you at my side, the world's my oyster!'

'You really need me?' He had found the argument that went straight to her heart.

'More than anything in the world!' He pulled her to him, gently, firmly. 'My little Carrie.' His kiss was expert, confident, undemanding. 'I shall go to your mother at once.' He put her back in her chair. 'She'll be delighted. So will your father. For the moment, we will tell no one else. Not that I don't long to boast of my happiness, but it is hardly fitting, with you so deep in mourning. What an age it will seem before I can call you mine indeed.' His eye lit on the dog-eared little packet of sonnets lying on the table beside her. 'In the meantime, no sonnets, please, my precious! But it did strike me, reading those effusions of yours, that you may have been more of an inspiration to Tremadoc than we any of us quite understood. From what I have heard, nothing he had done before prepared the world for the success of *The Downfall of Bonaparte*. Do you think, perhaps, that you and I might work together as you and he did? With you as my Egeria, who knows what heights I might not touch! Shall we give it a try, you and I?'

'Oh, Giles, do let us!' Something in her still held aloof, still rejected the idea of marriage to Giles, but this was an overwhelming argument. To be needed, to be at work again, this, surely would lift the grey all-inconclusive cloud of gloom that hung over her.

It did, for a while. It was wonderfully pleasant to be, for the first time in her life, totally approved by both her mother and her father. The Duke actually smiled, called her a good girl, and made one of his inconclusive remarks about something handsome and his man of business. And Frances Winterton plunged with enthusiasm into the matter of a trousseau. 'We will do everything as it should be this time. I have carte blanche from your father.'

'I wish he woulɑ say just what the "something handsome" is to be,' said Giles, when Caroline told him this. 'The more I think of it, the less I fancy the idea of my Bloomsbury Square house as the abode for a Duke's daughter—or a future Member of Parliament, come to that. I've been looking about me for a house nearer this end of town, but with prices the way they are, we've not a chance unless the Duke comes down handsomely.'

'There's the Tremadoc house.' Caroline was relieved that he seemed to have given up the idea of moving into Chevenham House.

'Quite ineligible! A widow's nook for retirement; not the least bit right for a young couple rising in the world. I've suggested to James that he look about him for a buyer.'

'Without consulting me?'

'Dear little Carrie!' He planted a kiss on her forehead. 'Man and wife are one flesh, you know.'

The new ministry was announced a few days later. 'Portland and Fox.' Giles had brought the news to Chevenham House. 'Your mother is disappointed, I am afraid.'

'Disappointed?'

'Do you pay attention to nothing, Carrie? Surely you know she hoped the Duke would be First Minister. And so he would have been, I think, if the Duchess had not died. Poor Frances, I hope she never understands how much harm she has done him by sitting tight here. He'll have to marry her, of course, in the end, but the harm's done.'

'Does she know you call her Frances?'

'Yes...no. I don't know. I am sure she would not mind it. My future mother-in-law. How I wish we could be married tomorrow, Carrie!'

Caroline did not. But then, she wished nothing these days, looked forward to nothing, felt nothing. Was it because of this that the new canto of *The Downfall of Bonaparte* was going so badly? Or was it, as she began to fear, because it was impossible to work with Giles as she had with Tremadoc?

Work with? Work through? What it came down to was that where Geraint had been happy to accept her words as his, Giles had a will of his own. Surely this was good? Looking back through the mist of her unhappiness, she recognised that in her marriage to Geraint, she had always really been the leader, though of course she had had to let him think he was. Tired and sad, she thought it would be marvellous to let the burden of herself slip on to someone else's shoulders.

Giles's shoulders? He was making decisions for her already. The Tremadoc house was up for sale, and he had given Mrs. Jones notice without consulting her. When she had protested about this he had had his usual answer ready: 'Man and wife are one flesh.' It was his duty, he said, to spare her every possible burden of decision. 'Especially just now, little Carrie.' He made no secret of his impatience with her continued state of listlessness. He was right, of course. If she could not even make up her mind what dress to put on in the morning, how could she expect to make more important decisions?

Tireder and tireder, she could not sleep, but lay awake, hour after hour, listening to the distant voice of the watchman, or, if she dozed off, plagued with anxious dreams. She was running, but her feet would not touch the ground. She was flying, but her wings beat the air in vain. Always, she was trying to get somewhere, to someone whose face she could not see. Once or twice, she woke up crying. She had been in her garden, her lost garden, she was sure of it. But which garden? At Llanfryn? At Cley? And whose hand had held hers?

'Really, Carrie, try for a little commonsense!' She and Giles were having one of their increasingly unsatisfactory sessions on *The Downfall of Bonaparte*. 'We must have a new hero, now Nelson is gone. Who would Tremadoc have chosen? Surely you cannot have lived for more than a year with a powerful mind like his without gaining some insight into it! Now, think: apply yourself! The Prince Regent, perhaps? Fox?'

'I don't think there is a hero,' she said slowly. 'I think, perhaps, we have to wait, to hope that one will appear.'

'Nonsense! I have promised the new canto for the late summer. You must see, child, that if it was outlined by Tremadoc, the canto must be ready this year.'

'Yes.' It was true, of course. She put a tired hand to her head. 'Give me a little time. I'm so tired . . . It's hard to think. I wish I could go to the country, to Cley. London stifles me.'

'You think about yourself too much.' Giles took an impatient turn about the room. 'It's over four months now since Tremadoc died. You must quit these self-indulgent fancies, and think about the future. Our future. I want a wife, not a memorial statue. Look at Frances! There's an example for you. She has lost her dearest friend, but she does not pine and mope and grieve. She does her best to spread happiness around her.'

'Yes. She said that to me too.'

'Carrie! I don't like your tone. That is no way to speak about your mother, the best friend you have ever had.'

'I suppose that is what she says too. It's not true, you know. The Duchess was my best friend. Oh, Giles, I miss her so.'

'I never heard such nonsense in my life. Everybody knows about the Duchess. A crazy gambler; a woman in debt to every moneylender in town. And as if that was not bad enough, she has reached from her grave to harm the Duke now!'

'What do you mean?'

'Letters she wrote to that lover of hers, what's his name? Mattingham, Trappingley, something like that. I met him once at your house and wanted to throw him out neck and crop. Lucky for him he's gone off to ruralise, or I'd have done it sooner or later. All his damned airs and not enough sense to burn the Duchess's love letters. The word in the clubs is that some cunning devil of a blackmailer has got hold of them and is bleeding the Duke dry. Published, they'd make your father the laughing stock of the town. And Mattingley with him, of course. I'd like that. By what I hear, it was more the threat of the letters than any indiscretion of poor Frances's that cost the Duke the post of First Minister. The Duchess wrote pretty freely to her good friend Mattingley. Her views of everyone. The King, the Prince Regent, Pitt, Fox! A very lively pen, I understand. I think poor Frances is anxious about what she may have said about herself and the Duke, and can you blame her? What a saint of a woman that is!'

'A saint!' This was too much. 'Mistress of her best friend's husband! That had gone on for ever, Giles. Mr. Mattingley must have been a boy when my mother and the Duke...' Hot colour flooded her face. 'I'm eighteen. All those years... Can you wonder the poor Duchess turned somewhere else for comfort? That's horrible about the blackmailer... Obscene. How could anyone?'

'Money's a powerful argument. All very well for you, who have grown up with a silver spoon in your mouth. And that reminds me, has the Duke said any more about what he means to do for you?'

'I should have thought you would know better than I, Giles, such good friends as you and my mother are these days.'

'Good God, I do believe you are jealous!' Giles let out a great self-satisfied roar of laughter. 'Bless your little heart, of course I am good friends with my future mother-in-law. Poor little Carrie, this waiting is coming harder on you than we any of us imagined. I think we must put our heads together and see if we cannot advance our happy day. That's what you need, my precious, a husband's strong arms round you. No wonder you are indulging in these megrims!' He pulled her to her feet and held her close. She could feel him stir against her, and felt, in pure horror, that he meant to take her where she stood.

Stop him. How? She pulled her mouth from under his rough lips and spoke. 'You're thinking of my mother!' How had she known it?

'Nonsense!' But he let her go.

22

'I CAN'T MARRY him.' Caroline went straight to her mother after Giles left. But how could she convince her when it was so impossible to give her reason?

Frances Winterton laughed impatiently. 'Anyone would think you were a miss out of the schoolroom, not a widow! I tell you, child, I have no patience with this affectation of nerves, and nor, let me warn you, has your Giles.'

'Not my Giles! I don't love him, and I do not believe he loves me. I have made one mistake, and regretted it bitterly; I'd rather die than make another, and with my eyes open too.'

'Die indeed. Such heroics! What you need is to set up your nursery and then maybe you'll become a rational creature again. We'll talk no more of this, and I warn you, not a word, not a hint to your father. I don't like to think what he would say! I have just talked him round to considering a figure for your dowry. We don't want to do or say anything that will give him second thoughts.'

'But mother, please!' Had she ever called Frances Winterton mother before?

Frances Winterton reached out for a hand bell. 'The subject is closed. None of us can afford any more gossip, and that's the end of it.'

Back in her own room, Caroline raged at herself for not having been firmer. How had she let herself get to this pass? And what was she going to do? Giles and Mr. James had dismissed the servants from the Tremadoc house and put it up for sale. She should not have let them, but it was too late to be thinking that now. She could not go back there. Where else could she go? She had asked Giles, a few days before, whether she was not due further payment granted the continued sales of *The Downfall of Bonaparte* and he had laughed, called her a little Shylock, and told her once again that man and wife were one flesh. Situated as she was, it would be very difficult indeed to make him pay her what she was sure he must owe her.

So, she had hardly any money. And friends? She could not turn to Blakeney for help. Charlotte hardly spoke to her. She thought for a moment, longingly, of Oldchurch. Would Mrs. Bowles take her in? If only her good friend John Gerard still existed, but she had lost him when she discovered he was Mattingley. And now, she had lost Mattingley too. What was he doing all this time, so silent, in the country? Still mourning the Duchess? Or had the blackmail threat driven him out of town? No. He would not let it. She knew him too well both as Gerard and as himself to believe that for a moment. What good friends they had been. How sad it was.

All hopeless. At least Giles thought he needed her. Perhaps, when they were married—if they were married—she would find a way of writing with him as she had with Tremadoc. Was she not overvaluing herself after all? What if Giles was infatuated with her mother? What right had she to mind? She did not love him either. Women had made unloving marriages through the years, and made the best of them. Why should not she? It would be so much easier to give in. She felt the grey mists close round her again. To do nothing. To go with the tide.

It was Giles himself who offered her the chance of escape. Calling next morning, he made no mention of her appeal to her mother. Perhaps, for once, he had come to her first. He was certainly looking serious. 'I've had a letter from Sophie.' He had kissed her and told her she looked very much more the thing today. 'Poor fool, she is in trouble as was to be expected. Tom Staines was killed in a hunting accident the other day.'

'Oh, I am sorry!'

'I should just about think so. Young fool; he left no will. Saddles her with a pair of illegitimate brats and makes no provision for her! It would serve her right if I left her to the fate she deserves, but I cannot bring myself to do so. Only— it's difficult! The Staines family's man of business is here in town and I must bring what pressure I can to bear on him. So there is no way I can go to the silly girl, and from what she writes I fear she may do something stupider still . . . something really foolish. Just look at her letter.'

It was hysterical, blurred with tears, frightening. 'Oh, poor Sophie,' said Caroline. 'Giles!' Inspiration struck her. 'Let me go to her!'

'Would you?'

'I'd like to! Poor Sophie . . . and the little girls.' And I'll get away from you, she thought. Get myself time to think.

'It's like you, Caroline.' He thought for a moment. 'I think it would do. She needs family support, public support. I'll make time to drive you down there; show that we intend to stand by her, but come straight back myself to take up her case here in town. How soon can you start?'

'I'll need a companion for the journey.'

'Your fiance, Carrie?'

'You know I must have a woman. My mother was speaking, just yesterday, of the need to avoid further scandal.'

'Prudent little Carrie! Shall I ask Mrs. Jones to come with us? I think I know where I can find her.'

'Oh, yes, please, Giles, that would be beyond anything. I have felt so unhappy about her.'

'That's settled then.' He rose to his feet. 'I'll find her out at once, and plan to call for you tomorrow morning. Don't pack a million trunks, Carrie. I'll hope to fetch you all back to town quite soon. I doubt the Staines family will let Sophie and the brats stay long in the house. Imagine not seeing to it that he made a will!'

'Perhaps she tried,' said Caroline.

'She should have succeeded.'

'An excellent notion.' Frances Winterton approved of the proposed journey. 'It will give you time to set your thoughts in order, and we can get the rest of your brideclothes together when you get back.'

Caroline did not argue with her. It would be time enough, when she got safe down to Llanfryn, away from Giles, to say that she did not mean to marry him. Perhaps she would find an old friend in the west who needed a housekeeper. She plunged into a daydream of an unmarried, elderly vicar. She would keep his house and walk in her lost garden again. Or perhaps she and Sophie would decide to set up house together. She longed to see Sophie's two little girls and felt a warm stirring of gratitude to Giles for unwittingly giving her this chance of escape. It was good of him to go to his sister's help, surprisingly good. Had she let herself get into a bad habit of doing him less than justice? Might she even find, away from him, that she could marry him after all?

She woke next morning to the muffled sounds and unmistakable, thick smell of a London fog, and it was hardly surprising that Giles was very late. He arrived at last just when she had finished a light luncheon with her mother. 'That's good,' he said. 'Now we can press on until it is full dark.'

'Has Mrs. Jones eaten?' But Giles had turned from her to say goodbye to her mother.

Busy packing, Caroline had not been out all morning, and had not realised just how bad the fog was until she and Giles emerged into the courtyard, to see his carriage waiting, a dim shape outlined by glimmering side lamps. 'It's worse than I thought,' she hung back on the top step. 'I had no idea it could be so thick, this late in March. Should we not perhaps wait until tomorrow?' She turned to consult her mother, but Frances had already returned, coughing, to the house.

'Nonsense.' Giles took her arm to guide her down the shelving steps. 'It will be clearer as soon as we get out of town. I sent a note by the night mail telling Sophie when to expect us.

We must not disappoint her now, or I don't like to imagine the consequences. She was always impulsive, poor, silly Sophie and I really fear she might do herself or the children a mischief.' He helped Caroline up the carriage step as a footman held open its door.

It was dark inside, and it took her a moment to realise that the carriage was empty. 'But, Giles,' she turned as he got in behind her. 'Mrs. Jones?'

'We are picking her up on the way.' He sat down beside her and the carriage door clicked shut behind him.

As they emerged from the main gate of Chevenham House a confused noise she had been hearing explained itself as one enormous traffic block, with frightened drivers shouting angrily at each other, the scream of wheel locked against wheel, and the startled neighing of horses. It seemed to take for ever for the carriage to edge its way out into the stream of carriages and turn right, towards the west.

'It will be better when we are out of town,' Giles said again.

'Where does Mrs. Jones live?'

'Lord knows! I certainly don't. Did you really think I was out scouring the streets for her? Not very flattering to me, your affianced husband, that you should insist on a chaperone, and in such an emergency.'

'But, Giles!' She was caught in her own device. This was not at all the moment to tell him she did not mean to marry him. What should she do? To travel on with him would commit her beyond recall, but she knew him well enough now to be certain that nothing she said would shift him. Try and escape? It would be both dangerous and useless to try to leave the carriage as it pushed its way through this mass of impatient traffic. Giles would prevent her, and be alerted. She must wait until they stopped for the night, then seize the first chance to escape him and make her own way to Sophie. The fog that made it impossible now might make it easier then.

She had hardly any money. The thought struck her like a blow. She had asked Frances Winterton for a loan only that morning and Frances had laughed and said she had not a feather to fly with herself. She had meant to ask Giles, once more, in the course of the journey, for some of the money she was sure he owed her, but that was impossible now, like everything else. Hopeless. All hopeless. She felt the inner fog close round her, thick as the one outside. Give in? Let Giles take her over? If she let him have his own way he would be a tolerant enough sort of husband. She would never have to make up her mind about anything important again. She would never have the chance. He would not only take her over, he would take her poetry too. That was a stiffening thought.

'You're very quiet, Carrie. Not in the dumps again, I hope?'

'Just thinking.' If she really meant to escape from him, she must not give him any idea that she was not his obedient companion. 'About the poem,' she went on. 'About a new hero for it. Have you thought of anyone?'

'A foreigner perhaps? The Czar? He would make a striking figure, after all.'

'No. It must be an Englishman. I am sure that was what Tremadoc intended.' Keeping the discussion going with half her mind, she was beginning to wonder just what route they were taking. It was hard to tell in the fog, but she had taken the west road often enough to visit friends who had country places along it and this did not feel right to her. The carriage was off the stones now and the traffic was thinner as they wound their way along country lanes.

The fog was thinner too. 'Gracious!' she exclaimed. 'Isn't that Paddington Green? Giles, where are you taking me?'

He took her hand. 'Where my heart tells me.'

'What do you mean?' Instinct made her let her hand lie passive in his.

He pressed it a little. 'I'd not meant to tell you so soon, but you are too acute for me, little puss. I had quite forgotten that you had travelled this road before. I promise I'll make a better companion, and a better husband too, than Tremadoc did.'

'Tremadoc? You can't mean?'

'We're off to Gretna, love. But this time with the full consent of your father and mother. We have been anxious about you—putting our heads together to decide what's best for you, and this is our answer. Since you and I cannot properly be married so soon in town, we are off on a romantic pilgrimage to Gretna. It will merely enhance the whole touching story of our marriage, the poet's widow and his publisher, her longtime friend and foster brother. No need to fret. We will be forgiven for being perhaps a little hasty. I have dropped a word in certain quarters. The world will understand that you need me at your side.'

He sounded enormously pleased with himself, and it was hard to let her hand lie meek in his. 'But Sophie?' she ventured.

'Has made her bed and must lie on it. Oh!' Carelessly. 'If

you like, we might give her a look in on our way back from Gretna. I know I shall want to prolong our honeymoon.'

'Will you, Giles?' At all costs, she must keep him talking, keep him sure of her.

'You know I will!' His hand squeezed hers again.

Why was she so sure that he meant none of it? That, in fact, he did not love her at all? 'You really have my mother's permission?' She felt his hand twitch on hers.

'And your father's too. What a woman your mother is! One in a million. And so kind! So caring about you, Carrie! She's been so anxious for you, while you've not been yourself. We'll make it all up to her when we get back to London and set up housekeeping. She'll live with us, of course.'

'Will she?' She thought she was beginning to see it all now. This elopement was her mother's idea. Had she perhaps decided that it had been a mistake to import her into Chevenham House? That she could bring the Duke round her thumb more easily if she was alone with him? Or had Giles become too obviously devoted to her? Had she perhaps tried to make the Duke jealous and decided it would not work? Or was she even planning a new *menage à trois*, with herself and Giles?

'Of course she will! We'll be the talk of the town, we happy three.' He laughed, a little self consciously. 'It was she who suggested the Czar as our new hero.'

'Was it?' If Caroline had had any doubts left about her predicament this would have settled them. At all costs, she must escape from him before night. But the fog had been lifting steadily since they left the Thames valley and the carriage was travelling faster. She must wait until they stopped for the night and hope for a chance to slip away, find help, hide.

But who would help her? If she managed to give Giles the slip, it would be without money, without baggage. I am afraid, she thought, I am most horribly afraid.

'You're tired, child.' Giles's voice roused her. 'Not long now, my patient puss. I like your confidence in me! No questions! No doubts! We are to stay tonight with old friends of your mother's,' he went on carelessly. 'She thought it would be more eligible than a public inn.'

'You and she have thought of everything. Do I know them?'

'I think not. Drummond, the name is. She knew them abroad, I believe, when she was quite a girl. They have a house near Colney Heath. They live very quietly, she says, but will be delighted to see us.'

'They are expecting us?' Her thoughts were racing. If they were to stay in a private house, could she not afford to let the night pass before she tried to escape? It would mean that she was farther from London, when she did get away from Giles, but it would also give her more time to make him sure of her. And she had heard that the farther you got from London, the kinder people were.

'I'm so tired, Giles, so very tired.' She made herself slump a little against him. 'It's all been such a shock.'

'Poor little Carrie. A happy one, of course.' He was in no doubt of it. 'I am sure Mr. and Mrs. Drummond will understand if you wish to go straight to bed when we get there.'

'Oh, I'd like that, if they did not think me too rude.'

'I shall explain to them.' She thought that this suited his book very well and wondered just what he and his mother had told the Drummonds.

They were a kind, middle-aged couple, full of sympathy for Caroline and loving questions about Frances Winterton. 'Only to think of her remembering us after all this time,' said Mrs. Drummond over and over again as she took Caroline up to the comfortable bedroom that had been made ready for her. 'Of course you must rest if that is what you wish. Such a romantic journey as you are on, you naturally wish all your strength for its happy conclusion.' She insisted on helping Caroline to bed, with a stream of comment on everything from the silverbacked hairbrushes the Duchess had given her to her extreme thinness. 'I vow you'll be plumper and pinker in the cheek when you visit us on your way back from Gretna,' she said at last, leaving Caroline in peace to make herself eat some of the luxurious supper that was sent up to her.

She had dismissed all thoughts of escape from here when she saw how lonely the house was, set well outside a tiny village some distance from the Great North Road. As she drifted off to exhausted sleep her mind was still puzzling over the problem that had been with her all day. If she was right in thinking that Giles was not in the least in love with her, but, in fact, infatuated with her mother, why in the world was he so set on marrying her?

She woke to country silence, a fine morning and a new sense of determination. Something about Mrs. Drummond's coy comments the night before had brought home to her the full horror of marriage with Giles. Today, at whatever risk, she was going to get away from him.

She joined the party at breakfast, smiled and blushed at their innuendoes, and let Mrs. Drummond tell her that she must quite long for the journey's end. Leaning on Giles's arm as he led her out to the carriage, she asked casually how far they were going today. If only he would mention where he planned to stop for lunch and the night she would have some basis for planning.

But he merely laughed, and pressed her arm, and told her he was quite as anxious to get to Gretna as she could be. He had caught a hint of the Drummonds' ogling vulgarity and she thought that he had always been someone who took his tone from his surroundings.

Her long night's sleep had done her good. She leaned forward to look out of the carriage window. 'Oh, look, Giles, wild daffodils! How pretty! I wish we could stop.' They had just passed through a small village and she had a quick, wild idea of asking to pick them and running away from him.

'Nonsense, Carrie,' he said.

She subsided into silence, but went on gazing out of the window, enjoying the green haze along the hedgerows that spoke of spring and watching eagerly for signposts that might tell her where they were.

She saw one at last pointing down a narrow tree-lined lane: Lower Hallam, it read, Three Miles.

Hallam? The name was familiar. Of course. It was where Mattingley's country house was. She remembered the last time she had seen him. He had been summoned home, he had said, to Hallam, and Giles had said something sneering about being lucky to have a country estate. Would Giles remember? Had he seen the signpost? And was she really thinking of trying to get away and going to Mattingley for help?

Not Mattingley. Her friend John Gerard. If only they really were two people. If she did manage to get away, and turned to Mattingley for help, would he feel in honour bound to propose to her again? Well, if he did, she could but refuse him. Her hands were hard fists in her lap. She would ask him to send her to Sophie. It was comfortable to know how entirely she could trust him to do what she asked.

But first she must get to Hallam. 'What time is it, Giles? We've been driving for ever! Could we not stop for a luncheon at the next likely inn we see? I really need to stop.' She put a faint tremor into her voice.

'Oh, Carrie!' He sounded merely irritated. 'It's early yet! Must you?'

'Please, Giles?'

'Oh, very well, but it will make a long afternoon.' He leaned out to tell the coachman to look out for the next inn. 'God knows what we'll get to eat! I had planned to get much farther, to an inn the Drummonds recommended. Just my luck to get a coachman who doesn't know the road! I can't think why your mother could not persuade the Duke to lend us one of the carriages that stand idle at Chevenham House. It would have given us consequence!'

'And made us notorious,' said Caroline. And thought that that was just what he wished. But in fact she too had been bitterly disappointed that they had not used one of the Chevenham carriages. She was good friends with all the inmates of the stable yard and thought they would have helped her. 'Look,' she pointed. 'There's a church tower on the hill ahead. It looks like a thriving little town. Do ask the boy what it is?'

The boy, questioned, said it was Upper Hallam, and, yes, he thought there was a good enough sort of inn, though it was not a post house.

'Please, Giles?' Caroline had held her breath to see if the name Hallam suggested anything to Giles, but apparently it did not.

'Oh, very well then, but upon your own head be it if the food's uneatable.' His tone of elaborate patience suggested to her that he yielded on small points because he did not intend to do so on important ones.

The Hallam Arms was on the far side of the village green from the main road and Caroline's hopes leaped up as the carriage edged its way through a narrow gate into the yard. The old-fashioned, rambling inn with its thatched roof and bits of Tudor beaming seemed to run straight out into the countryside. As Giles helped her down from the carriage she looked beyond barns to a field with sheep and then a little wood, with a footpath and stile.

Looking eagerly about her, she saw a couple of carts and a neat, light gig, whose owners must presumably be eating in the inn. Could she persuade one of them to give her a lift to Hallam House? Or could she make Giles think she had done so, and walk there? How long would he go on looking for her? And, most important of all, would he remember Mattingley's connection with Hallam?

The landlady had come out into the yard, smiling effusively at the sight of gentry. She promised Giles as neat a luncheon as he could wish for, and bent her head to Caroline's shyly whispered request.

'Yes, ma'am.' She pointed. 'Through the yard and down the garden. You can't miss.'

A path led past the privy to a gate on to the sheep field and Caroline felt a moment's wild temptation to run for it there and then. But it would be madness. She must eat first, and try to find out how the land lay without alerting Giles. It was a pity the landlady had not shown her the way, and laid herself open to questioning, but there it was.

Emerging from the privy, she saw a boy whistling his way towards her across the sheepfield. Here was opportunity. She walked towards him, pulling on her gloves. 'A fine morning.' She smiled at him. 'Can you tell me where Hallam House lies?'

'Squire Mattingley's place?' Her heart leapt up as the boy pointed back towards the wood. 'Back there a piece. Longer by road, a 'course.' His accent was so thick and strange that it was hard to understand.

'How far on foot?'

'I dunno.' He scratched his head and stared at her, overwhelmed by her elegance. 'I never bin there. Quite a way, I reckon.' He thought about it, eager to please. 'My ma used to work there,' he offered. 'Left early, she did, when she come home.'

She dared not delay longer. Pausing to pick a few primroses, she thought she had learned a good ideal. She knew that Hallam House was within a long walk, and which way to start. She walked back up the garden, noticing that none of the inn's public rooms seemed to look out on it.

Back in the yard, she found Giles standing in the inn doorway. 'You took long enough.' Impatiently.

'I picked you a buttonhole.' She reached up to tuck the primroses into his coat. Another gig had just driven into the yard and its burly owner had thrown the reins to a lounging boy and strode past them into the inn, calling for ale.

'Touching. We're to have a pig's face and pickles,' he told her. 'What that will do to my digestion!'

'Oh, Giles, do you have a digestion?'

'After all those years in India.' He had forgotten the scold he meant to give her for keeping him waiting.

'I'd like to wash my hands and make myself tidy,' she said

as they moved into the dark interior of the inn. 'Our first meal together.' She managed to sound almost as coy as Mrs. Drummond.

It earned her a smile. 'Don't be long then. The girl will take you.' He snapped his fingers at an aproned maid. 'And a pint of porter for me,' he added.

To her surprised delight, the girl led her not upstairs but down a long, dark corridor towards the back of the house. Passing a door open on to the yard, she saw a man climbing into the gig that had been parked there when they arrived. He was in neat black, a country lawyer, perhaps, or a doctor. If only she could have asked his help.

Perhaps he could help her yet. 'Who's that?' she asked the girl.

'Mr. Sanders? He's the bailiff, mum.' She opened a door and showed Caroline into a neat little bedroom overlooking the garden. Pouring water from jug into basin, she explained further. 'Not from Hallam; t'other way.'

'Thank you.' Not Hallam. Caroline breathed a sigh of relief. 'I can find my own way back,' she said. 'Just look at my hair!' She pulled out the pins and let it fall round her face. 'Tell the gentleman I won't be more than five minutes.'

'Very good, mum.' The girl curtsied and left her alone.

Not a moment to lose. She bundled her hair up anyhow, opened her reticule and got out the pencil and paper she always carried to note down ideas for *The Downfall of Bonaparte*.

'I'm sorry, Giles,' she wrote quickly. 'I find I cannot face another trip to Gretna. A kind man is giving me a lift in his gig. I am going back to London, to my mother. Forgive me.'

The less she said, the better. She folded the note, wrote *Mr. Comfrey* on it and put it on the washstand. Then she threw up the sash window and climbed out into the garden, praying that she was right and it was not overlooked by the public rooms.

Down the path, through the gate, across the field. Her shoulders stiff with the expectation of Giles's angry shout. It did not come. Had he perhaps been given his pint of porter?

The stile was high, and she hitched up her petticoats ruthlessly to climb it and wished she was wearing stouter shoes. Once into the wood, she let herself look back and saw with joy that the inn was no longer visible. She took a deep breath and started down the narrow, muddy path.

23

'SHE'S GONE WHERE?' Calling early at Chevenham House, Mattingley had insisted on seeing Frances Winterton.

'To Gretna, the dear child! The most romantic thing. You are absolutely the first to know, and I rely on your discretion as an old friend of the family. She's been quite in a decline since Christmas. The Duke and I have been afraid for her. She only came alive when Giles Comfrey called. I really think she must have loved him always. Sir Walter advised marriage as the only cure for her mopes, but of course to tie the knot here in London would have been quite ineligible. With poor Tremadoc not dead six months! And, poor child, exposed to scandal as she has been!'

'And you think a second runaway match to Gretna will not cause scandal?'

'Oh, a nine days' wonder of course! But marriage at the end of it, and the Duke's support. We shall brush through well enough. Comfrey's a clever man. He has good friends in the newspaper world. They'll stand by him.'

'If you believe that, you will believe anything!' He did not know when he had been so angry. 'It was a hint in the *Chronicle* brought me to town. No names, of course, but it fitted, and I did not like the tone of it.'

'So soon?' He had surprised her.

'When did they leave?'

She hesitated, then, 'Yesterday,' she said. 'They will be well on their way now. Giles Comfrey meant to lose no time.'

There had been a little pause after the Giles as if she had almost omitted the surname. 'You're very thick, you and Comfrey.'

'My future son-in-law? Why, yes. A coming man. I'm happy for Caroline. He'll put an end to her dismals.'

'Dismals?'

'I never saw anything like it!' Impatient, she sounded genuine for the first time. 'Peaking and pining over that Tremadoc! Well, a sad end, but from what I hear no great loss. But, Caroline! It was like having a ghost in the house! More than the poor Duke could bear, I can tell you, missing the dear Duchess as he does.'

'I'm sorry.' Formally. 'I should have condoled with you.'

'Or I with you.' A very knowing look. 'As for the Duke, he is inconsolable. It is sad for him to lose his daughter, too, at this moment, but to tell truth, and between old friends, her mopes were becoming more than he could bear. I really thought it best to encourage Giles Comfrey in carrying her off, though of course I miss her sadly.'

False again, he thought. What had been going on here? If only he was not too angry to think clearly. Caroline gone off with Comfrey. Carried off? He had been so sure of her. Too sure? Don't think about that now; not with this acute woman watching. 'I suppose I should congratulate you. Frankly, I think Mrs. Tremadoc would have done better to wait out her mourning, but that is her affair.'

'And Comfrey's. They had our permission after all. The Duke's and mine. I hope you will stand their friend, Mr. Mattingley. You've always been good to my poor little Caroline. You'll not let this rash start of hers count against her?'

'Of hers? Or of Comfrey's?'

'It takes two to make a marriage, Mr. Mattingley.'

Did it? If he stayed any longer with this devious woman he would lose his temper and say something he would regret. Lose his temper? It was lost long since.

'Mr. Mattingley!' He had come striding furiously down the balustraded stair from the family apartments, now paused, dark brows drawn together, in the lobby.

'Yes?' It was a footman who had made bold to stop him.

'Sir! Might I speak to you?'

'You seem to be.'

'You was a friend of her ladyship.'

'The Duchess? Yes.' Reminded of their relationship, he sounded angrier than ever.

'She loved Miss Caroline,' said the man, surprising him. He was sweating with fright, big drops forming under his wig. 'So do we.'

'So?'

'Sir! She thought she was going to Llanfryn.'

'*What?*'

'She told her maid. Going home, she said.' His face suddenly became wooden, and Mattingley, turning, saw the groom of the chambers looming behind him.

'Come to my house.' He gave the man a guinea, smiled formidably at the groom of the chambers, and left.

Driving too fast across the Park, Mattingley raged inwardly at Frances Winterton, at Caroline, at himself. He had been so sure of her. So sure that he had spoken too soon and got the setdown he deserved for it. But, surely, she must have known that he would come again just as soon as was decent? That he had gone to the country because he could not bear this waiting time? Well, not only that. The Duchess had died. His mother had been ill. He had had to go, but it had suited him well enough. He had been busy redecorating his house to suit his bride, planning a garden that he thought would surprise and please her.

And she had gone off with Comfrey. Possible? Impossible? He pulled his horses to a sweating halt outside his house and strode indoors to the glum, dust-sheeted rooms. 'A man will be coming from Chevenham House,' he told a footman. 'I'll see him at once.'

How long? He rang and ordered his bags repacked and his curricle kept ready, with fresh horses. Could he really mean to go after Caroline? Crazy. She and Comfrey had two days' start on him. But—something false, one of Frances Winterton's many false notes, when she told him that Giles Comfrey would travel fast? Caroline had told her maid she was going home to Llanfryn. She must have believed it. He had learned one thing about her when he had been her friend, as John Gerard. She could not tell a lie. It was the real reason why he had not told her who he was. He had known she would be unable to keep his secret. He regretted it now. But she had been a married woman. It had been better to remain her good friend, John Gerard.

What story could Giles Comfrey have told to persuade her to go to Llanfryn with him? Did he really believe this was what had happened? He rang again and had a messenger sent to Comfrey's Bloomsbury house. Normally an easy master, he noticed with savage amusement that his servants were beginning to look frightened. I'm frightened myself, he thought. More frightened than angry now. He was beginning to believe it possible that Giles Comfrey and Frances Winterton between them had deceived Caroline. Lured her into starting on a journey that must end in marriage. A second disastrous trip to Gretna Green.

I'll kill him, he thought. I will have to kill him. He was cold, now, with fear for Caroline. 'Yes?' He almost shouted it at the man who had scratched at the door.

'It's the man from Chevenham House, sir.'

'Good.' He looked the man up and down. 'You took long enough.'

'I had to hand in my livery, sir.'

'Sacked?'

'Yes.'

'I suppose so.' No time for that now. 'Tell me about Miss Caroline.' Why had he called her that?

'Yes, sir. She's been ill, see. Not herself at all. Moping. Writing away at all hours till her candle burned out. And crying, sir. Well, deep mourning. Only, we got thinking in the servants' hall it was funny, see.'

'Funny?'

'You wouldn't know, sir. How could you? But we . . . we see a lot in the servants' hall. Well, there was Tench.'

'Tench?'

'Her maid, from way back. Went to Oldchurch with her when she was married. Come back to the House last winter, with a new husband, asking for work. The Duchess give it them, of course.'

'And?'

'Sacked when the Duchess took ill, sir. The pair of them. And then, Mrs. Jones.'

'Who's she?'

'Housekeeper at the Tremadoc House, sir, until Mr. Comfrey put it up for sale. From what Miss Caroline's maid heard, he didn't even ask her first. Just put it up for sale and got rid of the servants. So she couldn't go back there, Miss Caroline. And her not well, sir. Couldn't make up her mind what to put on in the morning, her maid said. Funny, that. Writing away, and crying, and couldn't make up her mind.'

'And she thought she was going to Llanfryn?'

'That's what she told Prue, sir. Her maid. Going home, she said.'

And would have learned her mistake too late. Where was she now? What would she do? What *could* she do? He turned to greet the man he had sent to Comfrey's house. 'What did you find out?'

'Not much, sir. He's gone north, that they know. Hired carriage; two horses; none of his own servants. They don't love him much. His man showed me a letter he'd found in one of his pockets. From a Mrs. Drummond, saying she'd be glad to see him and his young lady.'

Drummond. He had met them, years ago, at Chevenham House and thought them fit friends for Frances Winterton. They had lived somewhere north of London. Colney Heath, was it? If Comfrey had taken Caroline there, he was very far from travelling with the speed Frances Winterton had suggested. Well, after all, why should he hurry? He must feel sure enough of Caroline. Where could she turn, poor child? No time to lose. He rang and gave his orders.

'Let me come too, sir?' said the man from Chevenham House.

'You'd like to?'

'Please?'

'Very well.'

His curricle. Four horses. A man sent ahead on horseback to arrange for post horses all the way to the border. A quick note to his mother to tell her he was detained on urgent business. The man from Chevenham House riding a spare horse. Surely he would catch Comfrey before he reached Gretna Green. He was comforting himself with vain hope, and knew it. Two days' start was a formidable advantage. But he must try, or go mad. If he has laid a finger on her, he promised himself, I will kill him. But what comfort would that be?

Waking, Caroline could not think, for a moment, where she was. Then, staring up at the smoke-blackened ceiling so close above her hard bed, she remembered yesterday's long nightmare. At first, it had been enough to have escaped from Giles. She had hurried along the little path, listening for sounds of pursuit, hearing none, breathing again, and then, gradually, becoming aware of her other problems. Of hunger and cold, of bruised feet in soft, unsuitable half boots, and, gradually, of creeping exhaustion, and of fear.

She saw nobody, which was just as well, since she must present an odd enough spectacle in her muslin dress and the soft pelisse that would slip off her shoulders. Her reticule was surprisingly heavy and combined with the pelisse to make her walk awkwardly. Trying to push its strings further up her arm, she missed her footing and fell heavily in mud. For a moment, she just lay there, giving way to the old despair. She had not come far. If she stayed here, sooner or later, Giles would find her.

Giles. She pulled herself to her feet, shook out mudstained skirts and started steadily forward again. How very strange that now, thinking about Giles, she was suddenly certain that it was he who had got hold of the Duchess's letters to Mattingley, and was blackmailing the Duke. Blackmailing the father of the woman he meant to marry. There had been something in his tone when he told her about it that had struck her at the time. An element of gloating?

He should not gloat over her. And he would, she thought, if they married. Man and wife are one flesh. He would dictate not only her life but her writing. The thought kept her walking steadily forward for an hour or so through the quiet woods. She began to wish she would meet someone. Suppose she had been walking, all this time, in the wrong direction? When the path forked, she had taken, always, what she thought was the major branch, but could easily have chosen wrong.

A trailing bramble caught her hair under the bonnet and she let out a little, involuntary cry of pain. Don't. She made herself stand still and coolly disentangle her hair. If I start to cry, she thought, I am lost. Lost? She was lost already. But at least she should be safe from Giles.

And on the thought, turned a corner and saw that her path joined a country lane. No signpost, of course. And no one in sight. Which way? Or should she cross the lane and continue along the path? Suppose Giles had discovered that she had not gone off with the bailiff? He might well be scouring the lanes in his carriage, looking for her. She gave a little sigh and crossed the road quickly to plunge back into sheltering woods on the other side.

Now the path was less well used and she had to pick her way with care. The woods stretched around her, high and lonely and oddly quiet. The hush before a storm. The sky had darkened and rain began to fall in heavy, single drops, then finer and faster until she was wet through, her soaking skirts draggling round her ankles.

Her boots had not been meant for real walking and had rubbed sore places on both her feet. How long before they fell to pieces and she was reduced to going barefoot. And would that be much worse than her present misery? I must find a house, she thought. I must find help.

What was she going to say? How explain herself? A carriage accident? I'm tired, she thought. Too tired to think. Too tired to plan. If I sat down here, in the rain, would I ever get up again? I am not going to. She straightened her back and shifted the awkward reticule to the other arm. I am going to get myself out of this. Presently, I will be by a fire, eating hot soup. I could eat a horse.

When had she last been hungry? When had she last been tired like this? She pulled the sodden remnants of her bonnet off her head and threw them into the bushes. She was cold, and wet, and hungry, and her feet hurt and yet suddenly she was filled with a surge of the old, unreasoning happiness. I'm free, she thought. I'm myself, and free. One day, I will put all this into a poem. Somehow. Some way. I'll use it.

Another lane, and this time the path did not continue across it. Right or left? The rain had slackened, but there was a hint of dusk in the air. I must find shelter. She turned to the right. Would Giles have remembered about Hallam House? Did he know that Mattingley lived there? Suppose she found it, and found Giles waiting for her at the gates? Happiness ebbed . . . drained away.

Don't think like that. Think of a fire, and food. Think of the bend in the road ahead. Around it, there might be a snug village, a rectory, with a friendly parson's wife. Her feet hurt too much. She sat down on a stone and took off her sodden boots. Both heels were bleeding. It felt better, barefoot in the muddy lane. She got to the bend, turned it, and saw another bend.

Her back ached. She felt it more, now that her bare feet hurt less. If she started to cry, there would be no stopping. Cry? Why should she cry? I am here because I mean to be. How strange to remember those lifeless, listless days at Chevenham House. I am alive. I have escaped.

Another corner. A little, humpbacked, thatched cottage huddled by the road. No lights, but a plume of smoke from the central chimney. And the sound of a carriage, driven fast, somewhere behind her. Cross the road. Knock on the door. An old brown face, peering out, frightened.

'Let me in, please. Please let me in?' Had she actually pushed past the old woman, made her pull the door to behind them? They had stood together, in the darkness of the little room, listening to the approaching carriage.

Had it been Giles? She would never know. After that, it

had all been a blur. Questions, exclamations from the old woman, hard to understand, but kind. Bread and dry cheese and all she could say was, 'tired,' and 'Hallam House', and 'in the morning'.

And here she was, waking in the old woman's bed, aware of movement, of the wrinkled face peering anxiously down at her.

'Much better.' She smiled up at her rescuer. 'Thank you.' And then, her thoughts beginning to make sense. 'Hallam House?' she asked.

The old face creased into a toothless smile. 'I've sent,' said the old woman. 'My boy went at first light.'

She did not remember a boy. Did not remember mentioning Hallam House for the matter of that, but must have done so. She was lying in her shift on a straw pallet. 'My clothes?'

'So fine!' The old woman moved over to where they were drying by the fire. 'So beautiful!'

They did not look it to Caroline, torn and mudstained as they were, but they were dry and she put them on, surprised to find the old woman neatly buttoning her up the back. A lady's maid once? What kind of message would she have sent to Hallam House? Combing her hair, she was glad she had not thrown away her reticule in the course of yesterday's nightmare walk. Would Mattingley be at home? Would he come for her? What would she say if he did?

Dry bread and a little thin ale for breakfast, and it did her good. The old woman sat across the table from her, smiling and saying nothing. She must have lived alone a great deal, Caroline thought, and lost the habit of talk. It was restful not to be questioned, but she still could not think what she was going to say to Mattingley. If he came.

The old woman had washed and dried her bloodstained stockings, but the half boots were beyond service and she was glad to accept a pair of shabby wooden clogs. I look a fright, she thought, but I am alive. And safe?

When they heard a carriage, they both hurried to the cottage's one window to peer out. Had the old woman caught Caroline's fear? She smiled reassuringly. 'Hallam's,' she said, and opened to the groom who was knocking on the door.

'Well, now, Granny Biggs, what's this about a young lady?' He saw Caroline. 'Beg pardon, ma'am.' His features were wooden, the mask of a well-trained servant. 'The mistress sent me for you. Master's from home, and she's not well. She begs you will come to the house and let her know how she can serve you.'

'Thank you.' Mattingley married? Was that what had kept him so long in the country? She thanked her kind hostess mechanically and got into the carriage.

Why should she be surprised to learn that Mattingley was married? She had known, when he had asked her to marry him, that it had been out of pity, Mattingley, the unmarrying man. Mattingley, whose magic touch could make any woman his slave. He would have married a brilliant figure, a younger version of the Duchess, a society hostess who would shine at his side.

I shall never marry, she thought. I shall grow old, and silent, and strange like Granny Biggs. But I shall live my own life. And, at least, she told herself, Mattingley married would be an easier friend. He would find her a lawyer Giles could not bend around his thumb as he had Mr. James. With the proceeds of the sale of the Tremadoc house, and what she was owed for *The Downfall of Bonaparte*, she should be able to find herself a country cottage. To live in a tiny, quiet way, and write. She would need another publisher too. But first she must find her own voice as a poet. *The Downfall of Bonaparte* had been her tribute to Tremadoc. What should she write for herself?

It was a fine morning after the rain. The woods gleamed wetly; blackthorn shone white in the hedges. She remembered the fog in which they had left London. Just two days ago. If I can help it, she thought, I will never waste the spring in London again. I am going to manage my own life. Mrs. Mattingley would send her to Sophie. Perhaps there would be a cottage at Llanfryn. How strange it was to find herself thinking forward again after all the listless months.

Mrs. Mattingley. She looked ruefully down at her torn and mudstained skirts. What was she going to tell her? Well, the truth. Most of it, anyway. 'Truth is always easiest,' Mr. Trentham used to say. She would like to go back to Llanfryn, to live again in his benevolent, remembered shadow.

It was a long drive. She could not possibly have walked it. But then she might well have missed her way. She ached a good deal today and was both tired and hungry when the carriage turned at last through neat lodge gates and up a tree-lined drive. The house was rambling brick, with a forest of writhing Tudor chimney pots. A gentleman's residence, comfortable, unpretentious. Mattingley's home. Mrs. Mattingley's home.

She swallowed a knot of tears and put a quick hand to her hair, wishing for the bonnet she had discarded. Ridiculous. She straightened her back, put up her chin and climbed a little awkwardly out of the carriage, the borrowed clogs heavy on her aching feet.

The front door was open and a woman in black stood at the head of the steps to receive her. A housekeeper, sent to look her over. She felt her glance, from bonnetless head to clumsy feet and stiffened a little.

But the woman's voice was civil. 'Welcome to Hallam House, ma'am. Mrs. Mattingley is not well and begs you will forgive her for not greeting you herself. She asks how we can serve you.'

'Not well? I'm sorry.' Pregnant already? 'Not well enough to see me?' Bad enough to tell her wretched story to Mattingley's new wife, but to his housekeeper... 'I'm Mrs. Tremadoc,' she went on. 'I've known Mr. Mattingley a little. I badly need help. As you can see!' A wry glance shared the housekeeper's unspoken comments on her appearance.

'Come in, Mrs. Tremadoc.' The housekeeper had come to some sort of decision. 'I am sure Mrs. Mattingley will see you. If you will come this way?'

No chance to tidy herself. Well, it would take some time. She followed the woman up a polished flight of stairs, her clogs clacking awkwardly at every step. The house smelled of potpourri and beeswax. Family portraits in the upstairs hall had hints of Mattingley.

'If you would wait here a moment?' The housekeeper pointed to an upright chair in a chintz-hung dressing room, went on herself through a further door.

'Mrs. Tremadoc?' A deep voice, raised in surprise. 'I'll see her at once.'

A room full of crimson shadows, velvet curtains drawn against morning sun. A huge tapestry-hung four poster bed. The marriage bed?

'Draw the curtains, Smart,' commanded the voice from the shadow of the curtains. A beautiful voice, full of character. I shall like her, Caroline thought, God help me.

'Welcome to Hallam House, Mrs. Tremadoc.' The curtains swished back and Caroline saw a tiny old lady propped against piled up pillows. Brilliant black eyes studied her keenly. 'My son has spoken of you. But...' she had taken in Caroline's appearance. 'Child, what has happened to you?'

'Your son?' she gasped. 'I never thought . . .'

'Good gracious.' The dark eyes so like Mattingley's sparkled with amusement. 'Never tell me you expected a wife? You cannot know my son very well, Mrs. Tremadoc.' A shadow crossed her face. 'But that's nothing to the purpose. Sit down, child, and tell me what in the world has happened to you. And, Smart, a glass of madeira for Mrs. Tremadoc.'

'If you please, ma'am, if it could be milk?'

'Milk and a luncheon, Smart, and I'll take madeira. That's right.' Caroline had subsided on to a gilt chaise-longue. 'Put your feet up, child, and take off those terrible clogs, and tell me about it.' And then, as Caroline hesitated, wondering how in the world to begin. 'Naturally, I know some of your sad story. I condole with you for the loss of a brilliant husband, Mrs. Tremadoc. I have read his poem, and the last canto, for which I understand we have to thank your good memory, but what in the world can have happened to bring you here, in this plight?'

'It's a long story.'

'So much the better. I love long stories.' And then, as Caroline still hesitated. 'If it helps at all, I saw a piece in the *Chronicle* just the other day, in that shabby gossip column of theirs. I do not normally read it,' she said severely, but did not explain that she had read the entire paper wondering what it was in it that had taken her son in such a rage to town. Now, she began to think she knew. 'A nasty knowing little paragraph about Mr. C the publisher and Mrs. T the poet's widow. I take it you are Mrs. T, so what have you done with Mr. C?'

'I ran away from him at an inn in Upper Hallam,' said Caroline. 'He said he was taking me to his sister in Llanfryn. Oh, ma'am, she's in such trouble, poor Sophie. I had hoped that Mr. Mattingley would do something for her. Perhaps help me to get to her?'

'First we must get him home,' said his mother. 'Mr. Comfrey said he was taking you to his sister,' she prompted. 'And where was he really taking you?'

'Gretna Green.'

'Good gracious! But, forgive me, my dear, have you not been there before?'

'Yes.' Caroline met the black eyes squarely. 'I could not let it happen to me again, ma'am. I knew I must get away. I could not think how. I had no money, you see. No friends. My mother . . .' She coloured.

'I know all about your mother. Never mind her. And, you have friends now. But how did you get away?'

Caroline laughed. She could now. 'We stopped at an inn in Upper Hallam. Then I just walked. I saw a signpost, you see, that said Hallam. I remembered Mr. Mattingley had a house there. He's always been kind to me.' She felt her colour higher than ever.

'From Upper Hallam to Granny Biggs' cottage? You walked a long way. Ah, here's your luncheon. Smart, the blue room for Mrs. Tremadoc and she will be wanting a hot bath. And ask my dresser to look her out a suit of clothes that will not be too ridiculous.'

'Oh, thank you, ma'am!' Caroline took a long pull at the milk, and looked hungrily at a tempting plate of cold meats.

'Eat away, child. I doubt Granny Biggs had much to give you, and you must be starving from a walk like that. But don't stop talking! Tell what happened to Mr. Comfrey.'

'I don't know, ma'am. But I heard a carriage, just as I got to Mrs. Biggs' cottage. I think he may be looking for me.'

'I hope he comes here. I'll see him, if he does. He must love you very much, poor man.'

'I don't think he does, you know. Would he have done such a thing to me, if he really did?'

The old woman shrugged among her pillows. 'Men are a mystery, and that's all there is to it. But, talking of men, I think I had best send for my son. And get dressed. If your Mr. C should come, I wish to be ready to receive him.' She rung her bell.

'But should you get up?'

'I'm better. I think I was ill with boredom before.' Or with Mattingley's absence. 'Have you finished? Then off you go, child. Have your bath, change your clothes. If you'll be ruled by me, we'll do nothing until Charles gets here. Of course I'd like to have Comfrey horsewhipped . . .'

'But I can't stand another scandal,' said Caroline. 'I know it, ma'am. I think that's why he thought he had me. Thought I would not dare try to get away. And I was frightened. At first.'

'You're not now?'

'Now, I've met you? No.' And then, with her usual incorrigible honesty. 'In fact, I had decided already what to do. Giles can't hurt me any more. No one can. I'm going to live in a cottage and write.'

'Poetry?'

'I hope so.'

'Brave. And end up like Granny Biggs?'

'Exactly! Oh, ma'am, I'm glad I found you.'

'And I you.' But Mrs. Mattingley was beginning to have quite other plans for her.

Driving hell for leather up the Great North Road, Mattingley paused to send the man from Chevenham House to Colney Heath to establish that Comfrey and Caroline had really stayed with the Drummonds.

'Yes, sir.' The man returned to the curricle. 'Left bright and early, planning to lunch at an inn of Mr. Drummond's recommendation at Dunstable and make a long day of it. I told them Mrs. Winterton had sent something after Miss Caroline,' he explained.

'Ingenious,' said Mattingley. 'You must come and work for me when this is over. Not a chance of catching them at Dunstable. You didn't learn where Comfrey meant to spend the night?'

'No, sir. I'm sorry. They didn't know.'

'Pity. But not your fault, man.' He must look as savage as he felt. 'We'll just have to enquire at all the likely inns. They'll stop where they change horses of course. We're bound to find them.' And if they were sharing a room, passing as man and wife, he was going to kill Comfrey. 'They lunch at Dunstable,' he was making himself think calmly. 'We'll find them racked up for the night somewhere round Stony Stratford. But we will start enquiring for them well south of there, just to be on the safe side. It's going to mean driving all night.'

'Yes, sir. The girl I talked to at the Drummond's house said Miss Caroline wasn't well. She went straight to bed when they got there. Had her dinner sent up to her room. She looked proper poorly. They won't have got far. Not if he's any kind of a gentleman.'

'But he's not.' Mattingley had taken the man up in his curricle and they were driving forward at breakneck speed again. 'You're not afraid for your neck, I hope.'

'Not when I think of Miss Caroline, sir.'

The light was beginning to fade as they bucketed through Dunstable, and Mattingley did not even bother to stop at the inn where Comfrey had planned to lunch. As long as the light held, he kept his horses close to the nine miles an hour that was expected of the mail coaches to which everything else on the road had to give way. But with darkness, while his anxiety for Caroline reached fever pitch, he had to slacken speed or risk an accident that might put him out of the running altogether.

'You'll be no use to Miss Caroline with a broken neck, sir,' said the man from Chevenham House at last, and Mattingley swore, and fought back the image of Caroline defending herself from Comfrey's advances, and slowed his horses to a safer pace.

24

GILES COMFREY DID not appear at Hallam House, and Caroline thought Mrs. Mattingley was disappointed. There was no chance, she said, of her son's arriving until next day. 'We will just have to entertain each other as best we may in the meanwhile. Tell me all about yourself, child.' She reached out to pat Caroline's hand. 'I know about your father, of course.'

'Everyone does,' said Caroline bitterly. 'Sometimes I wonder why we even pretend to pretend.'

'Does your mother?'

'Pretend? Not really. Oh, ma'am, do you think she encouraged Giles to take me off because she wanted to be alone with my father? To make him marry her?'

'I expect so,' said Mrs. Mattingley. She was really beginning to hope that she was entertaining her future daughter-in-law and welcomed any signs that she was not particularly devoted to her undesirable mother. 'She'll marry the Duke in the end, I think,' she said. 'She's a clever woman, your mother.'

'The Duchess was worth ten of her,' said Caroline. 'I loved her.' And then blushed crimson, remembering that Mattingley had too.

'I'm glad,' said his mother, noticing everything. 'Yes, one could not help loving the Duchess, though one could not entirely approve of her either.' She changed the subject. 'Tell me about your brilliant husband and his poetry.'

An acute woman, she read a great deal more behind what Caroline had told her than Caroline imagined. 'You took it all down at his dictation?' she asked presently.

'Yes.' What a barometer the child's colour was. She was beginning to recognise when she was unhappily skirting around the exact truth. 'He . . . he liked it that way.'

'So you were able to write the last canto from your notes? I like it the best, I think.'

'I'm glad.' Again that quick rush of colour. 'I . . . It was his memorial.'

'He could not have a better one. Poor man, what a tragic end. And what an escape you had!'

'Thanks to Mr. Mattingley!'

'I wish I could have seen him dressed up as an old philosopher in a full-bottomed wig,' said his mother. 'He even deceived me, you know, wretched boy. Sent me letters full of vivid descriptions of St. Petersburg, supposed to have come in the diplomatic bag, and all the time he was entertaining you in his library down at Oldchurch.'

'He didn't tell you?'

'No indeed. When I twitted him with it, afterwards, he said the only safe secret was the one told to no one. So I have forgiven him, and I hope you will too.'

'Oh! Forgive!' exclaimed Caroline, and blushed and was silent.

It was beginning to get dark when Mrs. Mattingley was brought a note.

'From Charles.' She opened, read it rapidly and gave Caroline one of her glances of sparkling amusement. 'He's been called out of town on urgent business. He'd not had my note. I wonder where he has gone in such a rush. His writing is always difficult, but I have never seen anything like this. Oh, well, child, we will just have to make shift with each other's company until he thinks fit to return. But perhaps you would like to write a note to that poor girl in Llanfryn?'

'Oh, yes, please.' But she found it surprisingly difficult to decide what to say. Did she really want to suggest that she and Sophie set up house together? It had seemed a good idea in the first shock of Sophie's sad news, but now, thinking about it, she remembered that the two of them had never really got on. And besides, did she want to go so far from London? She knew enough about publishers to know that they were given to last moment crises. Imagine correcting proofs from Llanfryn.

She picked up the pen and put it down again, angry with herself. The surface of her mind might be occupied with Sophie, but underneath was a great surging tide of irrational happiness. Mattingley was not married. Well, until today, she had never imagined that he was. And he was still the Duchess's mourning lover. Why had meeting his mother, coming to his house, changed her feeling about him so? Or had it merely made her recognise how she did feel about him? I should not have come to his house, she thought. Throwing myself at him. And yet she was glad that she had. Was she? She was glad she had met his mother. Seen his house. But she could not stay here, meekly waiting for him to arrange her life for her.

That was it. Now she had found it. She put down the pen and sought out Mrs. Mattingley. 'Ma'am?'

'Yes, child?' Caroline would have been amazed if she could have known how exactly Mrs. Mattingley had anticipated her chain of thought. Having left her safely occupied with the letter to Sophie, she had descended to the servants' quarters to cross-examine the man who had brought Mattingley's note. Learning of her son's enraged return from Chevenham House, she had smiled to herself and sent another man to seek him out on the Great North Road. 'You'll find him easily enough. He'll have ordered horses ahead. Track him through them.'

'Yes, ma'am. But what am I to tell him?'

'Ah.' That was the question. If she simply asked him to come home, would he obey her? She rather thought not. 'Tell him Mrs. Tremadoc is here and we need his advice,' she said. And knew from the man's expression that the servants' hall had come to the same conclusion as she had. Well, nothing must go wrong now.

And here was Caroline, behaving exactly as she had expected she would. 'Forgive me,' she was saying. 'I am more grateful to you than I can say, but I think I ought to lose no time in going back to London. I ought to see my mother before Giles does. She is my mother, after all.'

'Yes. What would you say to her?'

'That I do not intend to marry.' There came the betraying tide of colour. 'That I mean to set up house by myself in the country somewhere, I might get Sophie to live with me.'

'You don't think your mother might just hand you back to Giles Comfrey?' asked Mrs. Mattingley.

'I won't let her.'

'I don't think you will. Very well, I think you are quite

right, though I shall be sorry to see you go, and I am sure my son will be sorry to miss you.' How soon would her messenger catch him? 'Too late for you to start tonight,' she went on. 'But I will give orders for the morning. If you are sure you will not stay and give Charles the meeting? I am afraid I cannot hope for him until tomorrow night at the earliest.' She devoutly hoped she was wrong.

'Dear madam, I really think I should go.'

'Then it is high time you were in bed. You must be exhausted. Sleep well, dear child.'

She sat up for a while herself, wondering what was best to do. Having been furiously anxious about Caroline, Mattingley would no doubt arrive furiously angry with her. She remembered enough occasions in his childhood when this had happened to her. Let the child go back to town and face her mother? In many ways it might be best. She understood exactly how Caroline felt about seeming to throw herself at Mattingley. In the heat of terror, it had seemed the obvious thing to do. Now she was safe, she was beginning to feel a fool.

But she did not trust Frances Winterton, and that was all there was to it. Mattingley had told her about the blackmail attempt over the Duchess's letters and she was privately certain that Frances Winterton was involved. Capable of that, she was capable of anything, most certainly of saying something to Caroline about Mattingley's long affair with the Duchess that would make Caroline think she could not accept him.

Very well, she thought, delaying tactics: gave careful orders to the servants, and went to bed.

Caroline woke to sunshine and the sound of birds. Late birds. This was no dawn song. She lay for a few moments, collecting herself, aware of stiffness, of sore feet, of a great reluctance to move. But she must. Mattingley might be home this evening, his mother had said. She must be well away before then, off to town to confront her mother.

She did not want to go. They might say things they would both regret. But she must. Go to her father first? Well, why not? She reached out and rang the bell. Mrs. Mattingley had ordered breakfast in bed, and she was grateful for the respite.

Dressed at last in a severe riding outfit worn by a much younger Mrs. Mattingley she put on the soft slippers that were all she could wear and went downstairs to seek out her hostess.

'There you are, my dear. Did you sleep well? Are you sure you are strong enough to go back to London?' She wished now that she had sent for the doctor. Caroline looked transparent with strain.

'Oh, yes. I must. If you really can spare me the carriage?'

'Of course, but I am afraid you will have to wait a little. One of the horses has cast a shoe and we've no smith on the place. It won't be long, and it will give us time to get together a basket of goodies for Granny Biggs.'

'Granny Biggs? Oh, I'm ashamed. I must go and thank her.'

'I thought you'd want to. I've told Smart to get a few things together. Come and see the gardens while we wait. You will be glad of a breath of air before you start on your journey.'

'Are you well enough? I should have asked . . .'

'I'm myself again today. You've done me good.' It was true, but she wished Mattingley would come. *I'm old*, she thought, *I want things settled.*

The gardens lay behind the house, sloping away to the east, and they walked together into morning sunshine. 'This is the knot garden.' Mrs. Mattingley bent to pick a sprig of lavender and hand it to Caroline. 'Charles had it put in order for me when he came of age. He's a good son.'

'I'm sure he is,' Caroline said warmly, and then, 'Oh!' They had come out from among trim, strong-smelling box hedges to where the slope grew suddenly steeper down towards a little stream that ran along the bottom of the valley.

'It's Charles's new project,' said his mother. 'He's been busy with it all spring. A wild garden, he says.'

'Yes, but . . .'

'You do recognise it? I'm glad. I told Charles no one would for years, but I'm delighted to be proved wrong. Yes, it's the wild garden at Merton from your husband's last canto. You think it will do?'

'Oh, *yes*,' breathed Caroline. And then, 'Mrs. Mattingley, do you think the carriage will be ready now?'

They kissed each other goodbye and Mrs. Mattingley felt Caroline close to tears, and longed to urge her to stay. Instead, 'Give my thanks to Granny Biggs,' she said. 'And you won't mind it, my dear, if the coachman does one errand for me while you are with her?'

'Of course not.' *What else could she say?*

Mattingley reached Hallam House half an hour later, dust-stained and haggard from his two days' desperate search for Caroline. Having overshot them at Upper Hallam, he had never even encountered Comfrey, and had been at his wits' end when his mother's messenger caught up with him.

'Mother!' She was waiting at the door. 'She's here? She's safe?'

'Safe, Charles, but not here. She felt she must go back to London and face her mother.'

'Damnation! You could not make her stay?'

'She's not someone one makes do things, I'm glad to say. As Giles Comfrey found, thank God.'

'How did she get away from him?'

'Walked. But she'll tell you.'

'I thought you said—'

'She only left half an hour ago, Charles. She's gone to see Granny Biggs on her way to town.'

'Granny Biggs?'

'She spent the night with her. Night before last. After she walked away from Comfrey. I sent her to say thank you, and told the coachman to leave her there for an hour or so. She'll be getting restless now. You had better hurry or she'll walk off again. That's a very determined young woman.' She put out a hand to detain him. 'Just one thing, before you rush after her. Don't take anything for granted, Charles.'

'No.' He was controlling his impatience with a visible effort.

'She's decided to live in a cottage and write poetry.'

'Has she, by God?' She had his full attention now.

'Yes. And if you bully her, she'll do it.'

'Bully her? I?'

'Yes, Charles. You. Now, off you go and bring her back to me. I like her, Charles. I like her very much.'

'That's lucky.' He kissed her warmly and strode back down the steps to where his curricle waited. 'You, Frank!' The man from Chevenham House was holding the horses' heads. 'It's the end of the chase. You had better come too.'

'Thank you, sir.'

Bored with her visitor, Granny Biggs presently drifted off into a light doze, and Caroline left the basket beside her and went out into the lane to watch for the carriage. There was actually some warmth in the sun and she lifted her head to take deep breaths of spring air. Charles Mattingley had made her garden, the one she had happily written into her last canto. That was what he had been doing all the long winter while she sat in the fog in London. Why? And how did he know it was her garden, not Tremadoc's? Could he have been to Llanfryn? Could he have seen it there? Or was her description in that last canto really so good? Giles had never recognised the garden, and Giles had grown up in it.

Giles. She looked up, listening. That was not the heavy Hallam House carriage. That was something much lighter, faster. Giles? She looked up and down the narrow lane, then at the cottage. No, I won't hide. I'm tired of running away.

She stood there, chin up, waiting as the curricle swept dangerously round the corner and Mattingley pulled his horses to a savage stop.

'I thought you were Giles!'

'I nearly ran you down.' He threw the reins to the man from Chevenham House. And then, jumping down. 'Giles Comfrey? You were waiting for him?'

She smiled at him. 'I was going to tell him what I thought of him.' And then, 'You've seen your mother? You know?'

'I knew before that.' He had taken her arm and started them forward down the lane, away from the cottage. 'Your mother told me. God, it seems a lifetime! I've been looking for you.'

'Looking for me? What did my mother say?'

'That you'd gone off with Giles Comfrey.'

'But you didn't believe her? You came looking for me?'

'Caroline, I nearly did. Believe her. I was so angry. So wretched. I nearly left you to your fate.' He laughed. 'But you saved yourself. My mother says you just walked away from him.' He looked down at her. 'You're lame!'

'A little.' She paused. 'This is a very strange conversation.'

'Yes. You were going back to London?'

'I am going back to London.'

'To face your mother?'

'And my father.'

'As you were going to face Giles Comfrey?'

'Yes.'

He put both hands on her shoulders and looked down at her. 'Do you need to?'

'I thought I did.' She met his eyes squarely.

'Do they matter?'

'I don't know. She is my mother.'

'And Comfrey was your publisher. We'll have to find you a new one. My mother says you are going to live in a cottage, and write.'

'Yes.'

'Caroline.' His hands were urgent on her shoulders. 'Would you consider living in Hallam House and writing? It's not a cottage . . .'

'No. You're making my garden.'

'You recognised it?'

'Oh, yes, Charles, I recognised it.'

'Caroline!'

'Charles!' His arms around her were the most natural thing in the world. His kiss was like nothing that had ever happened to her: a beginning, an ending, a whole new life . . .

'I have asked you twice before.' He looked down at her at last, the smile she remembered in his eyes. 'Is third time to be lucky, Caroline?'

'I hope so.' And then, an ecstatic, endless while later. 'Charles, do you know we are in full sight of your curricle? And can you tell me why you have a man from Chevenham House with you?'

'That's not a man,' he told her, his arms still firm around her, 'that's an angel. It was he told me you thought you were going to Llanfryn, not Gretna.'

'He's a very amused angel at the moment. Perhaps we should go and thank him. But, first—Charles?'

'Yes, my love?'

'You really understand? When I saw the garden, I thought you must. But how did you know?'

'That you were the poet? My darling, I am not entirely a fool. When you came once a week and sat in John Gerard's library and picked my brains, I had the advantage of you; I knew who you were. Then I read your husband's poem and found myself quoted so extensively . . . so flatteringly. Well . . . I wondered. But it was your last canto that settled it. Do you remember consulting me about Aboukir Bay? I offered to look at the notes you'd taken from Tremadoc's dictation, and you blushed crimson and looked like a naughty child. How I longed to kiss you.' He smiled down at her. 'Do you know, our tactful angel has turned the other way?' This time the kiss was longer, easier, a whole wordless conversation. 'I think I've loved you always,' he said at last.

'Always?'

'Yes. Ever since that first night at Chevenham House. Only, for a while, I could not see it.'

'Because of the Duchess?'

'Yes, Caroline, because of the Duchess. You'll not mind it?'

'I loved her too.'

'I know. I'm glad. She was such a loving person, Caroline.'

'And so unhappy. I'm glad you gave her some happiness, Charles.' She pulled away a little to look up at him. 'Do you think they will marry now?'

'The Duke and your mother? I expect so. She's a very clever woman. But it will be no concern of ours.'

'None at all. I do like your mother.' It was very far from being a *non sequitur*.

'And she you, my darling. I'm a very lucky man.' He traced the fine line of her eyebrow with a loving fingertip. 'There's just one thing: Do you want me to kill Giles Comfrey?'

'Good gracious, no! He's got troubles enough as it is. He didn't even want to marry me, you know. That's why the whole abduction was so absurd.'

'Caroline, you're laughing. I love you.' But he thought she was near tears too. 'I would have killed him if . . .'

'Don't. Let's not talk about it. Only . . . one thing I thought of when he told me where we were going. I think he's your blackmailer, Charles.'

'You know about that!'

'He told me. And there was something about the way he told me . . .' Safe in his arms, she smiled up at Mattingley. 'Charles, why do you think he wanted so desperately to marry me?'

'Not for your *beaux yeux*, you think?' He kissed her again, in a friendly spirit this time. 'How good it is to like you so much as well as loving you, love. And as to your poor Giles, I think he's near bankruptcy. Put all his publishing eggs in one basket and has been on the thinnest ice since Tremadoc died. And, another thing, I heard some talk about your mother-in-law the other day. A downy old bird, someone was calling her. Do you think she might have saved more of her fortune from the crash than she let her son know?'

'Of course! Mr. James, the lawyer, called me an heiress once and I remember thinking it was an odd word to choose. He and Giles were very thick; I expect he told him. That explains everything!' She laughed. 'Not my *beaux yeux*, my expectations! How very unflattering.'

'Very like Giles Comfrey. As to the money, no need for you to take it if you don't want to. I've enough for us both, and then there will be your earnings which I imagine must be considerable. I expect Comfrey had that in mind too. He must surely have seen how the land lay.'

'Oh, no, he had no idea. He just hoped we were going to be able to go on cashing in on the publicity for a while. That was all. Charles, would you mind if I took Mrs. Tremadoc's money after all? I . . . I sort of promised her . . .'

'Promised her?' He touched her cheek with a loving finger. 'What a delicious blusher you are! Come on, love, chin up, and break it to me gently. What in the world did you promise that old tartar?'

'I didn't exactly promise. She told me . . . She thought there was to be a child. "For Geraint," she said. "For little Geraint." Charles!'

He was roaring with laughter. 'Now I've heard everything! I'm not to kill the man who abducted you, because he's your publisher, and I'm to call our son after your first husband! Tell me, love, may we call him Charles too? After me, of course.'

'She'll be a girl. Charles!' Now it was a protest.

'You're right.' He let her go. 'I'll tell you one thing, my darling, and that is that we are going to be married directly and be damned to the gossips. What do you say to a trip to Gretna?'

'Oh, no!'

'I quite agree with you. I rather fancy the chapel at Cley myself, with your father giving you away and your mother swooning in the front pew. Would you mind that?'

'Do you know, Charles, I think I'd enjoy it. If your mother will come?'

'Oh, she'll come all right. Why do you think she sent you round by Granny Biggs' cottage?'

'Oh?' Her eyes were sparkling with something between anger and amusement. 'You mean she knew?'

'She's no more a fool than I am. Less, in fact. She told me to take nothing for granted.'

'Oh, Charles, you can me.'

'But I don't intend to,' he said.